I0564510

CAVE MARIE

La Llorona

Rise of a Mafia Queen

First edition

ISBN (paperback): 979-8-9875526-8-1
ISBN (hardcover): 979-8-9875526-7-4

Cover art by Glen Edelstein

This book was professionally typeset on Reedsy.
Find out more at reedsy.com

For little bird...
You are stronger than you know.
You are an amazing woman: flawed, scarred, emotional, and fierce.
Your trust means everything to me.
I can't fight your fights or take away the burdens you carry, but I will always be your bruja; your agony aunt to call; your supporter and hype woman.
Te amo.

For little bird...
You are stronger than you know.
You are an amazing woman: flawed, scarred, emotional, and fierce.
Your trust means everything to me.
I can't fight your fights or take away the burdens you carry, but I will always be your bruja; your agony aunt to call; your supporter and hype woman.
Te amo.

Foreword

Before you continue reading any further, this is your warning that there are triggers ahead. This book contains depictions of domestic violence, attempted assault, psychological and mental abuse of a partner, and other violence.

Although this book is a work of fiction, domestic violence happens everyday. Domestic violence isn't just about physical abuse. Victims are often controlled emotionally, psychologically, or financially.

Regardless of where we come from, all people deserve to be loved and supported. If you or someone you know are the victim of domestic violence, there is help out there. Whether you are a man or a woman, it is a universal human right to expect and deserve dignity and respect.

Below are some national-level support contacts, courtesy of Safe and Together Institute website. The phone numbers are a mixture of 24-hour hotlines and business-hour helpline services. The listed phone numbers are local to that country.

(Australia) National sexual assault, domestic and family violence counselling service:

https://1800Respect.org.au Ph: 1800 737 732

(Australia) Lifeline: https://www.lifeline.org.au/ Ph: 13 11 14

(Australia) Men's Line: https://mensline.org.au/ Ph: 1300 78 99 78

(Australia) Kids Helpline: https://kidshelpline.com.au/
Ph: 1800 55 1800

(Canada) Shelter Safe: https://www.sheltersafe.ca/
(provides a list of domestic abuse shelters in each province
and territory with phone numbers)

(Hong Kong) Hong Kong Federation of Women's Centres:
https://womencentre.org.hk/ Ph: 2386 6255

(New Zealand) Women's Refuge: https://womensrefuge.
org.nz/ Ph: 0800 REFUGE or 0800 733 843

(New Zealand) It's Not Ok Campaign: http://www.areyo
uok.org.nz/ Ph: 0800 456 450

(New Zealand) Lifeline: https://www.lifeline.org.nz/ Ph:
0800 543 354

(Northern Ireland) Northern Ireland Women's Aid:
https://www.womensaidni.org/ Ph: 0808 802 1414

(Scotland) Scottish Women's Aid: https://womensaid.sco
t/ Ph: 0800 027 1234

(Singapore) Association of Women for Action and Re-
search: https://www.aware.org.sg/ Ph: 1800 777 5555

(UK) National Domestic Abuse Helpline: https://www.na
tionaldahelpline.org.uk/ Ph: 0808 2000 247

(UK) National LGBT+ Domestic Abuse Helpline:
http://www.galop.org.uk/domesticabuse/
Ph: 0800 999 5428

(UK) Respect Men's Advice Line: https://mensadviceline.
org.uk/ Ph: 0808 8010327

(US) National Domestic Violence Hotline: https://thehotl
ine.org Ph: 1-800-799-7233/1-800-787-3224 (TTY)

(US) StrongHearts Native Helpline: https://www.strongh
eartshelpline.org/ Ph: 1–844-762-8483

(US) The National Deaf Domestic Violence Hotline:

https://thedeafhotline.org/

Videophone: 1-855-812-1001

(Wales) Welsh Women's Aid: https://www.welshwomens aid.org.uk/ Ph: 0808 80 10 800

Acknowledgments

Merriam Webster defines an exotic dancer as a person who dances or performs in a seductive or provocative manner while skimpily dressed… to the accompaniment of music.

Exotic dancers are not whores, sluts, or prostitutes.

For the women who embrace their beauty and refuse to adhere to archaic societal stigmas and constructs, this book was inspired by you. You are intelligent, driven, beautiful, amazing, and so much more than the skin you bare. Thank you for trusting me with your stories.

Flaunt and own your power as a woman.

Prologue

"Shit, Tacie. Who messed you up like that?" My sister asked, staring at me from the phone.

I didn't need to see my face to know it was bad. Domenico and I got into it again yesterday. He didn't like my dancing, but we couldn't afford the rent without that income. He swore we could make things work, but I had gone from pulling twelve grand a month to three hundred a week.

Mister macho wasn't able to hold down everything like he promised. Shit wasn't getting paid, and I wasn't willing to lose my lifestyle for his ego. I started dancing again in secret. My first week back at the club, I took center stage in time to see Domenico leaving the club with another woman.

We'd fought for weeks the last time I stripped because he was crazy jealous. He'd screamed about I had gone back on agreements. How I had emasculated him, by stripping to begin with. I thought we were good again. We had been for nearly a month.

"I fell," I told her.

She stared at me for a minute before just shaking her head. "You seem real fucking clumsy all of a sudden. You sure you didn't have help falling?" she asked, arching an eyebrow at me.

She knew Domenico and I were toxic as fuck together. When he was good, I felt like a Queen. When we were bad, I was just another whore warming his bed.

"Don't look at me like that," I grumbled, shutting off my camera so she couldn't see my face.

"Like what?" Jada asked, staring intently back through the screen.

"Like you are my mother."

Jada snorted. "If our mother were still here, she would cry, hermana."

I didn't want to continue this conversation. Jada always hit right to the heart of shit, and I didn't want to deal with that right now.

"Are you going to cover for me or not?" I asked her. It was the only reason I even called her. Jada and I had different fathers, but we could pass for twins with the right make up. Right now, I needed her to pull my shift at the club so that I could get my face healed.

I only worked two nights a week at the club in Baltimore, but it pulled enough to buy me everything I wanted. New car. Stylish clothes. Fendi, Gucci, Louboutin, whatever I wanted, I bought it.

I made enough in a weekend to afford this bougie, high end fucking crib in town. Surrounded by all the professionals, politicians, and 'family men' who so loved to pass me their paychecks every Friday night. It was one of the reasons I fought with Domenico. One of many.

He swore I was fucking the neighbor across the hall because the man said, 'Excuse me,' after bumping into us. Ignoring the fact that he was the cheater. Last week, I got accused of flirting with a delivery man when the guy wished me a great weekend. Before that, Domenico accused me of stealing from his fucking profits.

Ha! Like I needed his fucking drug money when I was paying my bills long before he started sleeping in my bed. Domenico would be crazy for a week before getting into his feels and then filling my head with sweet dreams of our future together. My problem was that I would never be equal with him in any future he mentioned.

He wanted a trophy wife. Candy to put on his arm and use to sweeten deals when it suited his business. He wanted me home while he ran around with a side piece, gambled away money, or partied. Last night I refused to play docile lamb. I wasn't drunk. I wasn't high.

For the life of me, I was sober for the first time in who knew how long. I couldn't even remember what got him started when we left the club together. I just wanted to sleep when we got back, but he wasn't having it.

I couldn't tell you who threw the first punch, but the fight ended when he pulled his gun and held it against my head. In that moment, that second before I heard the empty chamber click, I thought it would finally be over. All of this shit would just be done, and I could stop fighting.

I never closed my eyes. I stared up at him as he held me down by the throat and growled every hateful name he could call me. I didn't miss the hatred in his eyes. I don't know how I ever saw love in them before. It was not there, if it ever was.

He may not have shot me last night. But he damn sure killed the woman I was. When he left this morning, I had a couple guys from the old neighborhood take and pawn everything of value that I owned. Domenico's knuckles were messed up from beating my ass, and my blood was all over the apartment from our tussle. I drained all of my accounts, and added enough into the shared account with Domenico to cause suspicion.

Jada covering my shift was the last step. Once she left, I was fully trashing the apartment and disappearing. The District Attorney didn't need a body to prosecute foul-play in Delaware. It was one of the reasons I insisted on taking up residency in the state.

Domenico thought he was in control? I would burn his fucking world down if it was the last thing I did.

Chapter 1

Why was it so hard to find a job?

I had applied to three boutiques, two convenience stores, and a fast food joint. Every one had signs posted that they were hiring, but not a single place would hire me.

I was 17 with a general education certificate instead of a high school diploma. Why? Because I dropped out. They inevitably asked why I dropped out, and saying due to personal reasons wasn't enough to satisfy them. Do I want to tell them I had to drop out because I was bullied? *No.*

Do I need to explain that my life was threatened when I reported the assholes who did it? *I shouldn't have to.* I finished my education requirements ahead of my intended class, and it meant *shit.*

"Anastacia, can you run to the store for your grandparents?"

I folded up the adverts page and set it neatly with the rest of my documents. My mom's parents were always finding errands for me to do so they could justify slipping me money for gas or other spending cash, or trying to help with one thing or another.

Didn't matter how much I declined their money, they would find a way to hide it in my jacket, shoes, or car. I just had to shake my head. It was sweet that they wanted to take care of me, but I wanted to be my own woman and earn my own way in life.

Coming out of my room into the kitchen of our small apartment, my mom was busy preparing dinner. I walked up behind her, and hugged her. "Did they say what they needed, Mami?" I asked, resting my chin on her shoulder.

She paused in her movements to lean into me. "You know they don't tell me. Nana wants you to pick her up and take her out. She has a list of things she needs and places to go."

I couldn't help but chuckle as I pulled away. "I'll take her, but she can't pay me. I'm not her taxi, I'm her granddaughter. She needs to stop shoving money at me like I'm a stranger."

My mom didn't say anything, but nodded. She knew what I was talking about. Her parents weren't rich, but they weren't poor. They had a nice house that my mom and aunties had grown up in. They drove nice cars, and had nice things in general. Her sisters too. Then there was us.

We lived in a rough part of town, in a sketchy apartment complex. Our apartment was a two bedroom, single bathroom. The kitchen, dining and living rooms were listed as "open concept," but, in reality, there just wasn't enough space for a sofa and dining table in the flat. One or the other would fit.

We made it work. My mom raised us to be clean and tidy. We had painted the apartment and decorated it to the nines. Nothing in it was high end, but it looked really nice. It looked so damn good, the owner used pictures of our place when he advertised available units. Nobody's apartment looked as good as ours. Not that that said much when you live in the poorest part of town.

It was still a shit part of town, in a crap building that was not taken care of. Mami's parents thought we needed every penny they could spare us, but Mami insisted we were fine with the money we had. We were here because my mom decided 18 was the right time to have kids. She left home to marry Mr. Right, only to be left holding the carriage later. After that, she met my dad. He was juggling multiple women, knocked up two at the same time and chose to marry the other instead of my mother.

Then there was Mr. Cool. Mr. Fix it but forgets it. Mr. Sticky Fingers. Mr. Junkie. She thought we didn't know about the many in between, but we did. Mr. Junkie was the worst though. When he was sober, he was an amazing partner for her and they talked about everything. When he was high, he stole from everyone in the house. He had wrecked four of Mami's cars, claiming it was an animal jumping out in front of him every time. In reality, he was high.

We were living in this shithole because we couldn't get a lease anywhere else. When I was getting bullied at school, she was bailing his ass out of jail. When I was struggling with life, she was running off to help him get into and out of his next, last rehab. Jada was rock. If it weren't for her dragging me forward, I would have stopped long ago.

"When does Jada get home?" I asked, grabbing my bag and keys from my room.

"She should be home by nine o'clock tonight," Mami answered.

Jada was my older sister by eleven and a half months. We shared the same mom, but different fathers, and yet still looked like twins. My grandparents said it was thanks to

3

their genes that we look so much alike. What they left out was how my sister and I were born so close together by two different donors. I loved my mom, but she made some messed up choices that still affected us.

"Ok, I'll make sure I am back before that!" I said and left to go play taxi for my grandmother.

* * *

"Stacia, love, would you be a dear and help me into the car?" my grandmother asked.

I couldn't help but raise an eyebrow at her. "Nana, you keep stuffing money in my pants, I'm going to get the wrong impression," I told her.

Her face flushed beet red as she huffed at me. "That- That. I am not stuffing money in your pants!" She disagreed. "I twisted my knee, you brat!"

I just smirked, "Uh-huh. And how did you do that?"

Her face flushed a darker red. "That's none of your damn business!" she whispered.

I was confused for a second before I caught on and then I started laughing. "Go, Nana!! You and pops are still rocking the rafters at your ages..."

"Oh, for the love of God! Anastacia we are not talking about my sex life!" she shouted, drawing the attention of her nosey neighbor Ms. Helen.

I kept laughing after she was situated in my little sedan. I was still chuckling twenty minutes later when we arrived to her first destination. She had no problem getting out of my car, so I could only assume that money was stuffed somewhere in the seat. I locked the car and followed her into the store, shaking my head.

Her list included the cleaners, the butcher, a farmers' produce market, and finally a salon. I had nearly forgotten that she wanted to get her hair cut and styled for some party she was attending with Pops.

I sat in the waiting area reading a magazine while she was shampooed and pampered by a team of stylists. "I love your nails," a woman sitting across from me commented.

"Where did you get them done?" she asked.

"Hello?"

I realized that she was talking to me when she tapped my leg. "I'm sorry, what did you ask?"

She looked like she was in her mid 20s and had more money than I would ever see in my lifetime. She smiled. "I asked where you get your nails done. They're to fucking die for!" she complimented.

I felt my face flush up. "Thank you. I do them myself," I admitted. *How to get by with nice things when you're poor, rule number 2: Learn to do for yourself.*

"Shut up!" she yelled, causing several people in the salon to jump.

"Tara, you need to control your volume," a stylist chastised. I was guessing the stylist was a manager and Tara a regular client.

"Mary, have you seen this girl's nails?" The woman named Tara asked, now holding my hand up in the air.

I had coffin nails with intricate patterns of crisscrossed lines over faded rainbow ombre. It wasn't my best work, and I was planning to change it this weekend. The woman I thought was the manager came over to look at my nails.

"Shit, those are gorgeous. Where'd you get them done?"

she asked.

Tara answered for me, "She did them herself! Look at this shit. You need to poach her from whatever joint she's working in!"

The stylist looked at my nails and then back at me. "Are you licensed?" she asked.

I shook my head. "No. Just poor. I taught myself so I could save a few bucks every month."

I watched the stylist bite her cheek, run her tongue over her teeth, and finally purse her lips. "I can't hire her as a technician. I'd lose my business license," she sighed. "I'm sorry. I'd hire you in a heartbeat and straight up steal you from another salon if you were licensed."

I nodded in understanding. Another job I wouldn't be getting.

Tara wasn't hearing it though. "Stop it, Kammie. Madonna can do the nail work. She doesn't need a license to paint nails. Log her hours as an apprentice, Madonna certifies her training, and you sponsor her testing fees after a 90-day probation."

The manager named Kammie narrowed her eyes at Tara. "Did you set this up?"

"I have no idea who she is," I admitted before Tara could say a word.

It was just then that Nana walked out. Her hair was styled in a neat, turned under bob. She looked ten years younger with the way they blended her make-up to create a softened look.

"Nana, you look so hot!" I gushed at her.

She rolled her eyes and tried to wave me off. "Kammie, you keep asking where I get my nails done. Meet my technician,

Anastacia. I set this up. You hire her, or I find a new salon."

My jaw dropped. "Nana! You can't be serious," I whispered. I knew how much she loved her stylist here. She had followed the woman to four different salons over the past ten years.

Nana puffed out her chest. "I'll take my stylist with me when I leave, too," she threatened.

Kammie's head jerked as she looked over Loan-Thi. The woman was a miracle worker with hair. Didn't matter how crazy or damaged your hair was before you sat in her chair, because when you left it you had a head full of silken locks.

Loan-Thi just smiled and sashayed away from her station to the break room. Kammie turned back to look at me.

"Fine. She starts Saturday. Apprentice rates, but she keeps her tips. I'll sponsor her certification after 90 days and hire her as a senior tech if she passes her licensure."

Nana smiled and shook hands with Kammie. Tara was grinning from ear to ear, and I was still sitting with my jaw hanging open. The only reason I didn't have my license was because of my age, not because I didn't pass the licensure exam.

My grandmother must have seen the wheels spinning in my head, because she interrupted before I could say anything. "That will do perfectly. Thank you so much for this opportunity. Come along, Stacia."

I followed along behind her, a mix of gob smacked and chuffed to bits. "Nana, I already took my test," I whispered when we were both in my car.

"I know. And now you have a means to recoup those fees. This is also working smarter not harder. You turn 18 in ten weeks. This gives you a little income in the meantime. Not to mention what you could do with a few hundred back in your account at the end of it," she explained.

"Your mother told me that you have been struggling to get past the gatekeepers because of your age. I got you in the door, now it is up to you to make a go of it," she continued.

I felt my eyes burn. I didn't want to cry, but this was so much more than I was expecting today.

"Thank you, Nana," I whispered, pulling out of the parking lot to head back to her place.

I had a job!!

* * *

"Happy birthday, baby girl!" My mom cheered, bouncing onto my bed with me. I wasn't ready to get up yet, but this was what she did every year.

"Thank you, Mami," I whispered, giving her a hug.

"I can't believe you are 18! Where did my time go?" she whispered back, brushing the hair out of my face. "You are so beautiful, Tay. See? Do you see how beautiful we made you? The world is yours, baby girl. Anything you want," she gushed, peppering kisses all over my face.

"Ew, Tay. Your breath," Jada wretched leaning in to hug us. "Mami, don't fill her head with bullshit. The world *is* going to fall at your feet, passed out from your stank breath. Go brush your teeth!" She continued while poking at me.

Our mom jumped up from the bed. "Jada Marie Rivera! How can you talk to your sister like that? Come here!" Our mother yelled, chasing Jada out of the room.

I listened to the sound of them squealing and hollering before Jada burst back into our room and pounced on the bed. "Did you enjoy it? Did you enjoy those extra ten minutes in bed on your birthday?" she asked, grinning ear to ear.

"They were the best!" I exclaimed stretching.

"You little shits!" our mom yelled from the door.

We laughed and chased each other around the apartment for another 30 minutes before the real world needed to be addressed. Mami had to get to work. Jada was driving me to Dover to pick up my state cosmetology license. There were a lot of things I couldn't do, because of my age, only being 18, but I could do nails as a fully licensed technician. I couldn't wait to start pulling in real money to buy myself a new car.

By the time we got back from Dover, and I was at work it was already two in the afternoon. Madonna knew that I would be late today, and adjusted my schedule. She was waiting at the employee entrance when Jada dropped me off.

"Let me see it!" she demanded.

I pulled the yellow parchment paper from its folder and passed it over. "When did you take test?" she asked, realizing my certification date was my birthday.

I bit my lower lip and smirked, "Five months ago."

Madonna's stony face broke and she laughed. "You grandmother is so sneaky. She make Kammie pay for your test! I'm happy for you. Now, go work!" she yelled, passing me my certificate.

I was pulling on my apron as I walked out to my station, and stopped when I looked up. My station was replaced with a brand new one. The tools, the lighting, everything was brand new. "Is this for me?" I asked, eyes watering up as my hands caressed everything.

Madonna suddenly came up behind me and smacked my hand away. "You crazy?!? That my shit! I buy with all the money you make me! You take my old station," she grumbled, pointing to the station next to hers.

I felt like such an ass. Of course they wouldn't buy me thousands of dollars of equipment for getting certified. My face felt so hot. "I am so embarrassed," I whispered under my breath.

"Why? You can have all nice things too, when you make the big money," Madonna replied, patting my back.

I sat down at my new station and opened a drawer to pull out a mask. The drawer had been neatly organized and restocked. The casing with my masks was embellished with pink and gold rhinestones that spelled my name. I opened the next drawer and found new tools wrapped with pink and gold bows. Each drawer was filled with the same. Brand new tools, files, polishes, gels, each wrapped with a bow.

I started blinking rapidly to flush away the tears. I looked up to see the entire staff standing around us. Kammie was holding a cupcake with a flickering LED candle on top. "Happy Birthday!" they cheered all at once.

I couldn't hold back the tears any more and started crying. "You guys are so nice to me. Thank you," I whispered, my voice cracked and broken with emotion.

Kammie shrugged it off. "It was the least we could do. You made us too much money, so I had to write off some of it," she snorted.

My jaw dropped and I stared at her.

Madonna smacked her leg, and berated her. "You so full of shit!"

The entire salon burst out laughing as Madonna continued her tirade.

"You want her to have my new station! You tell me, 'train her, and I buy new stuff for everyone.' Now you say it tax write off? I say bullshit! You big softie like marshmallow. You want to spoil us rotten! Don't lie. You say it! You big marshmallow!"

Kammie laughed even harder, listening to her best friend of 20 years fuss and carry on. "Fine! I admit it! I am a squishy marshmallow! Now get back to work before I cry and smudge my make-up!"

It took me 30 minutes to set up all of my new stuff how I wanted it. The rest of the day flew by, and before I knew it Jada was back to pick me up.

Kammie handed me an envelope as I went out the door, reminding me that I was opening the salon with Loan-Thi the next day. I stuffed it into my bag and left. Jada and I ordered pizza for dinner, and camped on the sofa with Mami. I should have felt happy, but I couldn't. Not entirely. In my short 18 years, nothing good came without a balancing bad.

I woke up the next morning feeling like something was *off*. I didn't have a fever, but I didn't feel *right*. I grabbed a bottle of water and ran out the door when I was dressed. I arrived at the Salon two minutes after Loan-Thi and we started preparing the salon.

I folded and stocked the fresh towels, prepped all of the coloring bowls and brushes, and reorganized the color trays for the stylists. Loan-Thi went through the waiting area and wiped down all of the seats and tables with an orange & vinegar spray to disinfect the surfaces. I opened the till and made sure that the previous day's charges were reconciled, printing out a receipt for the day prior's transactions.

Most places did it the day of a transaction, but Kammie always did it the next day to account for glitches with the system that occurred. The receipt went into the journal under the front counter after I locked the register up again. I set up the beverage counter with fresh coffee, new cups and bottled water. Turning to look at Loan-Thi, it was time to start another day.

The whole day was slammed with one walk-in after another. Kammie called out because her kids were sick. The new nail technician that should have started didn't show up, and Madonna had no way to contact her because she was Kammie's hire. I didn't want to complain because the tips were good, but I was exhausted when my shift finally ended.

I was barely out of the parking lot when my car was suddenly slammed forward into traffic. An oncoming car hit the driver's side of my car, and I went rolling down the highway. When the world stopped spinning, my car had landed on its side and I was staring at traffic on the opposite side of the road.

I reached down to unfasten my seatbelt but the buckle was stuck. I had glass cuts on my hands and face, and my body felt numb. "Help!" I tried yelling, but it came out so faint at first.

I heard someone yelling for help, but I couldn't see anyone coming yet. "Help!" I tried yelling a little louder.

Someone was yelling for people to shut up. There were sirens in the distance.

"Please? Can anyone hear me?" I called as loud as I could.

"Oh my god! There's a survivor! Quick!"

Suddenly, my vision was filled with men trying to crawl into my shattered car. "What's your name?" one asked.

"Anastacia," I replied.

"Can you move at all?" he asked.

"My belt is stuck."

The guy nodded. "My name is Joey. I know you're a bit freaked out, but just hold tight. I'm an EMT. I'm just going to check you over while we wait for the ambulance. Do you know what happened?" he asked.

I thought I was hit from behind at the intersection, and my vehicle was thrown forward. I didn't see who hit me from behind, let alone the car that sent me rolling further down the highway. He kept talking as the voices around us were drowned out by the sirens.

His hand held my wrist to check my pulse, I was assuming. He asked me questions to keep me talking, intermittently yelling information to people gathering outside of my vehicle.

"How bad is it?" I asked him. I knew my car was totaled but I was worried about the other driver.

"Not the first one that hit me. The other one. Are they okay? They didn't really have a chance," I clarified.

Joey smiled a bit. "I'm not really sure. They'll check them out. I'll be right back. I'm going to talk with the emergency responders who are here okay?"

"Okay," I whispered. The sounds of shouts and sirens soon quieted down and I was left in silence in my car. *Did they forget I was in here?*

"HELLO?!?" I yelled, becoming more and more nervous the quieter it became outside.

"PLEASE! DON'T LEAVE ME IN HERE!!" I shouted. I heard movement outside of my car again, and the sounds of metal scraping on metal.

The noise was so loud it felt like my head was being crushed. My car suddenly jerked and dropped onto a righted position, causing me to fling to the right. A yelp came out of me.

"Holy shit! There's someone alive in this car! Call the paramedics over here!"

"Sweetie, are you okay?"

"What's your name?"

"Do you know what happened here?"

The barrage of questions came at me, one after the other. I didn't understand what was happening. "Joey. Where's Joey?" I asked.

"Jesus Christ! We have a missing passenger!" someone yelled.

"No! He was here. He checked on me when you came. He said he was an EMT," I clarified, as the paramedics began bracing my neck and preparing to remove me from the vehicle.

"Do you have any identification, Sweetie?"

"My bag. My purse. My ID." I muttered, becoming nauseous as they pulled me from the car. I blacked out a few times between coming out of my car, the ride to the hospital, and waking in the emergency department.

The good Samaritan named 'Joey' had apparently stolen all of my money from my bag and dumped it near my car. I wanted to cry. I felt like I had been violated twice. *Why would someone take advantage of an accident scene for a few bucks?*

After spending the night in the hospital, I was released with a concussion and a very battered body. My mom was beside herself. Two days later I was asked to come to the police station to sign my statement. I asked if I needed a lawyer or anything like that, but they assured me that I was the victim. The police had me describe the accident over and over and over again.

They kept asking if I had met Joey before, or how I knew Joey. I finally looked up at the officer and asked if I was crazy. "Did I imagine him?"

The officer leaned back in his chair and then shook his head. "No. You didn't imagine him. We believe he was the driver of the first vehicle," he finally said.

"What do you mean?" I didn't understand what was going on.

"After going through the security footage around the shopping complex, we found an image of your car being hit from behind as you described."

"I told you!"

"The problem is, that you were talking to the man before the accident. So it looks rather staged."

"I didn't talk to any man. I left work. Got in my car, and then I was hit trying to leave the parking lot. I didn't talk to anyone," I whispered, confused as to how this had turned to me doing something wrong.

The officer pulled up a computer and showed me grainy footage from outside the salon. There I was talking animatedly to someone. A moment later I waved goodbye and Joey could be seen walking away just behind a woman.

"I wasn't talking to him. I was talking to her. She wanted a coffin set with gems. I have a picture of her on my phone! She was my last client before I left. I wasn't even supposed to see her, but the other girl no-showed!" I explained.

I pulled up my damaged phone to show the officer the pictures from my Insta. "I know it's hard to see, but that is the woman I was talking to. You can pull up my account on

15

your computer, and verify her information with the salon!"

The officer took my phone and left me alone in the small room. If they thought I had anything to do with this…. I knocked on the door until another officer answered. "Can I get you something?" he asked.

"I would like to make a phone call."

"I'm sorry-" he started to deny me before the first officer came back.

"Let her make a phone call. She's not being detained."

I smiled politely as they led me to a phone in the hallway. I didn't want to call my mom and freak her out, so I called Nana. She would know what to do.

Chapter 2

After two months of back and forth with the police and my insurance company, I was cleared from any and all wrongdoing in the accident. They were able to track down each one of the customers I saw the day of, and confirm my statements. My accident turned out to be a botched car-jacking. Rather than giving me a bump, my car was propelled into speeding traffic and hit by three other vehicles before rolling to a stop on the opposite side of the highway.

Joey turned himself in after pictures were released on the news of him climbing in and out of my overturned car. I didn't understand what I had done wrong to be targeted. It made me anxious to think about going back to work. Joey could have picked anyone, but he chose to target me. *Why me?*

In all of that, I was home on sick leave because my neck and back were messed up. The doctor said it was just whiplash, but it felt so much worse. The spasms in my neck and back made it impossible to sit over my station and do my job. The thought of coming back to work was so stressful.

"Are you sure you are ready to go back?" Jada asked, sitting with me to eat breakfast.

"Yes, she's going back to work," Mami answered.

"You don't get to decide, Mami. Stacia is eighteen. She decides if she's well enough to go back or not," Jada fired back.

"She can't stay here and just sleep. She needs to make her own money!" Mami argued. "The only way to get past her fear is to face them."

I loved my mother's tenacity, but it also rang hollow. She forced us to face fears but never faced her own. She hid here in the ghetto and pretended that this was living. "I will go back if the doctor clears me. Not before that," I grunted at the two of them

"How are you getting there?" Mami asked.

"Hitching?" I retorted.

"Nana is taking us," Jada clarified before our mother could lose her shit.

The down side of the accident was that we had no car. We couldn't use our mother's. Ever.

"She's coming here?" Our mother asked, suddenly looking flustered.

"Yes, but she's not coming up. We're meeting her down at the corner," Jada explained.

We grabbed our things and left after that. I kept my mouth shut until we were out of the building. "Why'd you lie and say Nana was picking us up?" I asked.

"She doesn't need to know that we have another car yet."

I didn't see the big deal and told her as much. She had her own wheels, we had ours.

"If you don't want to go back to the salon, I can get you a job with me."

I looked over at my sister as we drove to my appointment. "In the warehouse?" I asked. Jada nodded. *I'd have to think about that one.*

An hour later, I was given release to return to light work. The doctor wasn't thrilled that my job required me to sit hunched over. However, working in a warehouse was considered worse, according to him. I didn't want to go back to the salon. I had anxiety thinking about it. I almost died because somebody thought I had a little extra cash in my bag. It may have been strange, but I felt safer in the ghetto than I did in the rich salon.

Jada called her boss and got me an interview. I gave Kammie my notice, cleared out my station and followed Jada to work. They hired me on the spot to work as a runner. I didn't have to load anything. I just drove a cart around a factory and delivered parts. The pay wasn't nearly what I made with tips at the salon, but it was a consistent check that I could budget around.

That night we heard Mami whispering softly through the apartment on her phone. Didn't know who it was this time, but she only whispered like that when she was seeing someone and thought we didn't know. I just hoped this one was better than the last guy. He was a straight junkie. Nice enough guy, but he was still a junkie.

Jada looked at me and rolled her eyes. "He's out," she whispered.

Hello, Junkie.

I didn't want to live like this. Why were we struggling like this when everyone else in our family was thriving? How did our mom end up like this, when her sisters seemed like they were put together? It made no sense. It made me fucking angry. Our mother made it seem like everyone else had done this to her. Like her sisters had used her and cast her aside.

As if her parents were not willing to help when she really needed them, so she learned to do everything on her own.

Blah. Blaah. Blaah. The truth was undeniably that our mother made selfish choices her whole life. She was doing God's work by helping those around her. She was being the bigger person by not turning her back on the friends she had. Meanwhile, we were strung along like accessories. We had to look pretty, and say, 'thank you.' We had to pretend that she was a paragon, and never ever tell the rest of the family know how bad it really was.

"We need to move," I whispered to Jada. She just nodded.

If our mother was talking to Mr. Junkie again, we were going to be homeless in less than a year. While we whispered our plans quietly, Mami burst into our bedroom in tears. "Girls, I have some bad news. Mike's dad passed away last night. You know his mom, Valery, died just a month ago, and now Charlie is gone too."

Jada and I both moved to give her a hug. "How is Mike's sister?" Jada asked.

"Rachel is just devastated. It was so much to deal with their mother's estate, so they are releasing Mike to help. Rachel's hands are full with their grandmother's property, so Mike is going to take over their parents' house until their wills are settled," she explained, teary eyed.

"Who is watching the house until then?" I asked, knowing he still had another year of time to serve.

"Mike's being released on Friday, so that he can attend the funeral. You'll both need to take off work on Tuesday to attend the funeral with us," she continued.

"Why are we going to the funeral?" I asked without thinking.

Like a switch had been flipped, our mother went from grieving to irate. "What the hell is wrong with you? We go to pay our respects to family-"

"We met them once when I was fourteen. They weren't family. They were the parents of the dude you fucked for five years-"

I never saw her move, but the crack of her hand slapping my cheek made my ears ring. My head jerked to the side and I fell to the floor. "You will not disrespect me in *my house!*" she growled at me.

I couldn't see straight. I couldn't even look up. Jada helped me up and shuffled me out of the apartment while our mother was screaming and ranting about every slight she had ever endured because of *me*.

"I can't live here any more," I stated as we drove around aimlessly. "I can't, Jay." I didn't have tears left to cry.

"I know. Papi said we could live with him while we saved up."

"Seriously? Isn't he married to that crazy woman? The super religious freak? No. No, I am not moving in there." I wouldn't move from one crazy to another.

"Well, the other option is we rent a place and find a third to share the rent with," she offered.

"Who is going to rent a place to 18 and 19 year olds?" I asked.

"Then what do you suggest?" Jada asked, pulling into a random parking lot.

"Ask Nana?" I offered, looking at her skeptically.

"No. We can't ask her," Jada shot down that idea.

"That leaves Titi or the Bruja."

Our mother had three sisters, of which she was the

21

LA LLORONA

youngest. The eldest sister, Maria, was a nice lady but we rarely ever saw her. There was a huge age gap between her and Mami, so they were never close. The second, Tetiana or Titi, was the closest to us. She and Mami had been the two doing the most together our whole lives.

The last was the dark horse in the family, Antonia. We called her the Bruja, or witch, because she always knew when shit was going to happen, even without talking to anyone. She had a crazy sixth sense about shit that was just uncanny. We would be safe with either of them, but the Bruja had too many rules to her house.

We didn't have to say anything more. Jada pulled back onto the main road and drove us to Titi's house. We sat in Jada's car until Aunt Tetiana got home that evening. I knew my face was fucked up. My cheek had swelled throughout the day, and now it was discolored. Titi looked like she was going to cry when she saw me.

"Get in the house, both of you. Jada, start some coffee. I'm going to get changed from work, and then we'll talk," Titi directed us as she ushered us into her house.

Half an hour later we were seated around the table explaining everything that had happened. "Jesus Christ," Titi swore. "I'll empty the office out. You two can move in there. I'll talk to your mother."

She took another sip of her coffee and left the room to call her sister. She didn't call our mother first. She called the other two. We listened to her explain how things were becoming too much for us in that part of town. She described the lengthy commutes, the costs, the stress for me personally since the accident, and then asked for their help to move us into her house.

Once the logistics were settled she called our mother. Titi was a master at work. She talked our mother down from her ire, hearing out all of her grievances, before offering double sided suggestions that gave both parties face. She rendered condolences for the loss, and offered to send flowers from 'all of us.' By the end of the conversation, our mother thought she had asked Titi to take us in, and was thanking her for agreeing to it.

She hung up the phone and Jada rushed over to hug her. "Thank you, Titi," she whispered.

Titi looked over to me. "Your mouth is going to be the death of you one day."

"I didn't say anything wrong," I argued back.

"Not every truth needs to be said out loud to be acknowledged. There is a way to make the point without disrespecting your mother. Now, call your fathers, both of you. Apparently, my sister's flair for the dramatic knows no ends. They both think you two are abused in a ditch somewhere."

My jaw fell open. "What did she tell them?" Jada asked, sounding angry for the first time.

"Apparently, you two were so overwhelmed with grief that you got into it with each other, and she couldn't break you apart. Stacia's face got hit *by accident* when my *valiant* sister attempted to separate the two of you," she explained, using air quotes to highlight our mother's wording choices.

"This was not an accident!" I yelled, jumping to my feet.

Titi looked at me sadly. "We know, love. We all know. Your aunts will be here Saturday morning to start moving you in. Until then, you'll need to help me rearrange the house a bit to make room for you both."

23

"Did she talk to Nana and Pops?" I asked.

Titi smiled. "Don't ask stupid questions. Now, call your fathers before *they* call your grandmother and wind her up."

* * *

I slept like the dead at Titi's place. The bruja said it was hypervigilance due to lack of safety that kept me from sleeping properly before. When I asked what she meant, she explained how soldiers in combat zones develop hypervigilance because they are constantly looking for the enemy threat. Living in an unsafe or hostile environment is just the same. The brain and body never truly shut down, because they know they need to be prepared to respond and act quickly.

"Then how come I sleep so well here?" I asked.

"This is sanctuary, love. Even in your jaded heart of hearts, you know you are safe here," she stated quietly, taking a long drag of her cigarette.

I looked up at the house Jada and I now called home, and thought about it for a moment. "Maybe," I acknowledged.

"No one is going to steal from you here. No one is going to sneak into your rooms at night and put their hands on you. This is your sanctuary. No 'maybes' about it," she retorted, exhaling a long puff of smoke.

I reached over and took her cigarette. I took my own drag and exhaled, feeling the nicotine immediately giving me a buzz. I didn't want to equate living with my mother to being in a combat zone, but I couldn't give any other explanation. "I love my mom. I am who I am because of how she raised me."

Bruja reached over and took her cigarette back. "No one is denying that you are a force of nature, Tace. You are an amazing young woman," she nodded. "But don't sit there and tell me you're thankful for how my sister raised you. You shouldn't look like a battle hardened veteran at the age of 18." She took another long drag of her cigarette before putting it out on the ground and walking back into the house.

I sat there angry but not really sure who I should be angry with. My mom had put us in some seriously shitty situations over the years, most of which my grandparents knew nothing about. I hated her, but I hated anyone else talking bad about her. I was taught to love my mother, forgive my enemies, forget old transgressions, move forward, don't hold onto the past, yada yada yada. But I was angry. I held grudges. I couldn't forget.

Titi leaned out the door, "Stacia, the guys are coming over. Jada asked if you wanted to go bowling with them."

I stood up and jogged the short distance to the door. "Hell, yeah!" I cheered. I had known 'the guys' since I was seven or eight. My mom had dated some dude who insisted we play sports, and I met the guys playing little league baseball. Eric, Drew, Beau, Jackson and Brad were 'the guys.'

We would roast marshmallows after games and play together at the park whenever we could. When I was fifteen I convinced myself that I had a crush on Jackson. I asked him to date me in secret to see if things could work out between us, without destroying the friendship. It lasted for a while. I called him my boyfriend for months, truly convinced that he was it. We talked every day, and kissed and cuddled when no one was around. I didn't want to hide us anymore, but Jackson insisted it would ruin our friendships.

Then Eric found us making out behind a car one weekend and lost his shit. He told the others and there was a huge fight. Jackson broke up with me after that, and we didn't talk for almost two years. Not Jackson. Not Eric. Not even Beau, Drew, or Brad would talk to me. Then they showed up after my accident just like it was old times, and have been hanging around ever since. I understood but I didn't, and at the same time I didn't care. When Jada and I needed our brothers, they showed up. That was all that mattered.

* * *

"TACE! How are you so bad at this?" Brad yelled as I launched yet another gutter ball down the lane.

I turned around red faced as they all laughed at me. I couldn't be angry though, because I had 68 points whereas Brad had a score of 52. "How am I still kicking your ass?" I asked, smirking at him.

"OOOOOH!!!! She got you there, B!" Drew cackled, messing up Brad's perfectly styled hair with a headlock and a noogie. The two pretended to struggle a bit before Drew released him and we all just laughed.

"I'm going to get a slice of pizza. Anyone want anything?" I offered, grabbing my wallet from my bag.

"Grab me a coke?" Jada asked.

Drew and Brad also wanted pizza, so we decided it would be easiest to just order a whole pizza. I was halfway to the concessions counter when I heard someone yell, "Wait up."

I turned around to see Jackson jogging up behind me. I won't lie and say I felt nothing for him. My heart was still hurt that he ghosted me two years ago.

26

"I can cover it, Jackson. You guys paid for the lanes, I can cover the food," I said as he fell into step beside me.

"Well, I can help carry everything back!" he offered seriously.

I realized he was going with me one way or another, so I just kept quiet. After I placed our order, I started back to our lanes. They would call out my order on the public announcement system once the pizza was ready. There was no reason to hang out at the concessions and wait.

"You look good, Stacia," Jackson whispered quietly. I just gave him a sideways glance and kept walking. "I mean it. You were always beautiful," he continued.

I stopped dead in my tracks, refusing to look at him. "Don't," I said.

"Tace," he started and I turned to look at him. He looked sad. The kind of sadness that someone has when they really fucked up.

"Stop. You want to be my *friend*? Be my friend. You want someone to hook up with on the side? *Fuck off*," I growled at him. "*This?*" I said, gesturing back and forth between our chests. "Never gonna fucking happen. You ghosted me without a fucking word. I appreciate that you all came back when I needed you…. But there will never be anything more than friendship here. I will never trust you with my heart again, Jackson."

"Everything ok?" Beau's voice suddenly came up beside me.

I looked over at him and smiled. "No. This asshole wanted anchovies and black olives on the pizza," I lied.

Beau's eyebrows shot up in shock. "BRO! We *talked about this!!!*" He yelled at Jackson, then pulled him into a headlock

27

and dragged him the rest of the way toward the lanes.

"What the hell did he do?" Eric and Drew asked, almost in unison.

"Black olives and anchovies!" Beau announced to the group.

The tension between Jackson and I disappeared as everyone took turns heckling the toppings. The conversation devolved into gross concoctions for drinks, and other food pairings. Jada laughed and cackled at the guys' reaction to our love of french fries and chocolate milkshakes. It didn't seem that nefarious until I clarified that we dip the fries *in* the shake.

"Large pepperoni, lane 26," was announced over the thunder of balls and pins colliding.

"That's us," I said and stood to collect our food. Jada pushed me back into my seat and ran off with Drew to the concessions counter. "We got this!" Drew yelled over his shoulder.

Brad and Beau sat on either side of me, looking at Jackson and Eric. Beau put his arm around my shoulders and pulled me into a side hug. "You okay?" he asked quietly.

I nodded and leaned into the hug. "I'm good, B." I couldn't help my eyes looking at Jackson. Of course it was not missed by Beau.

"You know he was fucked up after you left him," Beau continued quietly so that only I could hear. "We weren't sure if he would come back from it. If I'm honest, I didn't think you were a savage like that, Stacia."

I stiffened and pulled back slowly. *What the fuck had Jackson told them?* "Is that why you all left us without a word? 'Cause of how *I* did *him*?" I asked in barely a whisper. I could already feel my body starting to tremble from anger.

"What did you expect, Tace? He's our boy," Beau declared quietly.

"And what if it was him who ghosted me, because you all found out about us?" I asked.

Beau chuckled, "That would be some fucked up shit. You're like a baby sister to us. We'd have kicked his ass!"

"Then I guess it's a good thing I'm the bad guy in his scenario," I stated, pulling away from him completely just as Jada returned with the pizza.

"Tace. Tace!" He called me, but I kept moving away from him.

"J, I'm gonna head home," I told my sister as she tried to pass me a slice of pizza.

"Um, okay," she said, furrowing her eyebrows in confusion. "Everything okay?"

"Yep. I just remembered that I need to study my history lessons," I retorted as I removed the rental shoes and pulled my chucks back on.

Jada immediately looked at Jackson and shook her head. "I'll head back with you. I may need to study as well, it would seem." My sister knew me. I didn't have to say shit else, because she just knew.

I didn't wait around to hug the guys like I normally would have. I simply grabbed my shit and left without so much as a glance over my shoulder. I was standing outside Jada's car when the rest of them came out about ten minutes later. It sounded like the guys were arguing with each other, and then Jada lost her shit.

"Shut the fuck up!" She seethed at one of them. "You want to be an inaccurate historian? Tell your version of facts to save face? How about this? Jackson fucked my sister and then ghosted her for two years. He broke her fucking heart after taking the V card from her. So, fuck you cocks for believing the asshole over the angel. Fuck you all!" she screamed in their faces.

"*JADA!*" I shouted, absolutely mortified that she would just scream my business to everyone in the parking lot. That I *slept* with Jackson. She turned to look at me and immediately realized what she had done.

"Tace, I'm sorry," she said, running over to apologize. "I shouldn't have said anything. I'm so sorry!"

"Just get in the car. I want to leave," I whispered back, refusing to look at any of the guys now staring in disbelief at my back.

"Tace!" Eric called out. "Tell them the truth!"

My back straightened, and I turned slowly to look at the guys now standing twenty feet away from me. "Tell who *what truth?*" I asked, staring Eric in the eyes. He flinched.

Jackson couldn't even look at me. Beau took one look at me then looked over to Jackson and Eric. He knew in that instant, Jackson had lied, Eric knew, and Jada told my truth.

"With friends like you, who needs enemies? Right?" I asked, sarcastically. "Sorry, I'm not interested in repeating any mistakes with you. And fuck you for never asking my side of shit," I stated before climbing into the car and slamming the door shut.

Jada jumped into the driver's side and left the parking lot a minute later. "I'm sorry, Tace. I am so sorry," she repeated over and over.

"Stop. You didn't do anything," I replied, staring out the window as she drove back to Titi's house. I just wanted to bury my head in a hole.

Chapter 3

I felt like I had been betrayed all over again. Sleep was elusive as I kept replaying my memories of times with Jackson over and over in my head. What had I missed? What had been said or done that could have tipped things in my favor? Was it my fault for keeping shit a secret in the beginning?

"Anastacia, you have company," Titi called from the door. I grumbled, and rolled out of bed, "Tell them to wait, I'll be down in a sec."

After emptying my screaming bladder and washing my face up a bit, I trundled downstairs to see the guys waiting for me. They looked the worst for wear. Jackson had a black eye and a split lip. Eric's face wasn't much better, looking like his nose had been broken. Beau and Brad had matching panda masks from double black eyes, and half of Drew's face was swollen. All five were sporting bloodied knuckles.

I sat across from them in a wingback chair, while they were crammed on the sofa. "I'm here. What do you want?" There was no emotion in my voice.

Beau was the first to speak. "I'm sorry, Anastacia. I had no idea."

I smirked. "What exactly are you apologizing for, Beau? For ghosting me? Or for calling me a savage? Are you apologizing that you dropped me like a hot potato without ever giving me a chance? Tell me, *brother*, why *you're* sorry."

"I-" Beau started but didn't finish. He looked over at Brad and Drew, but they just shook their heads.

"And you, Jackson? Did you tell them the truth yet? What about you, Eric?" I asked. I knew I had to look like a queen interrogating some mother fuckers… "Can't say shit now that I am here to defend myself? Can't lie about me to my face, chicken shits?" I goaded them. "Just leave. With "friends" like you dicks," I said with air quotes. "Who needs fucking enemies? Get out. I have nothing to say to any of you." I stood up and started walking back to my room.

"Wait!" Eric called out when I was halfway to the second floor. "I didn't know you two were dating. I thought Jackson was cheating on his girlfriend with you, and lost my shit. I was pissed that he would treat you like a side piece."

I stopped in my tracks and turned around slowly. "Why would you think I was the side piece? We were always together."

Eric scoffed. "No, Tace, you weren't. There was you, and then there was the girl he brought around us when you weren't around. I didn't know she was the *other*…"

I looked at Jackson. "You cheated on me?" He couldn't even look at me. "How long did it take? We dated for like six months, Jackson. How long did it take?" I asked, closing the distance between us as my voice raised.

"It wasn't like that!" He protested. "They knew I was seeing someone, but you wanted to keep it quiet-"

"Bullshit! *You* didn't want them to know. *I didn't care who knew!*" I yelled in his face. Then I turned to look at the other four. "So? Who was it?"

33

Drew looked at me guiltily before whispering, "Hillary."

It was like a punch to the gut. Hillary had tormented me so brutally in school that I had to drop out. It wasn't just verbal abuse either. I was bullied on social media, fucked with during school, nasty letters left in my locker, cornered and jumped when teachers weren't around. My knees buckled, and I dropped on the floor staring at Jackson in disbelief. Brad, Beau and Drew jumped from the sofa to help me.

"You didn't," I accused in a hoarse whisper. "Do you have any idea what *she did to me?*"

Eric scooted away from Jackson. "We didn't at first, but they 'broke up' when we did. I didn't know how to face you, Tace, knowing everything that he had done."

"And the rest of you?" I asked, looking at the three men surrounding me on the floor.

"We didn't hear either version of that shit. I knew you were seeing each other. You were shit at hiding how you felt, Tace." Beau admitted. "He told us you dumped him, and said you didn't want to be friends with us because of him and Hillary."

"Then he said you were dating someone new. We didn't believe him, but then we saw you out with a guy who was hugging you and shit..." Drew added.

"Jackson is the only guy I have ever dated," I told them, shaking my head in disbelief.

"Tace, don't lie. We saw you hanging all over a guy outside Nana's. Nobody batted an eye at you two. We knew it was true," Brad interjected.

Now I was confused. Who would I have hung on that these idiots would have confused for a guy my age? "When?" I asked.

"It was last year, after your birthday," Drew stated.

"I wasn't seeing anyone," I said again, becoming defensive. "*I'm* not lying. I don't know what you think you saw, but I wasn't seeing anyone. I was heartbroken!"

Beau, Brad and Drew were insistent that they saw me with a guy. Jackson looked relieved that I may have been equally unfaithful, and Eric sat quietly in disgust. We argued over each other for nearly fifteen minutes before the Bruja walked in the front door. "I can hear you from the street. Shut up!" she yelled over us.

We all fell silent. "Tace, go help your cousin Rob get his bag out of the car. He's on leave for a week."

I pulled away from the guys and ran out the front door. Rob was Maria's son. There was nearly a ten year age difference between us, so he always felt more like an uncle than cousin when I was growing up. I threw myself in his arms when he saw me barreling out of the house at him.

"SQUISH!!" he yelled and scooped me into a big hug. "Look how much you've grown!" He gushed, squeezing and shaking me in a bear hold. "I didn't know you were here. How have things been? You doing okay? You need anything, you just ask me," he continued before returning me to my feet.

"I'm good," I said honestly, smiling up at him. "Can I help you with your bags?"

Rob chuckled. "No…. But you can get the door for me."

I agreed and moved a few steps ahead of him to hold the door, completely forgetting for a moment that the living room of Titi's house was packed with drama. So as Rob walked in with a bag on one shoulder and sack in the other, his smile dropped with both bags on the floor.

"You've got to be fucking kidding me," Rob growled, seeing the guys now standing in the living room. "Who let these assholes in here?"

"Who the fuck are you calling *us* assholes?" Jackson barked back.

Bruja stood smiling. "Boys this is Anastacia's and Jada's cousin, Rob. My sister Maria's boy. He's been in the military for nearly a decade now, so we don't get to see him that often. Be dears and let us have some family time, would you?" she asked sweetly.

It looked like someone had taken the wind out of their sails. Brad, Drew and Beau looked like they were going to be sick. Eric just looked devastated, and Jackson... Well, he looked like he was going to piss himself. Jackson had heard enough stories about my cousin to realize how badly he fucked up. They all had. Jada and I idolized Rob, and talked about him all the time when we were younger.

Beau looked at me wide eyed. "This- This is Rob?" he asked.

Rob pulled me away from the door to stand beside him. "The one and only," he answered. Then Rob looked at me. "I thought you said you didn't know any creepers or hooligans."

I felt like someone had slapped me in the forehead, suddenly remembering Rob telling me that he would protect me from creepers and hooligans. He had gone on to say that he had already scared off three dipshits that were looking at me funny. "These were the idiots you were referring to? Rob!! That's *the guys!*" I whined at him, smacking his arm.

Rob looked back over at the five beaten and bruised men in front of him. "Seriously?" he asked with a bit of uncertainty. However, before I could answer Jackson stormed out of the

36

house, leaving Eric, Beau, Brad, and Drew staring at me and Rob.

"Jesus, Tace. We fucked up," Brad admitted, stepping forward and pulling me into a hug. "I don't know if you can ever forgive me, but I am truly sorry. I am."

I reluctantly hugged him back, not really willing to just forgive and forget with just a few words. "We'll talk another day." It had to be enough. There was just too much to unwrap right now.

"Ok," he responded and left. The other three followed suit, and gave me a hug while apologizing profusely before they walked out the door.

When they were gone, the Bruja smiled at Rob and I. "Ok, loves. I have to get to work myself. Talk to you later," she said, giving us each a peck and walking out the door.

After everything was quiet, and everyone else was gone, I sat back down. "How does she do that?" I asked, looking at the door.

Rob just shook his head. "I have no idea. It's crazy, right?"

"Definitely crazy," I agreed.

Rob moved his bags out of the entry, and sat on the sofa. "Come here, squish. Tell me what's been going on. I'll order something for delivery and we can just chill out today."

I moved over to sit next to Rob on the sofa, leaning into his side. "I feel so stupid. Why are guys so dumb?"

Rob sighed and wrapped an arm around me. "Start from the beginning. Tell me what's going on, and then I can translate 'dumb dude' for you."

I chuckled. I started from the beginning and told him everything that had happened. From the guys my mom dated, to meeting Beau and company at little league, to leaving school because of my bullies. I cried and told him about falling for Jackson, and how things ended. I told him about getting my school degree early even though I was a dropout. Nothing about my life in the nine years he had been gone was left out. Accidents, work, stress, depression; everything was laid out while we sat and ate breakfast, lunch, then dinner.

By the time we were done, I was exhausted. I felt like I had been dragged through an emotional ringer. I didn't know when I fell asleep, but I woke when Rob carried me to my bed. "Shhh. We'll talk tomorrow, Tace. Just sleep," he whispered, tucking me into my bed. I closed my eyes and let the world slip away. Tomorrow I had to go back to work. Tomorrow I had to face everything that went wrong. Tomorrow I had to pretend like I wasn't broken and aching inside.

* * *

"Morning, Anastacia!" Justin greeted me as I clocked in.

"Hey, man. How's it going?" I asked, trying to be polite. Justin didn't seem like a bad guy. He was always nice, and made an effort to greet everyone he saw. Everyone liked him, so I let my guard down a little bit each time we interacted.

"How was your weekend?" he asked, loading parts into the back of my cart.

"Not too bad. Went bowling with my sister," I offered.

"Really? You can bowl with those talons of yours?" he asked, pointing at my nails.

I looked down and laughed. "I did chip one…" I admitted, holding up my middle finger at him.

"Ouch! That hurt!" he gasped, clutching his chest like I had actually wounded him.

I laughed even harder. I couldn't help it. "There you are," he said, smiling. "Don't take shit so seriously, Anastacia. You have to remember to laugh every once in a while."

I bit the inside of my cheek and nodded. "I'll try to remember that. Thank you, Justin. It's…appreciated."

The rest of my day flew by. It seemed like Justin and Jada were competing to see who could make me laugh the hardest. By the time the end of day rolled around, I no longer felt the weight on my shoulders. I walked a little taller and felt myself smiling about life, something that didn't happen often. Tuesday flew into Wednesday and before I knew it, it was Friday night again.

Jada wouldn't be home until late tonight because she had picked up an extra shift in the warehouse doing inventory. Titi was working until closing at her second job, so she wasn't going to be home before midnight. The guys, minus Jackson, had each reached out and asked if I wanted to meet up. I didn't want to go out. I didn't want to deal with people tonight. I just wanted to Netflix and chill.

When I got home, I changed into the biggest comfiest pair of sweatpants I owned, fluffy socks and a tank. Titi made chili con carne in the slow cooker while we were all working, and it smelled delicious. I made myself a bowl with a dollop of sour cream and guac, and curled up on the couch to watch TV.

Unfortunately, sitting home alone just gave me time to get in my own head. Despite the positive up swing at work, the laughter; I still felt hollow. I didn't even know what the hell I was watching. My brain was replaying the blowout with the guys. Jackson had cheated on me with Hillary.

I told them about her. He *knew* that she was making my

life hell, but he still went out with her. He fucked her after he fucked me. He stayed with her, after he ditched me. After all of our years of friendship, he threw me away. Why couldn't I be enough for him? Why wasn't I pretty enough? Was I not funny enough? Not assertive enough? *What was so fucking great about Hillary?*

A sudden sharp pain pulled me from my thoughts. I looked down at my leg and saw blood seeping through the pant leg. It took me a minute to realize that my nails were dug into my leg so hard, I broke the skin.

"Shit," I muttered, standing to go clean up my leg and change my pants out. I was halfway through cleaning the blood out of the pants before I realized the obsessive thoughts from earlier were gone. That small spark of pain pulled me from my spiral. I looked at the nail marks in my thigh. They were high enough that no one would see them, unless I was in a bikini. That wasn't going to happen.

I put some ointment on the small cuts and decided to just crawl into bed. There was nothing I needed to ponder over tonight. I just needed to sleep and not think about this shit any more tonight. Lying in my bed, I felt my mind starting to spiral again. Tossing around, I accidentally brushed against the sores on my thigh. The sudden flash of pain caused me to suck in a quick breath, and in the same instant my brain stopped wandering. I pushed on my leg again, and let my mind just go blank.

It was enough. I closed my eyes and went to sleep.

Another week flew by. Beau, Drew, and Brad had showed up at the house every night with some stupidly huge apology gift each time. The first was a giant bear holding a sign that read, 'I'm sorry.' The second was a fruit bouquet from a shop in town. By the third day, Titi told me to forgive them or tell them to fuck off after a delivery guy showed up with dozens of flowers. I broke. I couldn't keep blaming the three of them for everything that had happened, but I was done with Eric and Jackson.

Saturday rolled around and we planned to spend a day at the boardwalk in Jersey. I hadn't been there in a minute, and I was looking forward to just hanging out. We loaded up into Brad's truck and drove the hour and a half to the beach. It was after Labor Day, so the traffic wasn't nearly as bad as it would have been during the height of tourist season.

"What do you want to do first?" Beau asked as we drove around looking for parking close to the boardwalk.

"You guys want to swim first or hit the boardwalk first?" I asked.

"Boardwalk first. I'm starving," Jada whined.

Several stomachs growled in unison, causing all of us to crack up. "Want to see if the breakfast burrito place is open yet?" Beau asked.

"YES!" Jada and I answered.

I couldn't remember the last time we had breakfast burritos on the boardwalk. The place started as a food truck years ago, but then they opened up a small shop right on the boardwalk after gaining popularity. My mom would swear they were the best hangover cures.

We climbed out of the truck, grabbed our bags and started down the boardwalk. This was the best time to come to the Jersey shore. The weather was still gorgeous but the hordes of tourists were gone. The majority of people now were locals who could finally enjoy the beaches without the crowds.

41

Jada and Beau were carrying on acting silly as we went. Jada would tag Beau then dodge between me and Drew to keep from getting tagged back. When she tried to hide behind me, I moved at the last second so that she got caught. Brad couldn't help laughing when Jada started whining that I didn't have her back.

"Sisters before misters!" she yelled at me, trying not to laugh.

I ran over and jumped on her back, hugging her fiercely. "I got your back, sis!" I yelled, making everyone laugh and she piggy-backed me the rest of the way.

By the time we found the place half way down the board-walk, we were all hungry and thirsty as hell. I loved this place because the burritos were all named after bands and songs from the 70s and 80s. My favorite was called 'the cure.' It was the one my mom always swore as the best hangover cure, but it was named for the band. It had eggs, tater tots, sausage, salsa and avocado. Jada preferred the Manic Monday, which had eggs, hash, and bacon with a shot of hot sauce.

I couldn't be bothered to see what the guys ordered because I was starving. Jada and I grabbed our food and found a table for all of us near the front of the shop so we could watch people going by.

"God, this so good," Jada mumbled with a mouth full of food, making me laugh as I dug into my

"Excuse me, you're at our table," a nasally voice commented next to me.

I looked up to see two girls who didn't look to be much older than Jada or I. The one closest to me was a Jersey girl with dark bottle hair and orange spray tan. Her friend wasn't much better looking. I glanced around the restaurant to see at least ten empty tables. "Sign said to seat yourself. They don't reserve tables here," I commented, taking another bite. We kept eating, and the guys quickly joined us, taking their seats at the table Jada and I by the window.

Not reacting to either girl standing next to our table, the guys started talking about what we should do next. That was not what Jersey Barbie wanted to hear.

"Move your skinny *'spic* asses out of our fucking seats, whores," Jersey girl squawked at us.

I stopped chewing and locked eyes with my sister. Jada shook her head, and I knew we were going to kick off if they continued.

The guys stopped eating and clenched their jaws. Beau set this burrito down and stood up, "Excuse me," he called over to one of the employees. "Do you know these two?"

The woman behind the counter sighed when she saw who he was talking about. "MARISSA! IF YOU ARE NOT GOING TO BUY ANYTHING, LEAVE," she shouted at the two girls. *"MY* restaurant. *MY TABLES!* You want to sit there? *Buy some food*, and *wait* til they're done," she barked.

We tried not to laugh, but they noticed that too and huffed out of the restaurant. "Sorry bout that. My friend's daughter acts a bit spoiled because her mom and I started this business together." The woman explained.

"No worries," Drew chimed in. "These burritos are worth the hassle!" He added, making the woman laugh.

"What did you get?" I asked, eyeing the burrito he was eating.

"The Wild, Wild, West. Eggs, hash, jalapenos, peppers, chorizo and hot sauce. Want a bite?" he asked, blowing his breath across the table.

43

"Ew. No! Your breath stinks!" I scrunched up my nose at him, causing everyone to laugh.

After everyone finished eating, Jada decided to hit the arcades while it was still early. We grabbed our stuff and started back down the boardwalk. We were just about to enter the arcades when someone grabbed my ponytail and pulled me back so hard I fell on my ass.

I didn't so much see what happened next as hear Jada screaming. By the time I got my bearings back Jada was beating the shit out of Jersey Barbie. I saw her friend going to make a move on my sister, and launched onto her back, punching her over and over in the face.

"HELP! HELP! CALL THE COPS!" the two girls started screaming.

It didn't take long for the beach police to show up and break us up. Jersey Barbie, *Marissa*, started crying and telling the police how we *attacked them* because they had asked for Beau's number.

"What the fuck are you talking about?" I yelled at her.

"You grabbed my sister first, bitch!" Jada screamed.

"Be quiet!" one of the cops yelled at us.

After taking everyone's statements, those two bitches had the cops convinced that we had attacked them first. Beau and Brad were pissed yelling at the cops as they put handcuffs on me and Jada. I was so fucking angry, I swore I'd finish that bitch's face if we ever crossed paths again.

The police started walking us down to their cars, when the owner of the Arcade came running down the wooden path, yelling for the cops to stop. "You're arresting the wrong ones! I have it all on video," he huffed when he reached us.

The cops looked skeptical, but agreed to look at the footage.

Jada and I were put into the back of one car, while the Jersey girls were put into another.

"I fucking hate Jersey girls, J," I said.

She laughed and put her head back. "Next time, let's go south. Jersey got too many crazies up here."

We sat in silence for nearly thirty minutes, according to the clock on the police dash. I honestly didn't want our mom to find out if we got arrested. I didn't want to call Titi or anyone, because I was so fucking ashamed. I didn't even realize I was crying until Jada leaned over and bumped me with her shoulder.

"Come on, put your bean down on my lap, Tace," she offered. I tipped over and dropped my head on her legs. And that was how the cops found us when they opened the door.

"I'm going to help you out of the vehicle, miss," one of them offered, because my hands were still cuffed behind my back.

Another cop pulled Jada out the other side and released her cuffs as well. "The owner of the Arcade is pressing charges on the other two for attacking you in his establishment. If you want to pursue battery charges as well, you'll need to come down to the station and file a formal complaint. We have the video surveillance, so it's pretty clear who started the fight."

"So everything we said was true, and those two bitches were lying.... But you didn't believe a fucking word we said, when we had witnesses corroborating our side, and you still handcuffed us?" I started mouthing off.

"Miss, I'm sorry. We can only go off the information on hand at the time-" he started.

"That's some bullshit and you know it!" I continued. "You

45

believed beach barbie over the two *Latinas*, cause that would make more sense. Right? How about this, I'm coming down to the station with you and filing a report for racial profiling, and premeditated assault."

"I thought you said you didn't know any of them," another cop stood next to the first.

"What are *you* talking about? I'm talking about those two skanks who attacked me. They threatened me when we were eating burritos, obviously followed us down the fucking boardwalk and waited for a chance to attack me. Ask the owner of *Mary's!* She'll tell you. She even comped our food because *Jersey Jenny* was making a fucking scene over a fucking table!"

I was screaming so loud, my throat was becoming hoarse. Drew and Brad came over and held me until I calmed down. The cops told us to meet them at the police station to file my report. I was still shaking when we got to the police station. Four white cops had almost arrested the only two obviously *not white* people in a brawl. It didn't look good for them.

The sergeant came out and tried to say that it was procedure to put everyone into the police cruisers until they had all of their information. When I asked why my sister and I were cuffed while the other two were not, he had nothing to say.

By the time we left the police station, it was already four in the afternoon. The whole day was fucked. I didn't want to stay there any longer, and we headed home. I leaned against Drew on the way home, and hissed when he rubbed the back of my head.

"You okay?" he asked.

"It hurts, Drew. Everything fucking hurts," I whispered,

crying myself to sleep on his shoulder.

Chapter 4

After the fight at the beach I stayed in bed the rest of the weekend. I didn't want to be in public and get the weird looks people always gave women who were banged up. The sad, 'I see you, but I don't see you,' look. Titi just asked if I had given as well as I had taken. Jada was quick to give her the play by play of the whole ordeal. I just wanted to forget it.. I wanted to forget being ambushed. I wanted to forget being treated like my word meant nothing and forget being handcuffed like I had done something wrong.

By the time Monday rolled around, I did my best to hide everything behind layers of make-up. From a distance, you couldn't tell that anything was wrong. Anyone who didn't know me, would not suspect a thing. Up close, for those who knew me, it was obvious that my face had been fucked up.

I kept my head down the whole week, just working and sleeping. By Friday, the swelling in my lip and around my eye had gone down enough that I didn't need quite so much cosmetics to cover up the bruising. I went bowling with Jada and the guys, and attempted to get life back to normal.

Before I knew it, it was nearly Halloween and everyone was talking about this party or that, what they were wearing or where they bought what. Jada convinced me to join her and a bunch of people from work for a costume party.

What she really meant was they needed a designated driver to carry their lushed asses home. I had nothing better to do, so I agreed. Jada and I had found two costumes online and decided to dress up as light and dark angels. Of course, Jada was the dark angel. By the time we had our make-up done and costumes on, we looked amazing.

The party was held at Justin's place, which was actually much bigger than I thought it would be. He had a nice two bedroom flat in town, and the place was packed by the time we got there. Jada and I walked in and were immediately greeted by the host, and introduced to several of his friends from trade school. I kept to myself for the most part, saying hello to the few people I recognized from work, and did my best to avoid some of the handsy drunks circulating the place.

It wasn't a bad night all in all. I found myself talking to Justin a lot as the night went on. He was kind of funny and kept me laughing, despite my anxiety about being in such a crowded place. Jada was pretty drunk by the end of the party having helped herself to the cooler of beers several times throughout the night. All I could do was shake my head at her.

By eleven o'clock the party was winding down, and I started driving the people that I knew home. Jada stayed at Justin's, as she was pretty drunk and had crashed in his guest room. By the time I got back, it was nearly well after midnight, and only a few people were still hanging out. Justin offered me a drink, saying that I was in good company if I wanted to let my hair down for one night.

After checking on Jada, I decided to have a few drinks with Justin and his friends. We played bullshit and laughed for hours. I don't know how many drinks I had before the last of his friends called it, and went home. I laid back on his sofa, feeling my head swimming. I had snuck drinks with my sister before, but I had never really let myself get hammered until tonight.

I leaned over on a cushion and decided to sleep on the sofa, letting the alcohol numb everything that ran rampant through my head.

I woke up feeling someone move me and tried to protest. I just wanted to sleep. Trying to swing my arm, it wouldn't move. I whimpered and struggled in my drunken stupor to move back to my comfortable position. Something warm covered my mouth, and my consciousness faded away again.

The next time I woke, I felt like I was being pressed down by a heavy weight, and my body was shifting uncontrollably. I tried to cry out, but my mouth was covered. I blacked out again.

Finally, I woke up to the bright sun shining in my face as I lay on Justin's sofa. My head was pounding, but that was the least of my pain. I stood up from the sofa and stumbled to the guest room where Jada was sleeping.

"Wake up," I urged her.

Her eyes blinked open slowly, and began taking in the room around us. "Did we crash here?" she asked, sitting up.

"We need to leave. Now," I whispered, pulling her out of the bed.

To her credit, she got to her feet quickly and followed me out of the apartment minutes later. I ran straight to the bathroom when we got to Titi's and threw up. Somewhere

50

between the retching, I started sobbing.

"Tace?" Jada called through the door. "Your phone is blowing up, sis. Did something happen last night?"

I retched again, holding my stomach.

Jada opened the door to find me huddled by the toilet crying uncontrollably. "Shit. TITI!" she yelled over her shoulder as she ran to pull me into her arms.

My aunt came running into the bathroom and stopped dead in her tracks. One look at me, and she knew. She saw my shame. I recognized it in her eyes. It broke me, and I sobbed harder.

"Jada, leave your sister here and go get my car. Call the Bruja and tell her to meet us at the hospital."

Jada's head whipped to face our aunt and then turned back to me. "No," her voice came out broken and hoarse. "No."

No. Each time she repeated the word, my heart shattered further. I was oblivious as to how I moved from the bathroom to the car or to the hospital. My thoughts were swirling, trying to piece together what I could of the previous night. Nothing made sense.

Three nurses came in and pulled me out of my costume. A social worker sat beside me while they collected my clothing, my soiled panties, and evidence in their rape kit. Everything touching my body was placed into a bag labeled *evidence*.

They took pictures of the bruising around my thighs, my wrists, and did all kinds of tests. I was numb as they moved and positioned me.

Yesterday, I was laughing with friends. Today, I was in the hospital because I was ra-.

I retched violently, and began throwing up again. The word turned my stomach. I felt like I had been hollowed out,

51

and left an empty shell. *Why me? Why did shit always happen to me?* Why?

My aunts whispered quietly with the nurses and the doctor while I lay curled in a ball on the bed. They gave me a plan B pill in case I *may* have been assaulted.

They had run a full scope of tests for sexually transmitted diseases and started me on antibiotics *just in case.*

"I didn't ask for this," my voice finally broke. "I didn't ask for this," I cried out, shaking.

Someone tried to hug me and I flinched. I didn't want anyone to touch me. Someone gave me a set of scrubs to wear and I waited to die.

When we were finally back home hours later, I ran straight to the bathroom and turned the hot water on in the shower. I didn't wait to test it, and just stepped under the scalding stream. I scrubbed my skin with the rag until it was cherry red. I kept scrubbing long after the water had turned cold, but I still couldn't wash away the feeling. I still felt dirty.

Bruja came in, shut the water off, and wrapped my shivering body in a towel. "She's in shock. Grab the electric blanket and set it up in her room," she said to someone as she guided me out of the shower.

"What the fuck happened?" someone whispered behind me as Titi held me tucked against her chest.

"Do as I asked," she stated firmly.

It felt like I was watching a movie in slow motion. My body wouldn't stop shaking. When I looked down at my arms, they were covered in bloodied scratches from my own fingernails. My skin was red, having been scalded and then chilled under the shower.

Titi laid me down on my bed, and I was quickly covered

with a warm blanket and held.

I didn't want to deal with life any more. It was too exhausting. When would something good happen for me? I closed my eyes and let the darkness swallow me up.

* * *

The sounds of whispering voices brought me out of the dark.

"How long has she been like this?"

"Since we got back from the hospital…"

"Call your boss. Tell them she is sick, and won't be in the next few days."

"They're going to ask why."

"Tell them she was in the hospital, and they said it could take up to a week to recover. Do not say a word to anyone outside this house about what happened. Do you understand?"

"Where's her phone?"

"Um, it's in her room. The battery died, so I set it to charge."

"Turn the sound off. Don't touch it again before she wakes up."

I didn't want to hear any more and let myself drift back into the dark.

"Anastacia, you need to eat."

"Anastacia, you need to drink."

"Anastacia, we need to get you into the shower, love."

"Anastacia, take your meds…"

"Tace, you need…"

"Tace…"

I felt like a puppet being moved and manipulated against my will. Drink water. Eat food. Sleep. Brush your teeth.

53

Wake up. Sleep. Was I okay? How was I feeling?

Drink water.

Eat.

Sleep.

I wanted to die.

"WHERE IS SHE?" my mother's shrill voice filled the quiet of the house. "HOW COULD YOU LET THIS HAPPEN TO YOUR SISTER? I TRUSTED YOU TO LOOK AFTER HER, AND YOU LEFT HER TO A MONSTER!!"

That last word was accompanied by the crack of skin on skin. Then my sister's sobbing pulled me out of the dark. I stumbled out of my bed, and made my way downstairs. My mother was standing over my sister, and Jada was holding her face and sobbing.

"She didn't do anything wrong," I stated clearly. There was no emotion in my voice. I may have been numb in my body, but I knew my sister had nothing to do with what happened to me. Jada and I loved each other more than anyone else in the world.

"Oh, my goodness! Baby, are you okay?" My mother cried, pulling me into a hug.

I pulled away from her and went over to help my sister up. "Jada didn't do anything wrong, Mami," I said again.

Jada was just as innocent as I was. She didn't wish this on me, any more than I had asked for it to happen.

"She's older than you. She should have been looking out for you instead of getting drunk at a stranger's house!" our mother insisted.

"Just leave. I don't need this right now," I told her pointing at the door.

To our mother's credit, she shut up and left. I pulled Jada

54

onto the sofa with me and just snuggled up next to her. She cried softly against my hair, and apologized over and over.

"It's not your fault, J," I soothed as she quietly sobbed.

It was Saturday already. A week had passed. I had lost an entire week.

Jada and I stayed curled up together the rest of the day. We talked quietly between us, and watched stupid cartoons. Sometimes we liked binging true crime documentaries, but I started shaking each time so we stuck to the G rated shows.

That night, I sat with my phone and began going through the many missed messages and calls.

Suddenly, I felt a chill run down my spine. There were nearly 30 texts since Sunday from one number in my contacts.

[I'm sorry.]

[I shouldn't have done that.]

[Please, talk to me.]

[I don't know what I was thinking.]

I felt the color drain out of my face. His smile filled my memory.

"Tace? Are you okay?" Jada asked. "Titi!" she shouted, before pulling me into her arms again and holding me.

My body was shaking uncontrollably. "He did this to me?" The broken crackles in my voice made it almost impossible to get out any sound.

"We don't know who it was, Anastacia," my aunt whispered, running to hug me from the side opposite of my sister.

"He did it," I repeated.

"Tace, we don't know who-" Jada started again.

"Justin raped me," I whispered, dropping my phone as I ran to the bathroom. I could feel the bile on the back of my

55

teeth as I scrambled to get to the toilet in time.

Justin. Justin raped me.

I threw up. His face was there suddenly in front of mine in the dark whispering how sexy I was as he raped me. My memories were broken, but I remembered *him*.

"Tace?" my sister called out as I bent over the toilet.

There was nothing left in my stomach. Everything I had kept down, was now back in the toilet. Every time I closed my eyes, I saw it all over again, and heaved into the porcelain bowl. It felt like an endless loop of torture.

* * *

Monday morning was shit. Titi and Jada insisted that I file a police report, but it was humiliating enough that our whole family knew I had been assaulted. I just wanted to forget it. I wanted to go about my life and pretend that it never happened.

The rain was pissing down when Jada and I got to work. We ran from the parking lot to the building, hoping to get in without being soaked, our shared umbrella doing nothing to keep the downpour at bay. Between the rain and the crowd around the time clock, I didn't notice the person approaching behind me.

"Anastacia?"

It felt like someone had grabbed my throat and choked me. I couldn't breathe. My eyes widened, scanning the room for my sister. My only life line at that moment. I watched as she turned round at my name, her eyes widening in recognition.

"Can we talk?" he asked.

I couldn't move. I couldn't breathe. It felt like the room was crashing in around me, when suddenly all hell broke loose. Most of the people around us had been at the Halloween party.

"Are you fucking kidding me?!?" Jada was screaming. "You don't get to talk to her! You don't even get to look at her!"

"I'm not talking to you!" Justin yelled back. "This is between us!"

Between us? Did he really just say that?

I found myself repeating his words. "This is between us." Jada looked like I had slapped her, until she heard my next words. "You raped me and then say it is between us?"

I still hadn't turned to face him. I didn't need to face him to know that he heard me, because every single person around us stopped talking. They slowly crowded around me, and I felt my body being pulled away from him.

"Anastacia. Tace-"

"YOU DON'T GET TO TALK TO ME!" I screamed, turning to face him. "YOU'RE A FUCKING RAPIST!" I lunged at him with everything I had and knocked him to the ground. Before I could scratch his eyes out multiple sets of hands were pulling me back. "RAPIST! RAPIST" I repeated at the top of my lungs.

"Take her home!" a manager yelled at my sister, pushing his way through the crowd.

"Why does she have to leave?" someone in the crowd asked.

"She just assaulted an employee!" he barked back.

"Well, he's a rapist!" Jada screamed in his face.

I watched as the words settled in. The words processing, his eyes scanning from my hysterical form to Justin's disheveled mess on the floor. When he looked at me, I knew that he knew.

"That's a civil matter for the police to handle. I can't have employees attacking each other in the factory. I'm sorry, Anastacia, but you have to leave today," he explained.

Whatever last bit of dignity I held, broke. "Why? Why do I have to go home? Why do I have to hide while he can go around smiling?" My voice trembled, but I couldn't stop it.

"I'm sorry."

Jada grabbed my arm and walked me back to the car. She didn't bother with the umbrella this time, so we were completely soaked by the time she had shoved me into the seat and closed the door.

"He's right, Tace," she said, starting the car.

I couldn't understand what she was saying. My mind was still trying to understand why I was being sent home. I was the victim. Justin was the bad guy, not me.

"This is a civil matter. We're going to the police. I'm taking you there now, and we're filing a police report. Then we're getting a restraining order against him," she continued as we pulled away from the parking area and onto the main road.

Jada held my hand as we entered the police station. She held my hand as I uttered the words I never imagined ever saying out loud. *I was raped.*

The officer took us aside and set us in a small conference room until a detective could take my statement. The man had tried to get Jada to leave the room, but I started shaking. I didn't want to be alone in that room with any man. He stormed out of the conference room muttering something that I couldn't make out, and returned with a female officer.

Jada was then asked to leave, as the female officer took my statement. I told her everything, from how I met Justin to when I started working at the factory. She asked if I knew

58

that it was illegal for me to have been drinking.

"Is that really what this is about?" I asked back, no tone in my voice.

She must have realized how her words sounded to me, and her eyes softened. "It's a common tactic used by predators. I meant nothing by it. Please continue," she encouraged me.

I told her everything that I could remember. From the moment we arrived at that apartment to when I was dragging my sister out the front door. I couldn't stop my hands from trembling.

"Without any evidence, this might be a hard case to prove. I want you to know that," she admitted.

"My aunt took me to the hospital. They t-too-" I couldn't get the words out. Every utterance evoked memories of that weekend. I was reliving everything all over again.

"You went to the hospital?" she asked, looking more positive.

I nodded my head and bit my lip.

"Did they do a rape kit?" the officer asked.

I just shrugged my shoulders. They had done a lot of stuff.

She placed her pen down on the table and set her hands in her lap facing me directly. "You probably don't know what that is so I'm going to explain, and you have to tell me yes or no. You can't just nod your head, understand?" she explained.

I nodded.

"I need to hear your words," she repeated.

"Yes."

"Did they take your clothes?" Yes.

"Did they examine your body?" Yes.

"Did they do a pelvic exam?" Yes.

"Did they take pictures?" Yes.

"Did they run tests for transmutable diseases?" Yes.

"Did they give you a case number? Did you tell them any-thing about the incident? Have you had any communication with the individual since that night?"

Yes. Yes. Yes.

"Was it verbal or text?"

"He texted me and then tried t-t-to talk to me at work," I stuttered.

"May I see your phone?" she asked.

I unlocked my phone and passed it to her. She opened the messaging app and started scribbling notes.

"Show me which ones were from him."

I pointed to the contact listed and she opened up the chain of messages back and forth. I watched her scribbling notes as she read. 37. He had apologized 37 times since Sunday. Before that we had exchanged a total of 8 messages between us, and those only dealt with work related matters.

"Have you deleted any messages?" she asked, looking at me now.

I started shaking my head, "No."

"Ok. My name is Sergeant Jaines. I'm going to give you my card. Detective Williams, the man who was here earlier, is going to be the lead on your case, but if you are not comfortable speaking with him just call me."

Sergeant Jaines passed me two small business cards, one for each of them. I stared down at the cards, feeling absolutely unsure if I was doing the right thing.

"What happens next?" I asked.

"Next we investigate. Someone from the prosecution's office will be in contact with you in the next two weeks. I have your name and contact information here, so that is what they are going to use. Do you have any other questions?" she asked.

I just shook my head. "I want a restraining order. We work in the same factory, but I don't want to see him."

Sergeant Jaines nodded. "I'll take you over to the clerk so that you can file for the order. It usually takes a few days, but I will ask that they fast track this one," she explained, standing from her seat. "Follow me, and we will go over there."

* * *

The courts denied my request for a restraining order against Justin. My shift was changed at work so that we would not have to interact with each other, but it didn't stop him from trying to talk to me. The more days that passed, the cockier and less apologetic he became. The last straw was hearing him talk about me in the break room a month later.

"She's a lot hotter on the eyes than she was in the sack."

"No way. I don't believe that for a second. Her ass is too tight to be a bad lay," another guy commented.

I couldn't move. I stood there frozen in the doorway, stunned. I listened as Justin went on and on about what a shitty lay I was to every guy in the room. My chest felt so fucking tight. Somewhere in those few minutes the sorrow and depression that had eaten at me disappeared. I became a wrathful burning inferno. I took out my phone and began mashing keys. When everything was done, I threw my drink across the room hitting Justin in the face. Blood immediately gushed from his nose, and everyone around him backed away, knocking over chairs.

"Did you tell them how unresponsive I was while you fucked me, Justin?" I asked, staring at him.

His eyes were wide as saucers, watching me strut across the room directly towards him.

"Hmm? Did you tell them how you tied me up that night?" I winked, looking around at the other men in the room.

"No? You didn't tell them how you got me drunk, then sedated me and raped me in your house after I was their designated driver?"

Several jaws dropped and wide eyes turned to stare back at my rapist. Justin looked like he was going to throw up. *Too bad, I'm not done yet.*

I stepped up onto a chair and stood looking down at every person in that break room. "That's right. I was a shit lay... BECAUSE HE DRUGGED AND RAPED ME!! YOUR COLLEAGUE HERE IS A FUCKING RAPIST! RA-PIST!" I screamed, dragging out every single word.

"WHILE I MADE SURE THAT EVERY ONE OF YOU ASSHOLES MADE IT HOME ON HALLOWEEN. WHILE YOU WERE SAFE IN YOUR BEDS, THIS MOTHER FUCKER WAS RAPING ME!!!"

"ANASTACIA!" a manager yelled from the doorway. "This is not appropriate!"

I looked over at the man who had done the bare minimum through the past month to help me. "What's inappropriate, *Dick?*" I asked my manager, Richard. "That you refused to change the rapist's schedule and made me change mine instead? That not one mother fucking man in this warehouse had the balls to tell this lying sack of shit to shut the fuck up? What's inappropriate about defending myself against a man who brutally raped me? HUH?!?!?"

"Do you have any proof?" someone asked.

I started laughing. "Do I have proof? Yeah. I have proof. I just posted all of my proof on my instagram account before walking in the door. There's copies of my medical records, the pictures of the bruising on my body, screenshots of him apologizing and admitting to raping me the day after. There's also a video of every single one of you egging him on, that I sent to corporate," I said, smiling at them.

"Oh yeah, I also shared it with your wives, assholes. Don't bother firing me, *Dick.* I just had my lawyer contact corporate. I won't be coming back here." With that I stepped off the chair and kicked it back in Justin's face.

I walked out of there with my head held high. It lasted all the way until I reached my car, then I balled my eyes out. I needed a lawyer and fast. I called my mother and told her everything that had happened. If I didn't know better I would have sworn she was squealing on the other end. Before I had even gotten home, my mother was calling me back to tell me that I had an appointment with her lawyer and she was on her way to get me.

I told her not to bother, and just send me the address. One benefit of my mother's many fucked up relationships, she had an amazing attorney on retainer. Mr. Hughes was a no nonsense man who didn't care what you did, he gave his all to representing his clients. He made no bones about where the line lay between confidentiality and his duty to report criminal activities. For people living between the gutter and prison, he was a god-send.

My appointment with Mr. Hughes lasted 45 minutes. I gave him everything I had and access to whatever else he asked for. He filed a complaint for a hostile working environment against the company, and included the video I had taken. The man blazed through everything that had to be done for the work side of the house, and then called the assistant district attorney's office to inquire about the status of my case.

Unsurprisingly, she hadn't even heard about it. She told him to give her ten minutes and that she would call back. I thought she would blow him off, but she didn't. She called exactly ten minutes later, and asked to set up an appointment with me.

It wasn't like I had a job to get to, so we agreed to meet at noon. Mr. Hughes went with me to her office the next day for the appointment. The woman was older than she sounded on the phone. She introduced herself as Marcy Staniewicz. I couldn't pronounce her last name to save my life.

She just smiled politely. "Just call me, Marcy. Everyone does," she said.

We took our seats at a small table in her office, and she began going through what I could only assume was my file. There didn't seem to be a whole lot in it.

Once she was done, she excused herself and made a phone call to the police department. Detective Williams had never questioned Justin, let alone any of the other witnesses I had named. He had not even retrieved my rape kit from the hospital for processing in the six weeks since the rape. When she finished her conversation with the police she returned to the table.

"This isn't what you want to hear, but your case isn't as far along as it should be. I have given my expectations to the detective in charge, and I hope to be able to move forward with your case within the next month," Marcy explained.

Another month?

"What do I do until then? I don't have a job. He's telling everyone that I was just some horrible lay while apologizing to me for what he did!" I said, crying. "Why is he allowed to continue going about his life every day while I am like this?"

Marcy bit the inside of her cheek. "It sucks," she agreed after a minute. "The system isn't perfect, but it's one of the best in the world. Just give me some time and I will get you your justice. I promise."

Mr Hughes took me back to his office so that I could get my car, and I went home. I needed a job. I needed money to pay Hughes, and I needed something to distract me from the growing number of cuts hidden on my legs.

Chapter 5

I was spiraling and I didn't know how to stop the carousel. My legs were covered with shallow cuts. I couldn't keep my food down, so my weight was dropping. I went days without showering or even getting out of bed. I looked... *rough*.

"Tell me what you want to do?" my mother asked as we sat in the attorney's office.

It had been three months since the last time I had seen Marcy in person. Every phone call promised results, but seeing her face when we walked in, I knew it wasn't good. After the incident at work, Justin hired a lawyer of his own and doubled down on the 'it was consensual' bullshit. My skin crawled every time I thought about it that night.

I never thought of myself as stupid, but this nightmare was eating away at my confidence. I did everything they told us not to do as young women. I allowed myself to let my guard down, thinking I was among friends. I fucking drank and enjoyed myself for the first time in who knew how long, and what happened....

It wasn't like I was a naive little girl from a sheltered life. I grew up in one of the worst cities in our state. How stupid was I to trust someone I didn't know? Someone like Justin, a pretty boy with a pretty smile. They were always the worst, smiling in public while they abused the shit out of girls behind closed doors. I wasn't even his girl. We weren't dating. We weren't even talking like that, so why did he choose me? Why was I the easy target in his mind?

Why was I always the victim? First, I was bullied out of school by Hillary and her asshole friends. Then there was Jackson. The one guy I let in, but he just used me, too. Once he punched that 'V' card, I was dropped like a hot potato. Why was I never enough to be treated right?

"You'd have to take the stand, Anastacia."

I wasn't listening to anything Marcy was saying. "What?"

"I was saying that you'd have to testify in court," Marcy repeated.

"What does that mean?" My mother asked, reaching over to hold my fidgeting hands in hers.

My ears started ringing and I couldn't stop the pounding sensation in my chest. I could feel a cold sweat starting to run down my back.

"Anastacia would have to take the stand and tell her version of the story."

Mom nodded, as if she thought this was good news. "And then?"

As if she couldn't look any more uncomfortable, Marcy awkwardly shifted in her seat; the chair making a horrible squeaking noise. "His attorney would also question you, Anastacia."

"It won't change my story," I said.

Marcy licked her lips nervously, before she continued. "His lawyer will attempt to ruin your credibility as a witness. It is what any defense attorney would do. He will use any information they could obtain on your history, social media use, how you dress…. They may even get statements from coworkers, or others who were at the party to diminish the veracity of your story."

I finally understood her look when we came in. She didn't feel like they could win the case. My word, the evidence taken at the hospital; it wasn't enough. I wanted to cry, but I was just numb. If she pursued the case, my whole life would be brought under a microscope. Who I slept with previously, my home life, my way of dressing, what previous co-workers thought of me.

What she didn't say was I would lose because I came from a broken home. My family was poor, his wasn't. Justin grew up in a middle class stable household. My mother was dating junkies, so I must be one too. The way I do my makeup could be perceived as provocative. I had agreed to sleep at his house, so the leap could be made that I agreed to sleep with *him*. I *'seemed happy'* that night, so how could I have claimed rape the day after?

Marcy kept talking, but I had stopped paying attention. Everything that came out of her mouth just made my stomach turn further. I thought women had more power than this. How was it still a law in Delaware that the victim had to prove they didn't consent for a rapist to be tried? The bruising on my body was not enough. The abrasions and bleeding around my labias and vagina wasn't enough. The blood work that showed I was *still* three times over the legal limit of alcohol consumption hours and hours later…. Not enough?

The text messages of him apologizing… Not enough.

The voice mail messages of apologies and him begging to forgive him for what he did… Not enough.

Marcy was shaking her head sadly and apologizing to my mother and I for being unable to get me the justice that I deserved. What did I deserve? *Truly?* I thought I deserved to be happy, but that was bullshit.

When had I *ever* been happy? The few moments of my life where I felt safe between hell and torment could fit into the palm of my hand.

"Nothing."

My mother looked at me in shock. "What did you say?"

"I said, nothing. I don't want to do anything. I don't want to be here. I'm done," I said, grabbing my bag and pulling my jacket on.

Marcy looked like she would cry, but said nothing. She knew. This was her job after all. She would take the cases that she could win, and I was no winner.

My mother looked from Marcy to me a couple times before trying to persuade me to fight.

"Anastacia, you could still win this. You can't give up. Fight back. She just told you the worst cases, you can still do this!"

I shook my head and looked over at Marcy. "Are you finished?"

"Yes. Unless you have any questions for me?" Marcy offered, knowing that she didn't have a single good answer to give.

I couldn't help the angry chuckle that bubbled out of me. "No. I really fucking don't," I said.

"Anastacia!" My mother's voice pitched up for cussing. I was a grown ass adult of 18 years old, I would cuss if I wanted, because being good had gotten me nothing but abuse. She kept calling after me even after I walked out of the office and stepped into the elevator.

I didn't wait around to hear her apologize to the lawyer, the District Attorney, or anyone else. There was nothing that any of them would do to help me.

* * *

I drove around for hours after leaving the courthouse. In the back of my head I just wanted to get away from everything. I wished I could be someone else. Someone happy. Someone who didn't have to constantly fight to survive. I didn't want to be treated like shit. I didn't want to be poor and looked down on, like some worthless piece of shit.

I didn't realize how long or far I had driven until the gaslight lit up on the dash. I pulled over at the nearest gas station, my car sputtering to make it the final few feet to the pump. It wasn't until I was paying for the fuel that I realized I had crossed the state line.

I was in the center of Philadelphia, surrounded by bustling city life. I would love to live in a place like Philly. There were so many people, I could start all over. I could be someone else, and just start fresh. The thought stuck in my head the ninety minutes it took me to drive home. I didn't need to ask anyone for permission, because I was an adult. I didn't need to clear my schedule with anyone, because I didn't have a job. I could just pack up and start all over.

By the time I got to the house, I had decided to start job hunting in Philly. "Hey, Titi?" I called out as I walked in the door.

"Hi, sweetie. Your mom told me what happened at the lawyer's. Are you okay?" Titi asked, coming out of the kitchen to give me a hug.

I shook my head and then nodded. "I'm fine. Can I use your computer to look for a job?"

She pulled back and held me at arm's length, looking over my face for any signs of distress. "Are you sure?" she asked.

"Positive."

"My computer is up in my room on my desk. Let me know if you need help with anything," she offered.

I pulled her back into a quick hug, and then yelled a quick thanks as I ran up the stairs. I started with a quick search for available jobs in Philly. That was too many. I didn't have a resume, and other than doing nails or moving shit in a warehouse, I didn't have any real experience either. I started looking for nail technician jobs. I found ten, but four of them were too long of a drive.

I copied the contact information for the last six and printed them out. I wouldn't sit around and wait for calls back. I would drive to each of these places and fill out an application in person. As the printer spit out my paper, I realized how ragged my nails were. I needed to clean them up, if I was going to try and sell my skills.

I grabbed my nail kit out of my room and started working on my left hand. I decided to do a different technique on each finger, to showcase my versatility. I did a silk wrap, an acrylic, a gel tip, and a dip. On my thumb I used two different mediums, one white and one pink, so that it looked like an American manicure.

By the time I was done filing, sanding, painting and decorating, two hours had passed. My nails each looked pretty, but having different styles and colors on every single nail on the one hand looked crazy as shit. I cleaned up all of my stuff, put it away, and started looking for a nice outfit to wear.

I decided on a pair of black skinny jeans and a black top. Nana always said that clean and simple attire made the best impressions. Now I just needed to wash myself and get some sleep. I hid the list of job announcements in my bag before I crawled into bed. I had a plan to make my own way going forward, but that didn't mean I wanted anyone else's input or commentary. I was keeping this to myself until I couldn't.

* * *

"I'm really sorry, I would love to hire you. Truly, I would. But state law requires that our technicians are at least 20 years old," the manager explained.

"Could I at least work part time?" I asked, hoping that someone would be willing to hire me. I had been turned down at every stop because of my age.

Every single salon loved my work, and what wasn't there to love? My nails were gorgeous. I was just too young to be a tech in Pennsylvania.

The woman smiled sadly, seeing my desperation. I didn't have to say I was desperate for work, it was written all over me. I promised myself that I would not cry, but it was getting harder and harder to hold back the tears with every rejection. How would I move forward if I couldn't find a job?

"I appreciate your time," I said politely, forcing a smile on my face and standing up to leave the back office we had been sitting in for the past five minutes. This was the longest meeting so far, but it didn't matter if I wasn't getting a job.

"Look, I know there are a lot of salons looking for technicians, but you won't get hired because of your age," she started.

I did my best to maintain my smile when in my head I was screaming, 'No shit!'

"But I might know a place that is looking for someone. I can set you up an appointment if you'd like?" she offered, biting the inside of her cheek.

"I can't work in PA because of my age. I can't do anything illegal, or I could lose my license," I countered. "I appreciate the offer."

"It's not illegal!" She corrected, opening a desk drawer. "I can't hire you because of the transactions between customers and technicians. This other place, however, would be hiring you as a nail artist for their performers. It's not the same."

I stopped trying to leave and listened as she rummaged through a drawer looking for a business card. It was black and shiny with very little writing on it, when she found the one she was looking for.

"I don't understand."

"Think of a theater. They have their own make-up artists, costume design, and set builders. The workers are paid by the theater to do an hourly job, so they can get around the age restrictions that we can't," she explained. "Take this and tell them you were referred and vetted at my salon."

I took the business card and stared at it, flipping it over in my hand. There was a simple silver swirl across the front and an address on the back. Nothing more.

She must have seen the skepticism on my face, because she stepped forward to assure me. "I know the owner. It's good money, if you don't mind working odd hours around the *performers*."

I just sighed, and said thank you. What else could I say?

I was out of options and looking to break away from my whole life. If I wanted a chance to do something for myself, maybe this was it.

"If you want, I can give them a call and say that you are on your way over?" She offered.

I nodded. "I would appreciate that. Thank you."

I didn't wait around anymore and got to my car three blocks away. I would have to find a better solution for transportation, because parking in the city was a premium. I had been lucky to find an empty spot with a parking meter, and even luckier to find enough spare change rolling around in my car to pay for parking.

I was walking the final block when I saw someone circling my car. "Hey! Get away from my car!" I shouted, running down the side toward the guy.

I was absolutely mortified when he turned and I saw that he was parking police. "I'm so sorry, I thought you were about to steal my car! I'm not over my time. I'm leaving now. I was just here for a job interview," I rambled.

The guy was older and looked nonplussed. "Your meter just ran out. Get in your car and go, or I'll ticket you," he grumbled and walked off to check the next metered car down the line. I guess the city of brotherly love didn't extend to little sisters.

I didn't waste any more time, threw my bag in the passenger seat, and climbed into my car. I pulled the card out of my pocket and plugged the address into the navigation on my phone. It would take me twenty minutes to get there in lunch traffic, but it would be worth the hassle if I left there with a job. I didn't care at this point. I needed a job to make a clean break.

* * *

I pulled into a parking lot tucked behind the building indicated on the navigation, and immediately felt like I was being set up. None of the businesses were open in this area. I walked around for a bit until I found the door marked 'staff only,' and knocked as loudly as I could. In my mind no one would be manning the door so I needed to make sure they heard me.

The door suddenly swung open, and a girl not much older than me stood there looking confused. "Was that you banging?" she asked.

"Yeah, I wasn't sure if anyone would hear me. I'm here about a job?"

She looked me over for a few minutes and then smiled. "Come on in."

"Are you old enough to work in a place like this?" She asked, still eyeing me as she closed the door behind me.

"I was sent over by a salon near Franklin, the owner said you all needed a nail tech," I explained.

A look of relief washed over her face. "Okay, let me take you up to Marjory. She's the one who oversees all that." I followed her through the narrow halls and up a flight of stairs to the office.

"Hey, Marj. Got a girl here looking to work as our nail tech," she announced, as we walked into a small room set up with make-up stations. This was not the office I was expecting.

A woman who looked to be in her late thirties smiled up at me. She was probably one of the most beautiful black women I had ever seen. Her hair was pulled back in a messy bun of braided locks, and there wasn't a spot of make up on her face. I couldn't put my finger on what made her so stunning, but whatever it was.... She had it.

"What's your name, sweetie?" she asked.

"Anastacia."

"Who sent a little lamb like you into a lion's den?" She murmured, eyeing me over the same way the other girl had at the door.

"I was over at a salon on Franklin, but I'm not old enough to work as a tech in PA yet. So she sent me over here," I explained, holding out the business card.

Marjory seemed to recognize the card and her smile stiffened for just a minute before she recovered. It was quick, but I still saw it.

"Are you certified?" She asked, taking the card from my hand.

"I am. In Delaware," I added quickly.

"Why are you up here looking for work, instead of there. PA has stricter rules about age restrictions in certain industries."

"I need a job that pays well, and I couldn't find that where I was."

It wasn't even close to the truth, but I wasn't going to share that right out the gate. I needed a job away from all of the shit that was my life. I needed a clean start.

"What kind of experience do you have? You don't look like you're old enough to even have credentials," Marjory commented, passing the black card back to me.

"I took night classes, and passed my test while I was still in school. I got my credentials as soon as I turned nineteen. I can do whatever you need: silk, acrylic, gel, dips... I can do all of it," I explained calmly, even though my heart was racing.

"Do you have any examples?"

I held out my left hand to show her my work. It wasn't the usual samples people would expect from a nail tech, but if I could make my own nails look this good one-handed... Anyone with two eyes would know that I could put my money where my mouth was.

Marjory and the other girl looked over my nails. "You did this yourself?" The girl asked.

"Yeah, last night."

"Marjory," the girl exclaimed, thrusting my hand at the other woman's face. "No one does work like this for us. Please give her a chance!" She pleaded.

"Cherry, go get the other girls. It needs to be a consensus," Marjory said, jutting her chin toward the door.

The girl squealed and ran out the door. It dawned on me that she had never once given me her name since opening the door.

"Take a seat, Ana."

"Tace," I corrected. "No one calls me that. You can just call me, Tace."

Marjory smiled back at me. "Okay, *Tace.* Let me tell you a little about our business. I am the backroom manager. I am responsible for hiring whoever we need to make the show run smoothly. For the most part, the girls do their own make-up and costumes, but they can't do their own nails. This means thirty sets of nails to maintain, on call."

"What would the pay be?" I asked, getting right to the point. "I realize I won't be making tips, so I need to know how much money the job pays."

"How much do you want?" she asked.

No one had asked me that before. "Five hundred. A week. I'll be on call for whatever you need."

Marjory's eyebrows shot up. "That's a lot of money for nails," she commented.

"It's a lot of money for gas driving up here on a moment's notice. Girl's gotta eat and pay the bills," I retorted.

Before she could say anything else, a group of young women began filing into the dressing room. There weren't 30, but there were definitely more than 20. The space was suddenly filled with the noise of chatter, and I did my best not to shift uncomfortably as every set of eyes raked over me.

"This is Tace. She's applying for a job as the nail tech," Marjory explained, immediately silencing all of their whispering. "I need one of you to get your nails done, so we can determine if she's a good fit."

The women immediately began talking between themselves eyeing their nails. Whoever had done them before was good. They were gorgeously painted, some even had embedded gems in the thumb and middle fingers. At first I thought they would be fighting to get their nails done, but I quickly realized that they were arguing against letting me do their nails.

"Is she even old enough?"

"I am not risking my livelihood on some kid."

"Why are you looking at me to be the guinea pig?"

"Is she fucking serious?"

I rolled my eyes and started looking at their hands, seriously appraising the work that had been done.

"Your gel is cracked," I said pointing at one of the women.

"They didn't set the stone in correctly, so I'm guessing they get caught on shit all the time," I commented pointing to another with my right hand.

"They used weak tips for that style of nail, so they break easily."

"Their style of patterning should be cleaner."

"Her nails are too thick at the cuticle so they look fake."

"Too wide."

"Your nail is exposed on the sides."

I pointed out the flaws of every single set of manicured nails that I could find, making the whole room of skeptics pissed off instead.

"I may look young, but I am damn good at what I do," I said, holding out my left hand for them to see. "I'm not trying to screw you over, I just need a damn chance to prove that I deserve this job."

There was a long moment of silence as the women exchanged glances with each other, sharing some unspoken conversation among them.

"Let her do mine. She fucks it up, she gets black balled," a young woman spoke up. She had curly red hair that fell around face in wispy tendrils, and freckles for days. The other women looked shocked.

"Are you sure you want her working on your shit today?" One of the women asked.

The red head smiled at me like I was about to lose. "If she fucks up, she's black balled, Marjory."

"Before you get too high on your horse, Angel. Terry sent her," Marjory commented, watching as the red head flushed with irritation.

"Fine. I'll take that under advisement with the management when she's scurrying out the door. Let's go, little girl. My time is money, and you can't afford me."

Chapter 6

"I need to grab my kit out of my car," I said, walking toward the door Cherry had led me through. The others had all come from another door, which I was guessing was the main stage. Angel wanted her nails done right now, I would do her nails right now. "I'll need someone to hold the door for me."

The young girl named Cherry jumped up to help. "Come on. I'll help you," she smiled.

I stopped listening to the nagging voices in the room, as they were being drowned out by the louder one in my head. It was all me, telling me how stupid I was. How incompetent I was. I didn't want to hear it from anyone else, but hearing it from my own inner demons was harder to ignore.

I could feel myself starting to shake from the nerves. Suddenly, a warm hand grabbed mine. I looked up to see Cherry staring back at me.

"Angel may be a bitch, but her word goes a long way in this place and across Philly. Don't be nervous. Just think of her as something wealthy entitled witch you want to shut up. Take her money. To do so well, she has to eat her words," she whispered.

I nodded furiously, grateful for the small pep talk. I wiped

81

at my eyes, and made some lame excuse about the dust in the back halls as Cherry pushed open the door for me. It didn't take long for me to grab a travel suitcase and a tote from the trunk, and scurry back into the building. I handed the tote to Cherry, and followed her back to the dressing room.

The girl had cleared a table for me by the time we got back, so I was able to set up a station quickly. I set my portable UV lamp up to the side and took out everything I needed. "I'm ready when you are," I said, looking at Angel.

Angel sat down in front of me and passed her hands over so that I could inspect her nails. The work was beautiful, but there was serious damage down the midline of the thumb. I saw this a lot when people caught their nail inside car door handles.

"Do you want a full set or fill and repair?" I asked.

"Full set."

"Okay," I said, filling a bowl with acetone.

Angel moved to dip her finger into the bowl, and I stopped her.

"What the hell are you doing?" I asked.

Angel looked at me like I was an idiot. "I'm helping you soak the tips off, obviously."

I snorted and shook my head. "If you want to mess up your skin, we'll soak 'em all," I said as I stuffed the bowl of acetone full of cotton. "Or you sit back and let me remove the nails without damaging your skin or the nail beds."

Before she could say another word, I began topping her nails with the cotton balls and wrapping the tips with foil.

"Why are you doing it that way?" Another girl asked, scooting closer to watch what I was doing.

"It's too much work for the acetone in a bowl to work

through ten nails. By soaking the cotton and applying to where I want the acetone to work, I get a stronger and faster result."

"How long will that take?" She asked.

"Ten minutes."

This time Angel spoke up. "I'm supposed to sit here for ten minutes?"

"No, you're going to sit here for 40 minutes while I redo a full set," I corrected her, continuing the process of soaking and wrapping. "How do you want them done?" I asked.

Angel snorted, "Like they were before you started."

"Sorry, I can't do that," I started as I pulled out the silk wraps and gel powder. Before Angel could make another smart ass comment or insult me further, I finished the rest of my thought.

"I would never let a client walk away from my station with broken or shattered nails."

Angel sucked in like she wanted to retort, but there was nothing she could say. She thought I hadn't noticed the breakage, but she was sorely mistaken. I saw it, and called her on it to boot!

"I'm going to recommend a silk wrap with the gel tip. I noticed that you like them thin. This way you can keep the strength without the bulky thick nails," I explained, pulling the foil and cotton off of the first finger nail.

I always loved opening the little bundles to see just how much of the nail product remained. I was not disappointed with Angel's nails. They were practically melting into the cotton foil as I unwrapped them. I made quick work of removing the old acrylic and cleaned up her nail beds.

We didn't talk while I applied the new tips. She didn't

83

say a word when I applied the silk wraps or the gel cover. In fact, I didn't really hear anyone saying anything while I worked. It was a combination of my concentration, and the others talking quietly, watching me do my thing. I went with coffins, but had made the thumbs a bit shorter than I normally would.

If Angel noticed, she didn't say anything. When it came time to paint, I decided on an angels and demons look, with red flames creeping up to little wings on three of the nails on each hand. The odd two got small gems. When I finished, I couldn't have been happier. I put her hands under the UV lamp and began cleaning up my makeshift station.

"Why are the thumbs shorter?" Angel asked after not saying a word the entire time.

"You tend to jam your thumbs in tight places, like car doors. I made them a little shorter so they won't get caught in shit and break," I explained.

"Who told you about my car?" She asked, sounding defensive.

I stopped what I was doing and looked at her like she was an idiot. "I don't know anyone here, nor do I know anything about anyone's vehicle. I just know that fracturing on the thumbs, like you had, usually happens when they get their thumb nail caught in the door handles."

She pursed her lips and started looking at my work, now that the UV timer had gone off. "Why did you paint flames on them?"

"Because your name is Angel, but you're a hell of a pain to deal with?" I commented, smirking.

Whatever side chatter had been going on suddenly stopped. I could have heard a pin drop it go so quiet. It slowly dawned on me that I probably shouldn't have poked at this particular bear.

To my surprise, Angel arched an eyebrow and winked at me. "Don't you forget it," she smiled.

There was a group exhale, and then the others were swarming around Angel to see what kind of work I had done.

"These are so pretty!"

"I just got mine done, or I would have you do mine."

"How did she get them so thin?"

"Angel, you didn't even flinch once. Did it not hurt at all?"

"I'm due for a fill next week, but I think I want you to redo mine. Can you do a starry night? Cause my name is *Star?*"

I was overwhelmed by the positive feedback, but I didn't have a job yet. "I just came for an interview. But I can't work in PA because I'm only 19," I apologized, closing up my bags.

Angel gave Marjory a look and the other nodded. "Break time is over, back to rehearsals!" Marjory yelled, clapping her hands.

The group of women waved at me as they ran out the door they had come through after I arrived. I grabbed my bags and started toward the door.

"Walking away already?" Marjory asked.

"No, I was going to take my shit out to my car and then demand you hire me."

"I can't pay you five hundred a week, but I can cover three fifty."

"Four hundred," I countered, watching her watch me.

"Three fifty, plus tips from the girls."

I couldn't help the laugh that barked out. "I need five hundred a week, I can't make less than that."

"Well, considering you just received a hundred dollar tip for your first day, I don't think that will be a problem," Marjory chuckled.

My jaw dropped. "She tipped a hundred?" I asked in shock.

"Angel is one of the most demanding girls we have here. She takes her job seriously, and image is everything in this business. Getting her approval will have customers lining up from all over town to see you."

"But I can't work as a nail in PA," I repeated.

"You're not working as a nail tech here. I am hiring you to work backstage. Your hours will be eleven to eight, Wednesday to Sunday. Mondays and Tuesdays are off," Marjory continued.

"Eleven am to eight pm?" I asked.

"Yeah. For now. Your hours may get shifted later depending on how things go."

"When can I start?" I asked, unable to keep the shit eating smile off of my face.

"Tomorrow. I'll see you at eleven. We'll get you a key and access card so that you can let yourself in the back door. Employees do not use the main entrance," she said, winking.

"Ok. I'll see you tomorrow, Marjory!"

"One more thing before you go," Marjory called out as I was about to run out the door. "Here's my card. If anyone gives you any trouble, use it," she said, passing me a black card with a metallic red swoosh on the front.

I studied it for a minute. "This looks a lot like the one from the other salon," I said, looking up.

"Think of it like a collective. We look out for each other and our interests."

"Huh. Like a small business bureau?" I asked.

Marjory laughed. "Yeah. We'll call it that. I look forward to working with you, Taze."

I didn't waste anymore time, and lugged my kits back out to my car. Normally, I would leave my station set up where I worked, but this was my livelihood in my hands. I hadn't really started yet, and I didn't trust them yet.

I plugged Titi's address into the navigation and started back home. Soon I could live here in Philly and not have to worry about anyone messing with me. I could be whoever I wanted and start with a fresh new life. A life where I wasn't surrounded by memories of everything that had gone wrong.

By the time I got on the freeway, I was singing at the top of my lungs to Chun-li by Nicki Minaj.

"Ayy, yo… Look like I'm goin' for a swim."

I had a job.

"Dunked on 'em, now I'm swingin' off the rim."

I would be making more money than any place I had ever worked before.

"Bitch ain't comin' off the bench."

I'd need three months to create my savings buffer…

"While I'm comin' off the court fully drenched."

Then I could start looking for a new place to live in the city.

"Here go some haterade, get your thirst quenched!"

Holy shit. I had a job, and I was moving to Philly! I couldn't wait to tell Jada.

"SHIT!" I yelled.

I had to tell Jada. She was going to be so pissed that I made all of these plans without her. Could it wait until I got home to tell her? I looked at the time, and realized that she was probably still at work. I couldn't call her if she was working. My stomach settled a bit once I realized that I couldn't tell her anything just yet. I wasn't sure what she would think of all of this, but I knew she would support whatever I decided.

She was my ride or die sister.

* * *

"What is this all about?" Jada asked as we took our seats at the restaurant.

"I wanted to treat my sister," I said, smiling as I grabbed a menu.

Jada knew something was up. She left for work before me, but I came home a couple hours after every night this week. I had no idea how I kept this quiet, but I made it through my first week of work in Philly with seven hundred dollars in my pocket. The girls were amazing and had even referred a few of their friends my way.

"Spill it, Tace. What's going on?" Jada asked, taking the menu out of my hands.

"I got a new job," I admitted.

"Oh my god! That's awesome! Where at?" She squealed, truly happy for me.

My sister knew everything I had been through in the two decades of my life. The things that were shared, and even those that weren't. When I fell, Jada was always the first one to come pick me up. She'd tell me to dust myself off, and push me back out into the world.

"I'm working for an acting company in Philly. I got a job working backstage with costumes and shit," I told her.

"Seriously? Tace, that's so awesome! Is this why you've been out so much this week?"

"Yeah. I wasn't sure how it would work out, so I didn't

want to tell anyone until I was sure. But I really like it there," I confessed, unable to conceal the shit eating grin on my face.

Jada laughed and tapped me on the head with the menu. "You are such a worrier. Anyone would be thrilled to have you working for them. You have a great work ethic, and you're honest," she said. "Tell me about the place. What kind of plays do they do?"

I stopped for a second, unsure how to answer her. "Honestly, I don't know. They just hired me to do their nails."

"Really? You just do nails five days a week?" She asked, sipping her water.

Before I could answer, the waiter came up and took our order. We both ordered the fish tacos and decided to split an artichoke dip appetizer. We didn't always have enough money to eat out when we were little, but on special occasions like birthdays… Our mother took us out to eat. Over the years, it became our thing for every major event.

This was the first time I found a job on my own. It wasn't a fast food restaurant our mom had pulled strings to get me into. It wasn't a salon that Nana frequented, or a warehouse my sister worked in. I did this on my own.

"I'm moving to Philly," I said as the waiter cleared our plates from the table.

"Is this like a one day thing?" Jada asked, wiping her mouth.

"It is," I said.

"Well, one day I want to move to New York City," she whispered back.

"I'm moving next month, J."

My sister stared at me for a solid minute before saying anything. "Isn't that kind of fast, Tace? You just started working-"

"I'll make enough that I can afford it. A couple of the girls I work with have an apartment, and I'm going to rent a room with them-"

"Bullshit. You hate sharing a room with random people-"

"They're nice! And they aren't random!"

"Anastacia, you can't just run away from everything like our mother!"

"What did you just say to me?" I asked, no longer feeling like celebrating.

Even Jada looked shocked that those words had come out of her mouth.

"Tace-" she started, but I held up my hand to stop her.

"You of all people know better. You *know*, Jada. Dinner was on me. Thanks for making me feel like a real winner." I pulled a hundred out of my wallet and dropped it on the table. "Get your own ride home."

I left the restaurant and ran to my car. I didn't want her to see me cry. Saying that I could be anything like our mother was the worst insult that either of us could use to describe someone. I thought my sister would support me being independent, but she just wanted me under her thumb.

As I pulled out of the parking lot, I called Cherry. "Hey, it's me. Is it okay if I move after this weekend instead of waiting 'til next month?"

'Are you kidding? That would be totally fine!'

"Are you sure?" I asked, turning toward Philly instead of heading home.

'Absolutely! I'll let the girls know, and we can get your room ready. What changed your mind?'

"Let's just say I didn't get the support I was hoping for," I said, letting out a staggered breath.

'You okay, Taze?'

"No. Not really. Can I crash with you guys tonight?"

'Yeah. That's not a problem. I don't have to be in til later. I'll see you when you get here.'

"Thanks, Cherry. I'll be there in about thirty minutes," I sighed, feeling the weight of everything in my life.

After hanging up with Cherry, I shut my phone off. I already had four missed calls from my sister, and several messages I had no interest in reading. I drove the rest of the way in silence. By the time I got to Cherry's, I had nothing left.

She gave me a shirt to wear for the night and a big hug, apologizing that she had to run to work. I promised I would be fine, and I meant it. Despite wanting to substitute the pain in my chest with physical pain, I crawled into what would be my bed and cried. I cried for everything that I couldn't be, and for every wrong that had been done to me. The worst was feeling like my sister was gone. For the first time in my life, I didn't feel like my sister had my back and it broke something in me. Something I always thought was untouchable…. until tonight.

* * *

I woke up when the girls came in sometime in early morning. I listened to them giggling and chatting as they had their late night dinner, and prepared for bed. I didn't feel like saying anything, so I let myself drift back to sleep.

The next time I woke, the sun was up and the apartment was quiet. I assumed the girls were all fast asleep after their show the night before. I willed myself out of bed and got dressed in the same clothes I had worn yesterday. I threw the t-shirt I had borrowed in the wash and left a note saying I would be back later with my shit.

Cherry had given me a key when I got in last night, so I didn't need to worry about disturbing anyone when I came back. It was after seven already. By the time I got to Titi's, Jada and everyone else would have left for work. I planned on going in, grabbing my shit and leaving before anyone could talk to me.

The drive seemed like it went by in the blink of an eye. Suddenly, I was parking in front of my aunt's bungalow, and hoping no one was home. I grabbed my purse and went inside. The house was quiet, confirming that everyone had gone to work. Hurrying up the stairs to the room I shared with Jada, I grabbed my suitcase and began stuffing it with the few items I owned.

It took less than half an hour to remove every trace of me from the house. My bags loaded in the car, I ran back inside to grab my phone charger. I hadn't made it halfway down the stairs when the front door burst open. Jada was standing there with our mother and my aunts, each looking more crazed than the other.

"Oh thank god! You're alive," my mother sobbed, rushing up to give me a hug.

"Why wouldn't I be alive?" I asked, pushing her back.

"Your sister said that you'd been depressed and stressed about everything, and then you just disappeared last night! No one could reach you, and she thought you would do something to yourself!" Mami rambled on as she checked me over for any injuries. "But you're here now, and you're safe. I have an appointment already set up with a doctor to talk about medications."

Jada and my aunt looked mortified. I was guessing that not even half of what my mother was ranting about had been discussed with either of them.

"What the hell are you talking about?" I asked, sounding every bit as pissed off as I should have been last night. "I found a job, and a new place to live. That's what I told Jada. Why the fuck would you think I would kill myself?"

There was an eerie silence that filled the room. Jada wouldn't even look at me, and my aunt just looked.... *Lost?* I pulled my phone out of my pocket and turned it on. At least forty messages pinged, one after another. As I scrolled through them, one would have thought that I'd left a note promising my own demise.

They were pleading to reconsider, and begging me to come home. Nearly every single one, made me seem like a lost soul. As if I were a troubled youth lost on the streets again.

"I'm 19 years old, not 12," I said, returning my phone back to my pocket. "I found a job that pays well, and a place to rent. What the fuck have I ever done that would make you think I would kill myself over some asshole?" I was screaming now.

"IS THIS WHAT YOU WANTED, J? INSTEAD OF BEING HAPPY THAT I'VE GOT MY SHIT TOGETHER THEY ALL THINK I'M FUCKING CRAZY? ARE YOU HAPPY? DOES IT MAKE YOU FEEL GOOD?" I shouted.

"Stace, let's just calm down. There's obviously been a misunderstanding-" Titi began, but I was too pissed to hear her.

"Did she tell you that I was a disappointment just like you, Mami? Did she tell you that I was going to throw my life away just like you did?" I seethed.

Suddenly there was a loud crack noise, and everything flashed white before my eyes. When the ringing in my ears subsided, I realized my mother had slapped me across the face. My aunt and Jada were pulling her back as she began screaming.

"You ungrateful bitch! I gave up everything for you! Do you think I would have suffered so much if I had known you'd turn out like this? I should have just left you with your father's family if you were going to turn on me!"

I lunged off of the stairs and swung. When my fist connected with her cheek, I knew she was going down like a sack of potatoes. Her head jerked hard to the left with the impact and she went limp in their arms. She wasn't knocked out cold, but she shut the fuck up.

"I'm done being a fucking punching bag. You thought what? Telling me that I deserved to be molested instead of speaking up for myself-" I tried to take a deep breath. My chest ached so bad. This was my mother, the woman who should have loved and protected my sister and I. "You've been more worried about who you can fuck and keep your bed warm than you were about your own children. I deserved to be molested as a child because I wanted to get out of this shitty life you subjected me to?" I growled at the woman crouched on the floor holding her face.

"Consider me dead. Because I don't have a mother anymore. I fucking hope you fucking rot in your loneliness, because I will never speak with you again!" I screamed and stormed out the door.

My hands were shaking as I unlocked my car and climbed in. My whole body felt like it was vibrating from the adrenaline flooding my system. I hadn't just talked back to my mother. I swung back with everything I had and my fist.

I drove straight to my grandparents. I needed them to hear my side of the story, before my mother could get to them. I didn't have anyone in my corner, and it felt shitty. Since she had turned my sister on me, I would turn her mother against her. I wasn't keeping anymore of her fucking secrets. The whole can of worms was getting opened, and I was determined to let all of the dirty laundry get aired.

Chapter 7

"Hey sweetie. What brings you by?" My grandfather greeted me as he pulled me in for a hug.

"I needed someone to talk to. I don't know who else to turn to," I said, hugging him back.

My grandparents had always been a safe haven for us growing up. I used to sit under the table when I was little and listen to the adults talk while they drank coffee and played cards. Whatever hardships my mother and her sisters had endured as children, they agreed the grandkids would be spoiled with love and affection in this house.

This was just as much a home to me as any other place I had lived, except without the stress. I never had to worry about the police here. I never had to worry about being hit or yelled at in this house. Here, I had always been safe.

"Nana, just ran out to grab some stuff from the store. You want to sit for a bit? I know you don't like coffee but I can make you some iced tea," he offered, pulling me in and closing the door behind us.

Once we stepped into the house and I was fully illuminated by the lights inside, he saw the large red hand print across my face. He grabbed my chin gently and turned my head to get a better look.

"Who the hell hit you?" He asked, his voice dropping several octaves to nearly a growl.

"Mami."

He studied my eyes for a moment longer, and then nodded as if in understanding. "Let me call your grandmother, before she gets sidetracked. Have a seat at the table, I'll get some ice for that cheek."

I sat down and watched as he grabbed the phone, dialing a number by heart, while rummaging the freezer for a pack of frozen peas. He handed me the peas and a towel, and stepped out of the room for a moment, returning with an empty coffee cup.

"Hey, love. Anastacia's here."

They always greeted each other with such endearing terms, even after being married for forty years. It caused an involuntary smile to creep up my face. My grandfather noticed it, and smiled back at me.

"Can you grab something from the bakery on your way here?"

"She hasn't said anything yet, but she has a hand print across her face."

"I don't care what she wants to say right now, our grand-daughter is here, and this is where we need to be."

I could only hear his side of the conversation, but I knew my mother must have reached out to the one she thought would be most likely to give her sympathy. I honestly felt bad that I was asking them to choose me over their daughter, but she didn't need them like I did.

"She's a grown woman," he said suddenly, echoing my inner thoughts. "I won't, and neither will you. If you're done, come here first. Don't go there until after we have taken care of

Anastacia."

"Okay, we'll be here."

He hung up the call and returned the phone to its place on the table sofa. "Your grandmother will be here in a few minutes. How's your face?" he asked, pulling back the ice pack to look at my swollen cheek.

"I've had worse," I said, smiling sadly. "But I gave better than I got."

His eyebrows shot up. "Well, do you want to wait or do you want to tell me about it now?" He asked, sitting across the table from me.

"I might as well tell you," I started. "I found a job up in Philly."

"Why so far away? The gas prices will eat up your whole paycheck driving back and forth," he commented, sipping his coffee.

"I also found a place to live, so that I won't have to drive back and forth every day."

"Is it safe?" He asked, knowing that I had little experience living on my own let alone being familiar with Philadelphia.

"Yeah. I have three roommates. We all work at the same place, and they had an empty room for rent. It's not much to start, but the building is in a safe neighborhood. There's even a garage to park my car, so I don't have to worry about it getting messed with on the street."

He nodded approvingly, but couldn't comment further as Nana came bursting in the door with her hands full of bags. My grandfather jumped to his feet and ran to help her. "Why didn't you tell me you were here, love? I would have come out and helped you," he fussed as he took the bags from her hands into the kitchen.

I stood up from the table as Nana came into the room and reached out to hug her. She wrapped her arms around my shoulders and held my head to her shoulder. At that moment, all of the grief I had held back began trickling out.

"Shhh. It's okay, nena. Everything will be okay," she murmured softly against my hair.

When I finally released my hold on her, her face was filled with worry and sadness as she took in the state of my face.

"Put the ice back on so it doesn't bruise up too badly," my grandfather said, passing me the bag of frozen peas again.

We took our seats at the table again, as my grandfather poured the drinks for everyone. I was the only one in our family who didn't drink coffee. I could never acquire a taste for it, so I stuck with sweet tea.

"Okay, you want to start with what happened this morning?" Nana asked.

"No, but I will," I agreed.

Suddenly, everything just poured out of me. I told them again, about finding a job in Philly. When I explained why I wanted to work there instead of here, they looked like I had punched them. Rather than tell them I had been raped by a coworker, my mother had told them I was bullied at work. It wasn't entirely wrong, but the way she told the story made it seem like I was the one who had issues and couldn't cope with working under strict management.

I shook my head in disbelief. "Did she tell you why Jada and I moved into Titi's place?" I asked.

Again, the whole story had been slanted in my mother's favor when she retold it. So I told them everything they didn't know about our lives from my father's uncle molesting me, to the string of men who had come and gone from

99

our lives. I told them about the money my mother had spent bailing the junkie out of jail, paying his restitutions or legal fees, and about the winter we went without electricity because the previous guy left a debt in Mami's name with the electric company.

Once I started, I couldn't stop the flow of words from coming out of my mouth. Maybe some part of me loved my mother, but she had never done right by me or my sister. She never prioritized us in any of her decisions.

My grandfather stood up suddenly and began pacing the kitchen. It was obvious that he was furious. I was nineteen and telling them that they had been lied to my entire life. I told them how I was struggling to make ends meet because I didn't feel safe. In my sobbing mess of unburdening my soul, I confessed to cutting myself.

Nana was in tears, pops was in tears. There weren't enough tissues in the house for all of the snot and tears that came out in that discussion. "What about the money from the accident? The restitution?" My grandfather asked suddenly.

"What money? It was barely enough to cover the legal fees. I didn't get anything."

I watched as my grandparents exchanged a look. I had no idea what they were talking about, but I had a feeling I was not going to like it. It seemed like forever ago that I was involved in that hit and run accident. Had it been a year already? I was lost in my thoughts, when Nana suddenly smacked the table.

"Call her. Call her now. I don't believe she'll lie to me twice!" She yelled at no one in particular, the focus of her ire absent from the room.

Pops grabbed the phone again and rang my mother. Not

surprisingly, the call went straight to voicemail. I just shook my head.

"She probably went to the urgent care center to tell them how I assaulted her without provocation. It wouldn't be the first time she started shit and flipped the scripts," I commented dryly.

Nana's eyebrows shot up. She quickly grabbed her phone and texted my mother. I had no idea what she messaged, but it was enough to grab my mother's attention. The phone rang not two minutes later. My mother was calling back.

"Hello?" Nana greeted, and put the phone on speaker so that we could all hear the conversation.

"Mom, why are you so angry with me? I am in the hospital right now. They think my orbital bone is fractured!"

"Well, my granddaughter's eardrum was ruptured. We're waiting for the police to take her statement right now."

"What?! Where are you? I'm coming there right now!" Mami shouted frantically into the phone.

"You don't have to worry about it. We're here with her. Did you know she was robbed?" Pops asked, suddenly.

"What? When? I just saw her this morning! Oh, my god! It was those people in Philly! I knew they were just out to use her!" she argued into the phone.

"Your father is contacting a lawyer. Apparently, the one who handled the previous case never gave Anastacia the restitution money. We've called the District Attorney's office, and asked that they investigate."

"What?! NO! Mr. Hughes never stole anything from Anastacia!" Mami argued back.

I could hear the control slipping in her voice. Her pitch was becoming higher and higher. It was always her tell when she was caught in a flat out lie, and about to be exposed. I sat there quietly and shook my head.

"If he didn't steal from her, where the hell did the money go? It was ten thousand dollars!" Pops yelled.

This time my eyebrows shot up. Ten thousand dollars. *Ten thousand?* When did she have ten thousand dollars? What the hell had she spent ten thousand dollars on? She didn't have that kind of money when Jada and I were living with her. She was shit at keeping that kind of stuff secret.

Then it clicked.

"You used my money to bail him out, didn't you?" I asked out loud. "When Charlie died, and then Mike *suddenly* got released… That's how you did it? You *stole* my money to bail your junkie boyfriend out of jail?"

There was a moment of silence as my grandparents registered what I was saying.

"You have me on speaker phone?!?" Mami screamed, completely ignoring my questions.

"Where is the money?" Pops repeated.

"It was used to pay for legal fees with Mr. Hughes!" she screamed back.

"What legal fees? Because I paid him out of pocket for all of my expenses!" I argued back. "Nana, if that lawyer was double billing, isn't that illegal?" I asked loudly.

My grandparents had their eyes wide open now. "It absolutely is! It's called fraud, and it's a criminal offense," Nana commented.

"Stop! I am on my way over there right now! We can figure all of this out, just let me get there!" My mother was still trying to salvage her carefully constructed image, but it was too late.

She had benefited from all of my suffering. She had profited even. I picked up my phone and called my sister. As the phone rang, I wondered if she would even believe a word I said. Would she take my side in all of this or support Mami?

"Tace? Oh, my god. I am so sorry! Please can we talk?" Jada cried as soon as she answered.

"Did you know that I had received restitution from the accident a year ago?" I asked, no emotion left in my voice.

"What? Yeah, but it was barely enough to cover the legal fees from Mr. Hughes, so I gave Mami the rest," she admitted.

I switched my call to speakerphone, and sat down at the table again. "How much did you have to give her to cover the balance?"

"Um, I think it was like two grand. I have it in my bank statements. Why? How did you find out about all of this? She said not to tell you because it would make you feel depressed," Jada continued.

My grandfather disconnected the call with my mother, and shook his head. "J, the restitution was ten grand after Mr. Hughes took his cut."

"Bullshit! She showed me the bill! I wouldn't help her unless she showed me an actual fucking invoice," Jada argued back.

"Oh, I'm sure it was a real invoice. But it was to get Mike out of jail. She took our money to bail out Junkie," I informed her.

"No."

"I'm at Nana and Pops. She just admitted it on the phone, J. They know everything now," I said.

"Tace-"

103

Before she could continue, pops took the phone out of my hand and turned off the speakerphone function.

"Jada Marie, your mother is a grown woman. Stop covering up for her bullshit, and worry about yourself from now on. Nana and I will take care of everything."

There was a long pause before he continued.

"You don't have to worry about that. Anastacia is just fine. She's not. I promise. She's sitting right here, and she's okay," he commented, looking over at me.

"I will. I know. I love you too, baby girl. Okay. We'll see you tonight then. Okay. Bye-bye."

Pops hung up and passed my phone back to me. "I hope it was worth it," he muttered.

I spent the better part of the day with nana and pops after calling Marjory to let her know there had been a family emergency. By the time I was on my way back to Philly, it felt like I had gone days without rest, although it had only been several hours.

I lugged my shit out the trunk and made my way up to my new home. Maybe I was crazy for moving in with people I had just met, but I had known my mother all my life and she routinely screwed me over. Maybe I wasn't a great judge of character, but I felt safer with these women than I ever did living under my Mami's roof. They had strict rules that everyone followed.

First rule: No overnight guests. No friends of friends, no hook-ups, no family. No exceptions.

Second rule: No drugs in the apartment. Amazingly, this included tobacco and anything stronger than tylenol.

Third rule: Nothing illegal in the apartment. No weapons, stolen goods, or 'holding' for a friend. If you didn't buy it, it couldn't come into the apartment.

Final rule: No stealing. This wasn't just about money or clothes or jewelry either. No stealing meant don't take anything from someone else in the house. This list ranged from purchased food and snacks down to money and clients.

I had no problem with the last rule, because it meant that I had job security at work. They couldn't get a new person without my being fired first, nor could they see someone outside. I wasn't going to lie, the rules seemed really over the top; but at the same time, these women were living their best lives, and happily at that.

It took me three trips to get everything out of my car and up to my room. It didn't seem like that much when I was hauling it out of Titi's, but unloading it from my car and trying to unpack it all in my small room seemed otherwise. I didn't have the nicest clothes, compared to my new roommates, but I never got the impression that they looked down on me for that. Especially not when I offered to pay an equal share of the rent.

I wasn't stupid. It was a four bedroom apartment in a really nice part of Philadelphia. The rent had to be through the fucking roof, for any one of them to pay. They had given me somewhere safe to live, it was worth the money. And that's what I was saying up until they told me that my share was two hundred and fifty a week.

"This place costs four thousand dollars a month? To rent!?" My voice had squeaked at the end. I felt all of the color drain from my face and I carefully appreciated how really nice all of the furniture was.

"I told you, you could pay less, but you insisted," Cherry whispered, half laughing at my reaction.

105

"No. No, you're right. I need to be treated like an equal. Do you want the money weekly or monthly?" I asked the other two, affectionately nicknamed Spider and Lacey.

Spider laughed. "See that cookie jar on the counter?" she asked, pointing to a pink jar with hearts sitting beside the sink.

"Yeah."

"You drop in what you can, when you can, as long as it equals your share at the end of the month."

"Wait, that's the rent jar?" I asked, looking shocked.

"What did you think it was?" Lacey asked, chuckling.

"I don't know... Like a community savings or grocery fund?" I muttered, suddenly not sure what I thought it was. I had seen Cherry stuff money into the jar a couple of times, but hadn't really thought about it.

"So rent is paid in cash?" I asked, slowly understanding.

"Every month, on the second. No exceptions. We miss one payment, we're out with a week's notice," Spider explained. "So if you don't think you can afford your share, you need to let us know before we get to that point."

I had shaken my head. "No, I will make sure I hold up my end!" I had promised.

Lacey smiled from ear to ear at that point. "Welcome home, Taze!"

"Welcome home!"

"Welcome home!"

The other two had echoed Lacey and pulled me into a group hug. I couldn't help but laugh. I was home.

"Hey, Taze? You home?" Spider called through the apartment.

"In here!" I shouted back from my room.

A moment later she was peeking her head in the door at

the disaster of a mess I had created.

"Sorry about the mess, I'm sorting it all out as I unpack. It's a bit of a mess," I giggled, moving a pile of neatly folded clothes into the closet.

"Marj said you called out today because of some family shit, I just wanted to make sure you were okay. If you just needed time to move, you didn't have to lie."

I stepped out of the closet and looked at the woman straight on. "I didn't lie."

Whatever words she had prepared to berate me stuck in her throat when she saw my face. My left cheek was still swollen and had bruised up rather significantly throughout the day. Spider rushed into my room and pulled me into a hug.

"Oh, sweetie. We had no idea. You should have told one of us, and we would have gone with you to get your shit," she apologized, caressing my back in a very motherly gesture.

I chuckled a little. "If it makes you feel better, I heard I fractured their orbital bone," I whispered.

"YAS! That is what I'm talking about!" Spider smiled, pulling me under her arm and leading me out to the kitchen. "But we can't have you looking like this when you come into work tomorrow, so we need to treat your face."

"I had ice on it all morning," I explained, but Spider just scoffed at me.

"This is the best shit in the world for inflammation and bruising, but don't go crazy with it cause it's expensive as shit," she explained, dabbing a small amount of a cream on my cheek. The jar reminded me of something I would see on a lady's dressing table in the old black and white movies. The smell reminded me of Thanksgiving desserts with hints of ginger, clove and chamomile. Within a couple of minutes the persistent ache in my cheek had almost disappeared.

"Holy shit, that stuff is amazing," I commented, wiggling my jaw around, much to Spider's amusement.

"It is, but it's really expensive to buy. So be mindful of who you decide to piss off next time, okay? I'm only sharing because you fought back like a boss today. When you have enough saved up, I'll take you to buy your own," she promised, closing up the jar.

I nodded, again thankful for these women in my life. "Okay. It's a deal!" I said, skipping back to my room as Spider chuckled behind me.

* * *

Monday morning the girls drug themselves out of bed for brunch at a restaurant a few blocks away. Dressed down in sweats and hoodies, we walked the few blocks to our destination. I watched in fascination as they ordered all kinds of sweet breads and pastries, wondering how they kept so thin while eating so much junk.

Cherry seemed to understand where my mind was going and started laughing. "You should work out with us later. Then you'll understand why we can afford the calories," she said.

"When do you have time to work out?" I asked, because I couldn't see where they found the time to do it.

"Not yet, Cherry. Marjory doesn't want her involved in the shows," Lacey said, giving Cherry a warning glance.

Cherry responded by waving her hand to dismiss Lacey. "There's a great gym in our building. I go there before work.

You don't see it, because you clock in before us. I can see about shifting my schedule if you want to join in, but I have to warn you...."

"She's fucking brutal, Taze. Don't do it!" Spider gasped, waving her hands to discourage me. "This bitch almost broke me! Then she laughed and said it was just the warm up. I thought she was pulling my leg, but she kept going. Don't do it!"

I couldn't help laughing at their antics. Who knew the little waif of a girl seated next to me was such a beast in the gym.

"Okay," I agreed. Just as Spider was smiling triumphantly at Cherry, I finished my next sentence. "Can we start tomorrow, Cherry?"

"YAS!!" Cherry cheered, jumping out of her seat and drawing attention to our table. "Girl, we are going to get you so ripped!"

"Eh-ehm," a woman at the table near us cleared her throat, obviously not impressed with our shenanigans.

"Sorry," I whispered politely. "She takes her physical fitness very seriously."

The woman rolled her eyes, and shifted her chair so that her back faced us. Of course we all erupted into giggles. We continued talking and eating until almost one o'clock.

"Alright, ladies. I need to get to the bank for deposits before two. Either of you need a lift?" Lacey asked Spider and Cherry.

"Nah, I'm good. I have an appointment tomorrow," Cherry responded, wiping her mouth and pulling out a handful of cash to pay the bill.

"Here. This is for my portion," I said, trying to hand her

what little cash I had on me.

"Isn't she so cute?" Spider asked, reaching over to pat my head. "Trying to pull her weight. Cherry, how'd you find such a sweetie to live with us?"

I pulled my head back and swatted her hand away. "I'm not a freeloader. I don't want anyone to feel like I'm taking advantage just because you make more money than me," I explained indignantly.

Lacey smiled at me and pulled me into a side hug. "We know, Taze. That's why we don't mind treating you to your first brunch."

The other two nodded in agreement, settling the point by paying the waiter before I say argue further.

By the time we made it back to the apartment, Lacey ran in to change into nice slacks and a button down top. She stuffed a black bank bag into her tote, and ran out the door. I had never seen her put together like that. She looked grown up and professional.

"Why'd she dress up, just to go to the bank?" I asked.

"People are judgy. They'll judge how you look, what you drive and how you talk. Before you can even open your mouth, they'll have decided whether you're a good person or not. You learn to hide in plain sight by not sticking out," Cherry explained, flopping down on the sofa and turning on the tv.

"She's a freaking stunner! How do people notice her less when she looks like that?" I asked, not understanding her logic.

Cherry sat up and looked at me seriously. "Come here, Taze," she said, patting the cushion next to her. Say you worked in a salon, and two customers walked in at the same time. One is dressed like Lacey, the other like yours truly," she continued, waving her hand up and down her body to emphasize the overgrown hoodie, holy sweatpants, and messy top bun.

"Who do you think is gonna be the bigger tipper?" she asked.

I smirked, realizing the obvious answer would be Lacey but that was not my experience. "You know my answer is you, right?"

"Okay, what about your nana. Who would she rather see you hanging out with?"

I sighed, knowing damn well it would be Lacey. Nana wasn't judgmental, but she was with outsiders. She would wonder about everything I said, if I rolled up with Cherry and Spider, dressed as they were.

"Old people are all judgmental," I sighed.

Cherry nodded, happy that I was understanding her point as well. "Now imagine being a bank teller, and someone came in to make a deposit every week. Which one would you be more likely to be suspicious of?" She asked, flipping through the channels.

"You. I wouldn't bat an eye at a professionally dressed person coming in to make a deposit," I conceded.

"Exactly. So we hide in plain sight, and no one pays attention to the professionals in the room. The scrubs, on the other hand, stand out."

Chapter 8

I felt like I was dying. Inhaling hurt. Exhaling hurt. I couldn't understand how blinking hurt.

"Come on, Taze. That was just the warm up!" Cherry cheered as she walked over to the weight machines.

"Are - ser -us?" I wheezed out, unable to complete a coherent sentence.

Cherry laughed hysterically. "No, I'm just messing with you! Come on, we're done."

"Ser - us?" I asked, not believing her. She had pulled that shit three times already, and each time I got up to leave she had dragged me into another set.

"Promise. We're done!" She giggled.

"No lie?"

"Cross my heart! Come on, let's get you back so you can take a hot bath and soak," she promised, pulling me up from the gym floor.

Every muscle in my body hurt. My legs were shaking so badly that Cherry had to support me or I'd have fallen over. By the time we made it back to the apartment, I could talk a bit more coherently.

Spider took one look at me as we walked in the door and started cackling. "I told you! I warned you yesterday, and you didn't believe me! Now look at you!"

"Shut it!" I grumbled, stumbling into the bathroom I shared with Cherry.

I slammed the door behind me, and started stripping off my clothes. It was easier said than done. My arms were so weak I couldn't pull my sports bra over my head. I sat on the edge of the tub for a moment whimpering, before I realized I could shimmy the article down my body.

When the tub was filled, I lowered myself into a blend of Epsom salts and citrus oils. I still had shit to do today, and the citrus was a great pick me up. I leaned back in the tub and let the water relax my muscles before I attempted to sit up and scrub myself clean. I must have dozed off for a bit, because I woke when my skin became chilled in the cooled water.

I quickly scrubbed everything down, and pulled the plug. My muscles were still sore, but the fatigue had worn off, and I didn't feel quite as weak as when I had climbed into the bath. I shuffled out of the bathroom to a very quiet apartment.

How long had I been in there? A quick glance at the clock answered my question. I had been dozing in the tub for nearly two hours.

"Shit," I sighed at myself. I was supposed to meet Nana at two, and it was already one thirty.

I found my phone, fired off a quick message apologizing for my eventual lateness, and started throwing on my clothes. I chose a pair of loose pants, a comfy top and did my best to tame the craziness that was my hair. I tried braiding it, but discovered rather quickly that I couldn't hold my arms up long enough to get it done. My mop of brown locks went into a quick bun on the back of my head, and it was enough.

I reached Nana's a half hour later than we had planned to meet, but she didn't seem too upset with me.

"I thought today was your day off," she commented, hugging me as I walked in the door.

"It is. I went to the gym with one of my roommates and she broke me off. I fell asleep in the tub," I explained.

Pops heard me and started laughing from the other room.

"It's not funny!" I whined, making him laugh even harder.

"Well, it doesn't matter. You're here now!" Nana smiled. "Are you hungry? Did you want to stay for dinner tonight?"

This was why I loved my grandparents. They kept everything normal, even knowing that my life had gone to shit just days prior. Our interactions weren't awkward or forced, and I didn't have to pretend that I was okay with them either.

"What did you want to do today?" I asked, sitting at the table.

"I was thinking about having you help me pull things out of the attic, but now I have to reconsider," she grumbled at me.

I couldn't help chuckling. "I promise I will be fit and ready to help you on Monday," I promised, crossing a finger over my heart.

"Deal. How about we just relax today. You can tell me about your roommates and your new job instead," she offered.

I smiled and began telling her about Spider, Lacey and Cherry.

Spider, I quickly learned, was a true lover of arachnids. She was studying entomology, taking part time classes at university, and hoping to finish her bachelor degree next year. Lacey was a girlie girl. She grew up poor and had

114

always admired the girls dressed in fancy lace dresses at church.

Of course, lace dresses as an adult were only cute when you were walking down the aisle in it. So Lacey invested her money in the finest undergarments I had ever laid eyes on. She was wearing brands that reminded of the names of cheesy romance novels like La Perla, Perele and Agent Provocateur. The most scandalous, however, were specially ordered from a company called Bordelle.

They all felt like silk and satin on the skin, and they made her boobs look amazing. Not to mention she had zero chafing from the thongs, making me wish I could afford to shop the way she did.

Then there was Cherry. I tried to ask how she earned her nickname, but the others only told me that Cherry had to tell her own story. Needless to say, Cherry didn't say a word and left the room each time I asked. I caught on after the third time, and just stopped asking. She would tell me when and if she felt ready to tell me.

"What do they call you?" Nana asked as she refilled my glass of tea.

"Taze," I muttered, chuckling.

"Not Tace?"

"No, everyone calls me Taze. Because I am a small package that packs a mean punch," I explained, feeling my cheeks heat up.

"Did you get into a fight at work?" Pops asked, coming out of the living room to join us at the table.

"No. At first it was just a mispronunciation. But then we went to an arcade downtown, and they had one of those test your strength boxing things…" I started explaining.

Pops caught on right away. "What'd you get?" He asked, leaning forward with expectation.

"The first time, I only got a 743. But the second swing was 860," I trailed off, biting the inside of my cheek.

"That's my girl!" He cheered, trying to give me a fist bump across the table. "I told you those boxing lessons would come in handy."

I rolled my eyes, but still gave in to the fist bump. I hadn't had boxing lessons, so much as a grandfather who insisted that we knew how to fight if needed. From the time I was five or six, he'd sneak us down to the basement and teach Jada and I how to wrap our hands and work a body bag.

I was always too short to do the speed bag, so Pops made a modified lift that he'd lower for me to do the work. He made us swear to never fight unless it was a last resort. I didn't even punch the girl at the beach with everything I had, but my mother took it all. Punching my mother in the face was the second time in my life I had used what he taught me on another person, the first time was my father's uncle. I had broken his nose.

"So, *Taze...*" Nana chuckled. "What time do you have to be home? It's already five o'clock and I haven't started dinner yet."

I shrugged. "We don't have to be fancy, and I don't have a curfew."

"Sandwiches it is!" Pops chimed in. "Your grandmother bought me a new sandwich press. You want a Cuban?"

"That sounds perfect," I agreed, smiling as the two began fussing around the kitchen to make my favorite toasted ham and cheese sandwiches.

By the time I got back to the apartment it was nearly nine.

Cherry was on the couch eating popcorn, heckling at Lacey and Spider doing yoga.

"Your lines aren't straight! Tuck your ass in, Lacey!"

"Why don't you just shut up!" Spider was yelling back.

"If you're going to do it, do it right!" Cherry yelled back.

The two ignored Cherry, and continued following along with the video they were watching.

Cherry turned to greet me when I closed the front door and dropped my keys on the side table. "Hey! How are you feeling?" She asked, chuckling maliciously.

"I feel better than I did earlier. Sorry, I fell asleep in the bath."

Cherry shrugged it off. "It was to be expected. I just used the other bathroom. How was your visit with your grandparents?" She asked, turning back to the spectacle that was our roommates' attempts at yoga.

"Pretty good. They just wanted to make sure that I was doing okay, and not getting taken advantage of."

"It's good that you have people who care about your well-being," Spider commented, leaning into the downward facing dog position.

"I thought you guys had plans tonight," I said, dropping onto the sofa next to Cherry and accepting the offered popcorn.

"We do. This is it," Lacey sighed as they finished their routine.

"Yoga and heckling from the sofa gallery?" I asked, arching an eyebrow at the three.

"This is how we unwind before the start of every week. Work is crazy hectic enough. Sometimes you have to make time for yourself to just relax," Spider added in as she rolled up her mat.

We chatted for another half hour before I felt my eyelids getting heavier and heavier. I needed to sleep. My body needed to recharge.

"I can't do it any more. I'm off to bed! Marjory asked me to come in a little earlier, and I want to maximize my sleeping hours thanks to Cherry's introduction to masochism," I said, groaning as I stood up.

"Sleep well, Taze!" Lacey and Spider said at the same time.

"See you at nine for our next workout!" Cherry chimed in, causing me to whine and Lacey and Spider to cackle.

I asked for it. I was warned and I still asked for it. I had no one to blame but myself for the pain my muscles were experiencing. No one but me, myself and Cherry, my new sadistic trainer.

Tomorrow, Cherry was introducing me to day two of her ten day rotation. I opened my bedside table and dropped my jewelry into a small box I kept in there. I stopped wearing jewelry to sleep after waking up to one of Mami's exes trying to take things off of my sleeping body. I had screamed loud enough to take a building down, but she didn't believe me. It was the words of a child against those of an adult. To be fair, any rational adult believed me.

My mother was many things, but rational was not among them. I didn't have much jewelry left when that relationship ended. Now I owned a few pairs of earrings and a ring I had gotten as a graduation gift from Nana and Pops. My attachment to things waned each time I was told to stop crying about what was lost or taken.

I laid there in bed tossing and turning before reaching into the drawer and pulling my jewelry box out again. These were my things and I was in a safe space.

I fell asleep wearing my ring. It was the best night of sleep I had ever had.

* * *

It had been two months since I moved to Philly, and I enjoyed the routine. I worked out with Cherry every morning before going to work. The girls and I had Monday brunch, and I had dinner with Nana and Pops every Tuesday. The days in between were filled with nails, gossip, and an ever growing list of clients from various parts of the city

I hadn't talked to Jada or Mami since the fight, and although I didn't miss the drama, I missed my sister. It felt like something was missing in my life, but I didn't know how or if I wanted to fix it. This was all me. Jada hadn't stopped texting me, letting me know that she missed me or how things were going at work.

She had stopped working in the warehouse, and took a job as a cashier in some discount store near Titi's. Mami was never mentioned in any of her messages. It made me wonder if they too had had a falling out or if she was just keeping me in the dark and out of her drama.

[Truce?] I typed, and then debated whether or not to send it.

I deleted the message and threw my phone on my bed. Rather than focus on that drama, I needed to get ready for work. Marjory had had me cleaning up the back rooms for the past few days because some big shot was coming to visit. I assumed it was the show's producer, and just did what she told me to do. It's not like the place was filthy anyway. The

119

girls were super neat freaks, so there wasn't much to really clean.

Other than organizing the dressing room a bit and cleaning up the various vanity tables, I didn't have a lot of work. I left a note for the girls with three protein shakes in the fridge. They were all super health fanatics during the week, and only binged on what I would call normal foods on Mondays. I had never heard of such a diet plan, but they were all super trim so it must work.

As I parked my car in the back lot, I noticed a few extra vehicles than normal for this time of day. I didn't really pay attention to anyone else, as I learned a long time ago it was better to not notice other people than be noticed. I still carted my stuff to and from work every single time. Though I had found a much neater way to pack everything up, it still required one case on wheels and a smaller carry bag to haul everything around.

"Hey, Marjory!" I greeted, as I did every time I came into work. After nearly scaring the shit out of her my first week, I made it a point to announce my presence when I came in.

"Good morning, Taze."

"Did your bigwigs get here already?" I asked, dragging my cases to my station and setting everything up.

Marjory either didn't hear me or she was super distracted, because she suddenly looked up at me with a confused expression.

"I asked if your producer person was here today instead of tomorrow," I repeated.

"Taze, what are you talking about?" she asked, now giving me her full attention.

I found myself biting the inside of my cheek. "I've been

cleaning the backstage area, because of the bigwigs coming to visit. I saw a few extra cars out back and wondered if they were here early."

Marjory's entire demeanor changed in an instant, from her shoulders stiffening to her face becoming stony. She dropped whatever she was working on and stood up.

"Anastacia, go into my office and lock the door. Don't let anyone in, that you don't know. Is that clear," she stated quietly.

I nodded and ran into the office, slamming the door behind me. I had had enough experience with police raids, courtesy of Mami's exes, to know when it was not in my best interest to get involved in shit. I latched the bolt and dropped the steel bar in place, the way Cherry had shown me.

Cherry! They would be fine as they wouldn't come in until later, I reached into my pocket to grab my phone and realized it wasn't in my pocket. Had I left it at my station? My brain started racing trying to recall where I had set it down, and then I remembered.

My phone was still sitting on my bed where I had thrown it this morning. If something happened, I had no way of calling for help. "Shit."

Overwhelmed with a sense of guilt and worry for Marjory, I left the safety of her office and ran to the back parking lot. I came bursting out of the door in time to see a man hitting Marjory. It was an open handed smack, but it whipped her head hard enough to the left that it caused her to drop to the ground. Marjory had been nothing but good to me, and she gave me a chance when no one else would.

I saw red, and hurled myself across the alley at the guy. I started swinging before he ever saw me coming. My first

121

punch landed on his jaw, the second a hard upper cut into his ribs. As he hunched forward from the second hit, the third came down on his temple.

Every ounce of rage I had held back came pouring out of me. I kept swinging even though the man couldn't fight back. Soft arms pulled me back.

"It's okay. It's okay. You can stop," a woman's voice broke through my fury induced haze.

I turned to see Angel trying to hug me to her body. "It's okay, Taze. You can stop. He can't hurt me anymore," she whispered.

I hadn't even seen Angel when I came out the door. I had no idea when she got here, but as my mind cleared I saw what I hadn't when I came out. Angel's face was black and blue. Her right eye was swollen, nearly shut, and her lip was busted. I moved a hand up to check her face and winced.

My own hands were screaming in pain. I hadn't even noticed it when I was punching, but I had split several knuckles open. "Are you okay?" I asked Angel.

"I will be. Let's go get you cleaned up okay?" she whispered softly and led me back into the building.

I tried to turn around, but she pulled in under one arm and kept me moving where she wanted me to go. "Look what you did to her hands, Taze. You can't make money if you don't take care of yourself," she scolded gently as she led me into one of the bathrooms next to the dressing room.

"Are you really okay?" I winced, as she ran my hand under cool water to wash the blood off.

"I'm a lot tougher than I look. I've survived worse," she said, smiling softly.

"You shouldn't have to survive that. You shouldn't even

have to experience it," I replied just as quietly.

"Tell you what. You teach me to box, and I will convince Marjory to let you have your own office. Sound like a deal?" Angel asked as she patted my hands dry with a wad of paper towels.

I couldn't help giggling at the absurdity of the arrangement. "How does Marjory giving me an office become a payment from you for my time?" I asked.

Angel smiled. "Fair enough. We'll work something out. Even if I have to pay for your time, it would be worth it."

"There's a boxing club not far from here. I'll find out what their hours are, and see about reserving time that won't draw a crowd," I offered.

Angel looked confused for a second. "Why would boxing draw a crowd?"

"Angel, you are built like a bombshell. As soon as you walk into the boxing hall, every man in there will be offering to help you out of your panties. We won't get shit done!"

She nodded as if in understanding. A soft knock on the door broke us from our little bubble and brought me straight back to reality. I had beaten the shit out of some guy and I had no idea who he was.

"Taze?" Angel asked, as the world around me started to shrink.

"Marj! Get in here! She's having a panic attack!" Angel yelled, grabbing me before I fell over.

Suddenly the two women had me on my butt with my head between my knees. Someone was putting a cold compress on the back of my neck while the other rubbed my back and encouraged me to control my breathing. I couldn't remember ever having a panic attack in my life, now I was nearly hyperventilating in a bathroom.

"Call Cherry and Spider, tell them to come get her. She can't be here. Tell them to take the night off, I'll cover everything," one of them was saying. I couldn't even tell who was who.

"Get your ass up, Taze."

I felt like I had been snapped back into my body. I looked up to see Cherry standing over me in the bathroom. "You heard me. Get your ass up off the damn floor."

I shook my head like it would help to clear the fog, but it didn't. Not really, anyway.

"I have lived this long without having to carry a grown ass woman, I'm not about to start now. Get the fuck up!" Cherry said again, with more force.

I leaned forward and pulled myself up to a kneeling position before grabbing the sink and trying to pull myself up. The effort of holding the pedestal sent a shock of pain through my hands and I sucked in a deep breath, wincing.

"Good girl," she whispered and pulled me into a hug. "You're okay, Taze. We've got you no matter what happens. We're ride or die bitches for life."

Her words calmed me in a way I didn't think they would. As the fog of adrenaline and panic subsided, my thoughts cleared and I voiced the one thing I had in my head before everything went black and swirly. "Is he dead?"

Cherry's body started shaking, and I thought she was crying until she pulled back from our hug. The biggest shit eating grin was spread across her face as she laughed. "No, he's not dead, but I bet he wished he were! You beat *the shit* out of him! Why didn't you tell us you were some sort of hidden dragon?" She asked, pulling me under her arm and

124

guiding me back to the dressing room.

All of the women I had come to know since starting to work here were piled into the dressing room. I didn't know what to say. I felt ashamed for losing my shit and beating a man I didn't even know. I had jumped into someone else's fight, and it would probably cost me my job.

"I'm sorry I lost my temper. I have problems with anger issues," I apologized.

There was a moment of awkward silence before the whole group broke into smiles, and moved to hug me. I was overwhelmed by their support and outpourings of affection and concern for my wellbeing.

"Don't ever apologize for what you did."

"Here we've been walking on eggshells, and you're the most badass bitch up in this place!"

"Holy shit, I am your new fangirl, Taze!"

"Thank you so much for what you did for Angel and Marjory."

"No apologies for sticking up for another woman."

"Don't apologize. You did good, kid."

"I have a great cream that will help your hands heal."

"Taze the dragon! I am so proud to be your friend!"

As the last of the women backed away, Marjory stepped forward. "I couldn't be prouder if you were my own daughter, Anastacia," she said, pulling me into a deep hug. "You did good, young lady. You did real good."

As we pulled apart, I was overwhelmed by their praise. I didn't like the feeling of gratitude from others. It was too foreign and unsettling. "Does this mean I get a raise?" I asked stone-faced, waiting for Marjory's reaction.

I tried. I really tried to keep a straight face, but I couldn't.

I started laughing when she looked at me wide-eyed; like I had lost my damn mind to ask such a thing. In the next second, the room full of women were bent over laughing and giggling together. Marjory smiled at me for a moment.

"No chance in hell, you little shit bird," she said, and hugged me again.

"What happens now?" I asked, in barely a whisper.

"Nothing. It's all been taken care of, sweetie. You go home and rest with Spider and Cherry. We'll see you tomorrow."

I started my day with a workout and smoothies, had almost beaten a man to death, and now I was going home to sleep it off. As I climbed into the backseat of my car, I heard Cherry giggling.

"Hell hath no fury like our Taze."

Chapter 9

I spent the past three days at home, sitting on my thumbs. After cleaning the apartment from top to bottom and binging three seasons of true crime documentaries, I was officially going stir crazy. When was the last time I had nothing to do? As I laid in bed contemplating what else I could clean or organize, my thoughts came back to my sister.

She had been on my mind that day, but I put it off. What if I hadn't had the upper hand and been hospitalized myself? Who would have known to call my sister? The girls had heard me talk about my family, but they were clear that our relationship was fractured.

I grabbed my phone and began typing. This time, I hit send before I could second guess myself.

Me: [You good?]

J: [Yeah. You?]

Me: [Alright. How's Mami?]

J: [You know how she is.]

Me: [Does she feel even a little bit bad for what she did?]

J: [Slapping you?]

Me: [Stealing our money.]

J: [Do you want an answer?]

Me: [Guess that is my answer.]

J: [I miss you, Tace.]

Me: [I know. But you hurt me, Jada.]

There was a long pause where neither of us wrote anything. I figured she had nothing more to say and tossed my phone aside, opting to go to the gym instead. I did twenty minutes on a treadmill before heading back to the apartment. I had just finished showering and changing when my phone pinged with a new message from Jada.

J: [Truce? Like long enough to meet and talk in person?]

Me: [What did you have in mind?]

J: [Bowling?]

I hadn't been bowling in a long time. Maybe getting back to what we knew would be a good middle ground.

Me: [Ok.]

J: [When do you have off?]

M: [I have off Monday and Tuesday.]

J: [Ok. I can do Monday! The usual?]

M: [Yeah. Sounds good. See you Monday.]

I didn't even realize I was smiling until I walked into the bathroom and saw my face in the mirror. We had never gone this long without talking to one another, and it didn't really hit me how much I missed my sister until this moment.

"Taze? You home?" Lacey hollered from the front door.

I quickly finished my business and washed up. "Yeah, I'm here."

"Marjory wanted you to come in today to meet the owners. Do you feel up to it?" Lacey asked, looking over my slightly discolored hands.

I held them out in front of me and chuckled. "They really aren't that bad. How much time do I have?" I asked, looking out how professionally she was dressed. "Should I be dressed up as well?"

Lacey shook her head. "You don't have to impress anyone today. Just be yourself. But we need to leave in the next ten minutes."

"Why didn't you say something!" I shouted, running back to my room to quickly change into my usual black pants. I threw on a nice tank and a light sweater, and I was ready to run out the door.

"Taze," Lacey commented, looking at me like I was crazy.

"What?" I asked.

"I know I said you don't have to impress anyone, but you can brush your teeth... Not impressing is not the same as offending people with your nasty ass breath."

My hand flew over my mouth as I ran back into the bathroom, listening to the sound of Lacey's cackling behind me. "Is nah fu ee!" I tried to bark at her as I frantically brushed my teeth. Two minutes later we were heading out the door and on our way to meet the big bosses.

"What are they like?" I asked fidgeting nervously in the car as Lacey drove through Philly.

"They are people with money. People with money are all the same. Make them more money, and you remain in their good graces. Cost them money, and you are out," she commented off handedly.

Rather than park behind the building like I always did, Lacey pulled into a parking garage about two blocks away. When she noticed my look of confusion, she smirked. "The boss travels with an entourage. The parking lot'll be full."

I nodded in understanding. There really weren't that many parking spaces to be had. I didn't need to question it further. Lacey and I walked arm in arm up to the building. When

I turned to head into the alley, she pulled me to continue walking straight forward.

"I thought we couldn't use the main entrance," I whispered.

"When the boss is here, we don't sneak in the back door."

"I've never seen the theater side of the place," I whispered back, sounding slightly giddy.

My comment caused Lacey to stop dead in her tracks as she turned to stare at me. "What did you say?"

"I said I have never seen the front side of the house. I've only ever been backstage," I repeated.

Lacey looked like she wanted to combust. "Sweetie, do you know what kind of shows we do here?" She asked, observing my face.

Her question left me rather dumbfounded. Did I know? Not really. In fact, I hadn't ever asked either. "No."

Her eyebrows shot up, and I thought she would tell me then and there but she didn't. Instead she patted my hand and giggled. "Well, try your best to keep your ignorance from showing all over your face. If you walk in the front doors with your mouth hanging open in shock, you may not have a job tomorrow."

"What?!?" I nearly shrieked at her.

"Come on. Put on that resting bitch face you do so well, we're going in."

She didn't say anything else and marched us up to the front of a club. Although the lights were out, the sign above read, "Marquessa."

It wasn't until we were well and truly inside the club that I realized it. I worked for a gentlemen's club. And not just any club, but one of three in Philly that catered to high end clients. "Holy shit," slipped out under my breath.

At the center of the room, Marjory was seated at a table with another woman and two men. The woman looked like she bathed in money every single day. Her red bottom shoes cost more than I would ever see in my lifetime, no matter how hard I worked. Her handbag didn't have any markings on it, but that just meant it was too fucking expensive for me to be eyeballing.

The two men were older. Not like old men, but just older than me. They eyed me up and down as soon as we approached, and I honestly felt like a prized pig being sized up before the slaughter.

"Ma'am, this is Anastacia," Lacey introduced me to the woman. I had no idea that anyone knew my actual name, because it was never used. I had gotten used to just being Taze.

"Anastacia, please sit," Marjory beckoned, gesturing to a chair next to her. "Stephanie, that will be all. Thank you."

Lacey nodded, gave me a quick reassuring smile, and left for the backstage area.

"It was quite a mess you left for me to clean up," one of the men stated.

I didn't even look at him, and continued to look at the woman in front of me. "Good morning, ma'am. I would say it's lovely to meet you, but I don't know who you are or why I was called in on a personal day."

I tried my best to sound polite, while keeping my face as stony as possible. The woman's mouth twitched like she wanted to smile at my obvious snub to her men, but she kept an equally straight face.

"Fighting on the premises is not condoned," she said.

"It's a good rule to have," I replied.

131

"So how should I handle your violation of the rules of my business?"

My eyebrows scrunched in confusion. "I'm not sure which rule I have broken," I replied, honestly unsure about what the hell was going on.

"Fighting," the woman stated, slowly enunciating each syllable.

I looked at Marjory still looking confused. "I have never fought with anyone at work. I show up on time, do my job and whatever else is asked of me. Have you seen me fighting on work premises?" I asked.

Marjory shook her head, a small smile on her face. "No, Anastacia, I have not seen you fighting on these premises."

I turned back to the woman. "When was I supposed to have been fighting at work?" I asked her.

Suddenly one of the two men slammed his hands on the table. "You beat the shit out of a guy, and left him in the fucking alley!" He screamed at me.

For the first time in my life, I was thankful for the volatile shit I had grown up in. I never flinched, or cowered from his outburst. I kept staring at the woman across the table and smiled politely.

"Ma'am, there seems to be some misunderstanding. The premises, as stipulated by the signs all over the building, end five feet from the back door. The back parking lot is shared by three different businesses and is not part of this particular premise. I know this because if my car were to be broken into, my employer has no obligation to guarantee the security of my belongings in said vehicle…" I said, turning to look at the man who had screamed. "Because it is not parked on business premises."

The man had deep brown eyes and bronze skin. He was beautiful eye candy, and I was sure he made for great muscle to throw around. But I was not intimidated by the man whose ass I had kicked in the parking lot, and this man in front of me wasn't nearly as scary as the other.

I caught Marjory's head tipping to the side. That was her way of saying I told you so, without saying I told you so.

The woman smirked. "Regardless, three fifty a week is too high for someone just working backstage. Teach her the front of the house, or let her go."

Finally, Marjory had a reaction and it was anger. "We had a deal when I took on this job. I make you money. The girls are the best in the city, and we don't have problems here. In exchange, you leave the management of the people to my sole discretion. Are you telling me that our deal is now null and void?"

I had no idea what they were talking about, but judging from the sudden increase in tension…. Marjory had a serious fucking ace up her sleeve and they didn't want her to play it.

"You read too much into shit. You wanted an assistant. Now you have one. If words got out that I hired a nail tech who was only 19-"

"I was never hired as a nail tech," I interrupted.

"Are you fucking with me right now? What do you do here?" The quiet man asked.

"I was hired to work backstage. I clean the dressing rooms, and bathrooms. I organize the storage rooms. It's illegal for me to work as a nail tech in PA. The girls have been letting me *practice* on them, and paid me in tips to cover my materials. I don't even make enough to live on my own, I'm so pitiful," I rambled, looking as pathetic as possible.

The man stared at me for a moment, and then waved his hand at the other two. They promptly got up and left the table, taking positions at the door.

"I like this one, Marjory," he said, leaning back in his seat and crossing his arms across his chest. "Do you have a criminal record?" He directed at me.

"No."

"Why didn't you graduate high school?"

"I did. A year early," I countered.

"Why did you want to come to Philly? What was wrong in Delaware?" He continued.

I sighed and let go of the stony facade. "Look. I don't know you. If you want to fire me for beating that guy's ass, so be it. You want to fire me for defending my co-workers against an unknown assailant, possibly saving their lives... Fine. You're the boss," I stated politely.

"But you don't get to ask about my personal life, and my back story. My family life doesn't affect my work performance, and I don't bring any drama to the workplace. I'm punctual, polite, and I do what I was hired to do. If I'm fired, just say so. I don't like fucking mind games," I said, standing up from my seat.

"Anastacia, please sit back down," Marjory asked politely.

I chewed the inside of my lip for a moment before deciding to sit down again. Both of my hands rested on the table as I did so, drawing attention to the myriad of blues, greens and purples still coloring my knuckles. Before I realized what was going on, the man had sat forward and taken hold of my hands.

"What the hell-" I yelled and tried to pull my hands back.

He didn't pay any attention to me at all and ran his fingers over my joints, where my split knuckles were still healing. "Not a single broken bone?"

"No, can you let go of my hands now?" I demanded.

"Let her develop at her pace. I trust your judgment," he said, releasing my hands. "It was lovely to meet you, Anastacia."

With that he stood up and left with the other two on either side. I realized a bit late that the quiet one was the boss and the other two were his security detail or bodyguards.

"That went better than I expected!" Marjory cheered once it was just us.

"What was that?" I asked, looking very confused.

"That was a job interview. Congratulations, you just got promoted!" She said, patting me on the back as she stood up from the table.

"Does that mean a pay raise?" I asked excitedly.

"HA! No." Marjory continued laughing as she walked backstage to the offices upstairs.

"Not even a little?" I yelled behind her.

* * *

The bowling alley was a lot more crowded than I remembered. The guy behind the counter was polite enough to let me know that league nights had been moved to Mondays, but was happy to reserve the first available lane for me. I grabbed my rented shoes and decided to find a place to sit and wait for Jada.

She wasn't normally late. Jada was usually the one to show up earlier than me. I ordered a slice of pizza and water and waited. I sat and watched as the league players finished their games and left, one group after another. When my name

135

was called, I felt pathetic being alone bowling when every other lane was crammed full of people.

"Hey, I'm sorry. There's been a family emergency," I lied, returning my shoes to the same guy behind the counter.

"I'm sorry to hear that!" He responded. "Tell you what, take a voucher since you already paid. It'll be good for six months. Come back when you can, and I hope everything works out with your family."

I accepted the voucher and smiled sadly. I was beginning to doubt that things would ever be the same, let alone work out with my family. I checked my phone for any missed calls or messages but there were none. The only people to contact me were nana and pops. Scoffing at my own naive optimism, I decided to just leave. I had waited for two hours past our meet up time, which was more than polite enough.

Deciding to take a cruise down memory lane, as if I wasn't depressed enough, I drove around the old neighborhoods for a bit. I passed the house we had lived in when I was little, and tried not to cry. Why was everything so much harder as I got older?

The tears slowly trickled down my cheeks as I pulled in front of my grandparents house. Inside I could see my aunts and cousins seated around the table with my mother and sister. My whole family was having dinner together, and I had not been invited. It was the final insult to injury.

I put my car back in gear and decided to drive home to Philly. I didn't make it very far when my fuel light came on. "Fuck!" I screamed at no one, as my car puttered into a gas station.

I had given the guy at the lane all of my cash, stupidly assuming Jada would pay for the other half. I didn't even have a credit card to pay with. I rummaged through my bag and then sat there at the pump staring at my phone. I could call Lacey or Spider or even Cherry, and I knew they would take care of me. But I was forty minutes away from them, and two minutes away from my grandparents.

Rather than burden the people who actually had my back, I decided to go with convenience instead. I called Nana.

'Hello?'

"Hey, Nana. It's Tace."

'Hi sweetie! We were just talking about you!' She sounded happy even through the noise of voices in the background.

"I'm sorry to bother you, but my car ran out of gas. And I don't have enough to get home. Would it be possible for you or pops to run out and help me?" I asked, feeling absolutely mortified that I had fallen to this new low.

'Um, where are you? Is it safe? This isn't like you, Tace.'

"Yeah, I know. Jada invited me to go bowling and then she didn't show up. So all of my cash went to pay for a lane and shoes that weren't used," I explained, hating that my voice quivered when I spoke.

'Where are you, sweetie?'

"At the gas station down the road from your place. I was on my way to your house when my light came on," I lied.

There was a rustling noise as she covered the phone to speak with someone else. I'm sure that whatever choice words she used went down like a fart in church.

'I'll be there in a few minutes, love.'

"Thank you, Nana," I sighed, happy that no one else was coming.

I hung up before I could hear what shouting was going to happen when pops found out that I had been left out. Served them right. While I was gloating in their demise, Nana pulled up behind my car not five minutes later. I climbed out as she walked up, and gave her a huge hug.

"I had no idea, Anastacia," she whispered against my hair.

"I just need to get home. I have to work tomorrow," I lied again. It was becoming so easy to just say whatever I needed to push them away.

Nana eyed me suspiciously as she swiped her card at the machine. "I thought you had off on Tuesdays."

"I did. I was coming to tell my sister about my promotion," I said. That was true. I wanted my sister to know that I was okay, and that she didn't have to worry about me.

"When did that happen?" Nana asked, smiling from ear to ear as I filled my car.

"Um, last week. I had a meeting with the manager and the owner of the company. They want me to start taking on more responsibility. I don't get a raise yet, so I guess it's like a training phase type thing," I explained.

"That's so wonderful, Anastacia!" She beamed at me, and I knew she was truly happy for my success no matter how great or small. "You know I was just telling your grandfather that we should take a trip up and see one of the shows," she commented.

If I had been drinking, I would have sprayed it across my car. "Um, I think they are between shows, Nana," I said, not sure how to tell her my employer was a gentlemen's club.

"Oh? Well, you'll have to let me know when their next show is. We'll be sure to come up and support everyone," she promised, as I closed the cap on my car and returned the pump to its cradle.

"Yeah. Okay. I'll get their schedule and let you know," I

lied again.

We gave each other a quick hug, and I hopped back in my car. She stood by the pump waving good-bye until my car was lost in the darkness down the road. I didn't bother looking at my buzzing phone, because I knew who and what I would find. Turning the radio up, I screamed along to whatever song was playing until I pulled into the parking garage at home.

When I walked in the door the girls were all watching TV in the living room laughing and eating popcorn. I didn't feel like bringing down the happy vibe, so I beelined straight to my room and closed the door. Crawling into my bed, I pulled the blankets up over my head and cried. Eventually, I cried myself to sleep.

* * *

The next morning I woke to someone knocking on my door. I groggily looked over at the clock and started cussing. It was already after eight, which meant I was late for my workout with Cherry. I scrambled out of bed and swung the door open.

"Sorry! Sorry! I overslept!" I apologized, blitzing into the bathroom.

I washed up and brushed my teeth in record time, before running back to my room. I stopped running around when I realized it was Spider, not Cherry, sitting on my bed. She had this knowing look on her face as she patted the bed next to her.

"Cherry is getting coffee. We need to talk," Spider coaxed.

I climbed back onto my bed and sat awkwardly, waiting

for what felt like an intervention. "Am I getting kicked out?" I asked, feeling my eyes start to burn.

Spider looked shocked for a split second before sadness took over. "What did they do to you, baby girl?" She asked softly. "Come here. You're not getting kicked out. We were just worried about you." Spider explained just as Cherry came in with a tray of coffee cups and bagels.

"I thought you were meeting up with your sister last night, then you came home looking like someone died," Cherry said, passing me a mug. "What happened?"

I took a deep breath, and leaned back against the wall. "She never showed," I said, sipping my coffee.

I watched as the look of shock hit both of their faces. "Did something happen?" Spider asked.

I nodded. "Yeah. She had dinner plans with the rest of my family at my grandparents."

"Holy shit…" Cherry exhaled. "Taze, I don't even know what to say."

Spider just reached over and hugged me. "We were hoping that you two would make up, truly. I'm so sorry, baby girl," she whispered.

I just sighed and relaxed into the embrace. "That wasn't the worst of it," I said, chuckling in a deprecating manner. "First, I waited two hours. When she didn't show up, I decided to drive by my grandparents to visit instead. Imagine my surprise when my whole family was there eating dinner, happily without me."

"Shit," Cherry said again.

I chuckled again. "It gets better. I didn't take that much cash with me, so my car ran out of gas like two minutes from my grandmother's house. I had to call them so I could get

140

home."

This time Spider looked pissed. "Shut up!! Why didn't you call one of us?" She asked, staring at me intently.

What could I do but shrug. "It was forty minutes away. My grandmother unleashed pops on the whole lot while she came to help me gas up my car."

As I recalled the brief interaction with Nana, I couldn't help chuckling. "Oh! I almost forgot. Nana asked when she and pops can come see a show."

"What? Where?" Spider asked.

"NO!!!" Cherry shouted at the same time.

"Yep. Whenever they can get tickets, she'd love to see your show," I said with as much seriousness as I could muster.

Spider and Cherry started laughing hysterically. They made so much noise that Lacey came running in to join.

"What did I miss?" She yelled, shuffling onto the bed with her own coffee.

"Nana and Pops want tickets to our next show!" Cherry and Spider announced at the same time.

Lacey looked at me in shock. "What did you say?" She asked, eyebrows pressed up to her hairline.

"I told them you had just finished, so it would be a few months before the next show?" I said, shrugging slightly.

"TAZE! You would invite your grandparents to see exotic dancers?!?" Lacey asked, still not over the initial shock.

"Well, I didn't know that's what you did until last week!" I tried to defend myself, but only succeeded in making Cherry and Spider laugh harder.

"Stahp! Stahp!" Spider wheezed while still laughing.

"I can't breathe!" Cherry echoed, tears streaming down her face.

141

"Seriously? How did you not know?" Lacey asked, still fucking stunned at my ignorance.

"I'd never seen the front of the house! I leave before the show happens, and I clean during the day. Until you took me through the front door I had no fucking idea, and I didn't ask questions! OKAY?" I yelled back at them, trying to justify what I thought was an obvious mistake.

Lacey nodded as if that made sense. "Yeah, I can see how you thought that. But how many actors get paid in wads of cash each week?" She asked.

I opened my mouth to argue, and then felt like I had been hit with a stupid stick. All of the clues were right there in front of me. "Ohhhhh my god….." I gasped remembering the money bags for cash deposits. The hours they worked, and how they were dressed when they came in from work. I grimaced, "I'm such a fucking idiot!"

This time we all laughed at my expense. "Don't tell anyone!" I begged, as Spider slipped out of my room.

"Oh hell no! This shit needs to be shared. How are you so fucking innocent and brutal at the same time?!" She yelled over her shoulder.

I tried to run after her but Lacey grabbed my coffee cup while Cherry tackled me down to the bed. "Send it quick!" They both yelled down the hall to our deliriously cackling roommate.

"You guys suck!" I half screamed, half laughed.

"This is the best fucking end to my week!" Lacey giggled after we had all settled down almost twenty minutes later.

"Did she send that to everyone?" I asked seriously.

Cherry looked at me for a moment, before patting the spot next to her on the sofa. "Come here. What are you so worried about?" She asked.

"I don't want people making fun of me for being stupid," I admitted.

Cherry smiled and tucked a wild curl of hair behind my ear. "No one. And I mean NO ONE thinks you are stupid. There isn't a single one of us who even thinks you are weak, Taze. But knowing how much shit you have been through, and can still be so blessedly naive…" She giggled. "It was the most precious thing I could have heard. And not just me. You are an absolute ray of sunshine, Taze. Don't change that."

"What do I tell Nana about your show?" I asked, feeling the laughter about to bubble up again.

"Tell her the truth," Lacey spoke up from the kitchen.

"Seriously? You wouldn't be upset or embarrassed," I asked them.

"I have nothing to be ashamed of. I'm hot as fuck!" Spider chirped up, swiveling her hips in her seat.

"Liar! I've seen that fucking tattoo you cover with makeup! 'Harry STYLES 4 EVAH'!!" Lacey yelled running into the living room, point her finger at Spider's boob.

"Seriously?!" I yelled. "HARRY STILES?"

"Shut the fuck up! You don't know nothing about me and Harry!" Spider yelled back in defense.

"Why would you want a guy who's only as big as your thumb?" I asked, scrunching up my nose.

"He's over six foot!" She promised, assuming I meant his height.

"Yeah, okay. I didn't mean his height," I corrected her. "He's a white dude from the UK. Gonna be too thin and dainty for you, Spider," I added pointing down between my legs as I

143

raised an eyebrow.

"And who do you have on your list?" Spider snapped back.

"I mean if we're sticking with the Queen's land…. Idris Elba?" I offered.

"Damn. That's a good pick," the girls agreed.

"Seriously, though. My tattoo isn't about Harry Stiles, the singer, but my best friend from school, Harriet. She wanted to go to cosmetology school and become this high end stylist to the stars." Spider explained, leaning against me on the sofa.

"Her nickname was Harry?" I asked.

Spider nodded.

"Did she get into school?" Cherry asked, having never heard this story.

Spider shook her head. "She died before we graduated," she whispered.

I shook my head. What could any of us say to that? "I'm so sorry, Spider."

Spider looked at me. "I found out at her funeral that she had been fucking my boyfriend. Never trust a bitch with your boo."

Chapter 10

I stepped out of the vehicle at the airport, nervous as hell as the girls piled out behind me. The Marquessa was *under new management*, which meant the club was getting an overhaul. We weren't out of jobs, but given a week's paid vacation to the Virgin Islands courtesy of the new *owner*.

I didn't ask what happened to the man I had met three months ago, and no one offered up any information. We were just excited to be getting out of the city and off to somewhere exotic and wonderful.

"What time does the flight leave?" Angel asked, pushing her suitcase onto the curb.

"Flight leaves at eight," Spider repeated for the tenth time in thirty minutes.

"Let's go get checked in so that we can relax before then. Maybe we can grab some mimosas before boarding!" Lacey offered, smiling at everyone as we piled out of the shuttle vans.

I rolled my eyes. I was too damn tired. It was six o'clock in the morning, and my otherwise pleasant roommate was already trying to get drunk. I was excited about the trip, but I hated getting up this freaking early.

"Let's go," I grumbled, marching into the terminal to look

for our airline's check-in counter. A file of twenty women falling in behind me made quite the scene as we moved through the terminal.

"Why are you so grumpy? We're going on a paid vacation!" Lacey chirped next to me.

I gave her the most scathing side eye I could muster. "Nothing is even open yet, and you are looking to get drunk. Can we get there first? It's too early to carry you around, Lace," I said.

Lacey rolled her eyes at me. "You're no fun."

"Remember that tonight when you're praying to the porcelain god, and we're going out on the town!" Spider said, siding with me.

"Ha!" I chuckled, pointing at her.

As we each checked into the airline counter and handed over our suitcases, my nerves began to settle. I had never flown anywhere in my short existence, let alone left the country. The process went very quickly and soon our gaggle of giggling bombshells was marching to the security lines.

"Which gate are we flying out of?" A girl named Elektra asked.

"A22," someone said.

As the line moved through the security, I watched as one girl after another was waved through the metal detectors. I stepped forward to walk through with the rest, but the security guard stopped me.

"You need to wait until you are called to step forward," he barked at me.

I stopped mid step and backed up to the line. "Sorry, I was following my group."

"Right," he scoffed, motioning for another agent to assist

him. "Do you have any metal on you?" He asked.

"No, I emptied my pockets. I'm not wearing jewelry, and my shoes are in the bin going through the machine right now."

"Step forward," he barked at me again.

I didn't know what to expect, but the machine's loud beeping was not it.

The agent looked truly irritated by me and began scowling. "I just asked if you had anything on you, and now the machine is saying that you do!" He was talking louder than necessary given the situation, and I honestly had no idea what set off the machine.

"I'm going to need assistance for a physical check!" He yelled to another male agent walking up.

"STOP!" Angel yelled suddenly. "She requests a female agent to search her!"

The two men looked from me to Angel and then back. "Miss, you need to mind your own business. You don't know what she could be smuggling," the second agent stated.

If my face wasn't flushed in embarrassment before, it was now. How, in the long line of twenty plus people, was I singled out as a smuggler?

"Are you serious?" I asked, beginning to tremble.

"Taze, ask for a female and a witness!" Angel barked at me.

I didn't hesitate to repeat her words, much to the dissatisfaction of the two men standing in front of me. The woman behind the x-ray machine whispered something into her radio, and three more agents started approaching the security point. I looked helplessly at the women traveling with me, and nearly began crying.

"What's happening?" I asked Angel standing behind me.

147

"This is a routine check. They have to manually search every fifteenth or twentieth passenger. Don't let those men touch you if you aren't comfortable. Do you hear me? You have done nothing wrong," she stated softly but loud enough for everyone around us to hear her.

"Smith! I got this one," a woman's voice called over from another lane. She was a short black woman who looked like she could bench a volvo. As she made her way over to me the two men backed away like they were afraid of being hit.

"Step forward, hon," she beckoned, smiling politely at me. "I'm going to conduct a physical search of your body. That means I am going to place my hands on you and feel for any hidden material you may be concealing," she explained.

"I'm not concealing anything!" I argued back, fighting the tears welling up in my eyes.

"You're probably not, but I have to explain to you what is happening. Do you understand what I have explained?" She asked patiently.

I nodded, wiping away the tear now trickling down my face.

The woman continued talking me through everything as she went. From feeling my arms, searching my hair, to patting down my chest, legs, groin and back. She was thorough, but nothing about what she did screamed of impropriety. She was professional in everything she did.

"She's clear," she announced, looking up to see the group of women waiting for me.

She turned back to see the four or five women behind me and chuckled darkly. "Where are you off to sweetie?" She asked as she pulled my tray of belongings from the belt and did a cursory search of my carry-on items.

"The Virgin Islands. Our company hasn't had a vacation in a year, so the new owners paid for a group vacation. All of the employees are traveling and staying in the same hotel for a week while the building is renovated," I explained.

As she shuffled through my wallet two sleek black business cards slipped out. The woman stopped moving and stared at them. I didn't say a word too afraid of what would happen next. Her head dropped and her body relaxed, as she leaned both hands down on the counter. When she looked up, her entire demeanor had changed.

She put everything away exactly as she found it, and handed me the tray. "I am so sorry for your inconvenience, miss. I hope that you and your coworkers enjoy your conference!"

I watched in shock as she whispered something to the woman behind the x-ray machine. Suddenly, the entire staffing at the security line was replaced by women. I didn't hear what happened to the asshole named Smith, and I didn't care. As I joined the group waiting for me, I was pulled into tight hugs and checked over.

"Are you okay?" Elektra asked, wiping my dampened cheeks with a tissue.

"I didn't do anything wrong," I whispered back.

"We know, sweetie," she said, looking at the security agents. "And so do they," Elektra announced loud enough for everyone to hear.

"Can we just go?" I begged, feeling too humiliated to stand there any longer.

"Not yet," Spider whispered, taking hold of my hand.

"I'm very sorry for the inconvenience experienced by your companion," a woman was saying to Angel.

149

Angel looked as high and mighty as I had ever seen her. "This is not acceptable," she stated.

"It will be dealt with," the woman promised, bowing her head slightly before scurrying away.

"What was that all about?" I whispered back to Spider.

"That is what power looks like. No one will ever bully you again, so long as we are with you," Angel stated, walking away from the security gate with the remainder of our group.

"Now let's get to our gate, so we can put this shit show behind us and get on with the party!" Lacey cheered, causing a volley of cheering to go through the group.

I couldn't help but be swayed by their excitement. I found myself smiling by the time we reached our gate and were called to begin boarding. Angel and several others had upgraded their tickets to first class, thanks to whatever member clubs they belonged to. I was happy to sit wherever, so long as I could look out the window.

Cherry plopped into the center seat beside me, and pulled me into a side hug. We didn't need to say anything. She knew. All of my roommates knew the shit I had lived through. I hadn't let another man near me in almost a year. The thought of another stranger putting his hands on me….

My body trembled involuntarily.

"We got you, sweet baby girl," Cherry whispered, giving me a light peck on my forehead.

"What are you going to do when I'm not the youngest anymore?" I asked, pushing her away.

"My sweet Taze is growing up so fast!" She lamented, throwing the back of her wrist up to her mouth and falling back in her seat. "I member when you was just a wee little fearful thing!" She went on and on in the thickest southern accent I had ever heard. "You member, don't ya, Spidey? Look at her now. So grown, she can't be seen getting kisses from her, mama!!"

"You are so fucking weird," I laughed, unable to hold back watching her antics.

"There it is!!" Spider cheered from the other side of Cherry. "Stella's got her dimples back!"

I felt my face burning red. Whenever I smiled really big, my dimples would show up on either cheek. I felt like it made me look like a kid, but the girls loved it. "Shut up!" I yelled, covering my face. Of course that only made them cackle even harder.

Time seemed to fly by as the attendants made their rounds to conduct their preflight checks and safety demonstrations. Before I knew it, we were pulling away from the gate, and leaving my stomach behind with it.

"I don't think I can do this!" I rasped, feeling panicked and claustrophobic.

"Here, drink this. It'll help with your nerves," Cherry assured me, passing a glass of water my way.

I gulped down the cold beverage, and waited for the panic to subside. It wasn't a minute later that my tongue felt funny. I reached up to feel my tongue and my hand sparkled with different colors.

"Chwe-Charweee, ma face feel funny," I tried speaking but my voice sounded weird.

Lacey turned around in the seat in front of me. "What'd you give her?" she asked, smiling sweetly at me.

"Sparkling water with a touch of —," Cherry smiled lovingly at me, but I couldn't hear her words anymore as the world turned dark around me.

151

"Yuuuuu dwug may?" I asked as my eyes rolled into the back of my head, and I fell fast asleep.

* * *

"Taze?"

"Taze, you gotta wake up. We're about to land," Cherry whispered, nudging me gently.

I blinked groggily at the woman next to me. I couldn't remember falling asleep. How were we landing already?

"How long was I out?" I asked, my voice sounding hoarse.

"Not long, just a couple hours."

I looked out the window at crystal blue waters, and my breath hitched. It was the most beautiful scenery I had ever seen. Lost for a moment in the gorgeous view just outside the window, my memories slowly filtered in.

"You drugged me?" I asked, shouting at her suddenly.

"Not really," she giggled, patting my hand to calm me down.

"No. I heard you! You said you drugged my drink!" I shouted, pulling my hand away from her.

"I gave you draMamine dissolved in water. It helps most people with motion sickness when traveling. Helps them calm down. I had no idea you were going to be such a lightweight," she admitted, smoothing back my hair from my face.

"You shouldn't have done that," I yelled back.

"Taze?" Lacey asked from the row ahead. "Everything okay?"

"No. It's not okay. If I wanted people manipulating me with drugs and drinks, I wouldn't have left home!" I growled back at them.

152

"Taze-" Cherry started, but I smacked her hands away.

"You had no right!" I growled at her.

For the life of me, I couldn't understand why anyone who knew me, anyone I trusted, would think drugging my drink would be okay.

"Taze, I was just trying to help you relax," Cherry explained, looking truly apologetic. I didn't care though. I didn't care what her reasoning was. It didn't matter what excuses came out of her mouth, because I only heard one thing in my head.

"That's what he said, Cherry. That's exactly what he said to me when he raped me."

Cherry looked like I had slapped her. I wish that I had had it in me to do that, but I was too angry. I felt betrayed and vulnerable. The people I had come to love and treat like family had drugged me against my will.

"I hope you all had a good laugh at my expense. Because it won't happen again," I swore, turning to stare out the window.

I didn't say another word. Not when the plane landed, and they tried to coax me. I didn't speak as we gathered our bags or lined up to take the shuttle to the hotel. I was quiet right up until it was time to check into our room.

"Elektra? Can I share a room with you and the others?" I asked.

Elektra looked from me to the three women standing at the counter and nodded. "Yeah, sure. We have room for one more in our room," she agreed.

I gathered my room key and followed Elektra to the room she and two others were sharing. When we were finally inside, and dropping our bags, Elektra pulled me aside.

"You okay?" She asked.

153

I didn't know what to say and just shook my head. "I need some time."

I did. In everything that had happened to me, I had never given myself time. I had allowed others to drag me forward, listening as they explained what they felt was best for me. I ran from my family, when I couldn't face everything.

The only control I had was what happened to my body. It was my decision to fight, to flee, to laugh or to bleed. I needed to feel like I had that control, or everything I held back and bottled up would drown me. All of the emotional bullshit I kept tamped down was a tsunami waiting to overflow and crush me. I didn't have anything else in my life that was my choice except that little bit of control. It may have seemed insignificant to them, but it was the only way I knew how to survive.

A knock at the door had everyone scurrying around excitedly, discussing what we would do first. I didn't need to talk with anyone. I grabbed my bikini and toiletry bag out of my suitcase and walked into the bathroom.

By the time I finished washing my face, brushing my teeth, changing and pulling my hair into a high ponytail, the noise outside the room had quieted down. When I came out of the bathroom, Angel was sitting on my bed waiting for me.

"Do we need to talk?" She asked, raising an eyebrow at me.

"No. I'm fine. I'm going to the beach," I said, throwing my stuff into my suitcase.

Angel nodded, and stood up. "Okay. Let's go."

I paused for a moment. "You want to hang out with me when everyone else is having fun at the bar downstairs?"

Angel shook then nodded her head. "We just got here. I want to pace myself."

"Okay. Let's go bake, white girl!"

"I'm not white, you little shit!" She balked at me.

I nodded as if in understanding. "Yeah, yeah. I heard all about it. You're just as Latina as me. But can we at least own the fact that we're the two whitest Latinas in history?" I threw back.

Angel tried her best not to laugh, but it was no good. "It's true," she finally agreed, chuckling. "Let's go fix that, hermana."

"Vamos!" I cheered, holding open the door.

Three hours later, I was already a golden brown. I looked over at Angel and couldn't help but giggle. "You sure you're Latina and not blanca?" I asked.

"Shut up!" she grumbled, looking down at her pink skin. "I'm burnt, aren't I?" she asked, grabbing a colorful sarong out of her bag and wrapping herself up.

"It's not too bad yet, but we really should go in before it turns," I agreed.

Angel tipped her head back and sighed in frustration. "Why can't I tan?" she whined.

"You live like a mole?" I retorted.

Her head whipped up to look at me. "What the hell does that mean?" She asked.

I waved my hands in mock surrender. "You work crazy hours at night and you hole up during the day to do online classes. When does your white ass ever see the light of day?"

Angel chuckled as we walked across the beach toward the hotel. "Marjory tell you all that?" She asked, looking straight ahead.

"No. Lacey did."

"She should mind her own business," Angel scoffed.

"Lacey graduates in four months. She has been trying to convince me to sign up for classes," I commented.

Angel stopped walking. "Four months?"

"That's what she told me. Why?" I asked.

"Let's go mend some fences. By the time we get back, everything'll be different."

I had no idea what she was talking about, but I felt that there was a grain of truth in her words. By the time we reached the hotel, Cherry was staggering out of the bar with Spider and a random guy holding her up.

"Stacia! I'm so sorry!" She blubbered when she saw us. "I'm so so soooorrrrry. Please don't leave me."

I stood still in shock for a moment unaccustomed to the emotional outpouring from my roommate. "How many did she have to drink?" I asked Spider.

Spider shook her head. "None. She's fucking devastated, Taze. It was stupid. We fucked up. You're a huge part of our lives, and the thought of you leaving is fucking horrible."

"These two are cutthroat," Angel stated in approval.

"They're idiots," I commented, shaking my head in disbelief. Then my eyes focused on the man holding up my best friend. "Who's the dude?" I asked Spider.

The guy looked terrified. "I'm just a busboy! Your friend is on something. I saw her mixing some shit with her water. We can't have people high and unhinged like this. Get her up to her room, or management will kick everybody out."

Angel and I rolled our eyes at his dramatic overreaction. I would believe him if it were Lacey or even Elektra, but not Cherry. I marched over and took over supporting her.

"She's not high, dickhead! She's just emotionally fucking stunted," I grumbled, dragging Cherry toward the elevators with Spider. "Why is it that every time a woman has a bad day, she's gotta be high or drugged? Huh?" I chastised as we walked.

"Can't someone fucking grieve the dead without being accused of taking drugs?" I continued, as we stepped into the elevator.

The poor busboy looked like he stuffed both feet in his mouth and started swallowing. "You're a dumbass!" I threw out as the elevator doors closed.

Cherry immediately stood up and straightened her clothes once we were alone in the lift. She and Spider both looked nervous as hell, and unable to make eye contact with me.

I smacked the emergency stop button and stared at both of them. "Start talking. You wanted my attention, now you have it," I stated calmly.

Cherry shook her head, not really looking at me but at the closed elevator doors. "Start it back up."

"No."

"Taze, this isn't funny. Start it back up," Cherry growled more insistently.

I just stood blocking the buttons and shook my head again. "No. Talk."

"Taze-" Cherry started as the color drained from her face.

"You don't like being locked in here, Cherry?" I squinted my eyes, goading her on.

"Th-this isn't funny," she said, looking wildly around the small space enclosed around us.

"What's not funny?" I asked, tipping my head to the side.

"T-ta-taze! You know I don't like being boxed in!" She yelled at me.

"I do. I also know that Spider here is actually fucking

157

terrified of arachnids. Not quite as bad as your fear of elevators, but it's up there," I chuckled.

"Why are you doing this?" She wheezed, starting to hyperventilate.

"Because I needed you to understand," I replied, my expression stony.

"Understand *WHAT?!?!*" She started screaming.

"What it feels like when someone you love and trust inflicts your greatest fear against you."

Cherry dropped to the floor as I hit the button again to resume our trip to the sixth floor. As her face flushed with relief, her eyes filled up with tears. Understanding of what they had done finally settling in. They hadn't helped me, regardless of what their intentions had been. They had crossed a boundary, using my greatest fear to subdue me.

"When we get back, I'll find a new place to live," Cherry croaked at me as the elevator dinged and the doors opened to our floor.

"Get your ass cleaned up, Cherry. You're embarrassing yourself," I scoffed under my breath. "Nobody's moving, that I know of. Just know that I may look nice, but I can be a vicious enemy if pushed. You use my fears against me again, I will murder you in your fucking bed," I growled, walking to my own room down the fall from theirs.

Whatever they discussed after that, I didn't want to hear it. Reducing Cherry to snot and tears in a tiny coffin, suspended between life and death, made us even in my book. There would be no apologies from either of us, but we could move forward from this first bump in the road.

I dropped my bag by the door and opted to wash the sun and sand off of me. Recharging in the sun had done wonders for my body and mind. I jumped into the shower while the water was still cool, and sighed at how amazing it felt. Rubbing the soapy rag over my skin felt delicious. I had come in at just the right time between golden goddess and lobster bisque. Angel may not have been so lucky, but I was happy that my Latina roots were singing through.

I left my hair to air dry, rubbing in a little bit of leave-in on the ends. The girls had convinced me to dress 'hot' during this trip, so I decided to embrace the whole experience. My make-up was over the top for me, completely masking my smattering of freckles.

The green sundress made the nominal flecks of color in my brown eyes almost glow. I was looking forward to a night out with all of the girls on this trip, and I knew it was going to be a night to remember for all of us. They had never seen me dressed to the nines, because I stopped dressing up after the assault.

It was time to start living my life, and taking back everything that others had stolen from me.

Chapter 11

Time seemed to fly by. Our trip to the islands felt like a dream that ended too quickly. I stopped hiding my body in baggy clothes, and started dressing up when we went out. Among the many changes implemented under the new management, the dancers were required to give fifteen percent of their tips to the club each night.

I thought it was ridiculous, but Cherry and Spider told me that most clubs in Philly took thirty. For them it was a win, and just went to show how much I still had to learn. The new management also cut our workdays down from five to three, which I thought would slow business down. It didn't. We had a packed house every night, and the girls were making tips like crazy.

Angel and Marjory took me under their wings and started teaching me all of the behind the scenes shit needed to keep the club's customers happy. I took over ordering everything from bar snacks to liquor and built up my own network with all of the Marquessa's suppliers. I never met with anyone in person, so I wasn't breaking any laws by being under twenty-one. As for all of my added responsibilities, my own pay was increased so that I was finally making five hundred a week.

I stopped doing nails for tips, and set my own hours on

Mondays, Tuesdays and Wednesdays by appointment only. My clientele may have been limited to exotic dancers, but they were calling from clubs all over Philly and the outlying areas. I had saved up enough to finally buy myself a brand new car, and thought I had finally made it.

Seeing Cherry come home with three grand after the first night, however, was almost enough to make me consider dancing instead. Marjory wasn't opposed to the idea, but Angel lost her shit. Hearing her swear and rant about my innocence was enough to put the idea on the back burner. I just focused on learning what I could about the business. Before I knew it, four months had passed, and Lacey announced that she was giving her notice.

Lacey had finally completed her law degree and passed the Pennsylvania Bar exam. She was offered a job in a local firm in Philly, and, although the pay wasn't the same, it was enough that she didn't need both jobs. Not to mention, she recognized several of her new firm's partners as recurring customers. She was worried if they recognized her she would lose her job and footing in the industry.

Tonight was her last night, and all of the girls decided to hold a huge glowing-away party before the club opened. She didn't know it, but everyone had agreed to give her half of their tips for the night. She was moving into her own apartment, and could use the money to get her life started.

"To Stephanie Thomas, attorney at law!" Marjory announced, holding up her glass of champagne.

"To Stephanie Thomas!" We all cheered, holding up our own glasses to toast this amazing woman.

Lacey looked overwhelmed with the outpouring of love and well wishes for her future. "You guys are going to make me cry!" She gushed while sipping her own glass.

I stood up from my chair and smiled at the woman I had come to love like a sister. "When I met you a year ago, I was a terrified shell of myself. You were, and still are, this amazing glamorous goddess in my eyes. Words cannot express how much I love you, and support all of your future adventures. I wish you nothing but happiness and many wins in court! To Lacey," I said, holding up my glass.

"Cheers! To Lacey!" Everyone echoed, taking another swig of their champagne.

We sat around joking and laughing until it was time to start getting ready for the night. While everyone scattered up to the changing rooms or behind the bar, I cleaned up the evidence of our party and reset the tables and chairs for the night. As I finished taking out the trash, Cherry pulled me aside and snuck me into one of the less frequently used offices.

"Okay, sweet cheeks! Are you sure you want to do this? Angel will kick both of our asses, but it's for a good cause!" She repeated, passing me what looked like scraps of fabric.

"What the hell is this?" I asked, holding the garment up in front of my eyes.

"That's part one of your outfit. Here's your mask, tail, shoes and makeup bag. Spider and I will be guarding outside the door, so you don't have to worry about anyone catching you!" She promised and ran out the door.

I couldn't believe I was going to do this. No. I could. Unlike everyone else, I was doing one song and giving Lacey any money I made. It took me a minute to figure out the one piece ensemble Cherry had ordered from Bordelle. The outfit we chose was a deep red mesh bodysuit with a crisscrossed harness that wrapped around my body. It gave nothing away, but left nothing to the imagination either.

As it was nearly October, I decided to add a pair of devil horns and a red lace eye mask. With the addition of my makeup and heels, I doubted my own mother could recognize me. I had just finished putting my stuff away in my bag, when the door knob began to turn. It wasn't nearly time for me to go on, so I wasn't sure if Cherry or Spider were coming to check on me.

Holding my bag in one hand I pulled the door open. "Your timing is perfect, I just got changed," I said, not looking to see which one was there.

"This is a private office," a man's voice sounded. "Dancers are down the hall in the changing room."

I nearly fell over from the shock of being caught. "I'm sorry," I apologized, smiling sweetly at the man I hadn't seen in almost a year. The gorgeous man whom I thought was no longer the owner, was standing in front of me.

"You're new?" He asked, eyes slowly appraising my body.

"More like a trial run," I said, winking at him.

"Turn around," he directed, stepping into the office and closing the door behind him.

Deciding that I was already in for the pound, I dropped my bag on the floor and did a slow turn. I knew damn well my ass was on full display for this man, and turned to look over my shoulder at him as he studied my backside.

"What's your name?" he asked, moving to sit behind the massive desk I had just used as my personal vanity.

"I don't have one yet," I lied. Cherry and I had already picked out my name for the night, but I wanted to hear what he wanted to call me.

He leaned back in his chair and adjusted himself. Knowing that I was making that Adonis hard was empowering. It filled me with a heady feeling that I could see myself getting addicted to. "What's your name?" I asked, strutting toward his desk.

"Is that how we are playing this little game?" He asked, smiling at me. I would have thought he was amused, but the smile never reached his eyes. This man was pissed, and most likely trying to decide if I was going to be thrown out. Before I could answer him, my roommates were knocking on the door.

"Let's go, Lilith!" Cherry called as she walked into the room. Seeing my backside, she started whistling but stopped abruptly when she realized I was not alone.

Her demeanor changed immediately. "Oh my god! I am so sorry, sir! She's doing a surprise guest spot for Lacey's going away. I shouldn't have let her change here. I am so sorry!" She apologized over and over, pulling me back slowly from the desk.

There were exactly two times I had seen Cherry unsettled by something. The first time was in an elevator, this was the second.

"Lilith, is it?" He asked slowly, still leaned back in his chair. I smiled and bit my lower lip.

"Bye, handsome!" I said, waving as I bent over to grab my bag and strutted out of the office. Cherry closed the door behind us, and we sprinted in heels down the hall.

"Holy shit!" I gasped.

"Fuck, fuck fuck, FUCK!" Cherry murmured over and over. "He was pissed. Right? Did he seem pissed to you?" She asked.

I shook my head and giggled. He had no idea who I was, nor would he ever find out. "It's okay. I told him that I was a guest dancer for Lacey's going away. He may not have believed me at first, but you came in at just the right time! Who the hell is he? I thought the owner changed. Why is he still here?" I asked quietly, making sure that no one else could hear our conversation.

Cherry looked terrified for a moment. "How do you know that man?"

"He's the one I had to meet after I beat that dude's ass in the parking lot!" I explained.

"Oh fuck. Taze, that man is the most dangerous underboss in the tri-state area. The Marquessa has always been owned by women, until that man bought out Iryna in a sale of force," she explained. "This isn't good. We need to tell Marjory about this."

Before I could say another word, Spider had grabbed our hands and began leading us toward the stage. "You ready, Lilith?" she asked, waving over to a guy named Mike who handled all of our music.

"Gentlemen, you are in for a real treat tonight. As we say goodbye to Lacey, and helloooo to Lilith! Give it up for a one night only show you will not forget! Ladies! The stage is yours!!!" He shouted over the introduction to the song we had chosen.

Spider and Cherry pulled Lacey up to center stage and sat her down in a chair as my chosen song began to play. I waited about three beats and began my slow strut behind my girl.

Boom-tssst. Boom-tsst. Boom-tsst.

I had never felt so amazing and fucking invincible as I did

165

walking out onto the stage to *Closer*. I dropped into a deep squat behind Lacey, and ran my hands down the sides of her body to her legs. As the first words were uttered by the vocalist, *'You let me violate you'*, my hands were pulling her knees apart.

The men started whistling and howling as I turned her chair around and popped back up and rolled my hips in Lacey's face to, *'You let me desecrate you.'*

Lacey was grinning from ear to ear, not expecting to get a lap dance from another dancer on her last night. I moved in close to her body as the song continued, letting my own body ebb and roll around her to the music.

I was so lost in the dance I didn't even see the other girls come out on the stage to start dancing with us. There was a sudden screeching noise like someone dragged a needle over vinyl and the song changed to Pony by Ginuwine. On cue we all began dancing the piece that Spider had choreographed.

Instead of just me and Lacey on the stage, there were now twenty of us scattered around the club doing the same moves in absolute sync. I felt high, my endorphins were so elevated from the rush of being on stage. I looked out across the sea of hungry men and my eyes locked on a pair of eyes that almost had me willing to break my dry spell. I watched him watching me, and I went all out to perform for him rolling my hips and bouncing my ass for his enjoyment alone.

As the song ended I stood with the other girls to hug Lacey and left before that man could find me again. I ran to the dressing room, grabbed my bag and ran into Marjory's office. My normal clothes were quickly pulled over the skimpy suit, and I ripped off my mask and fake lashes.

I had just finished washing the makeup off when someone

knocked on the door. I kicked my bag under the desk and yelled, "It's open."

When the door opened, I was sitting over a stack of orders and invoices, checking off our stock against what was delivered. I didn't even look up, as I was normally a nobody in this club and I wanted to keep it that way.

"I'm sorry, do you know where I can find Marjory?" The owner's deep voice broke my fake concentration.

I looked up and shook my head. "She may be in the changing room, sir," I added.

"I'd rather not walk into their space. Would you mind checking for me?" He asked, politely.

I put down the receipts in my hands and smiled. "Yeah, I can check. Give me a second," I agreed, trying to scoot past him as quickly as possible and praying he did not recognize me.

Before I could get out the door, my body was pulled back and pushed up against the wall. The owner, whose name I still didn't know, was holding me by the throat staring at me like he wasn't sure who I was.

"The fighter, right?" He asked, watching my every reaction.

"Yes, sir," I admitted, not willing to make eye contact this time.

"Why aren't you fighting back?" He asked, tipping my head up so that I had no choice but to look at him.

"I'm on business premises, and you haven't hurt me. Will I need to fight back, sir?" I asked, now staring back into his hazel eyes.

He shook his head and released me to find Marjory. While I walked away looking confident and secure, the trembling started up as soon as I was out of that man's line of sight.

"Marjory," I croaked out. "Boss is looking for you."

"Where is he?" she asked, moving toward the door.

"Your office."

"Shit," Marjory cursed and started walking faster.

I stayed in the changing room until Marjory came back twenty minutes later. She immediately pulled me aside looking like she didn't know whether to be pissed or amused.

"Taze, do you know who the guest dancer was tonight?" She asked.

I nodded slowly, afraid to say a word.

"Is she going to be making anymore appearances in our club?"

There was a long pause as I considered whether I would dance again, and I had to admit... I was torn, but I still shook my head no.

Marjory sighed with relief. "That woman could ruin a fucking empire. I have never seen that man so fucking obsessed. If you ever pull a stunt like that again, I won't be able to help you," she said at the end before walking away.

Fuck.

Cherry and Spider came back shortly after to check on me. With one look they knew I was not doing well. "What happened?" Cherry asked quietly, changing her outfit for her next song.

"Marjory knows and I almost got caught by the owner!" I whispered a little too loudly, looking panic stricken.

Cherry's smile froze. "It was a one time thing, so we don't have to worry about that. Right?"

I nodded like I was a bobble head. While I felt like an iron woman on the stage, now... In my jeans and button down shirt I felt like a *nobody* who was about to be crushed by the mighty. Why was he even here tonight, of all nights?

I spotted Angel across the room staring at the three of us. She wiggled her finger at me, beckoning me to her side. "I have to go," I whispered and went to where I was summoned.

Angel sat there removing her makeup. "You know what you've done," she said softly.

I wasn't sure if she could tell it was me or not so I played stupid and shook my head.

Angel reached up and took the set of horns off of my head, and I nearly fainted. *Oh, my fucking god.* I had those things on my head the whole fucking time I was talking to that man! She saw the panic on my face and smiled.

"Guest dancers don't have the right to *gift* props to anyone. The next time you find yourself in such a position, you need to decline. People might draw the wrong conclusions and think you stole something," she said, placing the horns in a bag under her table.

"I will remember that in the future," I promised.

By the time the night was over, Lacey was walking out the door in tears carrying a duffle bag with nearly thirty thousand dollars. I couldn't believe that was half of the tips for the night. When we got home, Cherry clarified for me. Lacey walked away with half of the tips *after* the club had taken its cut.

"Holy shit," was the only thing I could utter. That was a lot of money for a single night. How rich was that guy? No. I couldn't think about that. I had a plan, and I needed to stick with it!

Lacey moved out the following Monday, and I cried. I don't know why I cried, because it wasn't like she was leaving the city. She was just taking a new job on the other side of town.

She paid for three movers to come and collect her stuff after we packed her up.

Before she left she pulled me aside and gave me a hug. "Make up with your sister, Anastacia. She was just looking out for you. You're not the same girl who moved in here. You can face them now. And before you say no, I already talked to Nana and she's setting it up!"

I smacked her back, regretting that I had ever introduced my grandmother to my roommates. "You suck," I muttered against her hair.

"You still love me!" she whispered back, pulling away from our hug.

"Shut up with the mushy shit!" Spider yelled, shoving me out of the way to give Lacey another hug as well.

"You two act like she's leaving the country! Let her go already so we can decide who's getting her room!" Cherry piped in from the other room.

Lacey rolled her eyes and we laughed a bit. "Ok. I really do need to go so I can let the movers in at the new place. Smooches, bitches!" She yelled and ran out the door waving behind her.

I closed the door to our apartment and pouted. Who would be our new roommate? We agreed that we didn't want just anyone moving in here and messing with our flow. After a long afternoon of cleaning and discussing, we decided to leave the room vacant for two months. I couldn't afford to cover one third of the rent, but Spider and Cherry assured me that it would be no problem for them to split Lacey's portion.

Going back into work on Wednesday was nerve wracking. I kept looking over my shoulder for the owner. To my shock and horror, he was in his office. The owner who never made an appearance at the club, was there every fucking day that week. Despite myself, I kept checking him out. I couldn't help it. Everytime he turned his back, I was staring at his ass and imagining what it would feel like in my hands.

I wasn't brave enough to do anything about my growing obsession with him, so I avoided him as best I could. I stayed in the store room, or cleaned the upstairs areas if he was in the club downstairs. It worked for two weeks. Then Halloween rolled around, and Angel called in sick.

She was scheduled to be our main event that night, and Marjory was frantic trying to find a suitable replacement. Cherry and Spider must have heard the wheels grinding in my head because they were suddenly in front of me shaking their heads.

"No. Last time was it, remember?" Spider reminded me.

"You almost got caught, and I don't even want to think about what could have happened if the owner found out. Not happening," Cherry seconded.

"What's not happening?" Marjory asked, walking up behind us.

Before either of my roommates could intervene, I spoke up first. "Cherry suggested calling Lilith to cover Angel's slot."

Marjory's jaw dropped. But then she became very serious. "I'll have to speak with the owner. Lilith isn't contracted with us, and he would want to be sure that there were no conflicts with any other club," she said slowly, giving me time to change my mind.

I knew that she knew it was me, but she also didn't want to lose money on such a big night. I nodded in understanding.

Marjory gave me one more look, and walked back to the owner's office.

I knew what he would say. I remembered the way he looked at me when he found me in his office, and I knew he would agree. There would be no conflicts with any other clubs, because no one knew who I was. Lilith was a ghost.

I didn't wait for Marjory's answer and decided to get changed. This time my outfit was a two piece from Bordelle's Keio collection. Lacey bought it for me when I turned 20, and I had never had the courage to wear it. The top was nothing but straps and rings, like something from an S&M collection with a thin piece of mesh tulle covering my nipples. The bottom was high waisted with the same straps creating a belt around my tiny waist, the thong in the back exposing my plump ass cheeks.

Unlike the one piece, this one was silvery in color and I loved the way I felt wearing it. When I put on my heels, my ass looked fuller. Cherry tutted beside me as I put on my makeup, waiting to say something but stopped when she realized I wouldn't change my mind. The finishing touch was a lace mask that matched my top and bottom, and a small set of wings attached to the back of my top.

Elektra came up behind me and whistled. "Jesus…" she sighed. "If I hadn't watched you change, I wouldn't have known it was you!"

Cherry and I stilled, our eyes both going wide. I turned and stood up from the vanity. "Elektra, love… If you say a word, I will kick your ass," I whispered softly.

Elektra looked shocked. "Does Marjory know?"

"Yes, but that's it. If the owner finds out, I'll be fired and so will Marjory. Please don't say anything," I said firmly, hoping that she would understand the severity of the consequences.

"I don't see what the big deal is," she replied.

Cherry pulled her aside and whispered something in her ear. I don't know what she said, but it was enough to startle the unshakeable Elektra. She looked at me concerned, and then nodded.

"It's nice to meet you Lilith. You can call me Elektra," she said smiling and holding out her hand for me to shake.

"Nice to meet you too, Elektra," I winked, shaking her hand.

I sent Mike a text message with my song choice. It was an old school choice, but I hoped that he had it in his system. I didn't care what anyone else thought of the song. I knew that once I started dancing, they wouldn't give a shit about the music.

Marjory peeked her head into the changing room and gave me a thumbs up. I nodded and made my way downstairs to the stage. There were two more sets before mine. I watched as the girls danced, there were two on side stages, and another named Trinity on the main stage.

"Why are you here," a man's voice whispered in my ear.

I recognized the voice and fought to keep from shivering. "I'm helping a friend," I said, not turning to look at the man behind me.

"Whose club do you work for?" He asked, sliding his hands from my waist to my hips.

"Would you believe me if I told you I only do special requests?" I commented, peeking over my shoulder.

"I can't have you working in my club," he growled, pulling me back against him so that I could feel how hard he was against my ass.

"Don't you like what you see?" I asked, batting my eyes at him.

He chuckled and let go of my body. "Too much. I don't fuck where I work, so this can only happen if you don't work here."

The words were a double edged sword. If I let this thing between us go any further, I would lose my job. If I declined him, it meant that I worked here.

"I don't fuck strangers," I replied, pushing my ass back against him and rubbing against the erection straining against the fabric of his pants. "Gotta go, handsome," I said as I walked onto the stage.

The synth music began and I strutted out onto the stage, and swirled around the pole as the opening lyrics began. *'Do you believe in heaven above? Do you believe in love?'*

I slowly lowered to my knees and looked over my shoulder for the man I knew would be watching. *'Don't tell any lies, don't be false or untrue,'* I sighed, rolling my hips and biting my bottom lip.

I slowly climbed back up the pole and twisted my leg around it so that it would hold my weight as the chorus began. *'Send me an angel... Send me an angel. Right now.'*

Three and a half minutes of that man's hazel eyes devouring my body, and I knew I was going to be dripping down my legs when I walked off of this stage. I laid back on the stage and arched my back up, my knees bent in the most provocative pose I had ever made. I couldn't help imagining him between my legs, fucking me with everything he had.

Between my sex crazed fantasies of my boss and the rumbling base of the music vibrating the floor, it was almost enough to make me come undone without anyone touching me. When the song finally ended I walked away as fast as I could hoping to avoid that man before reaching the dressing room.

I was almost there when two firm hands pulled me into an office. The door slammed shut and I was pressed against the door by a firm body behind me.

"Fuck, you are an angel and a devil," he murmured, burrowing his nose into my neck. "Please tell me that this is mutual," he asked, running his hands down my body.

"Yes," came out breathy and so much more seductive than I meant it to.

"Fuck, I want you so bad my balls ache, cara," he whispered as he pulled both of my arms over my head and pinned them there with one hand while the other caressed my ass. "You staring at me with those fuck me eyes, while every other man was fantasizing about doing exactly what I am doing," he continued, as his fingers reached forward into my soaking lower lips.

I couldn't speak. I couldn't utter a single word as he pulled my thong to the side and slid two fingers inside of me. I gasped, a moan escaping my lips when he began pumping those magical fingers in and out of me.

"You are so fucking responsive, little angel," he groaned, as he left open mouth kisses across my shoulders and down the side of my neck. "I'm going to make you come all over my fingers, and then you are going to leave my office before I bend you over my desk and fuck you."

"Ahh," I moaned, becoming more excited by the physical stimulation and the thought of him inside of me. "Fuck me," I whimpered.

Chapter 12

Suddenly, he grabbed me by the hair, and turned me toward his desk. I didn't need any more prompting. I walked to his desk and bent my ass high over the top, my legs spread wide. When I heard his belt coming undone, I peeked over my shoulder at him. He was fucking gorgeous.

"Keep looking at me like that, and this will end sooner than either of us wants it to," he growled, pulling out his cock.

I couldn't resist taunting him, shaking my ass a little and giggling. His reaction was a swift smack across my ass cheek. I squeaked and tried to move away, but he was already rubbing his bare cock against me.

"Condom," I rasped, realizing that I was about to have sex with a stranger for all intents and purposes. This was the first time in years I had a say in what happened to my body, and I wasn't taking chances.

"I'm clean, but I will respect your wishes," he whispered, caressing my flaming ass cheek. I heard him open the wrapper, and then he was sliding into me.

"Fuck!" I moaned loudly, as he filled me to the point of almost being too painful. Where my mind had been filled with visions of him wrapped between my legs, I was now overwhelmed with this sensation of being full.

"Fuck," he grunted at the same time, not moving for a few seconds. "Lilith suits you," he panted, pulling back slowly before thrusting back in. "You were made by the gods to tempt every man to his doom. Fuck, you are so tight, dolce."

I was lost in the feel of this man's effect on me. Bent over his desk, my thong was giving all the right kinds of friction across my clit. He pulled my arms behind my back and held me by the elbows so that my back arched up. Each time he slammed into me my hips pulled furthŕer at the constrictive bottoms. I couldn't stop the moans that came out of my mouth. I was a panting hot mess under this man, and I didn't want to stop.

"Sing for me, Lilith. Let me hear you," he grunted, beginning to pound deeper and harder into me, and sing I did.

I became lost in my bliss, coming so hard I thought I was blind for a moment. I had never been high before, but I assumed that this was what it felt like: a sweet high of euphoria exploding out from my core. My limbs tingled with the aftershocks, my lower end repeatedly spasming with every thrust as he chased his own finish.

"God, don't stop," I pleaded, pushing my ass back to meet him, loving the feeling of everything he was doing to my body.

"Just like that," he grunted, becoming impossibly harder and bigger inside me. He let go of my arms and grabbed my hips, slamming into me so hard I knew I would have bruises where my legs were repeatedly slammed into the desk.

I whimpered, almost unable to take anymore when he stilled and I felt him coming; his body trembling over mine.

"Shit," he whispered, caressing my back. "This can't happen

again, little devil."

"Then it won't," I agreed, pushing myself up from his desk as he pulled out of me to dispose of the condom.

Before either of us could say another word, someone knocked at the door. I made sure my bottom was back in place and gave him a look to see if he was dressed. He nodded and I opened the door to find the angry man who I assumed was his bodyguard.

I turned slowly and smiled back. "I'm sorry, but I'll have to decline your offer. Thank you anyway," I said, and strutted past the security guy to the changing room.

I needed a new job. I couldn't work here anymore. I had just fucked the owner, after swearing that I wasn't one of his employees.

* * *

By the time I got back to the apartment, I was spent. Physically, emotionally. I was torn between enjoying the feel of what I had done, and at the same time shaming myself for being so fucking easy. My head was telling me that I was still a good person. Women should not be shamed for having a sex life outside of marriage. But the years of indoctrination ruled my heart. Was I a slut now? I wasn't in a relationship with that man, yet I allowed him to have sex with me.

No. It was a consensual and mutual attraction that led us to that. I did nothing wrong. He did nothing wrong. Well, not knowingly anyway. He said he didn't fuck employees, and technically I was an employee. But Lilith was not. Lilith was not a contracted dancer for the Marquessa. She was her own woman. Her own lusty, slutty woman… Who happened to be me, an employee of the Marquessa. I was so screwed.

I had no idea when I fell asleep, but I woke to my phone ringing incessantly. I couldn't even see who was calling, and rejected the call.

My phone began ringing again. This time I was determined to sleep and rejected the call again, throwing my phone across the bed so I couldn't hear it vibrating. I was just falling back into dreamland when Cherry opened my door, light from the hall spilling right into my eyes.

"FUCK! Why can't anyone let me sleep?" I whined, pulling a pillow over my head.

"Taze, your grandmother is here," Cherry stated.

Not understanding what was going on, I mumbled something about calling her back when I woke up.

"Anastacia, you can come out of that room or I am coming in!" Nana's voice came from the hall behind Cherry.

I sat bolt upright, nearly falling out of bed. "Shit! She's here? I thought someone was calling me!" I mumbled, pulling myself together as I stumbled out of my bedroom.

She looked older, standing in my apartment. I still had dinner with her and pops every Tuesday, but she looked like she had aged so many years since the last time I had seen her.

"What happened?" I asked, knowing that she would not be here at seven o'clock in the morning unless something happened.

"Let's go sit," Nana offered, walking back to the living room.

Cherry made her way back into her room, offering to give us some privacy.

"I'm sorry, I didn't realize that was you calling me," I stated, taking a seat in the corner of the sofa.

"That was probably your sister, hoping to talk to you before anyone else," Nana said, a sad smile on her face.

"Are you dying?" I asked, not ready to hear the answer.

"No. I mean we all die, but I am fine," she said, looking at me like I should know something more.

"Just say it. What happened?"

"Your mother has cancer. She didn't want you to know initially, but it's progressed beyond what they can treat. Right now it's about quality of life, not quantity," she whispered softly, tears filling her eyes.

"Mami is dying? How long?" I asked, suddenly feeling like a lost little girl after all this time. My relationship with my mother may have been strained and broken, but she was still my mother. She had always been there though. She was a constant in my life.

"Three to six months."

"Shit."

"I know this is a lot to ask, but I want you to come home. My daughter can never make things right. What's done, can't be undone. But you... can you let her die in peace? Can you be there for her, Anastacia?" Nana asked, holding my hand and caressing my knuckles.

"I'll need to give notice at work," I admitted. In the back of my mind a thousand scenarios were going through my head, from how to hand over my tasks to how to give notice. "Is she in the hospital?"

"No, she's home. Well, sort of. Titi agreed to take her in. Jada packed up the apartment and broke the lease with the landlord. Everything is sitting in storage for you and your sister. Your grandfather and I have cleared out the spare room, so that you'll have a place to stay."

This was too much. In less the span of a night, I went from feeling like I could rule the world to being pulled back down to the depths of hell and despair. The worst part: I couldn't be angry with anyone. My mother didn't choose to get cancer. She wasn't choosing to die. My family was asking for me to come home. I couldn't mend all of the broken pieces, but we could heal what could be healed and move forward without 'what ifs'.

I called pops and told him that Nana was with me, and we would be at their house in time for dinner. Cherry and Spider helped me put fresh linens on the bed in Lacey's old room, and I convinced Nana to rest while I ran in to work to give notice. They weren't going to like it, but there wasn't much of a choice for them. I couldn't stay knowing that my mother might not make it to Christmas.

I showered and made myself look more presentable. With so little sleep, I couldn't be bothered to hide the bags under my eyes. After making sure that Cherry and Spider had Nana, I drove to the Marquessa for the last time.

It felt bittersweet knowing I would not come back here again. I loved everything about this experience, but knew that if I came back I would be ruined in this place. Lacey and Angel always told me to leave before this felt like home. I couldn't honestly say the Marquessa never felt like home, but the women here were my family.

Walking through the downstairs area was quiet. The night crew had already cleaned and scrubbed everything down, and set the tables and chairs back into their place. Seeing the club without the lights and music, took away the magic of the place. This thought made the decision to walk away so much easier. This part of the Marquessa wasn't what I knew. It wasn't what kept me here all this time.

I knocked on the owner's door, knowing he would be in like he had been. To my surprise the woman who I had met beside him that first time answered the door.

"What do you want?" She asked, almost snarling at me.

"Good morning, ma'am. Sir, do you have a moment?" I asked, looking over at my boss behind his desk. He looked every bit as hot as I remembered, but the look on his face was no longer one of desire but irritation.

"Sure, what can I do for you, Taze?" He asked, ignoring the woman strutting past me to sit on his desk.

"I want to apologize in advance, but last night was my last night here. I won't be able to continue working here due to-"

My words were cut short and the world spun as the woman seated before me suddenly slapped my face.

"FUCKING WHORE! DO YOU THINK YOU CAN HAVE HIM BECAUSE YOU QUIT?!?" She screamed, lunging to hit me again.

"Iryna! What the hell are you doing?" He yelled, jumping up to restrain her.

I turned and smacked her back, knocking her on her ass. "Shut the fuck up while the adults are speaking," I growled at her. The man behind the desk stopped and stared at me. Without even looking at him, I knew in that instant that he knew it was me and I didn't care. It wasn't going to change anything between or about us. Iryna, on the other hand, looked fucking terrified before recovering and pulling herself back up.

"My mother is dying. My grandmother came up last night to let me know. My family is asking that I move back home, and I agreed," I finished not even looking at the man who had me bent over this desk the night before, but staring at the woman beside him.

Before she could say another word to argue or insult me, Marjory came running into the office and pulled me into a hug. "Anastacia, I'm so sorry about your mom. Cherry just told me. Don't worry about anything here, just go be with your family," she murmured reassuringly against my hair.

I didn't cry when Nana told me. I didn't cry saying the words a moment ago. Yet, somehow, hearing the words confirmed again from Marjory made it all real. My Mami was dying. The tears fell and I sobbed in Marjory's embrace. Regardless of the shit in my life, my mother had always been there and soon she would be gone.

When she pulled me back to look at my face, the hot red handprint on my cheek was screaming for attention. Marjory turned on Iryna in a heartbeat. "You fucking hit her?!" She screamed.

The man moved to pull Iryna behind him, but Marjory wasn't having it. "I have tolerated your fucking shit long enough. This girl has done nothing but keep your shit above board for a fucking year, and this is how you treat her?" She continued yelling and pointing at the pair. "Do you know how fucking hard it's been for her to come here and tell you she is leaving? Do you have any fucking idea how the rest of us live outside your gilded fucking cage, Iryna?" Marjory berated the woman she once called her boss.

"Marjory, I think that's enough," the man started, but Marjory wasn't having it.

"Fuck you too, Roman! You just couldn't help getting your wife all riled about your flings… You think because you have

183

fucking money, you can do and say what you want to us lowly workers? I've got news for you, you fucked up this time. Consider this my notice. I'm fucking done with your bullshit. And your wife is *blacklisted*."

I didn't know what half of that meant, but Iryna looked like she had seen a ghost. She literally fell against Roman, the man who finally had a name. I had never seen Marjory so angry. I don't think I had ever seen her angry at all, come to think of it. And now she wasn't just angry, she was so pissed that she had quit her job and threatened the owners.

She pulled me under her arm, and guided me out of the office. "Let's go pack up your things," she whispered softly, guiding me toward the changing room and her office as if the screaming hadn't just happened.

"You shouldn't have quit because of me," I whispered when we were alone.

Marjory chuckled sadly. "I didn't. You aren't the only one with a family drama calling you home," she said. "I've put off my own shit long enough, too afraid to face the past. This was a good kick in the ass."

I nodded and began packing up my mini nail station. By the time I got back to the apartment, Cherry and Spider had already packed up my room. I had hidden here in my fantasy world long enough. It was time to face the real world.

When we got to the house, Pops helped me unload my car, and stuff all of my stuff into their guest room. I didn't even bother unpacking before heading directly over to Titi's to see Mami. The house was pin drop quiet when I walked in. I didn't know where anyone was, until I heard whispering coming from upstairs.

Titi came down seconds later and pulled me into a tight

hug as soon as she saw me. I just hugged her back. I hadn't spoken with her since the fight nearly a year ago. I hadn't spoken with anyone, except for Nana and Pops, but they hadn't reached out to me either.

"Come help me with the food," she suggested, pulling me into the kitchen.

"How is she?" I asked, unsure what to do until she passed me a jar with brown rice. As I cooked the rice, Titi prepared me for everything that would come after.

"She's lost a lot of weight, Tacie. *Es flaquisima,*" she started. "Some days are better than others. But most days, she's in a lot of pain."

"Did they give her anything para el dolor?" I asked, concentrating on my pot of rice.

"Si. She has morphine patches, and we got her some marijuana to help her keep her food down. Sometimes she confuses things, people…. Don't take what she says to heart."

"What does that mean?" I asked.

"Sometimes she lashes out with her words, when the pain is really bad. I can't tell you the things she said to your grandmother," she commented, shaking her head.

"Is she lucid? Sabes que está pasando?" I needed to know what I was walking into.

"Mostly. She's a little loopy for an hour when we change out her morphine patches, but then she sobers up a bit. She knows what's going on. It's just hard with the pain. You know?" Titi added.

Truly, I had no idea and I admitted as much. "I don't even know what kind of cancer she has. When was she diagnosed? Why isn't she getting treatment? There's chemo, radiation…" I rambled off before Titi gave me a look.

"We don't know when she was diagnosed. She didn't tell anyone until six months ago, and by then she was well into radiation treatments. She'd been wearing wigs and hats, so no one knew her hair had fallen out-" her words broke off, as she was mid sentence.

"Why didn't anyone tell me?" I asked, turning off the rice and leaving it to sit with the lid on the pot.

"Tacie, I don't have an answer. Your sister wanted to tell you, but you two had been on the outs. Your mother was certain that it would go into remission, but then... Here we are. No one wanted you to feel like you were being forced back home, but here you are anyway."

"Why did she stop treatments?" I asked, wanting to know just how bad this was going to be.

"It's in her pancreas. They hoped that because they caught it early..." Her voice trailed off. "It's aggressive, what she has. All we can do now is make her comfortable the best we can," Titi said, finishing up the vegetables she had prepared to go with the rice.

I stepped back, watching her place the brightly colored mix of fresh vegetables and brown rice. I would ask about diet restrictions later, for now I needed to help where I could, and watch and learn.

Titi loaded everything up onto a tray, and I followed her upstairs. There was a hospital bed set up in Titi's room, making the spacious room seem cramped. Whatever I expected, it was so much more than I anticipated. My mother, a woman who had been graced with curves for days from an early age, was practically a skeleton. The room smelled of chemical cleaners, and marijuana.

"Juana, it's time to eat lunch," Titi announced, setting the tray onto a small bedside table.

Mami didn't even budge. Titi walked over and caressed her arms while repeating the same words. "Juana, it's time to eat."

My mother moved a little, as Titi began adjusting the bed so that she could sit up. "Come on, hermanita. You have a visitor," she continued coaxing.

Mami's eyes fluttered open and she looked over at her sister. "Teti, I am too tired. Let me sleep," she whispered.

Titi sighed and caressed her cheek with the back of her hand. "You'll need to take your medicine, and you need food in your stomach."

I hadn't heard what medicines she was taking, but saw what looked like a small pharmacy of pill bottles on the dresser. "What does she need to take?" I asked moving over to the dresser, prepared to help however I could.

"You should be at work, Jada," Mami's hoarse voice called behind me.

"Juana, that's Anastacia. Jada is at work," Titi corrected her, trying to spoon a small bite of brown rice past my mother's lips.

"Why are you here?" My mother asked.

I turned slowly to face her. "Did you not want me here, Mami?" I asked, holding back the mix of conflicting emotions overflowing and clashing inside.

"You got away, nena. Why come back?" she asked, tears filling her eyes.

"You need me here," I responded, turning back to read the various pill bottles.

She had zoloft that was taken twice per day, eye drops that had not been opened, acetaminophen, a box of morphine patches, diazepam administered three times daily, and something called prochlorperazine which was administered as needed up to three times per day. I guessed it was time to take the diazepam and prochlorperazine pills.

"These two?" I asked, holding them up for Titi to verify.

"Just the diazepam. If she isn't puking, we don't need to give her the other," Titi corrected.

"You shouldn't be here," my mother insisted, barely chewing the half spoon of rice in her mouth.

"What are you going to do about it? Chase me out?" I asked, passing the pill to Titi.

Titi chuckled and stuffed the pill into a spoon of rice. Mami was too focused on me, so she didn't even pay attention to what her sister was doing.

"What about your job?" Mami asked.

"My boss quit, so I didn't want to stay there without her," I told her. It wasn't a flat out lie in my mind. Marjory did quit, but she quit because of how I was treated. Not the other way around.

"No-" Mami rasped.

"Yes-" I rasped back, mimicking her.

Titi looked like she was going to piss herself from either shock or laughter.

"You're impossible to deal with," Mami said finally, rolling her eyes at me.

"Well, now you get to deal with me a lot more. I'm here to the end," I said seriously, with my back turned to them. Both women looked like they wanted to say something profound, so I kept talking as I used a pen on the dresser to give myself a mustache. "Whoever laughs first loses," I said as dryly as I could, turning to face them.

Titi sucked in a sharp breath, and tried not to say anything. Mami on the other hand was turning beet red. "You are a shit, Anastacia!" Mami gasped, then covered her mouth so I wouldn't see her smiling.

"Mami… I mustache you a question," I stated in a thick accent, and plopped beside her on the bed. I faced her as I scribbled the pen along my jaw and cheeks. "Now that I have beard myself to you, I must know. Does this mustache make my ass look big?" I asked, quirking up an eyebrow.

Titi lost it and started laughing. Mami and I chuckled a bit, at her over the top hyena laugh. "Thank you, mi hija," Mami whispered, squeezing my hand.

Her illness would never change all of the shit between us. What was done was done. But that didn't mean I would kick a person when they were down. My mother was dying. There were no more harsh words or angry thoughts left in me. The worst fate that she could face had already been dealt. The least I could do was remove one burden from her shoulders as she made peace with her end.

I squeezed her hand back and excused myself to refill the water pitcher and ice chips that were nearly empty. I listened to the two of them whispering and giggling as I made my way into the kitchen. Titi followed behind shortly after and made herself a plate of food.

"She's asleep again. So we have a little time," she noted.

I nodded and then remembered hearing two voices when I came in. "Who else is here helping?" I asked.

Titi looked at me confused for a moment.

"I heard two voices when I got here. Mami was asleep, so I just assumed you weren't talking to yourself."

"Ah, Tia Antonia is in your old bed. We've been taking

189

shifts so that someone is always awake and available to help Juana. She has to go into work later, so she's getting a few hours of sleep before that."

I nodded. If Titi and the bruja were here, where was the eldest hermana? As if reading my mind, Titi continued telling me about everyone's schedule.

"Maria's flight gets in tomorrow. She's taken a leave of absence to be here with us. Rob is overseas, so he won't be able to come home before the funeral, sadly."

It made sense. Mami was an aunt and not even someone who had raised Rob. No matter how tight our family was, the military were sticklers for rules.

"If he can get approved for R&R, he might be able to get here after New Year's," Jada's voice came from behind me, causing me to nearly jump out of my skin and squeal.

"Don't scare me like that!" I shrieked in a high whisper, and swatted at her arm until she pulled me into a hug.

"Why wouldn't you call me back?" She whispered into my neck, squeezing me tightly.

"Why did you ghost me?"

"They called me at work. Mami had collapsed at the store, and they had to call an ambulance. She couldn't hide anything anymore after I got to the hospital. When she was released, I dragged her to Nana and Pops' so she could tell everyone. I thought you would come to Nana's when I didn't show," Jada whispered.

"I saw everyone inside and thought you all were blocking me out. Why didn't Nana tell me?" I asked, pulling back. "She came to help when I ran out of gas, why didn't she say something to me then?"

"Mami told everyone after Nana stormed out of the house.

She was so pissed when she got off the phone with you. She cussed me out, Tacie. I have never seen her so angry..." She explained, her eyes welling with tears.

"I tried calling you all night to tell you, but you blocked my calls after that. You stopped going to Nana and Pops for dinner on Tuesdays... I didn't know how to reach you, and then Mami said it was better if you never knew."

I shook my head and pulled away from my sister's touch. "That's bullshit and you know it. The whole fucking family sat around the table laughing and joking, and you *all* thought I didn't need to *know?*"

I wasn't pissed before but now I was getting there. My sister had decided that I didn't need to know our mother was dying? "Who the hell did you think you were making that decision, Jada?" I seethed.

"Stop it now," Titi barked at us. "You want to fight? Go outside. You want to point fingers? Start with the woman upstairs. You may be losing your mother, but that is my sister and she didn't fucking tell any of us.

"You want to be here to help, then fucking help her go in peace. We can all argue and bitch after she's dead. But you won't make her remaining days hell, because you have grudges to bear. I won't have it in my house. Do you two understand?" She asked, squaring off with Jada and I.

"All of you need to shut the hell up," the bruja commented, shuffling into the kitchen. "I just wanted three hours. Three hours of sleep," she grumbled as she poured a cup of coffee.

"What can I do to help?" I asked, looking from Bruja to Titi.

"There's a shopping list on the fridge, and an envelope full of money. Jada, go do the shopping, Tacie has the next shift

191

with Juana," Titi directed, accepting a cup of hot coffee from her sister.

I nodded and went back upstairs to sit with our mother. As I walked into the room, my mother was staring at me. "Are you okay, Mami?" I asked, moving to make sure she was tucked in.

"I thought I lost you. You went missing in a department store. I screamed and yelled for you, but you were just gone. The police were called and the whole store center was closed off while they searched for you," she whispered.

"I'm here, Mami," I told her, brushing her forehead to calm her.

"You were lost, Anastacia. *I died*. When I thought you were gone, I died," she confessed.

"But you found me," I reminded her, remembering the day I had decided to crawl under a clothing rack to take a nap. I was four years old, but the memory stayed with me from choosing to lie down to being awakened by a police dog who had tracked my scent.

"Yes," she agreed, nodding. "I always found you."

Chapter 13

With the arrival of Tia Maria, plus me added to the rotation, Titi, Jada, and Bruja were able to work their normal hours for the most part. I stayed with Mami during the day, and Maria, Titi and Jada took turns throughout the night. Bruja had to return home, but promised she would be back during the weekends to help.

It wasn't just about making sure that Mami ate and took her meds. She was too weak to make it to the bathroom by herself. Though when I suggested adult diapers, I honestly thought she was going to come up out of the bed and chase me out of the room.

"Anastacia? It's time to get up. I've already made coffee and porridge for your mother. Come down and eat breakfast before she wakes up," Bruja nudged me on the sofa. It was Monday already.

With Tia Maria here, all of the available beds upstairs were well and truly occupied. I chose to sleep on the sofa rather than swap with someone else each night. Even with the constant walking back and forth to the kitchen at all hours, I still slept as well as I could.

By the end of the second week, the gloves had come off. Mami became belligerent about the sheets not being cleaned, even though I had just changed them. She argued about the food making her sick, and accused Jada and I of stealing her money and hiding her man. I couldn't take it, and started screaming back.

Tia Maria came in and told me to go out for a while. I hadn't left the house in three weeks and I needed to take a break. It had been three weeks, twelve hours a day, without a day off. I wasn't physically tired, but my emotional state was fucking chaotic. The moments of lucidity with my mother always seemed to happen when I wasn't around. When I was there, she was abusive and vulgar.

I walked out the door, and didn't look back. Without even thinking about it, I drove to Nana and Pops's house. They made frequent visits throughout the week, but those trips weren't about me. They were losing their youngest child. While I was struggling to claim to be an adult, they were watching their child wither and die before their eyes. The guilt I carried with my growing resentment was almost tangible.

"What brings you this way?" Nana asked, hugging me as I walked in the door.

"I needed a break."

"Did Maria kick you out?" Nana asked, raising her brows in surprise.

"No."

"So, yes."

Pops and I both said at the same time. Nana looked from one to the other, and just shook her head. "Go upstairs, get yourself cleaned up and sleep. You look like hell, Anastacia," she added, before pushing me toward the guest room.

My grandparents bought this house from Pops's grandparents shortly after they had gotten married. His parents were already settled in their own home, but the family didn't want to part with the property. The house was originally a two bedroom ranch with a single bathroom that his mother had grown up in with eight siblings. After he and Nana bought it, they began renovating.

They added a second floor after Titi was born, so Mami and her sisters each had their own rooms growing up. As they aged and moved out the rooms were converted to a guest room, an office, and a playroom for the grandkids. Now that the grandkids were all grown, Nana packed up the play room and promised to set it up when the great grandkids eventually came along. There were six of us, but no one was even close to having kids any time soon.

I grabbed a change of clothes from one of my suitcases and stepped into the bathroom. I almost didn't recognize the woman staring back at me. There were dark circles under my eyes, and my hair pulled back in a sloppy mess of a bun. My face looked so fucking gaunt after eating and sleeping like shit for two weeks. I set the water as hot as I could stand it, I scrubbed my body from top to bottom.

With a hair mask setting on my long neglected locks, I proceeded to shave the wool pants off of my legs and the bushes growing under my arms. How had I not noticed how hairy and disgusting I had become? Deciding to give the whole body its due attention I continued up the legs and took care of the entire hairy situation downtown while I was at it.

Thirty minutes later, I felt like I had scrubbed a ton of weight from my body. My skin was humming with fresh air, and my face actually looked bright again. I was still too skinny looking, but at least I didn't look like death. After towel drying my hair, I rolled it around a long length of cotton fabric to curl it. It was still early enough that I could nap a bit and meet up with Cherry and Spider tonight, if they weren't too busy.

Before I could think too much about it, my phone vibrated. I smirked seeing there was a message from Cherry.

Cherry: [Going to Baltimore for Elektra's birthday. Wanna go?]

[Grab me on the way down?] I quickly texted back.

Cherry: [Be ready by eight! Send me the address]

I quickly sent her the address to Nana's house, set the alarm on my phone for 5pm, and crawled into bed. I slept like the dead. In fact I slept so well, I never heard the alarm on my phone going off, and only woke up when I felt someone caressing my face.

"You are so fucking cute when you sleep," Cherry was cooing at me.

My eyes shot open and I screamed, much to the amusement of Cherry, Elektra, Spider and Lacey.

"Holy shit! I overslept!" I squeaked and jumped out of bed.

"Relax, we're early," Lacey said, laughing and stopping me with a great hug.

I immediately relaxed and hugged her back. "I am so sorry, just give me like five minutes to get dressed," I promised them.

I didn't miss the looks exchanged between the four women in my room, and stepped back with a suspicious look on my face. "What are you not telling me?" I asked, eyeing each of them over.

"First, I am totally loving the whole bonnet look on you.

Two, we discussed it, and Anastacia needs a night off," Spider said first.

I bit my lips, remembering that I had put my hair up in twists before going to sleep. Then I thought about what she said. I did need a break. "Right. That's why I'm going," I agreed.

"Anastacia is going to sleep because she obviously fucking needs it," Elektra commented, taking out a bag from her tote.

"What the hell?" I asked, recognizing by now the Bordelle wrapping on the garments.

"Let Anastacia have a night off. We're here to take Lilith out for a couple of nights on the town," Cherry giggled, pulling an extremely revealing and racy, platinum two piece set out of its wrapping.

The lace material was decorated with a circular geometric pattern. The bottom was a low waisted thong, that I absolutely loved, paired with a matching balconette bra. I didn't bother hiding in front of them and immediately started stripping off my pajamas. When I had the top and bottom on, Lacey shook her head at me.

"It's missing a little something, something. Here, try this," she giggled, throwing a matching platinum harness at me.

I couldn't stop grinning from ear to ear. I looked wicked as hell in this lingerie, and it was everything I needed to pick me up. "Where are we going?" I asked, pulling on a button up blouse and black pants to cover everything.

"There's an expo going on, and we're going!" Elektra squealed, pulling five VIP passes out of her tote.

"Holy shit!" I squealed back. "How did you get VIP passes?"

Cherry shrugged her shoulders and chuckled. "Marjory knows somebody, who knows somebody, who knows somebody. Honestly, we didn't ask," she admitted. "Grab what you need to finish getting dolled up, we'll have space when we get there to finish getting ready."

I didn't need convincing and threw my make-up into Elektra's tote. "Wait!" I said, looking into my closet. "I don't have shoes for this. I always borrowed yours," I remembered as I stared at my selection of trainers and winter boots.

"We know. We got you covered…." Lacey started, then looked over to Spider who pulled out a platinum colored lace mask.

"From your toes to your nose!" Spider continued, showing me a pair of clear heels.

"You guys are too much," I said, feeling like I wanted to cry. "It's Elektra's birthday, and it feels like I am the one being spoiled."

Elektra furrowed her brows. "My birthday is in June, Taze."

I looked over at Cherry, and saw her cheeks pink up. "We were too busy to celebrate birthdays this last year, so now we're going to celebrate them all!" She announced.

I didn't need to hear any more convincing and the five of us were out the door, after a few quick hugs with Nana and Pops and promises to be safe. They knew I wouldn't be home for a couple of nights, but I wasn't alone.

The drive to Baltimore flew by as we all chatted and sang along to the radio in Lacey's SUV. For as long as I had known her, she preferred to drive sleek sports cars. But as a *young lawyer*, the SUV made her seem more serious and less entitled. At least that was how she tried to explain it. We all laughed hysterically at her bullshit logic. She was driving a freaking *Cayenne!*

I loved the woman dearly, but I couldn't understand

how a one hundred and fifty thousand dollar Porsche SUV appeared *less* entitled than the Mercedes SLS she had before. They were both grotesquely overpriced cars in my eyes, and one certainly didn't lose out to the other in terms of perceived prestige. Before we could argue further, Lacey was pulling up to a hotel valet in Baltimore's waterfront district.

I didn't ask questions, and we piled out of the vehicle as a concierge from the front desk came out to collect our bags on a cart. "Welcome back, Miss Thomas. Would you like me to have these things delivered to your suite?" He asked politely.

My eyebrows shot up in shock at the over the top formal greeting. I looked at Cherry and Spider, but they just smirked and subtly shook their heads, letting me know to keep my mouth shut until we were inside and behind closed doors.

Lacey just thanked the man politely, and tipped him two Benjamins before walking into the hotel leaving her car and all our stuff in other people's hands. We followed behind, giggling about what kind of trouble we would get into in the next twenty-four hours. Unlike the other four, I had never been to an expo of any kind, so I was looking forward to the whole experience.

"If you want, next year, you could set up a booth and do nails, Lilith," Cherry whispered. "A lot of dancers pay good money for their appearances, and your gel wrap technique is amazingly strong."

I looked at her in shock. "People can do that?" I asked.

Elektra laughed at my innocence and pulled me under her arm as we stepped into the elevator. "Oh, sweet baby girl, this is going to be so much fun with you here!"

199

I could feel my face heating up.

"She's so cute when she blushes!" Cherry cooed and squeezed my cheeks just as we reached our floor.

Lacey and the girls had rented a high end suite for the expo. There were two bedrooms, each equipped with separate ensuite and a huge living area connecting the two. Two bottles of champagne sat chilling in fancy ice buckets, with six fluted glasses arranged between them on the table.

"Who's the sixth?" I asked, realizing there were only five of us.

"Marjory couldn't make it down tonight. She'll be here tomorrow though," Lacey explained, grabbing a bottle and pouring everyone a glass.

"Ok, ladies! We have half an hour to get ready, and then we are going to have a fucking blast tonight! Bottoms up, bitches!" She said, holding up her own wine glass.

We each grabbed a glass and toasted before drinking the glasses empty in one go. I hardly ever drank and I hadn't eaten all day. A knock at the door signaled the arrival of our things, and the flurry to get ready began.

I had barely finished my makeup when I started feeling the buzz from the alcohol. "I need to eat something," I whined as my stomach growled angrily.

Lacey chuckled at me and grabbed her phone. "I ordered something for you. It'll be here shortly," she said two minutes later.

I nodded and finished my makeup. I took off the bonnet and began unwrapping my hair from the scarf. The hack did exactly what I wanted it to do. My hair fell in long spiraling curls down my back. I used my fingers to comb through them, separating the thicker pieces as best I could. I couldn't even recognize myself in the mirror.

"You look like a fucking goddess, Lilith!" Spider gasped when I turned around.

"Shut up, Spider," I giggled, smacking lightly at the air between us.

"Seriously, girl. You look fucking amazing when you clean yourself up," she continued staring at me wide eyed. I rolled my eyes and walked out of the shared bedroom to the living room.

"Holy shirt balls, Taze!" Cherry gasped when she saw me.

The other two immediately looked up and gawked as well.

"Guys, it's makeup and curly hair!" I said, feeling super awkward about the attention.

"I would totally fuck her," Elektra whispered not so subtly to Lacey. Lacey just nodded in agreement.

"Seriously?" I asked, staring wide eyed at them.

Cherry took my hand and led me to the full length mirror by the door. I had to do a double take at myself. Who the hell was the woman staring back at me?

"See?" Cherry whispered when my jaw dropped.

"Shit. We're not walking out like this are we?" I asked softly.

"No. You wear your blouse and pants, take the shoes in your bag. There's a place to change at the venue. Even if we could wear this out, I wouldn't let you walk around any city like this. You'd be snatched up before we reached the lobby!" Cherry continued.

I rolled my eyes at her theatrics and went to join everyone else. Lacey had ordered an assortment of finger foods from the hotel restaurant. There were sliders, fries, small sandwiches, cakes, cheeses, fruits and vegetables. I wasn't shy and dug in. The food was amazing.

"These are pulled pork sliders!" I moaned in ecstasy after taking a bite of one of the small sandwiches.

Lacey smiled and popped a small macron into her mouth, leaning back and moaning as the sweet almond meringue cookie melted in her mouth. "So good," she murmured.

It didn't take long for us to inhale the majority of the food on the table. I wasn't quite stuffed, but my stomach was pleasantly full. Tipping back a third glass of champagne, I was ready to go out and have some fun.

"Alright, touch ups and then we have to go. The driver just notified me that he's here," Lacey announced as I was washing my hands.

If the hotel treatment wasn't enough of a shock, seeing a limousine waiting for us was over the top. I had never in my life felt so spoiled and privileged. "How much did all of this cost?" I asked as I climbed into the back of the limo.

The interior was black with cream colored leather seating. One seat stretched out along the side, turning to make an L behind the driver's compartment. The opened side had a built-in bar, stocked with more champagne and fluted glasses. A single three seater bench faced toward the front from the back end of the compartment. It was all so *extravagant*.

Once we were all seated inside, Spider served another round of champagne and we just giggled and chatted about how bougie this whole experience was. What hadn't I experienced with these women? Aside from realizing financial stability and being able to buy my own new car, I had traveled to the Caribbean with them. Bared my soul and my ass with them at the Marquessa, and now we were about to parade through an Expo for Exotic Dancers and nightclub owners wearing mesh undies and a golden clasped body harness.

The limousine stopped outside the event center, and Lacey held me back until the driver came around to open the door. I would have rolled my eyes, but it really did look so much more jaw dropping to see someone opening the door of the limo for five bombshells than us just climbing out. Elektra passed everyone their event passes, each hanging from lanyards that coincidentally matched our undergarments.

A gorgeous man greeted us at the door. "Welcome to ED Expo. I see that you have private rooms reserved. If you lovely ladies would follow me, I would be happy to escort you to your space," he said, offering his arm out to Spider who was dressed in a black pencil skirt and white blouse. Come to think of it, we were each dressed in some version of sexy teacher/secretary fantasy wear.

The convention center was packed, so I was relieved when he escorted through a back corridor rather than through the crowds of people. I didn't say a word as the girls chatted him up the whole way. I had seen them in action before when we'd gone out to eat dinner, but this was different. This was a show they were putting on for him, and he was eating up everything they were serving.

"The open call begins at ten in Hall D. If you need me to escort you there, I would be happy to take care of you," handsome offered.

I wanted to ask what the open call was, but I wanted to show my innocent newbie card even less. Once he was out the door and we were alone, I started rattling the questions while stripping off my pants and blouse.

Cherry and Spider couldn't help but chuckle. While Lacey

just smiled dotingly at me.

"First, leave your clothes on until later," Lacey said, placing a hand over my arm to stop my stripping. "Now let's answer your questions one at a time. First, the event goes until midnight tonight, and there are classes tomorrow. Yes, there will be more food. Yes, you can take a bottle of water. The open call is like a dance off between the different clubs from around the country. Spider, Cherry and Elektra are representing the Marquessa. I am not dancing, and you are signed up as an independent contractor," Lacey explained patiently.

"Wait? What? You signed me up to dance without telling me?" I barked out, my jaw hanging wide open.

"Shut your mouth or someone'll stuff a cock in it!" Elektra shouted at me, causing me to immediately slam my mouth shut. Though my eyes had to be as big as saucers.

"You have a mask, and no one you know will be here," Lacey assured me.

"Do you want to hear some juicy gossip?" Cherry asked out of the blue.

"No. I don't want to hear about your vaginal discharge again!" Spider groaned, pushing Cherry away from her.

"You say that now... What if I told you that someone knocked boots with the owner?" Cherry asked, raising an eyebrow.

I hadn't been there in weeks, so I was curious to hear about what kind of drama went down since I had left. "What happened?" I asked, leaning closer.

"Well, I heard that Iryna was pissed because her sweet husband slept with one of the dancers in the Marquessa. Apparently, there was a huge blow up right after you and

Marjory left," she stated quietly.

"And how did you hear about all of this?" I asked.

"I happened to be passing the boss's office when she started screaming and slamming shit. I don't know what happened before that, but she was furious! Next thing I knew Marjory was telling me to get lost, and then flew into the office…"

"It was me," I admitted, staring at the other four.

There was a long moment of silence before they started laughing hysterically. I was waiting for them to call me out for breaking a cardinal rule, but instead they applauded my theatrical performance. They didn't believe me.

"Jesus Christ, Taze! You should be a fucking actress! Oscar worthy!"

"Holy shit! I almost believed you!"

"You almost had me!"

"Damn, I missed your sense of humor!"

Once their giggles had teetered off, and their makeup was touched up, we each donned our masks and heels and headed out the door. Dancing on a stage was one thing. Walking through a crowded convention center looking like sex on a stick was another thing altogether. Surprisingly, the majority of people were very respectful. The other women asked about our makeup or heels, and the men were passing out business cards, hoping to poach new dancers.

We stopped at several booths along the way. One offered insurance for exotic dancers and compensated lost wages due to injury. We each took a business card. Another booth had a DJ who offered personalized dance mixes and mashups for a reasonable price. The others kind of waved him off, but I liked his mask. I stayed there discussing a couple of song ideas, and left him my contact information.

I found the girls at another booth looking at costumes. These were nothing like the skimpy pieces we were wearing, but played to the fantasies of anime lovers. Cherry bit her lip and held up an outfit at me.

"What? You want me to dress up like Sailor Moon now?" I asked, arching an eyebrow behind my mask.

Cherry looked offended. "This is *not* Sailor Moon, Lilith!" She chided me. "You should have your mouth washed out with soap! This is obviously *She-Rah!*"

I bit my lips and kept walking to the next booth. They were advertising a special low wattage lighting. Another vendor specialized in state of the art sound systems, while yet another was offering cocktail samples in small plastic shot glasses. I grabbed one and gave it a sniff. It smelled fruity, but it wasn't sickly sweet either. Taking a small sip I was reminded of sour wine gummies.

The astringent sour hit the back of my tongue and made my jaw tighten up two seconds before the sweet blossomed in my mouth. "That's delicious," I stated, licking my lips.

A middle aged woman with a thick southern drawl thanked me. We stood talking for a brief moment before the others grabbed me so that we could start heading to Hall D. Lacey called Mr. handsome who was happy to escort us right to the hall, and show us to our reserved table.

I leaned over to Cherry and asked how this worked.

The first round was for novice dancers, second were the pros, and finally the pole dancers. There would be about fifteen women on the stage with numbers, and the judges sat below the stage with score cards. At the end of the night, the winners would be announced for each group. Cherry and Elektra were in group two, while Spider and I were in the third.

"Why did you sign me up to pole dance?" I asked, not understanding why I wouldn't be in the same group as them.

"Because we have seen you work a pole, and I want to see you win!" Cherry giggled evilly, while raising a brow in Spider's direction.

"Oh, it's on!" Spider cackled back.

"I'm surprised Angel didn't want to join you all for this," I commented, realizing that no one had mentioned her all night.

"It's kind of hard to dance with a pot belly," Elektra chuckled, earning scathing looks from the other three.

"What? I don't understand. What are you talking about?" I asked, leaning across the table toward Elektra.

"She's pregnant. She gave her notice the day after you did," Cherry whispered.

"Holy shit!" I gasped. "It wasn't the same guy, right?" I asked, remembering the guy who I had beaten up.

"No! No, no, no. This is a good guy. He's apparently a cop or security for some big wig in Philly. Something like that. She quit because he proposed when he found out she was pregnant," Lacey explained. I could tell there was more to it than that by the looks of the other three, but chose not to press further.

"Ladies and Gentlemen, we would like to invite our competitors backstage. Please follow the escorts with pink lights to the changing areas," the MC announced.

"Well, that's us!" Elektra beamed, taking my hand as we followed the others toward the pink glow sticks waving in the air.

Chapter 14

The novice round was not what I was expecting. If those were beginners, I didn't stand a chance of placing in any of the three competitions. The women were lithe and erotic, rolling their hips and bending for the judges. They had two minutes to grab the judges' attention to win. After the first round concluded, Cherry and Elektra were up.

Aside from the two times I showcased at the Marquessa, I had never really had an opportunity to just watch either of them dance. Not like this anyway. This was seductive and carnal. They each danced like they were doing a private show for a man who could take away all of their pain. Every movement promised ecstasy, obedience, loyalty….

"Fuck, it's so hot watching them dance," Spider whispered my exact thoughts.

"I have never seen any of you dance before. It's fucking erotic watching their bodies writhe around like that," I whispered back.

Spider gasped. "You seriously never snuck down to watch a performance?"

I just shook my head. "My shifts ended before yours, and I liked having my evenings to myself. Why would I hang out at work, after work, to watch my roommates working?" I asked, still watching our friends.

"You know, I never thought of it that way," she chuckled.

Standing backstage, my eyes wandered over to the judges table. I half expected to find a row of fat old perverts, but it was a mix of men and women. Two were obviously older than the rest, but the majority looked serious as they evaluated the performers. My breath caught as I recognized the man seated at the end of the row. Whatever butterflies I had before, they were gone now.

With the second round ended, the third round was about to begin. Spider and I joined a group of women as the stage was reset with two poles. For the final competition, the dancers drew numbers and competed in a process of elimination. Who we drew against was completely random luck of the numbers, and the lowest number in a pairing chose the music.

Spider was first, easily winning against the girl she went up against. Her competitor chose a song I had never heard before, but Spider never missed a beat. For as thin and svelte as she appeared, the woman was a powerhouse. Watching her do aerials on the pole was just mesmerizing.

I watched as four more women competed and it was finally my turn. Like Spider, the other woman had drawn the lower number, so I didn't have a choice on song selection. Thankfully, I recognized it as soon as the music began. I smirked as Banks' Beggin' for Thread began playing.

I stepped onto the stage and locked my eyes on the man at the end of the judging table. As the first lyrics filled the hall, I twirled slowly around the pole and dropped into a deep squat. With my mask on, I peaked over my shoulder. His eyes skittered briefly to the other woman, but then they were back on me as I rolled my hips.

The entire room disappeared, just like it had that night in the Marquessa. Memories of his hands on my body, prompting me to exaggerate every sway of my hips. I hoisted myself up the pole, and wrapped my legs around it, locking my position in place as my body arched back. I popped my chest up and exhaled, imagining what it would feel like to have my legs wrapped around his waist.

When the chorus hit, I slid down the pole until my body was on the floor. I spread my legs in a wide v and then twisted so that I was on my knees, my chest on the floor, and pole behind me. I rolled my body down in a wave, before spinning again and climbing back up the pole.

I bit my lip as my eyes scanned over the other judges at the table as the song ended. I had undivided attention. I smirked at the woman next to me on the stage and strutted away. Whether I could win on technical merit, I couldn't say. But if the judging was based on sex appeal, I even had the women drooling over my ass from that one performance.

When I got backstage, Elektra was the first to pull me into a hug. "You fucking slut! It was really you!" She whispered in my ear.

I pulled back expecting to see judgment or something akin to disgust, but her face was lit up like she had just discovered Santa was real. "Don't say a word," I warned, grinning back.

"Fuck, Lilith. Who would believe me?" she cackled. "Your own roommates didn't believe you, how would anyone else believe me?"

We watched as the final competitors finished their routines. The Marquessa and another club from Baltimore took the majority of the wins for the night. A few women who had traveled in from Los Angeles and Las Vegas bitched, but we just tossed it up to hometown advantage.

Looking back, years later. That night was what set everything in motion. While my friends and I drank and partied with dancers from across the country, eyes were already on me. Eyes that I would come to love and hate at the same time.

"Do you all want to go out with us?" A woman from one of the Vegas clubs offered. I had never been out in Baltimore, so the idea of getting wild and letting our hair down sounded fun.

"What'd you have in mind?" Spider asked.

"Couple of girls from town invited us to tour the bars around the inner harbor. The red head over there works at the Pussy Cat, and the blonde bombshell she's talking to works at Goddess," another woman explained.

Before a decision could be made, Lacey found us and squealed as she ran up to me. "You... Looked... Fucking etherial!" She said, pulling Spider and I into a group hug.

"Admit it," Spider giggled. "My ass is better than Lilith's, right?" She asked, turning and popping her ass at our friend. Lacey just cackled and spanked her.

"You know I can't choose favorites!" She whined back, still laughing. Then she turned to me. "Honestly, Lilith... If this had been five years ago, you would have won on fuck-me factor alone. I don't know who you were thinking about, but watching you... Even I was getting wet."

"Shut up!" I gushed, smacking at her shoulder playfully. My face felt so hot, I knew I was blushing crimson red.

"Seriously, you were like some sex goddess up on that stage! If you wanted to do this for real, you'd have your pick

211

of clubs in the country," she stated, pointing at several people crowded around the stage wearing shirts with various club logos.

"Stop. Listen, a bunch of local girls invited us to go bar hopping. You in? Or do you have other plans up your sleeves?" I asked her.

Lacey looked around the room. "How many we talking about?" She asked.

I grabbed the blonde and the red head, as well as the two girls from Vegas. The limo could easily seat fifteen, so adding five more bodies wasn't a problem. We all made quick introductions and decided to meet back at the main entrance in thirty minutes. Cherry and I exchanged numbers with the others while Lacey arranged for the driver to pick us up. We were walking back to our private room when one of the expo staff stopped us.

Although I had put my pants back on when we left Hall D, I didn't bother with the blouse. My mask had not left my face once since we arrived from the hotel. "Excuse me, Miss Lilith. There are a couple of organizers who would like to meet with you before you leave," he explained politely.

I looked over at the other four, unsure what to do. "Go. See what they have to say. We'll get your stuff from the room and meet you at the entrance," Cherry said, nudging me to follow the guy.

"Lead the way," I said, turning back toward the Hall we had just left.

The man was not very talkative and led me to what looked like a conference room not far from the hall. He knocked politely on the door and waited. After a few minutes, the door was opened by a man I recognized from the judging table. I stepped into the room without another word and looked around.

In total there were three people in the room. Myself, the mystery man with haunting dark eyes, and Roman... My former boss.

"How may I help you, gentlemen?" I asked, faking as much confidence as I could in my voice. Because I honestly was not feeling it at that moment.

Roman took a seat at the table and gestured for me to sit as well. I took the offered seat and leaned back waiting to hear what either of them had to say.

"Lilith, this is Domenico. He owns several clubs between New York, Atlantic City and Baltimore. He asked me to make introductions, so that he could poach you for his own clubs," Roman explained.

His voice was something else. The deep raspiness of it, remembering it whispering in my ear as he pressed me against his office door. God it did something to me. I couldn't help the smile that creeped at the corners of my mouth, watching him watch me. It took some effort, but I turned my attention to the other man in the room.

I tipped my head and sized him up. He was no less attractive than Roman, if not a few years younger. He had dark brown eyes that looked almost black, and thick black hair that fell in wavy curls around his face. He hadn't even said a word, but he didn't need to, the way his eyes were eating me up.

"That," he sighed after a moment. "I want you to look at me the way you looked at him."

"I don't know you," I stated matter of factly.

"What if we changed that?" He asked, taking a seat across

from me so that he was seated next to Roman.

"I'm sorry. I don't follow," I said.

"Why do you look at him differently than you look at me?" The man named Domenico asked.

"It's not obvious?" I asked, smirking.

"No. Make it clear for me."

"He wants what he can't have," I said, staring at Domenico. "I like that he knows that I know. I get off reminding him of that."

I looked over at Roman as he clenched and unclenched his jaw. "Isn't that right?" I whispered softly.

"See, Roman is a happily married man. He doesn't fuck where he works. In this industry, he's like a fucking saint," Domenico started. "Yet, sitting here listening to you, he's hard. So I ask again, how do I get you to look at me the way you look at him?" He asked again.

I sat back in my chair and thought for a moment. What would it take for me to look at this man the same way? He was an absolute stranger, whereas I had at least worked around Roman for several weeks before anything happened. It wasn't that he was gorgeous that did it for me. Eye candy was eye candy. Growing up poor, I learned that I could eat with my eyes even if my stomach remained empty.

This man asking for my attention was eye candy. Nothing more.

"Beg," I commented, barely above a whisper.

Both men looked shocked. Roman looked like I had slapped him and Domenico almost looked pissed. Their reactions only made me chuckle.

"It's true, Roman doesn't fuck his employees. But it doesn't stop him from wanting something he shouldn't. Knowing that he imagines pinning me down and fucking me, when he can't…. Ahh, it's why I look at him the way that I do," I explained.

"When I dance, I don't want to see all of the perverts vying for my attention. I find one man, and I give him all of my attention. I give him the fantasy he can't have," I said, whispering some bullshit that sounded like I knew what the fuck I was talking about.

Then I arched my brow and looked from Roman to Domenico again. "Or we fucked, and now, like an addict, he's jonesing for another fix," I confessed softly.

Domenico sat back and adjusted his pants. "What would it take for you to come dance in one of my clubs?" He asked.

"Nothing more than five percent," I stated.

"Five percent of what?" He asked.

"I'm independent. You want to invite me to dance in one of your clubs as a guest, you don't get more than five percent of my pull for that night," I stated with more resolve than I had in me. My heart felt like it was about to burst out of my ribcage. What the fuck was I demanding?? Who the hell was I to be asking this kind of shit from this man?

Domenico seemed to think about it for a moment. I looked down at my watch and realized that time had gotten away from me. I needed to leave now if I was going to meet up with the others for our night out in Baltimore.

I stood up from my seat and smiled. "I have another appointment, gentlemen. Have a good night," I stated, and walked toward the door I came in.

"What if I want more?" one of them asked from behind me. The voice was so low, I honestly couldn't tell who had said it.

When I turned around, however, my eyes locked with Domenico's. "Beg," I whispered, and then left the room before the shaking in my legs became super fucking obvious. As I walked quickly toward the main entrance, my thoughts were going wild. If Roman was a scary man, what kind of monster was Domenico that he could talk to Roman the way he did?

Shit!! I just told a club owner that he had to beg for my attention!

I couldn't stop the crazy that bubbled up out of me by the time I caught up with everyone at the entrance. Lacey looked absolutely fucking relieved that I had arrived in one piece and seemingly unscathed. Seeing me laughing as I walked up, her body physically relaxed.

"Everything go okay?" She asked expectantly.

Still smiling ear to ear, I shook my head. "It was an invitation to dance for another club," I told her as we climbed into the back of the waiting limo.

"What did you say?" Cherry asked, passing me a glass of champagne.

"Beg."

"What happened?" The blonde from Goddess asked, happy to listen to someone else's gossip.

"Lilith was pulled aside after the exhibitions in Hall D, and asked to meet with several owners. She just got back, and we're waiting to hear what happened," Lacey quickly explained, drawing everyone's attention.

"So start all over. Tell us what happened," Cherry urged me.

"It was Roman and some other guy I had never seen before,"

I started, licking my lips nervously. "He asked what it would take to get me to look at him the way I do when I dance. I told him he had to beg."

There was a moment of silence as nine sets of eyes stared back at me. Suddenly, like a band had snapped, they all started squealing and talking animatedly at me and each other.

"Holy shit!"

"That's some balls!"

"Hell yeah! That's my girl!"

"No you didn't!"

"Yeah, Lilith!!"

I felt my face heating up. "I think I fucked up…" I admitted.

"Who was the other guy?" The redhead asked.

I shrugged my shoulders. "I don't know. Some small time promoter," I lied.

The blonde nodded in approval. "You can't be too careful in this industry. There are some seriously amazing owners, and then there are the creeps. You didn't do anything wrong. You're not affiliated with a club, so you can get away with it," she stated, sipping her champagne.

Cherry and Spider smiled knowingly. They knew all of my tells, and they could smell the lie in my story. Even if they didn't know which part I had lied about, they didn't say anything more. We were in mixed company, and saying too much about what happened behind closed doors could be bad if taken out of context. Not just for me, but for all of the women I had come to call my friends.

"Miss Lacey, we've arrived," the chauffeur informed us as he stopped in front of a pier area on the Chesapeake bay.

"Thank you. I'll let you know when we're ready to be

217

picked up!" Lacey said, downing the remainder of her drink. "Let's go have some fun ladies!"

We each finished off our glasses and cheered for a night on the town. The first stop was a small club. The music was okay, but the vibe was not what we were looking for. After ordering one round of shots, we walked out and headed to the next stop.

After the fourth bar, I realized that we were doing a crawl and I wasn't feeling it. "Let's find a club. I want to dance and let my hair down," I whined, leaning my head on Lacey's shoulder.

The redhead exchanged a look with another woman in our group and smiled. "What's your flavor?" she asked, turning to me and Lacey.

"Anything we can dance to," came Lacey's reply.

"I know just the place!" the other woman smiled back. After discussing the distance and the time it would take to get there, Lacey called for the Limo driver to shuttle us the four blocks. The distance wasn't that far, but we weren't exactly dressed to be wandering around downtown Baltimore at almost midnight.

We gave the driver the new destination and ten minutes later we were stepping into a packed club. The bass vibrated through my body and had my hips swaying before we had even reached the dance floor. The interior was laid out with different levels. From what we could see, there were three different dance floors, separated by different levels.

Private booths were lined along the walls, and there was a VIP area with a balcony that overlooked the whole club. I beelined for the bar, and ordered a round of shots for everyone. I didn't wait for the others and took mine down, before grabbing Cherry's hand and moving to the dancefloor.

Needless to say, our group drew attention. Five of us wore masks, dressed like something out of an S&M - Victoria's Secret catalog. While the others in our group looked equally like sin in heels. I tipped my head back and let the music overtake me, my hips rolling and swaying with the music.

When the music changed to a Latin song, I couldn't stop the squeal. My body immediately began stepping and swaying to the upbeat salsa rhythm. A pair of hands rested on my hips, and I fell in step with the dancer behind me. As the song progressed, I leaned back and realized that I was not dancing with one of my girls, but a man. I turned around to meet the dark eyes of the man I had met earlier in the evening.

Even in my heels, he was still taller than me. When I didn't push him away, he pulled me closer and pressed our bodies together. Buzzing from the alcohol, I relaxed in his arms and let him lead me. After dancing three songs without a break, he pulled me toward a set of stairs that led to the VIP area.

I followed behind him, inspecting the rear view as he maneuvered us through the throngs of people. He had a nice ass, wide shoulders... I could do worse, I giggled to myself. Domenico pulled me next to him, placing a hand around my waist as we walked up the stairs. I didn't know if it was a show of dominance for anyone looking at me, or if he knew I was drunk and unsteady on my feet.

We took our seats in a private room with a window overlooking the club. I could still hear the music, but the volume was dampened enough that we could talk without shouting over it. A server came through and set a couple of drinks on the table. One was a short glass with brown liquid, which I assumed was a scotch or whiskey. The second was a cocktail in a taller glass, with salt or sugar around the wide rim. The final two items were unopened bottles of sparkling water.

"Tell me your name, princess," he stated, never taking his eyes off of mine.

"Why would I do that?" I asked, choosing the glass of scotch to sip. It was a mistake. I coughed as the foul liquid burned down my throat.

The man next to me chuckled and took his drink back. Still watching me, he downed the whole thing without batting an eye. I rolled my eyes, and picked up the mystery cocktail.

"What is this I asked," smelling the beverage without tasting it.

"It's a house specialty. It's called a Slip Slide. Try it," he encouraged me.

I gave it a sip and chuckled as the back of my jaw tightened up from the sourness, before the sweet flowed over my tongue. It was the cocktail I had tried in the Expo earlier in the night. "I like this one better," I admitted, taking another sip.

"Do you have any idea how lethal you are?" He asked, shaking his head and chuckling to himself.

"No," I admitted.

"When I saw you step onto the stage, I was fucking mesmerized. You commanded every single one of us to watch your every move. I wanted to stop the whole fucking thing and hide you away right then and there," he said softly as the back of his fingers trailed down my bare arm. The contact caused a chill to run through me, and I shivered against his touch.

220

"Can I kiss you?" He asked, leaning forward so that our faces were inches apart.

I smirked at him, and put my finger under his chin. "Beg."

"Please," he whispered as his arms were wrapping around me and pulling me onto his lap. I gasped as he now had me straddling his lap, one hand caressing my ass while the other tangled into my hair. "Please," he said again, rubbing the tip of his nose against mine.

I closed the distance between us and kissed him. It was tentative at first, our lips taking turns suckling the other's. He gripped my hair tightly causing me to gasp. When my lips parted, he pulled me in tighter so that his tongue could plunder deeper kisses. I moaned when the hand holding my ass pushed and pulled me against him. This man was rock hard beneath me and the friction was doing something to me.

The hand gripping my ass slid down the back of my pants, and I felt his warm fingers following down my ass crack. I reached down and unfastened the front of my pants, giving his hand more room to move along my backside. He growled into our kiss when his fingers discovered my wetness. I had been salivating over this man since I saw him from backstage.

He was gorgeous, and something about him made my heart stutter and my body ignite. When his digits dipped between my wet folds, I moaned. He withdrew his hand and then both hands were pulling my pants down past my ass.

I had a moment of clarity and pulled back from our kiss. "I won't fuck you."

He paused looking up at me. My words hadn't dissuaded him, but he slowed our rapid progression. "Too fast?" He asked, continuing to slowly caress my ass.

221

I shook my head. "I don't fuck nobody unless sober," I stated, watching his every micro expression as he processed my words.

"Ok. I won't fuck you tonight. But I can't have you leaving without being taken care of first," he whispered, trailing kisses down my neck and across my collarbone.

Before I could ask what he had in mind, one hand was slipping between our bodies and rubbing against my clit through the mesh of my thong. He watched me intently as his other hand trailed down my backside. His rubbed over my rear hole eliciting an unexpected moan from me.

"Tell me stop, and I'll stop," Domenico whispered against my chin.

I didn't want him to stop. "Make me come," I demanded, grabbing a handful of his hair and tipping his head back so that I could kiss him again.

He chuckled against my kiss, then lifted my body off of his. I thought he was going to stop, but instead he slid two fingers inside of dripping sex while the other hand put pressure against my virgin ass.

I ground down on his fingers, panting at the dual stimu-lation. "That's it, princess. Ride my fingers. Take what you want from me." His words were like a fucking catalyst.

My eyes fluttered as I rolled my hips on his fingers, taking them deeper.

"Just like that," he encouraged me. "Dance for me, baby."

I continued rocking against his fingers, taking them deeper until his palm was pressed against my clit. "Ahhh," a moan escaped me, as my core tightened around his digits.

The hand pressed against my ass pushed harder, and caused me to rock hard against the stimulation. Straddling this man with his dark eyes dancing in delight as I chased my high, was a high in and of itself. His fingers curled slightly and I whimpered, feeling like some new button had been pushed.

My body was glistening in sweat as I continued to ride his fingers. It felt like my whole body was being lit on fire. My heart was pounding in my chest and it felt like I was going to explode. The tightness in my core was winding up, like a spring ready to break at any second. When I slowed my movements, Domenico took over moving my body up and down with his hand pressing against my forbidden point.

Just as my body was tipped on the edge, he growled at me. "Come. Now."

It wasn't a request. It was a command and my body obeyed, exploding in bliss. The hand that had been guiding my hips flew up to grab my hair. Domenico's lips claimed mine and devoured my screaming moans, as my body shuddered and rode my orgasm. I was a panting mess when he finally released me. My head dropped onto his shoulder and it was all I could do to catch my breath, as my body collapsed against his.

"The next time, I won't waste a drop. I want you to ride my face," he whispered. The thought of his man's tongue drilling into me the way his fingers had made me shudder. "You like that idea?" He chuckled, lifting my hips so that he could pull his fingers out of my still spasming vagina.

"What makes you think there will be a next time?" I asked, slowly coming to my senses now that the alcohol and euphoria were wearing off.

Chapter 15

Domenico looked at me for a moment as if considering what I was saying. "You're right. You shouldn't have to wait," he said, before flipping my body onto the table so that my ass was positioned in front of his face.

"What-" I started to argue, but his hands were pulling my pants down to my knees.

My body tensed as I thought he was going to try to fuck me. The change did not go unnoticed. He immediately stopped moving so abruptly and began slowly caressing my body.

"I said it before. Say stop, and I will stop. You said no sex, so I'm not going to fuck you. You said there may not be a next time, so I am going to clean you up," he whispered, placing gentle open mouth kisses across my exposed ass. His finger released a clasp on the back of my thong, allowing the thin strip to come loose and exposing my entire pussy and ass.

"You were made to be worshiped," he murmured, flipping me so that I was lying on my back across a table, staring up at him. His eyes never left mine as his head lowered enough that he could place kisses on my mound. "Open your altar, and let me worship you."

As the words left his lips, his hands were pulling my legs

up and pushing them open. I sucked in a shaky breath as his tongue lapped my slick lips. "Ahh," I moaned as his mouth closed around my sensitive clit and sucked. My body was a pile of hot cinders waiting to erupt in fire again.

He pushed my legs up toward my chest and dragged his tongue over my ass, and I nearly came off the table. "D-don't," I stuttered.

"Your mouth is saying things your body doesn't agree with," he said, repeating the action of dragging and circling his tongue around my ass. My back arched and my traitorous body pushed my ass further into the sensation.

I had a death grip on the edge of the table, completely overwhelmed by the sensations this man was giving my body. His mouth returned to my slick and he devoured my pussy like a man starved. There was no more gentle prelude. Domenico was determined to make me come on his face, and my body was there for it.

"Fuck!" I moaned, when his tongue plundered deep and licked my inner walls. Enjoying the noises I was making, he continued to map out every trigger and erogenous point in my body with his tongue.

He had me panting and writhing on the table until he had me figured out. Then he went in for the kill. I was so fucking delirious with pleasure, I couldn't tell what was pushing me over the edge. The man was filling me, sucking my clit, and stimulating my ass constantly.

If his lips moved from my clit, his thumb was there to continue the pressure. His fingers drilled into me while his mouth lapped all of the juices pouring out of me. I was wailing on the table, unable to comprehend everything he was doing. I didn't just come once. I came over and over and over on his tongue. When he was finally full of my fluids, he let me recover.

"Where are you staying tonight?" He asked, kissing the insides of my thighs as he pulled my pants back up.

I couldn't even remember the name of the hotel. I had no idea what time it was or when the music of the club had stopped. I hadn't even told my friends where I was.

"Oh my god. I have to call my friends! They'll be worried shitless!" I yelled, trying to sit up or roll off of the table.

I could barely move, my body was so overloaded with endorphins from multiple orgasms. Everything I did felt like I was fighting through jello to do it.

"Relax," Domenico whispered, helping me to sit up. "Your friends know that you are with me, and they know that I will bring you back to your hotel. Tonight."

"How?" I asked, looking at him seriously.

"I had one of my guys let them know."

"Ok," I mumbled, not sure how to act now that I was sober and thoroughly fucking serviced.

"Let me see your face," he whispered, reaching up for my mask.

It was off before I even realized what he was asking. We stared at each other for a moment before he kissed me. I could taste myself on his lips and tongue. He had already owned my body, so this was a gentle soothing kiss that had my stomach in butterflies. He was seducing me.

"What's your name," he asked, pulling back from the kiss.

"Lilith," I responded.

He smirked and brushed my hair back from my face. "I want to know your real name."

"Why? Why do you need my name?" I asked, staring into

his eyes, unsure what he was hoping to gain from my name.

"I want to know what name to moan when I go back to the house and jerk myself off. I want to whisper your name when I am recalling your pussy riding my fingers and my mouth."

"Shit. That was not what I was expecting," I admitted, feeling breathless.

"Are you going to tell me your name?" He asked quietly.

I shook my head and giggled. "Not tonight."

He observed me for a second before smirking. "So when will I get to see you again?" He asked.

I bit my lip, not really wanting to give a set day. He sensed my hesitation and offered himself up. "Tell you what. I have off next Saturday. If you find that you are also unoccupied by other *obligations*, call me."

"Okay," I agreed.

Domenico led me down through the now empty club. I honestly thought there would be a few employees still cleaning up, but the whole place was deserted. We walked out a back door and into a small alley parking lot. I smirked remembering working at the Marquessa, and how I hadn't realized the types of shows they did.

"What's so funny?" He asked, opening the door of a waiting SUV for me.

Shaking my head, I didn't know how to answer. "I'm just wondering if every club has the same sketchy parking lot arrangement, or if it's just a big city thing," I mused.

He looked around the parking lot and shrugged. "Not all of the clubs have parking and some have parking only made available to VIPs. You wouldn't know it if you saw it, unless you were in the network."

227

"And you are?" I asked, chuckling.

Domenico smiled, but didn't say anything further. When we stopped at the hotel, I realized I was dressed like an exotic dancer, and there was no way they would let me through the lobby let alone up to a suite. Before I could say anything I spotted Lacey coming outside with a jacket.

The driver opened my door, and Lacey passed me the garment before anyone outside the vehicle could see what I was wearing. Although she smiled at me, I didn't miss the momentary look of panic that crossed her face when she saw Domenico beside me in the vehicle. I quickly said goodnight and followed Lacey into the hotel.

I didn't turn around, even when the elevator doors had closed behind me. Finally alone, just the two of us, Lacey gave me a look. I knew that look, so I just nodded. When we got to the suite, I beelined for the bathroom and took a long hot shower.

What the hell had come over me? First, I fucked my married boss, not that I knew he was married at the time… But now I had let an absolute stranger drive me to the moon and back with his mouth and hands inside a Baltimore club. What the hell was wrong with me?

I wrapped my hair in a towel when I was done, and crawled into bed. Coming down from a proper high had my head filled with the scariest, demoralizing thoughts. I wasn't completely deprecating myself, but the thought of going back into the bathroom to cut myself surfaced repeatedly. Eventually, I succumbed to my exhaustion and fell asleep.

When I finally crawled out of bed, the sun was shining high in the sky and filling my window with sunlight. I dragged myself out of bed and threw the towel I had wrapped my hair up with over a hook in the bathroom. Brushing my teeth, my mind replayed the night's events in my head. Over and over and over.

What the fuck had I been thinking?

Shuffling out to the main area, I found my four friends seated around the table playing cards. They all stopped and looked over at me, before resuming their game and whispering quietly. Not one said a peep to me as I grabbed a bottle of water, or filled a plate with fruit from what was left of a breakfast buffet. It wasn't until I sat down on the small sofa, that the cards were tossed down and the group ran over to sit around me.

"Despite our protests, Lacey insisted that we let you sleep. You slept. Now spill the fucking tea." Elektra was the first to whine at me.

I looked around at them in shock, stopping when I got to Lacey.

"Did you get some or what?" Spider giggled, pulling on my arm and nearly toppling my plate.

"I didn't fuck anyone last night... Or this morning," I added at the end, rolling my eyes at the lawyer.

The other three all looked at Lacey like she had some explaining to do. Lacey raised her eyebrows and stared back in my direction, telling me to spill it before she lost face.

Lacey held up her hand to stop me. "Before you start, don't say anything about how you met. Just skip to what happened at the club after you were taken upstairs."

I had no idea what to say or where to start. "After we went up the stairs?" I asked.

"Yes," the four responded in synch.

"He bought us each some drinks, and then asked if he could

229

kiss me. I allowed it," I said. Where I had been an open book when I first met them, I no longer wanted to share every aspect of what I did with them.

"Don't tell me you just kissed!" Spider complained.

Choosing my words carefully…. "I only kissed him," I responded vaguely.

Cherry shook her head. "She's not going to tell us anything. Lacey, who was she with last night?"

Lacey looked at me seriously for a moment before saying anything. "Taze, was here sleeping all night, ladies. Stop harassing this poor girl. If you want to know what Lilith got up to, you'll have to ask Lilith!" She said in a sing-songy tone.

"Lilithgotfingerfuckedandeatenupuntilshecouldn'tfucki ngseestraight," I said as fast as I could before shoving three giant pieces of fruit into my mouth.

The four of them looked at one another. I could see their mouths moving as their brains tried to make sense of what I had confessed. Unfortunately, Cherry was the first to jump up screaming!

"NO SHIT!!! LILITH GOT FINGER FUCKED AND EATEN UP LAST NIGHT!!"

"Oh my god, Cherry!" I nearly choked because of how loudly she was shouting.

Spider smacked my leg. "You said you only kissed! I'm calling liar, liar, pants on fire!" She yelled at me in a whisper.

"I didn't lie. *I* only kissed him. I just didn't tell you everything *he did*…." I explained, my voice trailing off at the end.

"Why didn't you go all the way? He was obviously into you," Elektra asked, stealing a grape off of my plate and popping

230

into her mouth.

"We never consent unless we're sober," Cherry explained before I could say anything.

Elektra just nodded as if the rule made sense. I managed to change the subject back to the expo, which we ended up ditching to stay in the hotel binjing movies.

* * *

Lacey drove me back to Nana's where I slept for the night. After two days away from my reality, I was back at Titi's to help with Mami. When I walked in the door, Titi was sitting at the table with Aunt Maria and Bruja.

"Is this an intervention?" I asked, dropping an overnight bag on the sofa.

Maria rolled her eyes at me while Titi just shook her head.

"We're discussing how to rotate our schedules so that we don't get burned out," Bruja commented, patting the empty chair at the table for me to sit down.

"Ok, so what does that mean?" I asked, taking the offered seat.

Maria was the first to speak. "You can't be here every day."

Her words were brutal and to the point. I nodded, despite my desire to scream at her. Regardless of the shit I had been through with my mother, she was still *my* mother. My fists clenched on top of the table as Maria continued.

"You and your mother are still not on good terms. I can't have you coming in here screaming and acting like a fool. She deserves to be treated with dignity, compassion-"

"Shut the fuck up," I whispered, cutting her off and creating a pin drop silence around the table. "You don't get to say

231

anything about my relationship with my mother."

Bruja reached over to hold my hand, but I pulled away.

"Do you think you get to suddenly show up after not being around for 15 years, and dictate how everything goes? What gives you the right?" I asked, staring at the table in front of me. I couldn't lift my head to face them. I knew if I did, I would just see more disappointment on their faces.

"Anastacia-" Maria started again, but Titi cut her off.

"Let her speak."

"Qué haces?" Bruja asked their eldest sister. "This is not what we discussed."

Maria had always been high on her horse whenever she came to town, and this was no different. The oldest always had a say in our family, but I wouldn't let a woman who didn't know me or my mother decide. Titi cleared her throat causing my eyes to shift up to look at her across the table. I was expecting to see her angry or even disappointed, instead she looked.... *Amused?*

She nodded at me in encouragement. The anger that was building in me, vanished. I wasn't going anywhere. I shifted my gaze to Aunt Maria and smiled sadly.

"Regardless of what you know or *think* you know, that is my mother dying. *Mi madre, no suya.* You don't get a say in what happens between us. You have no say at all here. You want to stay and help my mother, fine. You help. You have no voice in whether I am here, how often, or what I talk about with Mami," I continued.

Maria looked like a ripening tomato. When she started to speak, her sisters reached out and took her hands. "No. You listen, hermana," Titi stated.

"It's not healthy to have her attacking her!" Maria shouted

at them.

"Neither was telling my mother to make me forget!" I shouted back, slamming my hands on the table.

The three women at the table all looked confused, which just made me angrier. They all knew about what my father's uncle had done to me, but knowing and helping were two different things. Titi wanted my mother to get me counseling. Bruja shouted that I should have testified against him in court because it would have made me stronger.

Pops didn't even know what to say to me for a long time, so he taught me boxing and how to fight. Nana just held me when I was sad, and pulled me out of my shell when I was numb. They all did what they could to help me move forward. All of them except Maria.

Maria thought it was a 'shame' that I should not have to be reminded of, and advised Mami to not talk about it. 'Deja cerrada la caja de Pandora.' Leave the can of worms be. Don't embarrass my father's family further. Let him have some dignity. Of course, being the eldest, my mother listened to everything she said.

She canceled the therapy appointments, telling me that they said I didn't need it. She didn't drop the charges against my uncle, but she refused to allow me to testify which meant he went free. I wasn't allowed to talk about the past, because *we* needed to focus on the *future*.

"What was it you told her, Tia Maria? ¿Deja cerrada la caja?" I asked, my voice still quiet.

"Anastacia, that's not what happened," Titi started but I just shook my head.

"Tell them how you told my mother it wasn't right to *embarrass* my father by accusing his uncle. *We shouldn't open that Pandora's box.* Tell them how you personally came to town, took my sister and I out for ice cream, and then told me over and over that good girls don't dredge up the bad. We should smile and be tough...." I continued.

Titi pulled her hands back from her sister's like she had been scalded. "Maria, you didn't," she whispered in disbelief.

"I knew it. You just couldn't keep your fucking nose out of it, could you?" Bruja accused next.

Maria looked like she was ready to fight back, but I wouldn't let her.

"Did it ever occur to you that maybe teaching young girls to stand up for themselves would prevent the monsters from taking advantage of us? See, your way... There is a pedophile running the streets. The *right way*, I would have been supported instead of being shamed into silence. So, *no.* You have zero fucking say in what happens between my mother and I," I stated calmly.

Honestly, I don't know where the strength came from, because I was nearly shaking in pent up fury again. I had waited so long to confront these women, and now it was time. I was going to get my pound of flesh for all of the shit I endured because of Tia Maria's advice.

"Hermana, how could you tell her something like that?"

"Anastacia, go check on your mother. It should be time for her meds."

Titi and Bruja spoke at the same time. I gave one more scathing look at Tia Maria before excusing myself from the table and retreating upstairs. I didn't need to hear what they had to say to her. I didn't want to. Whatever words they had planned were going to cut so much worse than anything I could say.

234

They were sisters just like Jada and I. There were always dark secrets held between sisters. Secrets that, if ever aired in the light of day, could be wielded like weapons in a gladiatorial arena. Served her right for sticking her nose in shit.

Mami was watching the door when I entered the room. I could tell by the look in her eyes that it was a good day. She was lucid, her eyes clear.

"You're back?" she whispered.

"Yes. Aunt Maria kicked me out because she thought I was too toxic to be around you," I confessed.

Mami snorted, causing her to cough a little. "Que rico. Tell her to go home. I don't need all of them crowding around me like a fucking invalid."

I couldn't stop the smirk that quirked up on one side as I set out her meds for the day. It was smart keeping the notebook with the log of meds next to the bed. Whoever was here, whether it was the aunts, nana, Jada, the visiting hospice nurse or I, would know exactly when and what she had taken. I passed Mami a glass of water and the pills, and changed out her morphine patch.

"Don't you get bored staying up in this room all day every day?" I asked, adjusting her blankets.

"You have no idea," she muttered.

"How about we go for a ride to the park and run around for a bit," I offered.

"Mi hija, don't tempt me," Mami snorted.

"Okay. We'll stay up here all day then and stare at the paint," I countered sitting on the bed next to her and leaning back so that my head rested on her shoulder.

"They won't let us get past the front door," mami grumbled.

I smirked. She didn't know the shit storm her sisters were embroiled in downstairs.

"If I can get you out of the house, what do I get in return?" I asked.

"What are you five? If you can get me out of the house, I'll buy you a damn pony!" she wheezed.

"With what money?" I snorted back.

"My little pony is still a pony, Stacia!"

I couldn't stop the laughter that bubbled out. I laughed so hard that tears were streaming down my face. Seeing me lost in my own world made Mami laugh too. I loved and despised my mother throughout my life, but she was still my mother. The woman knew how to make me laugh, and lighten a room with a few words.

When I could finally calm down, I sighed. "Okay, Mami. We're getting out of here, and you had better not go cheap on me. I want the Princess Celestia pony!" I demanded, climbing out of the bed. Mami had lost too much weight to wear any of Titi's clothes, so I wandered into Jada's room instead.

It didn't take me long to find a pair of her sweatpants and an oversized hoodie. I grabbed them and a pair of thick socks and walked back to Mami. Pulling back the blankets I put the thick socks on her feet and then we worked together to get her dressed in the full sweatsuit.

Happy with my work, I told Mami to climb on my back so that I could carry her down the stairs.

"Are you out of your damn mind?" She asked, staring at me wide eyed.

"What? Jada and I would walk out like this all the time. No one's gonna say a word, until we are long gone. Come on," I encouraged her, swinging her legs over the side of the bed before turning my back to her.

"Stacia, I am too weak to hold on to you," Mami confessed.

I shook my head and patted my back for her to wrap her arms around me. She sighed in frustration, but still placed her arms around my neck. Reaching back on either side, I pulled a sheet up under and behind her. Once the sheet was tied across my chest, my mother was basically strapped to my back like a baby in a papoose.

"Relax, Mami. I won't let you fall," I promised, patting her hands as I stood up. I kept reassuring her as I stepped away from the bed. All of the months of working out with the girls made me look thinner, but there was only muscle left on my body. I was strong as hell.

"Okay, when we get to the door, you need to do the peace sign over your head with your hand. Don't say anything, okay?" I instructed her.

"Let's go, baby!" She giggled against my neck.

I slowly walked down the stairs, ensuring not to bounce mami too much along the way. She began trembling on my back, causing me to pause. "Are you okay?" I whispered over my shoulder.

"Hurry up!" She wheezed. I quickly realized that my mother was giggling like a naughty five year old because I was *sneaking* her out of the house on my back.

Picking up my step I walked straight to the door. "Tace?" Titi called out behind me.

Mami threw up her two fingers as I yelled that we would be right back.

"I thought Jada had work today," one of the aunts commented as I exited the house with my dying mother strapped to my back.

By the time we made it to my car, we were both in stitches laughing about our successful jailbreak. I had to lean back on the hood in order to untie our makeshift seat strap, and then help her climb down into the passenger seat. I could barely see what I was doing, tears cloudy my vision from laughing so hard.

"Shhh! You'll get us caught!" I chastised her, while buckling the seat belt over her chest and lap.

"Let's go get ice cream!" She whispered.

Chapter 16

The November weather was too cold for ice cream. Most of the small ice cream shops had closed for the season back in September. Thinking on it for a few minutes, I decided to drive to a seafood restaurant that made the best root beer floats instead.

"Where are you going?" She asked after a few minutes, realizing that I was driving toward the state line.

"The Captain's. Root beer floats okay?" I asked, looking over at her.

"Mmmm. That sounds perfect," she murmured, leaning back against the seat and slowly drifting to sleep.

The drive only took ten minutes, but she was out. It was normal whenever she had her pain patch changed out. If I had let her stay in bed, she would have drifted back to sleep right away, but the excitement of our escape had given her an extra push to stay awake.

I ordered two small floats and drove us to the park. Mami was sound asleep, so I pulled a small blanket from the back seat and wrapped it around her. Ever since coming back, I kept an emergency bag in my car filled with things that I thought I would need if I needed to take her to the hospital. There was a spare blanket to keep her warm, and other odds and ends to decorate her room if she were admitted. I sat there with the heat blasting and sipping my drink until she began stirring again.

"Hi. You took a little nap. You want to try some of your float?" I asked.

Mami nodded groggily. I leaned over and put the straw against her lips, reminding her to take a small sip. She ate so little, I was afraid the shock of something so cold on her stomach would have her doubled over in agony.

"Mmm. Yummy," she murmured, licking her lips. "That was worth it."

"I think it's a little too cold to play on the swings," I whispered, placing her drink back in the cup holder.

"How much time do we have?" she asked.

Looking at the clock on my dashboard, I guessed we had maybe five minutes before one of them called and asked where the hell we were. "Not long. Where do you want to go?"

"Drive to your dad's," she whispered.

I didn't ask any more questions and drove to my dad's. We hadn't even been on the road for three minutes when my phone rang.

Mami began giggling, "Busted."

I answered the call, "Hello, Titi."

"Everything okay?" Titi asked in a hushed whisper.

"Yep. We'll be back in a bit."

"Can you grab some milk on your way back?"

"Um… No. I'm not leaving her alone in the car."

"Oh, okay. Well, I will send your aunts out to get what we need here around ten."

That was her way of telling me when to come back. "Thank

you. I'll call when we are on our way."

Mami giggled again. "How much time does that leave us?"

"About thirty minutes," I responded, glancing at the clock again.

"It's okay. Let's just head back."

"Mami, you wanted to go there, I am five minutes away from his house. We're doing this," I encouraged her. "Do you want me to call him and tell him we're coming?"

"Yes. Tell him he needs to come out to the car."

I did as she bade, and convinced my dad to meet us outside his house. When I pulled up he looked shocked. I had not come to his house in ten years, and my mother, looking like a shell of her former self, was beside me.

I parked the car, and stepped out. He didn't hesitate to walk around the car and pull me into a hug. "I've missed you so much, baby girl," he whispered into my hair.

His acknowledgement of me as his daughter didn't lift the weight on my heart, but it lessened it a bit. I sighed and leaned into the embrace for another minute before pulling away.

"Mami wants to talk to you, so climb in. I'll be out here while you two talk," I explained.

Papi gave me a look of concern but did as I asked. As he closed the driver's door, the front door of his house opened. I looked over to see his wife, Rachelle staring at the car in concern. When she recognized me, her expression changed from confusion to recognition and then something akin to anger. She must have realized my mother was in the car talking to her husband.

Rachelle began a beeline for my car, but I stepped in front of her. "My mother is here to ask for amends. If you take

241

one more step toward that vehicle, I will lay you on your ass," I whispered, smiling at her.

She looked shocked to hear me speak to her in such a blunt tone. "What the hell does she want? He's not giving her a fucking penny!" She seethed back at me.

"Rachelle, my mom is dying. No one wants your fucking money, so shut the fuck up and go back inside," I stated quite calmly. Rachelle and I had never gotten along. She was the one my father had cheated on Mami with. When they first got married, I thought it would be nice to see how a normal family worked and looked forward to visiting them every weekend.

Unfortunately, Rachelle was a bitter woman. She took every opportunity to tell me how horrible my mother was, and urged me to pray that I never ended up like her. Rather than enjoying time with my dad, I began dreading every second I spent in their house.

Now standing in front of the woman who had bullied me and my mom for nearly a decade, I was happy to have an excuse to punch her in the face. Fortunately, Rachelle had never once imagined a dying woman showing up, and backed down.

"Would you like to come in for a coffee?" She asked.

"No. We won't be here much longer. I need to get her home," I said, looking back over at the car.

Rachelle stood beside me for ten minutes attempting to make small talk. My responses were perfunctory at best. I had no desire to kindle any sort of relationship with this woman. Those dreams died a long, long time ago.

"I wish we had a better relationship," she confessed suddenly, pulling me from my thoughts.

"Why?"

"We could be there for you, in the future. You know. After," she explained, glancing over at the car.

I followed her gaze and smirked. "You cheated with him for two years. While he was sneaking off with you, I was left to be abused. And when you had your chance to be something in my life, you just wanted to make sure I knew what a horrible person my mother was. When she dies, you're both dead to me," I clarified, looking her in the eyes as I spoke.

Rachelle's eyes watered up, but she bit her lip and just nodded. She didn't say another word and turned to walk back into their house. I walked back over to my car and tapped the driver's window. I needed to get Mami home to rest before her meds wore off.

Papi leaned across the seat and hugged my mother. I watched as he gave her a kiss on the cheek before climbing back out of the car. "Thank you," he whispered. His voice sounded hoarse with emotion.

"I'm sorry," he said, pulling me into a hug. "I will spend the rest of my life trying to make it up to you."

I pushed back and pulled out of his embrace. "I'm not a child. You made your peace with my mother, because that's what she needed. You will die before any of the shit between you and I is resolved," I whispered back.

He looked like I had slapped him in the face. The initial shock, however, quickly turned into understanding and resignation. The time he squandered was gone. There were no more second chances in my book of debts.

"I'll let you know when it happens," I offered, and then climbed back into my car. As I drove away, I never looked back. I didn't care how long he stood there or didn't. He didn't want to be a part of my life when I needed him the most, so he wouldn't be allowed in the future either.

I couldn't forgive him for taking his family's side over his own daughter. My mother may have been misguided by Aunt Maria's advice, but she stuck by my side throughout my life. Did we have it hard? Yes. Did we fight? *Absolutely*. But I never had a doubt that my mother would show up swinging if I needed her. The same could never be said about my father.

"Did you have a good talk?" I asked.

"No. But it was necessary," she responded, not saying anything more on the matter.

The rest of the ride to Titi's was silent. I didn't ask about what she said, and I didn't want to know. She had closure and that was all that mattered to me. When I pulled up in front of my aunt's house, I was surprised to see Rob waiting for us out front.

As I turned the car off, I stepped out and walked around to the passenger door. Rob walked down to the car, and gently lifted my mother out of her seat like she weighed nothing. I wrapped the blanket up around her, as she was sound asleep.

Rob helped me get her situated back into her bed before I woke her up to take her meds and eat a little bit of food. She ate a few bites before falling back to sleep. This had been the most excitement she had had in weeks, and it was obvious that it took it out of her. We left her to sleep, and went downstairs to talk.

"Where is everyone?" I asked, pouring us each a cup of coffee.

"Titi went to pick up prescriptions, and Bruja took my

mom to shop for Christmas gifts," he responded.

"When did you get in? I thought you were overseas and couldn't get back." I sat down at the table and passed Rob his coffee, taking a sip of my own while waiting for him to answer.

"Can you keep a secret?" he asked, taking a drink of his own coffee.

"You know I can!" I smiled.

"I accepted a new assignment so that I can be closer to you all," he confessed.

"That's so awesome! Where will you be stationed?" I asked, excited to have more time with him despite the circumstances that provoked the move.

"Uh, just in the D.C. area. Not super close, but close enough that I can get up here if you all needed a bit more help."

"Who else knows?" I asked, beaming ear to ear.

"Just you and my command so far, so don't say anything," came the response accompanied with a serious glare.

I made a motion to zip my lips and tossed an invisible key over my shoulder. Rob seemed content with my response and smirked, nodding in approval.

"I don't want my mom to know just yet. If she knows she'll start trying to house hunt for me, and buying furniture and all kinds of weird shit. I have what I need, and a realtor to do the rest. For now, I am on normal leave and have time to help. We'll leave it at that," he explained.

"No problem!" I giggled, taking another sip of my coffee.

Rob and I spent the next hour catching up and taking care of Mami. By the time I had finished prepping lunches for everyone, Titi and her sisters were back from their outing.

"How is everything?" I asked, moving to help bring in the

bags and groceries.

"Not good," Titi grumbled as she shook off her coat. The three women exchanged glances which made me all the more on edge about what had happened during our escape earlier in the day.

"Just tell her. We're going to need to discuss this with her and Jada at some point," Bruja commented, taking a seat on the sofa and patting the spot next to her for me to sit down.

"What's going on?" I asked again, now very serious.

Titi sighed and dropped into a chair. "Your mother's insurance will run out in three weeks. It's not a problem right now, but it will be. Her meds are expensive. Even the co-pay is two to three hundred if we have to refill everything. When the insurance lapses... I don't know how we're going to afford everything."

I sat there in silence, processing the information. "What do you mean her insurance ends?" I asked, sticking on that one key point.

"I mean, the pharmacy said that this will be the last time I can pick up her meds under her current plan. The next time, we have to pay the full price. I don't know what the hell is going on, and they won't talk to me," she explained.

"Who has power of attorney?" Rob asked.

The three women stared at one another for a moment before looking over at me. I didn't have a clue as to what they were talking about, so I asked what it was. Rob then explained the different types of powers of attorney from general to specialized, and the rights the wielder had with each. Then he explained the medical power of attorney. The weight of it all finally settled. My aunts' hands were tied because no one had a power of attorney.

"Jada and I will discuss it tonight, and get it all set up tomorrow," I stated.

"Stacia, this is too much. We'll take care of this," Maria stated softly.

I just shook my head. "You don't get to make decisions for her. Jada and I will decide who gets the power of attorney after we talk with Mami. For now, just leave it and don't say anything. If we need more money, I can work on weekends to cover the costs of the meds."

Titi looked shocked. I thought she would be upset with my direct control of the situation, but then she opened her mouth. "Stacia, the meds are going to cost over six thousand. We don't have that much between us," she explained.

"I know. But I have money saved up, and a long list of clients in Philly who will tip really well if I tell them why I need the money," I said, biting my lip. While my aunts assumed I would be doing nails, it was not the tip money I had in mind.

Bruja squeezed my hand in comfort. "Before we get to that, let's get the power of attorney settled first thing in the morning so that we can see about fixing the insurance issue. We'll worry about the money after we have spoken to the right people," she offered.

Everyone agreed, and we left it at that. I spent the remainder of the day helping my aunts decorate the house for Christmas. It was still weeks away, but we thought Mami would be happy with a little Christmas cheer around the house. By the time Jada got home, the house had been transformed into a winter wonderland of twinkling lights, garland and festive decor.

"Whoa!" She gasped as she came into the house. "What

247

did I miss?"

"A lot," I said, smiling. "Let's go talk upstairs, so I can catch you up."

Before my aunts could say another word, I dragged Jada up to her room and told her everything that we had talked about this afternoon. I also told her how I snuck our mother out of the house, which had her laughing to the point of tears. When there was nothing more to say, Jada and I just nodded in understanding. Mami needed to be part of this discussion because her opinion mattered.

Rob had made it clear that we needed to have her input in order to make the documents as iron clad as possible. There couldn't be any gaps for bureaucracy to manipulate in order to withhold information from us or benefits from Mami.

After the dinner dishes were cleaned up, Jada and I sat with our mother to discuss the need for the power of attorney. We decided to leave out the money issues and just focus on her care. I explained everything, as Rob had explained it to me, and encouraged her to give Jada power of attorney.

Jada stared at me wide eyed. "I don't want it," she confessed softly.

"J, it has to be one of us, and you are older," I said.

Mami shook her head. "No. Anastacia, you will have the power of attorney. You are here with me everyday. I don't want to put that on your sister when she is working as much as she is."

I looked at them both for a moment. "Are you sure you want me to make all of the decisions for you? We didn't talk for months, I don't want people to think I came back just to take advantage."

Mami and Jada both snorted.

"Anastacia, you are the most honest, selfless person in this family. No one will think that. You are a fighter. We know that you will only do what you think is right," Jada added.

I felt my eyes burning with unshed tears. Two months ago we had a broken relationship, and now they were telling me that I was their most trusted person. What the hell was I supposed to say to that?

"Okay. Rob is getting the papers printed out and then Bruja said she can arrange for a notary to come here to validate every-"

"No," Mami said, cutting me off. "We'll go in person tomorrow morning. Rob and Tetiana can go with us while Jada is at work."

Jada's eyebrows shot up. "You want to go out?" She asked in shock.

Mami looked from Jada to me and then back again. "It's not going to kill me to get out of this house. Ask your sister!"

I bit my lips and tried not to laugh. I had already told Jada about our excursion so she knew. Mami rolled her eyes and huffed like Jada was being dramatic, and I couldn't stop the giggle that escaped.

"See what you did?" Jada accused me. "Give her one root beer float and she thinks she's beaten cancer!"

I nearly fell over laughing when Mami gasped in shock and threw her hand up on her chest in mock shock.

"Do you see how she treats me, Stacia?" Mami whined at me. "This is why she can't be in control! She's so bossy! I've made up my mind. It has to be you, Anastacia."

The three of us erupted into laughter. This was what I missed in the months we were apart. The back and forth was effortless between us. We had been through so much together, the three of us, I regretted the time that I had been away. In hindsight, it was moments of time that I would never get back.

The next morning, Jada went off to work while Bruja, Rob and I shuffled Mami into Rob's SUV. He convinced us that his vehicle would be a better fit for this outing as no one needed to bend over to get my mother in or out of the vehicle. Aunt Maria had protested about going out, but she was quickly shut down by her sisters. Titi took Maria to buy groceries and we left for the county clerk's office.

When we got there, Rob had us wait in the vehicle while he ran inside. He came back out with a wheelchair, and set it up on the sidewalk where we were parked. Mami had dozed off on the drive and was sleeping when he opened her door.

"Tia Juanita, I need to pick you up and move you." Rob was a big guy, and hearing him speak so softly to my mother when he was normally so gruff and serious made my eyes water.

Mami's eyes fluttered open and she looked around. "Are we there?" she whispered.

"Yes. Rob got a wheelchair for you. He's going to move you now. Are you ready?" Bruja explained from the front seat.

"Mmm. I'm ready," she murmured. We had given her the pain meds on schedule, and she always drifted easily between sleep and waking for two hours after. We were still in that window of pain control, so it was the best time to get this done.

Rob gently scooped her up from her seat and lowered her into the chair. I was already out of the vehicle and standing by with a blanket to put over her. Bruja pulled two pillows out of the back of the vehicle and we wedged them on either side of her body so she wouldn't get bruised by the metal arm rests from sliding around in the seat.

I thought Rob would join us, but he explained that the vehicle couldn't stay where it was. He had only stopped out front to unload passengers and had to park in the parking garage down the block. The distance wouldn't be a problem for the three of us, but it was too cold outside to move Mami that far.

Bruja led the way as Rob drove off and I pushed Mami's wheelchair into the courthouse.

"Ma'am, this is a general power of attorney. Are you sure you want to give this much power to your daughter?" The clerk asked my mother. Bruja explained that this would happen, because a general power of attorney would allow the beneficiary to make any legal transactions in the other party's name.

"Yes. I understand," Mami responded.

"In that case, please sign right here and I will stamp it as the witness," the man directed, pointing to the spot she needed to sign.

Stamped and officiated, he passed over the documents. "Will that be all for you today?" he asked.

"No," I responded. "We also have a medical one that needs to be completed."

I passed him the medical power of attorney, which he quickly reviewed. I didn't know what he thought we were doing with the first, but I saw the recognition of the situation register as he read the second. The wording left nothing to doubt. My mother gave me sole discretion to make end of life decisions on her behalf. She did not want any to be

251

kept alive artificially, so a 'do not resuscitate' addendum was written into it.

The clerk looked at me and then looked back at my mother. "I'm very sorry," he stated quietly.

Mami smiled. "What can you do but play the hand God has dealt you."

"Cancer?" He asked.

Mami nodded.

"Cancer fucking sucks," he responded, stamping the power of attorney after it was signed. "What are you taking to help with the nausea, if you don't mind my asking?"

Mami didn't say anything. Everything made her sick.

"Trial and error," Bruja replied.

"Give me a second," the clerk advised and then disappeared behind the counter to a back office. I looked at Bruja in confusion and she just shrugged.

When the clerk returned there was a Sheriff's deputy with him. "Ma'am, this is a request form for the medical dispensary in town. The deputy here has to sign off, verifying your need, and then you can purchase medical marijuana to help with your symptoms."

My jaw dropped. I had heard of shit like that in other states, but I had no idea it was legal in our state. "Seriously?" I asked.

The deputy nodded solemnly. "It's not been announced officially, so we are testing out the procedures. I'm going to give you my business card, should you be stopped for any reason."

I filled out the paperwork with Mami's help and we got it all signed. The clerk issued her card and we were out the door with signed powers of attorney and a card that allowed us to procure marijuana, legally. Bruja had called Rob to meet us outside, so he was just pulling up as we exited the building.

"So where to next?" Rob asked once we were all seated in the SUV.

Mami thumped my arm, "Give him the address, mi hija."

"Seriously? You want to pick it up now?" I asked.

"I want to eat. Let's go get my weed," she nodded.

Rob's eyebrows shot up. "Titi, I can't be the one to help you with that. I can't even have that shit in my car."

Rob was still on active duty. If we were pulled over and his unit found out, it would not go well for his career. Bruja nodded as if in understanding.

"I have that covered. Here's a letter from the Sheriff's office for your command. It just states that you transported your dying family member to her appointments. If you test positive for anything, that's on you. But you can't get in trouble for being with us today," she explained.

It wasn't exactly a get out of jail free card, but it was enough that it settled Rob's nerves. He drove to the address of the dispensary, and waited in the car with Mami and Bruja while I ran inside. I was walking back out the door two minutes later with one of the employees.

The woman was sweet and bubbly, and extremely knowledgeable about her weed. She had a ten minute consultation through the car window, asking about previous experiences, medicinal tolerances, family history of mental issues like depression or mania. I thought we were just getting weed, but this was so much more.

"Ok, Juanita. I will start a card for you and it will help us get you dialed in to the product that best helps with your needs," she explained to my mother before looking over at me. "Are you her power of attorney?"

"Yes," I responded.

"Okay. Next time, bring us a copy to keep on file, and your mom won't need to be present each time. This is the best one for helping with nausea. When you come back, I'll need specific feedback to get her prescriptions just right. Let me know things like efficacy, duration, mood changes, and things like that. This should help her body relax so she can eat, but she shouldn't be tripping balls, if you know what I mean," the woman explained.

I couldn't help giggling, looking over at my mother. "Okay. Thank you so much for your help."

"No problem. Let's go back in and I will get her all set up."

I followed the woman back inside and left five minutes later with a water pipe, gummies, and two bags with weed in them. If anyone had told me that I would one day be picking up and currying drugs for my mother, I would have beat their asses. Now here I was, working as my mother's marijuana mule.

I got back in the car and passed Mami a gummy. "Here. Eat this," I directed.

She didn't bat an eye before popping it into her mouth and chewing it up. "*Pineapple*. Nice," she whispered.

"Really?" I asked, not sure what it would taste like.

"No, not really. It tastes like shit," she giggled.

Chapter 17

"I'm sorry miss, this is what it says in our database," the woman informed me politely.

"I understand that, but she wasn't fired. She has cancer," I repeated. "My mother collapsed at work and was put on sick leave because she has cancer. Now you're telling me that she was let go for not coming in to work?"

"Miss, I understand your frustration. But corporate policy is very clear. We covered her for ninety days, when we really should have stopped her benefits at termination."

"Isn't this a violation of the disabilities law? You fired her because she was too sick to come in? With *cancer...*" I growled for the fiftieth time into the phone. I didn't want to be rude, but I had been transferred four times already and spent a total of six days making phone calls between mami's former employer and the insurance company.

"She was terminated for repeated no-shows, according to her fi-"

"I'm going to stop you right there. My mother collapsed at work 62 days ago, and was given three months of sick leave. Where in that time was she reported as a no-show for a scheduled shift?" I asked, feeling my frustration rise.

"I don't have that information available."

"That's okay. I'll have our lawyer get it. One more question. If my mother was given three months of sick leave, which was endorsed by the regional manager, why are her benefits being terminated early?" I asked, checking off the questions that we had come up with.

"Her benefits were extended as a courtesy. They should have stopped when she was terminated-"

"And what was the date of the termination?"

"Um... I have the ninth of September."

"So let me get this straight. My mother was terminated on the ninth of September, but the district AND regional managers allowed her to continue working as a general manager for 28 days? Does that make any damn sense to you? She collapsed at work in October. Her sick leave was endorsed in October. How was she fired in September all of a sudden? Are you fucking kidding me?"

"Please refrain from cursing at me. I am trying to help you understand this situation as best I can, but you're being very-"

"Just stop talking. My mother has worked for your company for fifteen years. She worked through sexual harassment... She was robbed at gunpoint TWICE and assaulted by a fellow employee. Now, rather than letting her have SOME fucking dignity, you want to do her dirty like this? How the fuck do you sleep at night? My mother is dying, so you mother fuckers cooked your books to fire her?" I began screaming into the phone.

I heard a gasp through the phone but the woman named Felicia refused to say anything further.

"Hello? You have nothing to say now? Tell you what. Keep your fucking benefits. You'll hear from my lawyer anyway. And Feliz fucking Navidad," I yelled, slamming the phone

256

off.

Titi and Jada came running into the living room from upstairs looking wide eyed and weary. They had heard me go through this goat rope of a system for the past week, and we got nothing for it.

"What did they say?" Jada asked.

"Well, apparently Mami was fired back in September, like a month before they approved her sick leave, which means her ninety days of benefits are over. And because she has cancer, we can't get any insurance coverage to cover her meds between now and whenever she goes," I whispered, dropping onto the sofa and putting my head in my hands. My throat felt like it was on fire from the previous screaming and now choking back my tears. "How can people do this, Titi?"

My aunt looked at me helplessly. I had barely enough savings to cover her meds through the end of December, and now we were not only going into a new month but a new year with higher rates for the meds she needed.

"We can start a fundraiser?" Jada offered, taking a seat next to me and pulling me into a side hug.

"We wouldn't be able to make that much in time," Titi said, sitting to my other side. "Don't be down on yourself. We'll find a way to overturn this shit, and get her covered."

I was so exhausted, emotionally and mentally. Every day I called and called and called, and got nowhere. What good was I as her person, if I couldn't get shit done.

"I don't know if I can do this," I admitted as the first tears trailed down my cheeks.

"Anastacia, you are one of the strongest women I know. We'll find a way to make it all work out," Jada encouraged me.

"I'm tired. I'm going to go get some sleep," I sighed, leaving Titi and Jada on the sofa.

As I laid down, the exhaustion disappeared and my brain began running a mile a minute. I thought of calling Lacey, but she wasn't licensed to practice in this state. I definitely wasn't calling my mother's lawyer, because he was an ambulance chaser. As soon as my mother died, he would drop our case and that would happen sooner than we had a chance of getting into a courtroom.

We needed money, plain and simple. I just needed to make sure her expenses were paid. I sent a group message to the three people I knew could help me get some fast cash; Cherry, Spider and Elektra

Group: [I need a lot of money and fast. They cut off my mom's insurance and her meds are like 2k a week.]

Cherry: [I can send you a thousand through Venmo]

Spider: [Shit, girl. I would help, but Cherry and I are moving. All of my money went into buying a place back home. I feel fucking gutted.]

Elektra: [Dance.]

Cherry, Spider: [NO!!]

Elektra: [Why not? She needs fast money, and that is the fastest *legal* way to do it.]

Spider: [No. No, absolutely not. She's never been involved in this life, let's keep her out of it.]

Me: [I'm not looking to make a career change, ladies. I appreciate you two looking out for me, but my mom is dying. If I can't find a way to get her meds covered, she has to be hospitalized. So six to eight grand suddenly becomes a hundred thou. What would you do in my shoes?]

I didn't want to take money from anyone. I didn't like owing money or favors to anyone, but the thought of my mother suffering alone in a hospital fucking gutted me. Jada and I would give anything to make her healthy, but that wasn't in the cards for us. I knew because I had spoken with her team of doctors all week about her condition, prognosis, and medications. She was dying sooner than later, and the pain of pancreatic cancer would drive her to insanity before the cancer could kill her.

I dozed off as the three went back and forth discussing my options in the group chat, my head swirling with all of the bureaucratic bullshit I had been through since accepting the powers of attorney.

I woke up the next morning with a private message from Elektra. She could help me get a couple of gigs as a freelance dancer, but the clubs would take thirty percent of my tips. In her opinion, I was best off just taking a job as an exotic dancer with a club so that I could make more money.

I had thought about reaching out to the Marquessa, but that was off the table. I had already salted the grounds there as Lilith, and after getting slapped by Iryna, I didn't like the idea of going back. I called Elektra back.

"Hey, it's me. What clubs can I get into that Roman isn't involved in?" I asked.

"Shit, Taze. If you're looking to steer clear of him, you're limited to Baltimore or Atlantic City... And I would not recommend AC. Their girls get treated like shit," Elektra advised.

"Who do you know in Baltimore that can hook me up with a high end on short notice?" I asked, my mind committing to the plan.

"Don't you have connections?" She giggled. *"I mean you let a*

boss dine on your snatch. I don't see why you aren't calling him."

I was confused. "Who are you talking about, E?"

"Seriously? The guy you disappeared with after the expo? Mister hottie badass who had your pussy drip-"

"Oh my god! You are so nasty!" I squealed into the phone, feeling my cheeks burning. "How do you know he can help? I don't even know who he is."

Elektra was quiet for a minute before sighing on the other end. *"Look. That guy is... known. If you want to get a quick job with high yields, call him. He'll get you set up faster than any of us can."*

We talked for another thirty minutes about everything going on in our lives. I gave her more details about the bullshit of bureaucracy I was wading through, and she updated me on the gossip from Marquessa. I missed having my girls in my life everyday. I had only ever seen women compete and be cut throat. Working in that industry, I felt supported for the first time in my life. I needed more of that than ever before.

By the time I was cleaned up and ready to start my day, Bruja was already on the clock getting Mami situated with her morning meds and breakfast. I peeked into her room and nearly choked on the cloud of smoke billowing out.

"Hey Cheech and Chong, I'm going to run some errands today. Give me a call if you need anything," I laughed at the two passing a joint back and forth.

Mami looked up at me and giggled before waving me off. Bruja just smiled and asked me to pick up vanilla ice cream and A&Ws while I was out. I laughed and closed the door. By the time I got to Nana and Pops', I had committed in my head to calling Mister tall dark and yummy. His number was still in my hand bag from that weekend at the Expo.

It took nearly an hour of tossing my room before I found what I was looking for. It was a small slip of paper that he had written his contact information on. The more I thought about it, the less I wanted to call him to ask for a job. The man had his face between my legs. I could only imagine the restrictions I would have dancing in any club that he held sway over.

I crumpled up the paper and threw it in the trash. There was still another way, and it was the safest. I trusted Elektra, but there was one woman who knew everyone in the industry around here much better than her and I knew they would help if I called.

"Hello. I wasn't expecting to hear from you."

"Hey. Sorry. Things have been a bit hectic since I got back."

"Not so hectic that you couldn't go to the expo and dance, but just too much to call me?"

"I know, I know. I'm sorry!" I chuckled hearing the comforting voice through the phone.

"I know you didn't just call to see how I was doing, so spill it. What's going on?"

I took a deep breath and told Marjory about everything that had happened with Mami over the past few weeks. Everything from the fighting to the costs of her meds to the bullshit I had dealt with with her former employers was laid out. By the end I felt like I would cry, but I couldn't bring myself to shed anymore tears.

"That's a lot to take on. I'm sorry you have had to deal with all of this. It's tough," she commented sadly. *"I can call in a favor, but you'll need to really think this over before you call them."*

My heart leapt up into my chest. "Which club?"

"It's one of the older places in Philly. Very low key. The tips are really good and they do a decent job of looking after the girls there. Let me call them and then I will send you the details. How soon are you available?" Marjory asked.

"I can start tomorrow," I offered. Today was Wednesday. Jada, Titi and Bruja had already arranged for Mami to be with them Thursday night through the weekend. It was part of our no one gets burned out rotation.

"Does your family support you in this?" She asked.

"They don't know, and I'm not going to tell them before anything is guaranteed," I explained. "I don't want my aunt to mortgage her house for medical bills and my sister and I can't afford the alternative, so it is what it is."

"Okay, Taze. I'll send you the details when I have them... It was good talking to you, sweetie."

"You too, Marjory. Maybe we can grab a coffee the next time I'm up in Philly?" I offered.

Marjory chuckled. *"I'm out of town for a bit, but I'll let you know when I get back."*

"Oh. Okay. Um, thank you. For everything. I really mean it," I said, feeling guilty that I hadn't kept in touch with her after I came back.

"Don't worry about it. It's what we do for those we care about that matters. You're a good girl, Anastacia. I'm happy to help."

By the time I got off the phone with Marjory it was already lunch time. I felt like a huge weight had been lifted from my chest and I could finally breathe again. I got to work cleaning up the house and getting food ready for everyone.

Everything would work out. I just knew it.

* * *

I stepped into Infinity for my interview with the owner. Marjory had come through for me, like I knew she would, and got me in with a reputable club that paid well. I dressed like Lacey taught me whenever the owners of Marquessa were around and we were called in after hours. It was cold as hell outside just before the holidays, so I opted for boots instead of the heels I owned. I carried everything I needed in my bag, just in case I needed to perform to seal this opportunity.

The club was clean. Polished floors, neatly organized tables and booths. It all screamed high end clientele. High end clientele meant higher tips, which in turn meant my mother would be taken care of without ruining the family financially.

"We're closed until 10pm," a woman behind the bar hollered over to me as I walked through the main room.

"I know. I'm here for an interview," I stated, smiling politely.

"Infinity doesn't do interviews. Someone must have pulled your leg," the bartender chuckled, continuing to organize her station. "Just walking here dressed to the nines doesn't mean you can work here," she continued, wiping down the bottles on the shelves until they shined.

I bit my lip, fighting the nausea swirling in my stomach. Marjory wouldn't have given me bad information. I only hoped that this woman behind the bar was not informed.

"I didn't just walk in, promise," I started. "A friend of mine helped me get this interview, but she didn't tell me who I was meeting with."

The bartender nodded like she understood. "Well, you can wait here at the bar if you want, but I have to warn you... It might be a while," she said, glancing over at me.

"That's not a problem. I don't mind waiting," I admitted, letting out a sigh of relief. She wasn't kicking me out, so I still had a chance to meet the owners and get this job.

I set my bag down on the floor and took a seat at the bar, watching the woman shuffle back and forth in the narrow galley to wash glasses, stock beers, and prepare food items. After a few minutes of watching her carry two crates of beers from the cold storage I jumped up to help.

"Oh, you don't have to do that. I'm used to this," she said.

"I don't mind. I can't sit and watch someone else work and not do anything. If you have gloves, I can finish prepping your fruits," I offered, gesturing over at the knife and cutting board behind the bar.

"You really don't have to do that…"

"Anastacia. But you can call me Tace or Taze, and I really don't mind. I don't exactly have anything better to do anyway," I offered, introducing myself.

"Olga," she smiled back offering out her hand.

"Nice to meet you, Olga," I grinned, and began rolling up my sleeves as I walked around the bar.

Olga explained how she needed her bar set up, and I got to work cutting lemons, limes, and pineapple slices. She was easy to talk to and before I knew it, I had spent two hours following her around the bar, cold storage, and main floor cleaning and restocking the bar stations.

My phone pinged and I excused myself to check it. The message was Jada reminding me to grab a few extra items from the store on my way home.

"You got somewhere to be?" Olga asked.

"Yes. Not really," I said, trying to smile. "Just my sister, reminding me to grab stuff for our mom on my way home," I explained, tucking my phone back into my pocket.

"Your mom doesn't have a car?" She asked, drying her hands on a towel.

"No, she has cancer. Kind of the reason I need the job," I stated. "She made the mistake of outliving her initial prognosis, and now her insurance is about to end. Her meds are expensive and I don't want to burden the rest of our family with the costs."

Olga looked shocked. "Shit. I was expecting to hear that you had some debts to pay down or a terrible coke habit, but that... *Shit.* That's heavy. I'm really sorry to hear about your mom."

I tried to smile but it never quite reached my eyes. "It is what it is."

"Tell you what. Leave me your contact information, and I will call the owner. Tell them that I vetted you, and we'll see where it goes from there," Olga offered.

I couldn't contain my hope. "Seriously? You don't even know me."

"I'm a pretty good judge of character. You seem like a sweet girl, Taze. Now get out. You've been here all day, and you have shit to do!" She said, swatting at my backside with the towel.

I chuckled and thanked her for letting me hang out. The drive back to Titi's was not the happy ride I was hoping for. I wanted to tell them that I had gotten a job and could help pitch in with the rising costs of caring for Mami. Instead I was stuck in bumper to bumper gridlock for two hours.

My phone began ringing, and I had to rummage through my bag to find it. "Hello?"

"Hey, Tace. Where are you? You've been gone all day, and I didn't hear back from you earlier," Jada's worried voice filled my car.

I sighed. "I'm sitting in rush hour traffic three miles from the house. I should be there soon. I'm gonna stop at the market on Huntington on the way, so text me the shopping list."

"You sure? I can run out if you're tired," Jada offered.

"Please. I've been sitting around for two hours. I'll be there shortly," I assured my sister.

I hung up with Jada and threw my phone on the passenger seat. It pinged two or three times before I was able to get to the store, causing me to chuckle.

"How much shit do I need to buy, J?" I murmured to myself as I finally pulled into the parking lot outside the Hannaford's on Huntington. I grabbed my phone and wallet, and got to it.

Pulling up the unread messages, I saw one from Jada and two from an unknown number. I opened then unknown messages first.

UNK: [Hey, this is Olga. I got you an in if you can be here tomorrow night at 8pm.]

UNK: [Dress to impress.]

Holy shit! I bit my lips to keep from squealing in the supermarket aisle.

Me: [Thank you so much! I will be there.]

After sending off my response to Olga, I saved her number and went shopping for the list of items Jada had sent. I had a job.

Possibly.

Maybe.

Either way, I would have some income and be able to contribute to the medical bills piling up at home.

* * *

When Jada got home from work the next day, I was already ready and my makeup done up. I dressed in a pencil skirt that came just past my knees, a red blouse and heels. I left my hair down in soft curls down my back.

"Holy shit, Anastacia. You have a hot date?"

I looked up from the mirror and smiled. "No. Job interview."

"Where? You look like a runway model, hermana! Go show Mami how beautiful you look!" She gushed, pushing and pulling me to spin around for her.

"Don't say anything to anyone, J. I don't know if I have the job, and I don't want anyone to know yet. Okay? Can you keep this between us?" I asked her.

"You doing something illegal?" She asked immediately.

I shook my head. "No. Nothing illegal. I just don't want to get any hopes up before I know I have a job," I explained, not wanting to tell my sister that I was applying to be an exotic dancer.

Jada wouldn't judge me, but I couldn't say the same for everyone else in our family. Hearing anyone talk shit about what I did would just burn the bridges I was trying to mend at this point.

"Knock 'em dead, Tace!" She whispered as I pulled on my coat and slipped out the door before the aunts could see me.

I didn't park near the club, and had my car valeted at a garage a couple of blocks down the road. The walk in heels wasn't bad, but the biting wind at my legs was brutal.

"No pain, no gain," I muttered to myself as I finally reached my destination.

Having seen the club during its off hours was nothing like seeing it lit up at night before the customers came in. The DJ was going through the song mixes for the girls as they practiced on the various side stages.

"Not bad," someone called out.

I looked over to see Olga smiling and waving from the bar. I rolled my eyes and smiled back at her. "You said dress to impress, so I did."

She nodded in approval as she walked around the bar to greet me with a hug. "Not bad at all, little girl. Come on, I'll take you to meet the owner," she said, hooking her arm in mine and leading me down a hall behind the bar.

Stopping outside a large black door, Olga knocked and a deep voice barked that we needed to wait. We stepped back from the door and waited.

After fifteen minutes, Olga started to get fidgety. "Go," I told her. "I know you have last minute shit to do. You can leave me here. I will be okay."

She looked unsure at first, but I nodded in encouragement. It wasn't my first time going into an interview cold, and it probably wouldn't be my last.

Another ten minutes passed before the door finally opened. Two women quickly scurried out, looking like they were escaping the depths of hell or the devil himself. "Come in," the deep voice barked again.

I didn't hesitate to step into the office, but all of my bravado died when I saw the man behind the desk. He hadn't looked up at me yet, and I hoped like hell that I was a lost memory among the many women I was sure he would have dealt with.

"What can I do for you?" He asked, still not looking up from his paperwork.

"I'm here about a job," I stated clearly.

"Any experience?"

"Yes."

"References?"

"Yes."

"You clean?"

"Yes."

"Criminal record?"

"No."

"Drug use?"

"No."

"I don't like liars. I can smell the weed on you from here," he growled at me.

"My mother has terminal cancer. Can't be helped," I stated.

He dropped his pen and finally looked up at me. I prayed with everything in me that Roman didn't recognize me as the woman he bent over his desk. Although he had seen me many times, he only paid attention to me when I was Lilith.

"Do I know you?" He asked, staring at me, scrutinizing my face carefully.

"I worked as a nail tech at the Marquessa. Your wife slapped me when I gave notice," I reminded him.

"Shit. Anastacia, right?"

"Yes, sir," I responded.

"I'm sorry. Please. Have a seat. Let's talk about your desire to work at Infinity," he said, gesturing at a pair of wingback chairs set off to the side of the office.

I thanked him, took a seat, and tried my best not to fidget

when he moved to sit in the chair next to me. He chuckled for a moment and then looked over at me.

"If I had known that you were the favor Marjory called in, I wouldn't have missed our appointment yesterday. I'm sorry for making you waste your time," Roman stated.

I shook my head and smiled. "I appreciate that. My time wasn't completely wasted. I hung out with Olga and helped her stock the bar while I waited. Gave us time to get to know each other and bond a bit," I said, winking at him.

Roman leaned back and laughed, "Wow. It takes a lot to win over the iron-hearted Olga."

My eyebrows scrunched up in confusion. Were we talking about the same sweet lady behind the bar? "Who are you talking about?" I asked, honestly thinking that I had met the wrong person.

"Olga chewed my ass out last night about failing to keep my scheduling straight. Said I had left a poor sweet girl here without notice and it was really un-fucking-professional," he explained.

This time I laughed. "It wasn't that bad. Gave me an opportunity to decide if the club would be a good fit for me."

"And what have you decided? Is Infinity up to your standards?" He leaned back in his chair with an eyebrow quirked up.

"It is. But I don't know if you want to hire me," I confessed, feeling the nerves still bubbling up. He still hadn't realized who I was. Not really. I hoped I looked calmer on the outside than I felt on the inside.

"Nonsense. Consider it done. Were you wanting to freelance until things settle down, or?"

My stomach was in absolute knots, palms sweating. He had made it very clear before that there was a line between work and play that should never be crossed. I had crossed it. I had no intention of crossing that line again. I needed money and that need weighs higher than any personal desires I had for myself.

"No. I want a contract. Standard deductions for the industry, and an assurance that you won't fire me for anything that happened outside of Infinity," I stated.

Roman smirked. "Sounds a bit dubious, but I'll accept that. You're a good kid. I don't expect to have any problems with you working here. I'll pull up the contract now and you can sign it. You can start tonight if you want," he offered, moving to his desk to print out a new contract.

I couldn't help the inner sneer when he called me a kid. I watched his fingers fly across the keyboard as he typed in the information I provided him. I could see the screen, and I knew the moment of truth was coming.

"Ok, last item. Have you given any thought to what you want for a stage name?" He asked, looking up at me.

Our eyes locked, and the name slipped across my tongue. I watched his mind process it, two faces overlapping in his memory. His pupils dilated ever so slightly, and his breath caught.

"You're *Lilith?*" He asked, clearing his throat. Seeing me nod my head, he exhaled sharply. *"Fuck me."*

"Sorry, *I don't fuck where I work,*" I said, repeating his words from that night.

271

Chapter 18

Roman looked like he was torn between screaming and throwing me out the door, or throwing me down on his desk. I didn't sit still and wait for him to continue talking.

"Not to mention, I don't make it a habit of fucking married men, especially married men with expectant wives. So... there shouldn't be any problems with me working here, right?" I asked, trying my hardest to keep my bitch face up, but feeling the heat in my cheeks betraying me.

He looked like I had slapped him. The desire and lust immediately abated with my words. "You're absolutely correct. There won't be any problems with you working here, Lilith."

A moment later my new contract was printed and I signed it. Roman made a copy for himself, and I maintained the original. We shook hands and I moved to leave the office. I needed to get changed and talk with the DJ if I was going to start tonight.

As I was about to step out the door, Roman stopped me. "For what it's worth, Iryna and I have an arranged marriage and the baby isn't mine."

"I don't care, Roman," I whispered and walked away. Arranged marriages or not, they were married. I didn't care what color of hat he was wearing, from the outside looking in that was his baby and his wife. I wasn't going there again.

I made my way back to the bar to find Olga yelling at two men whom I presumed were bouncers.

"Don't look at me like I just kicked your puppy! You have one fucking job! Keep your fucking hands off my shit or I will break your damn fingers!"

"It wasn't like-" one started but she cut him off again.

"It wasn't like what? It wasn't like you were behind the bar helping yourself to shots before work? Get the fuck out of my face before I get pissed, and if I catch either of you back here again…" Her words trailed off when she saw me.

"Hi, sweetie! How did it go?" Olga asked, her entire attitude flipping like a switch.

Seeing that her attention had been diverted, the two men visibly shook and scuttled away from her as quickly as possible.

"Wow. What did I miss out here?" I asked, chuckling.

She turned to look for her prey but they had disappeared. Olga puckered her lips, making a tsking sound. "Those two are new and stupid. Caught them back here trying to nick a few beers for later. Idiots," she explained, waving her hand to excuse her reaction.

She then walked over to me and turned me around slowly, studying my entire body. "Well, you seem unscathed. How did the interview go?" She asked, arching an eyebrow.

"It went well. I used to work at Marquessa, so," I stated, smiling.

"Oh, you little shit! If I had known you had an inside string, I wouldn't have made such a fuss to get you back in here!" She complained, smacking my arm.

273

I couldn't help but chuckle as she continued to fuss at me about not being up front with my connections. "To be fair," I said. "I didn't know Roman was the owner of Infinity. I called a friend, and they set me up with the interview. I didn't know anything other than where and when to be."

Olga pursed her lips at me again before sighing. "Fine. I'll believe you because you seem like a sweet girl. Come on. I'll show you the dressing room and you can meet the others on shift tonight," she said, grabbing my hand and pulling me toward a hall that led behind the main stage.

"This area is called the tunnels," Olga explained. "This main hall leads to the main stage, but there are branches that can take you to either side of the club, and stairs that will take you up to the VIP lounges for private dances. Customers are not allowed in the tunnels, no exceptions.

"That door leads to the back alley, in case of a fire. Not that we have ever had a fire, but you should know where to run to save your own ass. This is the dressing room. There is only one dressing room so you will have to share a vanity," she continued as we stepped into the dressing area.

Several women were in various stages of makeup, dressing and or undressing. The back and forth chatter suddenly stopped after we walked in as eight sets of eyes turned toward us.

"There are lockers on the back wall for you to keep your personal shit. Not that anyone here is a thief, but you never know," Olga whispered at the end.

One of the women turned from her mirror to face us. "Fresh meat? She doesn't even look legal," she commented.

"That is Charity. She is not giving. She is not hospitable, and she is not nice," Olga stated seriously.

274

"That's fucked up, Olga!" The woman named Charity snapped back. "I'll remember that the next time you need a babysitter on short notice!"

I thought the two women would start to argue, but they laughed and hugged instead. "You know I love you, Char-bear!" Olga laughed.

"You are so full of shit!" Charity laughed, slapping the other's back and pushing her away from the hug. "Now, seriously. What do we have here?" She asked, directing the attention back to me.

"This is-"

"Lilith," I offered, smiling. "Tonight is my first night, so Olga was giving me a tour."

The other women stared at me like I was a fucking liar or an assassin. It didn't make sense until I remembered how Roman had described her. "Roman told her to show me where to be, so that I don't get fucking lost," I added quickly.

Their body language relaxed hearing that the boss had directed the mean lady to help me. Charity and Olga exchanged a quick look before Charity turned away to keep from laughing.

"Unfortunately, we have a full staff tonight, so you'll need to share vanity space," Charity continued, looking around the room and realizing that she had the only vanity not under double to triple occupancy.

Olga smirked, "You can use Charity's station when she's done. I'll leave you to it, ladies."

After Olga left the dressing room an awkward silence filled the room. I didn't pay any attention, remembering how hard it was to make friends with the women in Marquessa when I started there.

"Hi, I am Star," a perky blonde introduced herself. "How old are you?"

"Twenty-one. You?" I asked, beginning to strip out of my skirt and blouse.

"Twenty-one also! You ever danced before?" Star continued.

"Yes," I answered, deciding not to provide any more information.

"How did you get into Infinity?" Star asked, leaning against the lockers.

Seeing the other women leaning in to hear my responses, I couldn't help but be brutally honest. "Oh, I fucked Roman. You?" I asked, locking eyes with Star.

There was pin drop silence before I broke into a smile. "I'm just joking. I walked in yesterday and Olga put in a good word for me after making me work for her for three hours."

The women in the room laughed. "Holy shit, my heart just stopped! I almost believed you for a second there," one of the others commented, patting her chest.

"Can you imagine? Fuck!"

"Jesus Christ, I just got my fucking porny hopes up, and it was a lie?" another whined.

"Sorry, I'm really not that interesting," I said, winking at them.

"I would ride that all night if I had a chance. That man is fucking gorgeous!" A fourth woman added in.

I decided not to add any more to the conversation and just listened to the women go back and forth about their Roman fantasies. Didn't seem like the time to say, 'been there, done that.' There was still another hour before the club opened, so Star offered to introduce me to the DJ/MC for the club. I half expected to see Mike from Marquessa, but was shocked to see a woman in the booth instead.

"Rene, this is Lilith. She is starting tonight. Lilith, Rene is our guru. You want it, she'll find whatever song you want," Star said, making quick introductions before disappearing again.

"Nice to meet you, Lilith. You look familiar. Have you danced somewhere else?" Rene asked, as she organized her playlists according to the girls' requests.

"I was a guest dancer at the Marquessa," I admitted, but Rene just shook her head.

"No. That's not it…. It'll come to me," she promised. "Do you know where you are in the line up?"

Shaking my head, I looked over her shoulder at the scheduling. There was one spot open near midnight on the main stage, so I pointed at it. "I'll take that spot."

Rene's eyebrows shot up. "You sure you want that one?"

"Why not?" I smiled back.

Rene wrote me into the program and I gave her my music choices. Two of the songs I had picked were already taken but the third was not.

"That's a pretty good song. I'm surprised one of the others hasn't claimed it yet," Rene chuckled.

"Claimed it?" I asked, not really understanding but understanding at the same time.

"When a dancer debuts, that first song becomes theirs in a way. If it's a good night, and the dancer does well, no one else would be able to use the song without the customers complaining. If the dance is shit, the song becomes taboo," she explained.

"So this is going to be like my, what? My personal anthem?"

277

I asked, giggling because I couldn't remember anything like that at the Marquessa.

"Oh absolutely. You'll see it tonight. As soon as certain songs come up, and I'm talking about the opening chords, the regulars will move to get front row seats."

"Good to know," I said, making a mental note to pay attention to the songs that specific dancers had claimed. "Can I ask you a few questions while you work?"

"Sure. What do you want to know?" Rene asked, moving her headset from one ear down to her neck.

"How do the VIP rooms work?" I asked.

Rene looked stunned that I would ask such a question before chuckling. "If a client wants a one on one, they will request a VIP suite and a specific dancer. A bouncer is just outside the door at all times, and there are cameras in the rooms to protect the dancers and the client. Do not get caught having sex, giving hand jobs, blowies, or giving up your snatch in those rooms. This is not a brothel," she warned.

I snorted. "Don't have to worry about me there," I stated.

"None of the women here would either, but it doesn't hurt to lay the rules out up front," Rene added.

I thanked Rene for the information and found a side stage to warm up on. It had been a minute since I danced, and I didn't want to embarrass myself or my new boss. I kept my moves generic, moving to stretch and limber up my joints rather than provoke desires. Charity joined me after a couple of minutes and began mimicking my movements.

"Not a bad warm-up. I thought you were bullshitting me when you said you danced before. Sorry for the rough reception," she apologized. "You look really young and I

278

hate it when young girls come in thinking they can just strip, shake their asses, and make lots of money."

I stopped moving and stared at her wide eyed. "I can't?" I asked in a loud high pitched voice.

Charity bit her lip to keep from laughing. "Seriously, where did you come from and why the fuck are you here?"

I smirked and kept going through my routine. "I need the money. Plain and simple," I admitted.

"That's it? Just money?" Charity asked me.

"Yep. I like my body, I like my family... most days... It's all about the money. No mommy-daddy issues, or *Pretty Woman* fantasies here," I said, finishing my warm up.

"Good to know," Charity said, smiling as she thanked me for the warm up.

I smiled right back until she was out of sight and my smile dropped. I wasn't here to make friends, but I didn't need to be sussed out by every damn employee like I was a fucking narc. I stepped off the side stage and returned to the dressing room to finish getting ready.

"Excuse me, Miss?" An older man's voice called from the emergency exit door.

"Yes?" I responded smiling cheerfully.

"Could you get someone for me?" He asked, eyeing the dressing room door.

"Sure. Which bouncer did you want to show you to the front door?" I asked, batting my eyes at him.

"No, no. I don't need a bouncer, idiot. I want you to get a dancer," he huffed, still holding the door open.

The sweet smile stayed on my face, but the amusement left my eyes. "I'll tell you what, old man. You can let go of that door or leave your fingers while I grab that bouncer for you.

How does that sound?" I cooed at him as I stalked closer to the door.

"Listen here, honey. It's obvious you are new here, and don't know who I am-"

"You're right, I don't. But when you see Roman, tell him *Lilith* did it," I purred, cutting him off.

He looked confused for a second before asking, "Did what?"

I kicked the door outward knocking him on his ass, and then grabbed it again to slam it shut. As soon as I walked into the dressing room, the cold air from the corridor followed me in.

"Holy shit! Who opened the back door?!" Several of the women complained.

"Lilith might not have known the door needed to be kept shut," Star piped in.

I smiled at her, now knowing exactly which dancer had set me up. "You probably don't know, but this girl," I add, pointing at myself. *"Hates the cold.* I found some old man working as a doorstop, and, bless his heart, was committed to the task. So I kicked him out of the way, shut the door, and reset the alarm that had been disabled. Hope you don't mind."

Star looked like she had been slapped silly, when I faked a shiver.

"I may be new here, but I'm not the new girl you can fuck with," I warned Star directly.

The other women chuckled and shook their heads at Star for getting called out so quickly. I didn't pay them any more attention and pulled my shit out of my locker. I knew better than to leave my stuff out before it was time to actually get ready, because dancers loved to haze the new girls.

Donning a one piece sling shot I hadn't had the courage to wear yet, I paired it with leg straps that trailed from high thigh down to the ankle straps of my heels. I didn't need to hide who I was anymore, so my makeup was on point without the need to consider wearing a mask. I strutted out of the dressing room with the others like I had always belonged.

I had just stepped out into the main room when I saw the old man, surrounded by three bodyguards arguing with Olga and Roman. Olga shook her head for me to avoid the area, but I wasn't about to have another dancer fuck me over on my first day.

"Roman, this poor gentleman got confused and tried to come in the back door," I said, winking at the old man and Roman. Then I trailed my finger down Roman's chest, and batted my eyes. "You know how I am about men and a back door," my voice trailed off.

Roman looked surprised for a moment and then started laughing. I wasn't sure if he would remember the first time we met, but I had never forgotten it.

"Mr. Reynolds, be thankful she only put you on your ass. The last man who tried to get in the back door with Lilith was hospitalized," Roman stated, smiling menacingly at the old man named Reynolds.

He looked at me and then huffed in frustration. Before he could get too far, I stopped him. "Don't worry though, I made sure Star knew you were looking for her!" I said in the most cheerful voice possible.

Olga chuckled at my words, but Roman stopped laughing. "She's out," he ordered Olga who smiled even more.

"I fucking love you, Lilith," Olga whispered, as she passed me to find Star.

Roman looked at me and shook his head. "You're a troublemaker," he admonished.

I smirked. "Don't misbehave, and there's no need for punishment," I commented quietly.

"Lilith," Roman warned, eyes beginning to devour me. "Don't make me regret hiring you."

I bit my bottom lip and smiled up at him, and wiggled my eyebrows.

He chuckled and shook his head as I turned to walk away. I had only been on the front end of a gentlemen's club twice, and I never left the stage either time. This time, I walked around the club like I owned the place, talking to the customers, asking how they were enjoying their night.

When Olga's waitresses couldn't keep up with the drinks, I grabbed a tray and helped them deliver the orders to the right tables and VIP suites. When someone slipped cash into my leg straps, I thanked them sweetly and wished them a good night. Within an hour I was pulling cash out of my straps, because I looked like I was wearing spiky green chaps.

I tried to sneak back to the dressing room, but one of the bouncers stopped me at the door and gave me a two minute warning for my first song.

As I stepped to the side of the main stage, I watched one of the other girls finishing her number. Two bouncers quickly swept the stage, stuffing all of the money into a net for her to collect once she was done. Rene urged the guests to give a round of applause for the previous dancer named Candy, and introduced me… Infinity's newest temptation.

Unlike the other women dancing here tonight, I would be

stepping onto the stage covered in cash already. I waited until I heard Amarae's sweet voice cooing before I stepped onto the stage.

Oh there's dollars all around.

Dolla dolla bills yeah. Dolla dolla bills...

I slowly started rolling my hips from side to side as I walked. I grabbed the pole and spun slowly around, showing off my assets to every man in the club.

I feel like there's nothing in my way.

All this money on me. It feels Amazing.

I bit my lip and stopped spinning to run my hands down my cash covered legs and smiled over my shoulder with my ass in the air. My knees bent and I dropped to the floor, rotating my hips slowly as I went.

Unlike the other women in this club. My eyes scanned the crowd. I wasn't afraid to make eye contact; I looked until I had their undivided attention on me. I glanced briefly at Roman, and smirked as he adjusted his pants.

I rolled my hips again, as I pulled myself around the bar, hooking one leg with the bar just behind the knee so that my hands could run down my body. I arched and rolled my torso slowly, as my body twisted and turned around the pole.

I'm gonna get paid yeah.

Just gimme my moolah-la-la.

I crawled slowly forward on the floor, until I could just reach the pole behind me. I leaned back on my knees, my body arching backwards as it pulsed and waved between my hips and shoulders. One hand held my body suspended, while the other traced the empty straps on my suit begging for the moolah.

I really like your body.

283

Yo quiero sentirte inside of me.

My legs twisted out from under me, and I lay on my back on the floor before kicking one leg over my head and hooking it around the pole. It was hard to get the traction I needed with the cash stuffed in my leg strap, but it was enough for me to roll my body under so that my ass was toward the pole and I faced the hungry men in front of me.

Todo el dia imaginandote.

Lo quiero para mi toda la noche.

I licked my lips and rolled my hips flexing my back so that my ass was raised up just in front of the pole. I reached behind me and pulled my body back toward the pole again, arching my breasts out in the process

And I walk in like my pussy's so dangerous.

When I whisper to you in a couple of languages.

I didn't need to stare at the back wall when I danced. Wasn't trying to block out the men gawking at me, or making lewd sounds and gestures. I was feeding them everything they needed to feel like my dance was for their eyes only.

The previously cleared black stage was turning greener with every turn I made on the pole. I knew what my body looked like, having practiced with Cherry and Spider so many times during our training. Not a single motion or glance was unintentional in my movements. I wanted every man in the room drooling over me.

My body.

Y cuando termines te quedas por dentro.

My sighs.

I'm gonna get paid yeah.

I had the entire room's attention on me, including Olga behind the bar. As the song neared its end, I lowered myself to the floor again in a deep squat with my knees pushed out. I scanned every hungry set of eyes in the room, biting my lip.

Rene was silent for a moment before Charity finally got her attention, signaling that she should be introducing the next dancer.

Snapping out of it, Rene quickly changed out the lights. "Holy shit, gentlemen. Give up that moolah-la-la for LILITH!!!" Rene cheered, causing a flurry of cash to rain onto the stage. "Next up is your favorite bad girl, Charity!"

Three bouncers had to help get all of the cash off the stage before Charity's number could begin. As the three of them helped me sort everything in my tip bag, a banker's bag with a lock and key, one of the waitresses passed me a gold card with the number three on it.

"What's this?" I asked, unfamiliar with the process.

"You have a private dance request from a client. He's booked VIP room three, upstairs. Charlie will take you up when you are ready," she explained.

"Right. Thank you...?" I trailed off.

"Giselle," she answered.

"Giselle, thank you," I repeated, making sure to use her name.

The bouncer named Charlie was a big black guy who looked like he could bench a bus. He was quiet at first, but after cracking a few jokes at my own expense, he loosened up a bit.

"What is a sweet girl like you doing here?" He asked as we walked up the stairs.

"Need money, Charlie. Girl's gotta pay them bills," I responded.

"You're too nice for this life, Lilith. Don't let them take that from you," Charlie cautioned.

"I appreciate that, Charlie. Tell you what. You look out for me, and I will look out for you. Deal?" I asked, holding out my hand to shake his.

"Alright, small fry. I got your back. But I don't know how much damage a tiny tike like you can throw out there," he chuckled.

I smiled. "Think of me like a stick of dynamite. I look small and useless on a shelf, but fire me up and I'll lay waste to the whole fucking building."

Charlie laughed as we reached the VIP room. "You're alright," he said before knocking on the door and opening it for me to enter.

My heart stopped when I saw the man waiting for me.

"What are you doing here?" I asked as the door closed behind me.

"I could ask you the same," Domenico smirked.

"Obviously, I'm working," I commented, slowly sashaying around to inspect the room.

The room was luxuriously laid out with plush bench seating along two walls and a pole in the center of the room. A small table had a silver bucket with a chilled bottle of champagne inside. Beside the bucket sat two glasses, already filled with golden bubbly.

"Why are you here?" I asked again, spinning around the pole.

Domenico leaned back on the bench and watched me dance. "I was here for business, but I got distracted," he admitted.

"Mmm," I hummed. "Hate it when that happens," I

murmured, climbing up the pole.

"You never called."

"No, I didn't," I admitted, twirling around to the music playing softly in the background.

"You use me?" He asked, slowly beginning to rub the noticeable bulge in his pants.

"Do you want to be used?" I asked, facing him as my hips rolled around.

"Do you have any idea how fucking sexy you are?" He asked.

"I do," I admitted, biting my lip. "But I want you to tell me anyway."

"I don't even know your name," he complained, stroking his cock.

"Lilith-"

"Your real name," he corrected me, smirking.

"What's in a name? It's just a word. Will saying my name change how you feel about me?" I asked, leaning back against the pole and arching my body out.

"I want to know your name. I don't want to feel like one of these perverts fantasizing about a woman I can't have," he grunted, using more force to stroke himself.

"But I'm not some woman to you, am I? Unlike them, you've had my legs wrapped around your ears," I whispered softly, doing a split around the bar as I spun.

"Fuck. I would make you suck my cock right now if I could," Domenico seethed.

"Are you mad at me?" I pouted at him. "Are you angry that the girl didn't call you and fall at your feet?"

Domenico stopped rubbing his cock and stared at me. "Are you toying with me?" He asked, leaning forward to rest his elbows on his knees.

"No. I'm not. Well, maybe a little *now*," I admitted winking. "I don't have time to be your puppy. My life is complicated, and I need money more than I need to get fucked."

"What if you could have both? Right now?" He asked, smirking.

I stopped dancing and smiled at him. "Just because I let you get me off doesn't make me a whore, least of all *your* whore. You want to know my name? Treat me like a woman you want instead of a bitch you can rut."

Domenico sat back in his seat like I had slapped him.

"Time's up. Thank you for your favor, guest," I stated and walked out of the room.

Charlie closed the door behind me and escorted me downstairs to the tunnels so that I could change for my next song.

"He didn't get handsy did he?" Charlie asked, when we were out of hearing distance of the VIP suites.

"That guy? No. He only got handsy with himself," I chuckled.

"Be careful with the VIPs in this place. These people smile and act polite in public, but.." he trailed off as we reached the dressing room. "Just be careful."

I was stunned for a moment but recovered and smiled appreciatively. "I will. Thank you."

By the end of the night, I had been requested for three different VIP rooms after Domenico. Despite wanting to look for the man that made me feel hot, I did my best to *not* look for him. I had finished my first night as an exotic dancer in one of Philly's more elite gentlemen's clubs.

I got dressed in a pair of dress pants and a nice shirt, and took my bag of tips out to the main floor to have it counted. Olga called me over to her and started running the bills through a counter like they have at the bank. When it was all said and done, I had just under three grand for one night before the club took its piece.

I counted out five hundred and passed it over to the accountant for my share, and then handed Olga another two hundred.

"What's this for?" She asked, looking at me like I had three heads.

"It's the tips from helping the servers. Split it up like you normally would," I explained.

Olga laughed. "Oh, sweetie. The servers keep their tips. We don't split that shit. You helped them do their job, that's your earned wage. Keep it," she said, pushing my hand of cash back.

"Seriously?" I asked.

"Seriously. Keep your money, sweetie," she assured me.

I couldn't help but smile. "Thank you."

"No. Thank you! You didn't have to help but you did, so.... Have a good night."

I didn't know what else to say, so I said thanks and started to leave.

I was almost to the door, when Charlie caught up with me.

"You need me to call you a car?" He asked.

"No. I'm good. I'm just a couple blocks down the road in the parking garage," I assured him.

"Alright, Lilith. See you again tonight?" Charlie asked, giving me a fist bump.

"See you tonight!" I promised, hitting my fist against his.

Chapter 19

The walk to the parking garage was quiet. There were a few people showing up to the bakeries on the opposite side of the street, who nodded at me as I passed. Infinity was nestled in one of the less seedy parts of the city, surrounded by everyday shops and cafes, completely unnoticed by most people.

Seeing me walking down the street with my bag, I looked like I was off to catch an early train or something, not coming from a club. By the time I reached the valet, they were just setting up for the day. I had been one of their last customers when I showed up the night before.

"I'm here to collect my car," I informed him, as I passed over my stub. "How much do I owe you?"

The guy pulled up his phone and calculated the costs. "That'll be-"

"Nothing," a man's voice echoed through the garage.

The valet and I turned to see Domenico walking up, his sleek black SUV idling not far away.

The poor guy holding my car keys looked like he was going to piss himself. "Yes, sir!" He said, and ran off to collect my car.

"Let me guess… He works for you?" I asked, squinting my

eyes at the man now standing in front of me.

"In a manner of speaking," he acknowledged.

"You don't need to pay for my parking just because you called me a whore," I stated.

"I'm covering your parking because I want to say that I am sorry for what I said. It came out all wrong. I wasn't trying to imply that you were a whore," he said softly, tipping my chin up to look at him.

"How else did you think that was going to come out?" I asked, looking into his eyes.

Domenico's eyes scanned my face, his fingers tucking a wisp of hair behind my ear. "Let me take you out on a real date, so you can decide if I am sincere or not."

Before I could answer my car arrived with a very frazzled looking valet. Domenico sighed and stepped back from me. I smiled politely as the valet passed me keys over and then made himself scarce again.

"I'm free on Tuesday night. I'll call you and we can maybe get together then," I offered.

"Tuesday it is. I'll see you then," Domenico agreed, smiling like he just won a prize.

I rolled my eyes, shook my head at him, and started moving toward my car.

"Wait!" He called out, grabbing my arm and spinning me to face him. Both hands came up to either side of my face, as his lips brushed mine.

His lips were soft and warm in the cold night air. He alternated sucking on my bottom then top lip, before deepening the kiss. I felt like my body was being lit on fire, the sensation spreading from my face down through the rest of my body. My hands held his waist as he stole my words of protest away.

When he pulled away, I was nearly breathless. His thumb gently caressed my lips, as he smiled at me. "I couldn't resist," he admitted softly. "I'll see you Tuesday."

I nodded and tucked my lips between my teeth. "Yeah, Tuesday. Good night."

This time I turned and scurried back to my car before he could tempt me further. The man knew how to make me want him. He was gorgeous to look at, and said all the right things to get my attention.

My internal energy, however, quickly depleted by the time I got to Nana's. I was exhausted and just wanted to sleep. I grabbed a quick shower and crawled into bed. Visions of Domenico rubbing his cock while I danced filled my head as I drifted off to sleep.

The alarm on my phone sounded and startled me from my slumber. I had set it for ten o'clock so that I would have time to run to the bank. They had limited hours on Saturdays, and only dealt with business deposits.

I dressed quickly in nice pants and a sweater with my hair pulled up into a bun. The banker's bag of cash was placed inside a tote bag, and out the door I went. Thankfully, I got into the bank just before the security guard closed the door to stop more customers from coming in.

The wait wasn't long before I was standing before a teller, and handing over my bag. I expected her to make a face, seeing the stacks of cash, but she just undid the banding and ran them through the counter.

"Do you want to deposit all of this into the primary account?" She asked once it had all been tallied up.

"Yes, please," I responded.

I stood patiently as she typed up the information into my account, and credited my account.

"Do you need a receipt?"

"Yes, please."

"Here you are. My name is Tracey, and this is my business card. I work every Saturday and Monday. If you have weekly deposits, I can handle them by appointment so that you don't have to wait next time," she said, winking at me.

I couldn't help but smile back at the woman. "Thank you, Tracey. I appreciate that. Should I just call the bank or?"

"You can call my direct number or email me, and I will get back to you within three hours with an appointment time," she assured me.

"Okay. Thank you," I replied again, placing the receipt, bag, and business card away in my tote. The security guard let me out and I was on my way to Titi's to check on Mami.

"So how did it go?" Jada asked, when we were alone in her room.

"I got a job," I said.

"You got a job? Or the one you went out for?" She countered.

I couldn't help but chuckle. "I got the job that I went out for."

"That's so awesome! Tell me about it! I want to hear everything!" She giggled, pulling me to sit beside her on the bed.

"It's night shift on weekends, pays really well, but no insurance," I answered.

"Shit. I hoped you could add Mami to your plan. My enrollment period doesn't open until March, so I can't add her to mine," Jada sighed, flopping onto her back.

"Well, my pay is really good, so we should be able to afford Mami's medical expenses regardless," I added, laying back next to her.

"Tace, I really hoped you had a hot date last night, I won't lie," Jada admitted.

"Sorry to disappoint. I'm just boring old me," I chuckled.

Jada laughed and threw a pillow onto my face. "Shut the hell up! Can't you pretend that you are living some double life? Give me something!"

I threw the pillow back onto her face. "Not today, J. Speaking of boring me, I have to get ready to head up to work!" I announced as I sat up again.

* * *

Saturday night had been a blur of activity in the club. While I only had a couple of songs on the main stage, I was requested for six VIP rooms, one of which was a bachelor party. To my surprise, I received an additional three grand at the end of the night, after the tips were counted out.

"What the hell is this for?" I asked, shocked that I would be walking out the door with almost four grand.

"You handled the bachelor party, that's fifteen from them, and the other fifteen is from the other five," Roman explained.

"That seems like too much. Are you sure?" I asked again, feeling almost giddy with the number. "I didn't get anything like this last night."

Roman looked at me confused for a minute before snapping his fingers at the man with the ledger. With the book slid in front of him, he quickly flipped back a few pages to read the previous night's transactions.

"You're absolutely right. My apologies," Roman said to me. "Arch, payout for last night's VIP rooms was balanced, but Lilith never received her money. Where is it?" He directed at one of the men counting cash on a table.

The bald man named Archie, nodded quickly. "I didn't know who that was, so I dropped it into the safe in an envelope with her name. You want me to go get it?" He asked, half standing from his seat.

"No. I'll go pull it," Roman directed at Archie before turning to me. "If you don't mind, we can go get your money from the safe."

"Sure, after you," I smiled and fell in step behind Roman.

When we reached his office, the smell of tobacco and something else permeated the air. Roman stopped short and turned back to face me, jaw clenched in irritation. "It would seem that I already have a guest. If you don't mind waiting out in the main lounge again, I will bring your stuff out when I am done with this visitor."

I didn't say another word and walked back to the main floor to wait. Seeing Olga done with the other girls' pay, I decided to help her clean up behind the bar. The club was closed on Sunday nights, so there wouldn't be a need to restock everything.

We had all of the glasses washed, and I had started wiping down the tables before Roman came back out with an envelope.

"Lilith, I'm sorry for the delay. Get out of here. I'll see you Wednesday," he said, passing me the envelope.

"Thanks. It wasn't a problem," I stated, taking the money. "Olga, let me know if you want help stocking on Wednesday.

I'll come in early," I said, returning the cleaning supplies I had to the cabinet behind the bar.

"You don't have to do that. I appreciate the thought. Go on now, and have a good night," she said, giving me a quick hug.

By the time I reached the parking garage I half expected to find Domenico waiting for me again. Fortunately or unfortunately, it was just the valet from the day before. He seemed nervous as hell to be dealing with me, and ran to collect my car as soon as I entered the garage.

With my coat pulled tight around me, I waited for his return in the quiet parking garage. The valet didn't come after five minutes. Another five minutes passed, and my car still hadn't shown up. An uneasy feeling started to settle in my stomach, and I made the decision to go back to the club.

I didn't just turn and walk away. I sprinted out of the building and ran the three blocks to Infinity. The door was locked but I knew someone would still be there, so I banged on the door.

The sound of screeching tires had every hair on my body standing on end. I had barely turned to see who was coming when the doors opened and I fell into the club.

"Holy shit, Lilith. Are you okay? You look like you just saw a ghost," Olga gasped, kneeling down to help me up from the floor.

"My car... Um.. My car wouldn't start," I stuttered, not sure what I was saying or why I felt like I needed to lie. "And I really need to pee," I blurted out.

"Uh, okay.. You know where the bathrooms are," Olga chuckled, as I scurried past her into the tunnels.

I slammed the bathroom door shut when I got there and let

out a long exhale. What was I running from? Why did I run? Nothing about what just happened made any sense to the logical side of my brain, but every instinct in me screamed that I needed to flee.

Dropping my bag on the counter, I turned on the faucet and splashed my face with cool water. My racing heart slowly calmed down. I grabbed my phone and messaged Cherry that I needed a place to crash. I wasn't going back for my car tonight, and I didn't want to call a cab to drive the thirty miles to Nana's. A soft knock at the door reminded me that I was probably holding up others from going home just as my phone pinged.

Expecting to see Olga when I opened the door, to my surprise, I found Roman staring back at me.

"Charlie offered to take you home, if you are comfortable with that," he offered, studying my face.

I held up my phone and smiled. "No need. I have a friend on her way to pick me up."

"You sure you're okay, Anastacia?" He whispered softly.

Nodding my head, I continued to smile. "Yeah. It was really cold, and I really had to pee," I giggled.

"Lilith! Your ride is here!" Olga called from the front of the house.

"See? No worries. I'll see you on Wednesday," I said, and walked away with my bag on my shoulder like nothing had happened.

Cherry grinned from ear to ear when she saw me and pulled me into a hug. "Oh my god, I have missed you so much!" She squealed. "Come on. Your room is just how you left it. I already told Spider we are doing brunch later."

Listening to Cherry prattle on and on about normal life

relaxed me. I waved goodbye to Olga and Charlie, and walked out the door with my girl talking my ear off. Cherry kept up the bubbly chatter all the way to the apartment I had once shared with her, Spider, and Lacey.

As soon as we were in the door, the facade fell from both of our faces. She grabbed me in a tight hug and just held me as my body shuddered.

"You're okay. I got you," she murmured.

Spider came out of my old room a second later and joined the group hug. "She okay?" she asked Cherry.

"Yeah. Just a bad scare this time," Cherry acknowledged.

"Car?" Spider asked.

"Yeah."

"Shit."

"What are you two talking about?" I asked, though my voice was muffled by their two bodies.

"You got spooked, Taze. It's happened to all of us," Cherry said, rubbing my back.

"I wasn't-"

"Remember when your car died halfway back from the club our first week?" Spider asked, turning on the radio.

Cherry nodded laughing. My bag was thrown onto the sofa, and I was ushered into Cherry's room. Once the door was closed, her entire demeanor changed.

"Who the fuck did you piss off?" She asked suddenly.

My eyes turned wide as saucers. "I don't know, Cher. I don't know what I did," I whispered shakily.

Cherry eyed me for a second before pulling me back into a hug. "You were smart to go back to the club. Did you see anything? Anything that stood out in your mind at all?" She asked.

I shook my head. "No. I mean I only started there two days ago. What the fuck do I know about what's normal or not? What happened? Like, you weren't even there, but you seem like you know something," I accused, pulling back and sitting on her bed.

"There are whisperings that some of the big shots in the city are getting restless. I don't know anything specific, just what customers talk about in the VIP rooms when they think it's safe."

"What does that have to do with me?" I asked, not seeing the connection.

"Why were you so late leaving the club?" Cherry asked. "The dancers should have cleared out by three, but you were there until almost four."

I shook my head a second trying to recall why I had left so much later. "I didn't have all of my money. Roman went to get his from his office, but there was someone there… So I waited," I explained.

"Wait. Roman? Why was Roman at Infinity?" Cherry asked, arching an eyebrow.

"Because he owns it?" I replied, confused.

Cherry's face paled immediately. "Jesus Christ. They thought you were close to Roman, Taze. You leaving so much later, they probably thought you were special to him. Do yourself a favor and don't let him near you. Don't be civil. Just keep away from him, okay?"

My head bobbed up and down like a bobble head. Stay away from Roman. Not a problem. "What about my car?" I asked.

"It'll be in a chop shop before lunch. Is there anyone you can call to get you home? Someone you trust?" She asked, looking a little less worried now.

I couldn't think of anyone at first. Then a face appeared in my mind. "Yeah. I know someone I can call."

Two hours later I was standing outside of Cherry and Spider's building when a sleek black SUV pulled up out front. I didn't hesitate to walk out the door and climb into the passenger seat, the vehicle pulling away before I even had my seatbelt buckled.

"I didn't think you'd call," Domenico stated, not taking his eyes off the road.

"I didn't think you'd come," I responded, turning to face him.

"What happened to Tuesday? You get too antsy to wait?" He asked, glancing at me from the corner of his eye.

"My car was stolen. I was really freaked out, and I didn't know who else to call," I explained.

This time he turned to look at me. "When was your car stolen?"

"This morning. I went to the garage after shift, but my car was stolen. So I ran back to the club and had a friend swing by and get me. That's where you picked me up," I explained.

"Why didn't you call me from the club? I'd have come and got you."

"Honestly?" I asked. "She was on speed dial. We were roommates for almost a year, and her number was on the top when I hit *call*."

"Put my number on the top for next time," he replied, turning down a road I didn't recognize.

"Where are you going? I don't know this way," I commented, feeling like I left the frying pan only to jump into a fire.

"I'm taking you to get a new car."

My jaw fell open. "Wait. What? Domenico, I can't afford a new car."

He looked at me and chuckled. "Relax. It's just the car rental place by the airport. Your insurance will pick up the bill. You call the police yet?"

I shook my head, looking out the window. "No. I didn't know what to say. I think my car was stolen and I got chased after work?" I snorted, realizing how insane it sounded hearing it out loud.

Domenico suddenly jerked the steering wheel and slammed on the brakes, abruptly stopping on the shoulder of the road. "What the fuck do you mean you were chased?"

My body, having lunged forward against the seatbelt, suddenly slammed back into the seat's back, knocking the breath out of me. I coughed hard, trying to get my breath back.

"What the fuck?" I demanded.

Domenico ripped off his seatbelt and unfastened mine before I could get a second word in. His hands wrapped around my waist and pulled me into his lap before embracing my tightly.

"Domenico?" I whispered, unsure what was happening.

"I'm so sorry. Tell me everything that happened," he whispered against my hair.

I sat there on his lap, cradled against his chest, and told him everything I could remember. From the VIPs who had come in to not getting all of my money, and how Roman asked me to wait while he dealt with a visitor. I described the way the valet reacted when he saw me, and what made me run back to the club.

301

Saying it all out loud, I couldn't think of a single thing that should have made me bolt the way I did. Outwardly, there was nothing scary or any warnings that should have triggered for me. Yet…. I ran for my life just the same.

Domenico grabbed his phone and made a call. I didn't know who he was calling, and I didn't ask..

"*Yes?*" A man's voice answered

"You have a leak. Find it and fix it. My apartment is soaked."

"*Do you know which room the pipe may have burst in?*"

"I'm not a fucking plumber, but when shit smells bad it's usually a fucking leak," Domenico seethed into the phone.

"*Ah. Yes. That must be the main line. I'll take care of it today. I'll make sure that restitution is paid for any damages. Just send it through the insurance.*"

The call disconnected, the conversation short and to the point. Domenico was angry, his fist clenching as he tossed his phone onto my seat.

"What kind of car do you want? The insurance company is going to total your car," he asked, his demeanor softening as he looked down at me.

"It wasn't worth that much," I started, but was promptly shushed.

"What do you want?"

"Honestly? I want something that won't kill my wallet driving back and forth from Philly in," I admitted.

"Why do you have to leave the city to go home?" He countered, relaxing his hold on me.

"It's complicated," I stated.

"We've got time," he countered.

I looked around nervously, because he had just pulled over

302

to the side of the road suddenly. "Shouldn't you get back on the road? What if a cop comes up to ask why you stopped?"

"We'll be alright," he chuckled. "What's so complicated that you can't tell me?" He asked again.

Before a word could leave my mouth my stomach grumbled loudly. I felt my face heat up with embarrassment, and bit my lip to keep from saying anything.

"Why didn't you say you were hungry?" He laughed, giving me a light peck on my forehead. "Get back in your seat. Let me take you to get some food, then we'll get your car situation sorted. Deal?"

I nodded and scurried back into my seat. Domenico and I buckled our seat belts as my stomach complained again.

"I'm on it. I'm on it," Domenico laughed, pulling back onto the road.

We stopped at a small diner on the outskirts of town and found a booth in the back of the restaurant. The waitress, an older woman named Agnes, wanted to chat us up about the weather and lament about the lack of snow so close to Christmas.

I thought she was cute, but he seemed annoyed when she wouldn't stop talking to us. When she walked away, I kicked him under the table.

"Hey! What was that for?" He asked.

'Be nice,' I mouthed, causing him to scowl at me.

It didn't take long before our table was filled with hot pancakes, eggs, toast, bacon, sausage, and scrapple. I couldn't wait to tuck into my own plate, and moaned when the combination of buttery, sweet and savory melted in my mouth.

Domenico watched me eat before taking a bite of his own

303

meal. "Keep making those noises, and it's going to get really awkward when we leave here," he muttered, taking another bite of his pancakes.

I was mid moan eating my bacon and nearly choked, my face heating up immediately. My eyes diverted to my food, unable to make eye contact after that. *This man...*

When all of the plates were finally cleared, I felt like I could sleep for a year. My tummy was full, and all of the endorphins and adrenaline had seeped away sitting with the man across the table.

"That was sweet of you," I whispered, leaning into him as we walked out to the car.

"What was?" He asked, looking down at me tucked under his arm.

"Leaving such a lovely tip for Agnes."

Domenico responded by rolling his eyes, which only made me laugh. He walked me to my side, and opened the door for me. As soon as I was seated, he reached across my body to buckle the seatbelt. I couldn't help but suck in a breath when his face was suddenly so close to mine. Just when I thought he would kiss me, he flicked my nose instead.

"Stop overthinking," he chuckled.

My face immediately warmed up again. I stared out the window as he climbed into the driver's seat, too embarrassed to look at him. As we pulled back onto the main roads toward the airport, I felt myself drifting off.

"Alright, *Lilith.* Tell me about these complications," Domenico asked, but I was too tired to respond.

I woke up feeling warm and well rested. Stretching my body, I realized that I was in a bed. A bed with silky sheets and a body next to mine.

Confused and panicked, I threw off the covers to inspect my body and see who the hell was lying next to me.

"You're awake?" a husky voice, laden with sleep asked.

Suddenly a light switched on next to the bed. Domenico leaned back against the headboard dressed in a pair of trainers and a t-shirt. I looked down to see that other than my pants coming off, none of my clothes had been touched.

"I didn't take your pants off. They were on when I tucked you in," he informed me, taking in the sight of my bare legs.

I squeaked and jumped back under the blankets, finding my pants kicked down to the foot of the bed. "Where am I?" I asked him, trying to redress my lower half under the blanket.

"You fell asleep after we ate, and I didn't know where to take you, so you're at my place."

"I was really tired," I admitted, giggling.

"Are you rested now?" He asked, turning to face me. I nodded, realizing that he had been on top of the blankets the entire time.

"Do you need to eat again? Or can you talk?" He questioned me, causing me to giggle again.

"I need to pee, and then we can talk," I admitted, biting my bottom lip.

Domenico just pointed at a door and I ran to it. The bathroom was like something out of a catalog. Slate flooring, white marble countertops… Double sinks. It was the bathroom of my dreams. I admired everything while I did my business, noticing the separate rainfall shower and enormous soaking tub.

I washed my face and hands before returning to the bedroom and sitting on the end of the bed. "Okay. What do

305

you want to know?" I offered.

"Name."

"Anastacia."

"Complications?"

"Where do you want to start? There's a few."

"Single?"

"Maybe, I'm not sure."

"How are you not sure?" He asked, looking annoyed.

"I just met someone, and I don't know where it's going yet. We've only been out a couple of times," I admitted, smirking at him.

"That doesn't count as anything," he retorted.

"Then you can take me home now," I responded, no longer smiling.

This time he looked confused. "What just happened?" He asked.

"'I'm an idiot' is what happened. Take me home, or I can call an uber," I demanded, getting off the bed. Before I could take two steps he was behind me and pulling me back towards him.

"What just happened?" He asked again.

"This means nothing, so I am not wasting my time here, Domenico," I said quietly, feeling like I was a damn yo-yo. Hot to cold, something to nothing to being held again.

He was quiet for a few seconds before chuckling. "Wait, were you talking about this? *Us?*" He asked, turning me to face him.

"Who else would I be talking about?" I asked, poking him in the chest.

"Ok, let's rewind this a bit. You single?" He asked again, smirking down at me.

"I'm not sure, to be honest. I met someone but I don't know where it's going yet. We've only been out a couple of times," I said again, shrugging my shoulders like I didn't care.

"Hmmm. That's a tough one," he commented, looking very serious. "Tell me about these couple of encounters, and maybe I can help you decide."

I tried not to smirk and rolled my eyes. "We met up at a club the first time, had a few drinks and danced together."

"And the second time?" He asked, wrapping his arms around my waist.

"The second time… He surprised me after work and kissed me," I whispered.

"That's it? That's tough. Any other encounters?" He asked, leaning down and gently kissing my neck.

"One other," I gasped, feeling my toes starting to curl from the barest of attention on my body.

"Tell me," he ordered, pulling my shirt slightly so that his mouth could reach my shoulders.

"My car was stolen, and he came when I called," I panted, as his hands began roaming my body.

"That sounds a lot more serious than *maybe*. He's into you," he whispered in my ear, nibbling my lobe.

"H-how do I know?" I asked as my hands snaked up around his neck so that my fingers could thread into his thick dark locks again.

"Trust me. He's into you, Anastacia," he growled, turning and throwing me onto the bed.

"Say it again."

"He's into you, Anastacia," he said, leaning over my body.

"I'm sober."

"I'm also sober," Domenico retorted, pecking my lips gently.

"What are you saying?"

"Show me. Show me how much he's into me," I whispered back.

"Fuuuck," he swore just before his mouth crashed into mine in a demanding kiss.

Chapter 20

The clothing that I had rustled onto my body when I woke up, was now being pulled off. My hands were under his shirt pulling it over his head and tossing it to the floor. His mouth trailed kisses down every newly exposed piece of skin on my body, but I wanted his lips on mine. Grabbing his hair, I turned his head back to face me and crashed my lips into his.

"Domenico," I whimpered, when his mouth returned to my collar bone, my blouse ripped open and sent buttons flying across the room.

"What do you want?" He whispered, slowing his movements, pulling my hands from wandering down his body.

"You," came my response.

Everything seemed to slow down. Domenico slid back off of the bed, and took my pants down my legs with him. I lay on my back in nothing but my bra and panties.

"You are so beautiful, dolce," he murmured, leaning forward to kiss the inside of my thighs. He continued up my body crawling onto the bed until he knelt between my legs again. Hands caressed my sides, my breasts, his mouth following behind with soft kisses.

I wanted him to feel as beautiful as I did. Wrapping my arms around his neck, I pulled his body down to mine, kissing and sucking his throat. A chuckle escaped my lips when I bit his collarbone, and he hissed.

His head dipped as he pulled one of my breasts out of my bra and began to flick his tongue over my nipple, causing it to pebble up and a shudder to run through my body. I had worked his pants down to mid thigh, and reached between our bodies and took his length into my hands. A soft grunt left his lips as I stroked the silkiness of his cock in my hands.

I lifted my ass when his fingers hooked into my panties to pull them down. I didn't see where they went, and I didn't care. All of my attention was focused on the man in my arms, making my heart race and my body combust with every touch of his fingers on my skin. Without needing to say anything, he reached over to the nightstand and pulled a condom out of the drawer. I bit my lip, watching as the latex rolled down his length. His dick wasn't perfectly straight and arched up.

My mind was racing with what he would feel like. He leaned over my body, arms braced on either side of my head. I reached between us and guided him just where I wanted him. Neither of us needed to say anything further. The rest of the night was filled with soft moans and heated passion. Domenico didn't let me go until just before the sun came up again. By the time I fell asleep, I felt drugged.

When I finally made it back to Nana's on Monday morning, I was deliciously sore all over my body. Domenico had been relentless, twisting and turning my body to find new positions, eliciting new reactions from me, swearing each time was the last time.

There wasn't a single inch of my body that he had not kissed, sucked, or touched. I didn't know if it was the sexual tension of denying him when we met, or just the right compatibility at the right time... But my toes curled just thinking about it.

"What happened to your car?" Pops asked, looking at the rental I had parked in front of the house.

"It broke down," I lied.

"Wasn't it new?" He asked.

"It was. The insurance is taking care of everything," I said, walking up to my room. I was wearing a pair of training pants borrowed from Domenico's closet along with one of his oversized sweatshirts. Looking at the clock, I had just enough time to shower, change, get to the bank for my deposit, and then head to Titi's.

I had more than enough money to pay for Mami's meds this month, and possibly find a place for myself in a nice area. While I loved living with the girls in Philly, I needed to find my own place and learn to live on my own for a change.

"What happened to your car?" Nana asked as I came back down, dressed in a flowing pair of pants and a cashmere sweater.

"Broke down," Pops informed her.

"Next time buy domestic," she encouraged me.

"We'll see what the insurance says," I smirked. The car I had was what I could afford. It had been mine and mine alone, the choice made based on the funds I had at the time.

My next car would obviously be much nicer, given the increase in my monthly capital. I could afford to buy a higher end SUV or another sedan if I wanted. I had options from here on.

"I am running to the bank, and then I'll be spending the next two days with Mami," I informed them, giving each a

311

quick peck on the cheek before running out the door.

"Okay. Give her our love. We'll be by tomorrow for dinner like usual," Nana reminded me.

I yelled a 'love you' over my shoulder and scurried out the door.

Tracey was waiting for me as I rushed into the bank with my bag in hand. "There you are," she greeted me.

"I'm sorry. I hope I'm not late," I apologized, checking the time on my phone. It was exactly 10:45, my appointment time.

"You're right on time. Let's get you sorted so that you can get back to work."

Leading the way through the bank's main foyer, she walked into a smaller cubicle office rather than back to the front counter. On the desk was the usual counter and a safe deposit chute on one wall. Noticing me eyeing the change of scenery, Tracey smiled.

"These are the small business offices. They're considered safer than handling large amounts of cash at the customer counters," she explained.

I just nodded, unlocked my bag and set my cash on the table. I didn't know how much was in the envelope from the first night, so I was shocked when Tracey gave me a receipt for nearly six thousand dollars.

"Do you want me to recount it? Are the numbers off?" She asked.

"Um, no. The last envelope was a late bonus. I hadn't even counted it before coming here. Sorry," I apologized, feeling my face heat up.

"Ok, do you need anything else today?" Tracey asked.

"I'm not sure. Could I make an appointment to talk about

investing or saving money so that it gets better interest?" I asked.

Tracey perked right up with another gigawatt smile. "Absolutely! I would be happy to assist you with that. Just let me know what times you have available and we can schedule accordingly."

"Mondays and Tuesdays work best for me," I replied.

"Ok. I will send that in to our investment services and they will contact you in the next two days with your appointment date and time. Did you want to keep the same appointment on Mondays for your deposits? I can try to find a time that you can come and get both done on the same day," she offered, typing quickly on a small laptop.

"Yes, please. Thank you."

"Alright, Miss Martinez. You are all set to go," Tracey said, handing me my receipt and appointment reminder card for my weekly deposit the following Monday.

I glanced quickly at the piece of paper before I shoved the receipt into my bag. There were too many things to get in order today, so I went straight to the pharmacy to pick up Mami's medications. Three thousand dollars. It cost three thousand dollars to fill all of her prescriptions this time. The difference between being insured and neglected was astounding to me.

"Where have you been hiding all weekend?" Titi asked, giving me a hug as I walked in the door.

I smirked and handed her the bag of meds after she released me. "I got a job up in Philly, so I was able to refill Mami's meds," I stated, taking off my coat.

"It's not illegal right?" She asked, arching an eyebrow.

"No, it's not illegal," I chuckled.

"The hospice is sending out their doctor to check on your mother. He should be here soon," she informed me, heading back to the kitchen to fetch two coffee cups.

"What does that mean? Did something happen?" I asked, following behind her.

Titi wouldn't look at me at first. "She's not doing as well as we hoped. This weekend... It was a rough one, Tace," she admitted.

I felt like I had been punched in the gut. "Why didn't anyone call me?" I accused, rushing up the stairs to check on Mami. I had been gone for two days. How had she gotten so much worse in just the two days that I was gone?

Bursting into the room, I found my grandparents, aunts, and Jada seated around Mami's bed. Mami looked even thinner than the last time I had seen her. Her eyes were glassy when she glanced in my direction, and it was like she didn't even see *me*.

Why hadn't they called me? Why hadn't Jada called me? Why didn't my grandparents say anything when I saw them this morning?

"Why didn't you call?" I asked, directing my question at my sister.

"I knew you were starting a new job. We had things under control here," she replied, moving to pull me into a hug. "No one is upset with you, Tace. She's still here. It was just a rough weekend is all. It happened before, and it won't be the last rough weekend," she softly assured me, rubbing my back.

Aunt Maria moved from Mami's bedside so that I could sit with her. "Hi, Mami," I whispered against her temple, leaving a light kiss on her skin.

"Tay," she whispered softly back.

"Yeah. It's me. How are you feeling today?" I asked, rubbing my hands down her arms to check her temperature.

"Fine. Fine. Your brother was here earlier. He said you were coming," she informed me.

I stared wide eyed at my aunts and sister. Since when did I have a brother? Bruja shook her head at me to say that this was not the right time. I bit my cheek to keep my peace.

"Oh, yeah?" I directed back to mami instead, sitting beside her on the bed. "How is he doing?"

"Good. He said he has a room for me. I should stay with him for a while," she whispered, before falling back to sleep.

I stared at my family, tears brimming in my eyes. *'What the fuck?'* I mouthed at them. Since when did I have a brother and why hadn't anyone told me that he had been here?

My grandparents couldn't even make eye contact with me, staring at their clasped hands beside their daughter. Aunt Maria and Bruja looked like someone had smacked them both, their faces flushed and moist with tears. Jada was the only person who looked just as shocked as me.

There were so many questions to ask, but I didn't even know where to start. I opened my mouth to begin, and a tall man walked into the room with Titi trailing behind him.

"This is?" I asked, half expecting *him* to be my unknown brother.

"I'm Doctor Anderson with the hospice care team. I usually don't get seen until it's near the end. I'm sorry for intruding." He spoke so politely that I had nearly forgotten the confession from a moment ago, replaying his words over and over.

"The end of what?" I asked, not understanding the words.

He looked to my aunts for assistance, but they looked just as lost as he did for how to respond. Nana finally came around the bed and held my hand.

"It's nearly time, Anastacia. She's dying, sweetie," she said in a choked staccato of words.

"I know that. She has cancer-"

"She's dying, Anastacia," Bruja repeated.

"I know-"

"No, Tace. They mean today," Jada stated, tears streaming down her face.

I stared at them in disbelief. I had only been gone for two days. "What did you do to her?" I accused Maria. "She was fine on Friday. She was talking and she was fine. What did you do?"

I sat with her through the night. I refused to leave her side. My sister made me a small cup of chamomile tea, but after a few sips it sat to get cold on a small side table. I just wanted to see her open her eyes and look at me, to know that this was a choice she was making.

I wanted... No, I needed her to look at me, to see her daughter, and still give up living. Her eyelids would flutter open and closed, but she wasn't there. Her eyes were glazed over from the morphine patches on her body.

One by one, our family took their turn to sit opposite of me, and say their prayers for my mother. Soft murmurs of cherished memories, and old grudges they were letting go of... *For her.* We didn't talk to one another. No one spoke a word to me, only murmuring gentle words of love and support for Mami.

Just before midnight, she just stopped breathing. Jada tried to resuscitate her, but Maria and Pops held her back. I stood there in shock, still holding her hand as my sister fell apart, and my grandparents cried in each other's arms.

My mother, a sister, a daughter, was gone from us, just like that. I barely had any time with her.

"It's okay, sobrina. She's in a better place. She's not in pain," Titi whispered softly to me, holding me up.

I knew I was crying, but my body felt numb. How had it come to this? How was it that I suddenly had no mother? I kept waiting for her to open her eyes and talk to me, to laugh and say that she was just joking, but there was nothing.

Her body was so still and cold beneath my hands. The room filled with family, medical equipment, and furniture suddenly felt.... *Empty.*

I didn't know how I managed to call the doctor or any of the other phone calls that I made into the wee hours of the morning. The police were notified once the doctor confirmed that she had passed. Her official time of death confirmed two hours after she breathed her last breath. We didn't need an autopsy to determine a cause of death, so the police were fine with us turning her body over to the funeral home.

Her body.

Her remains.

"My mother," I corrected the woman at the funeral home that afternoon, as we sat to make the final arrangements.

"I'm sorry. *Your mother,*" the coordinator apologized, continuing through the process.

I didn't sleep that night or the next night either. I was days without sleep, but I couldn't stop to think about what my body needed. My mother had entrusted me to take care of her until the end. I called every company she had accounts with and notified them of her death.

Jada had already reconciled most of them when she moved Mami to Titi's, but there were still the banks to deal with. It wasn't much, but a few credit cards and two empty accounts. My sister and I had no joint accounts with Mami, so the debts our mother had accrued went unpaid after her death. They would never see a penny of it. I laughed when one of the creditors stated that a lien would be put against her estate for restitution of the balance.

"What money do you think she had?" I asked, delirious from the lack of food and sleep, and excessive coffee intake.

"It doesn't matter, I'll make sure it is found-" the man on the other end of the line started, but I cut him off.

"My mother died of cancer. Her entire body was *eaten away* by the disease, and you are threatening *me for money?* THERE'S NO FUCKING MONEY, ASSHOLE! YOU WANNA KNOW WHY? CAUSE SHE FUCKED UP AND LIVED TOO LONG!" I screamed at the end.

Suddenly, the phone was ripped out of my hands and I was pulled into a hug. I couldn't hear what they were saying after that. My body shut down as day four without Mami came to a sudden end.

* * *

The funeral was somber but the outpouring of love from family and friends would have made her smile. There were so many people she had helped over the years, whether it was ten dollars to get fuel, food for a house full of kids, or taking the time to help people get through the systems they needed to get through to get clean, get help, back on their feet, or just a clean break from toxic shit.

My mother had helped so many people, in spite of all the shit it subjected us to because of her efforts. She never lost her faith in people or the system's mechanisms to do what was right and take care of people.

I hated her for it.

I hated myself for thinking it.

It was selfish. *I was selfish.*

Standing there listening to so many random people praise the great things she did; I wished that my mother had loved and supported my sister and I, the way she apparently cared for and supported absolute fucking strangers.

"I can't do this," I whispered, feeling my face dripping in cold sweat. My body was shaking with rage and grief, and I wanted to scream at my mother.

"Eat this," Maria whispered, passing me a piece of candy.

I popped into my mouth without even thinking about it. There was a bitter astringent flavor with something akin to orange and chocolate. I almost spit it back out, but Maria slapped her hand over my mouth.

"Chew it up and swallow it," she whispered, pulling me out of the receiving line of the church.

"It's fucking gross," I whined, looking for a trash can.

"It's a gummi. Just swallow the damn thing."

Reluctantly, I did as I was told and swallowed the vile candy. "I can't do this," I whispered looking at the line of people still waiting to come into the church.

"What can't you do, Anastacia?" Maria asked, sizing me up.

"I can't stand in front of all those people and claim how amazing my mother was. Who she was to them is not who she was to me, Tia. It's a fucking lie," I explained, shaking my head.

To my aunt's credit, she looked just as lost as I felt. "Thank, Christ," she muttered, before remembering where we were and quickly crossing herself and whispering an apology to the Lord. "I thought it was just me."

I stared in wide eyed disbelief at my aunt. First because she swore in a church, which was just so uncharacteristic of her.

Secondly... Because she was radiating light.

Like she was an angel glowing in the soft golden light of God. "You're so beautiful," I whispered breathlessly, my eyes watering in awe at this unexpected revelation.

Maria looked at me and smiled, and my knees buckled. I had never seen anything so beautiful in my life.

"Did she eat it?" Another angel approached, smiling down on me.

"Yep, she did," Maria responded, still radiating her heavenly grace.

"Thank God for small mercies. Let's get her into a pew before anyone else notices," the angel whispered before turning their shining light unto me.

I couldn't stop the smile from spreading across my own face.

"How much did you give her? *She's high as fuck,*" a third angel whispered before taking me into their arms.

"I smashed three together," Maria whispered to the other two.

"Hay dios!" Bruja whispered loudly. "Venga, Stacia. Sit with me."

I followed obediently and sat down compliantly. My eyes

wandered around the interior of the church and basked in the shining colors emanating from the love and adoration of the people sitting in the pews.

"How come you aren't an angel?" I asked, looking at Bruja.

"Just sit and enjoy the colors, amor."

Jada spoke for both of us about the woman we knew and the life that ended too soon. When I finally came down from the edibles, Mami was buried in the ground and we were accepting visitors at my grandparents' house.

Maria walked by and passed me another gummi. I swallowed it whole without batting an eye. I wanted to feel *love* more than the loss and grief.

I had no idea what time everyone left, or how long it took to clean everything up. I passed out long before that, tucked under piles of blankets on a guest bed, crying in my sister's arms.

"Hey, Lilith. I'm sorry to hear about your mom," Rene whispered quietly, pulling me into a hug.

I had been gone for two weeks, and now I wanted to make it all go away. I wanted to be Lilith for the night, and let Anastacia mourn in a dark corner of my mind.

"Thank you."

"You're sure you want to do this tonight?" She asked, looking me over.

I said yes, but shook my head no. "I just need a break from everything, and that's always been work for me. I just don't want to feel all of the sadness and be reminded of everything. Does that make sense?"

Rene nodded. "Yeah. Yeah, it does. What are you feeling like tonight?" She asked, pulling up her music list.

"Something that will make me feel colors," I responded

before walking off to the dressing room.

When I arrived at my station there was a gift bag sitting on the table. I opened it and found a delicate one piece bodysuit from La Perla. The piece was nude with faint cream colored lace to cover my most essential bits. I knew from living with Lacey that it wasn't a cheap garment, and looked around the room to the other women getting ready for the night.

"Did someone leave this on my vanity by mistake?" I asked, holding up the bag.

"No, that was left for you," one of the women responded with a smirk.

I looked into the bag and found a small card tucked inside. *'I've missed seeing you. Wear this for me.'*

I had no idea who would have missed seeing me in this club, but it was just the right kind of distraction I needed to get my mind off of my life. I changed into the one piece and matched it with a pair of nude heels in my bag.

By the time I had finished with my make-up, Rene sent me a message letting me know that I had twenty minutes before my first solo up on the main stage. Flipping my hair over my shoulder I strutted out of the dressing room and into the club. The black out lights near the bar made the lace seem like a vibrant paint against my skin, whereas the nude mesh of the body piece disappeared completely.

I did my part and sashayed between the guests and smiled politely. Inside I was a wash of conflicting emotions. My mother never knew that I was dancing to pay for her medical bills. My family was comforted that she died in comfort because of the cash I brought to the table. They didn't ask questions.

Now I had no one to tell me about my life choices. No

one to judge where my money came from or how I spent it. There was no one to worry about my love life, and whether I would settle down. I was and would be whatever I wanted to be, and no one could say a word.

"Lilith!" Olga called from behind the bar.

I smiled and moved to meet her as she stepped out from behind the bar. "Please, don't give me the *'sorry about your loss,'* talk. I don't want to cry at work," I whispered so that only she could hear me.

"I won't do that to you. Rene said you needed a pick me up," she explained, grabbing my hand and pulling me behind the bar.

She handed me a shot glass and a small pill. "Bottoms up," she cheered, tipping back her own drink. I didn't know what the pill was, but the drink was nothing more than seltzer water. "You have five minutes and then you are going to see music and feel colors. Enjoy the break," she whispered, turning me back toward the stage.

I didn't need five minutes.

Fuck this felt good.

"Now coming to the stage is Lilith!" Rene announced, as the music began to change up.

As I stepped onto the stage the strumming beat of a bass began. *'The boy I love's got another girl... He might be fuckin' her right now.'*

My hand grasped the pole as I strutted behind it, stepping out with exaggerated kicks to accentuate my ass. *'I don't have an apartment,'* I locked eyes with Rene as I began to spin around the pole, my leg tucking the pole behind my knee as I spun.

'Thought if I was smart, I'd make it far.... But I'm still at the

start.'

As the lyrics of the song continued my mind flooded with everything that I had been through in my life. Images of the carjacking gone wrong. The rape. The look on the DA's face when she let me down. The look on my mother's face when I finally confronted her. The feelings I had every time people fucked me over, let me down, and used me.

t's too quiet in this room.... I need noise!'

My body lowered to the floor as I raised one long heeled leg against the pole. Whatever Olga had given me was fucking magical.

When the vocalist sang, *'I need the buzz of a sub. Need the crack of a whip. Need some blood in the cut,'* I felt it in my bones.

My body rotated around the pole as I came up on to my knees with the chorus. My back arched out from the pole, and I rolled my hips. *'I need noise. I need the buzz of a sub.'*

Chapter 21

"Oh my god! I love this song!" Olga cheered, turning up the volume on the speakers.

"YOU MAKE ME FEEL LIKE A NATURAL WOMAN!" We all sang loudly.

Tonight was our monthly girls' night. It was the only time I got to spend with Spider, Elektra, Cherry *and* the few friends I made working at Infinity. Olga and I had clicked from the beginning, and Charity decided she liked me after I had put several women in their places.

"Puck and pass, bitches!" Charity called out, sliding a small round canister down the table.

Cherry stopped it, took out a pill and passed the tin around the table. I didn't hesitate to pop a pill into my own mouth and swallow it down. Spider stared at me in shock.

"When did you start popping Molly, little girl?" She asked, popping a pill into her own mouth.

Olga laughed. "This one likes to taste colors and see music."

The music changed and then so did the conversation topic, much to my amusement. "Are we going out or what?" Elektra asked.

"Fuck it! Let's go have some fun on the town," Cherry agreed.

We were all half drunk and high as fuck by the time the car service arrived to take us to the clubs.

"Where to, ladies?" The driver asked once we were all in.

Olga gave him the name of a club and we were off. The car was filled with our cackling laughter, and indecent innuendos the entire trip. By the time we stumbled out of the car, I felt like I was floating on cloud nine. Walking into the club, we commanded a bit of attention.

"Drinks?" Spider asked.

"Shots," Charity confirmed, and we made our way to the bar.

The bartender recognized Olga and served us immediately, leaning over the bar to give her a quick kiss on each cheek.

We downed our shots and then strutted onto the dance floor. Hands up, hips rolling, my body moved of its own accord to the music vibrating through my bones. I felt my phone vibrating in my bag, but I couldn't be fucked to answer it now.

"He's here," Charity whispered, pulling me against her body and dancing with me.

My eyes scanned the room until they landed on the man she was referring to. I didn't know what to call us.

We went out. He said all of the right things, filling my head with all of the words I wanted to hear from a man. We fucked, and he worshipped me like I was a goddess. But it wasn't all there. I always felt like I was missing something. Mami would say that it was my gut telling me to walk away, but my heart and pussy were all in with this man.

I let my eyes continue to scan the room, realizing he hadn't seen me yet. Olga passed me another shot glass and I downed it, prepared to ditch my girls to go home with him. I had taken two steps forward, when I stopped dead in my tracks as his arms encircled another woman's waist. I watched her giggle and flirt as he whispered something in her ear.

"I'm done here," I said and started for the door. Charity glanced quickly and saw what I had also seen.

"Fuck him! We were here first!" She shouted over the music.

Why the fuck was I going to run and hide? I didn't do shit wrong. He was the one fucking around on me. I strutted through the crowd until I reached him. I didn't hesitate to rip the other woman off of him and push him back against the bar.

He started to say something, but stared wide-eyed when he realized it was me.

"She's cute. Does she know that taste on your lips is my cunt?" I asked loud enough for the girl to hear.

She started to say something, but I turned to stare her down. "Say something and we're going to kick off. You didn't know he was with someone, so I'm gonna forgive you. Now walk the fuck away," I stated, smiling like we were best friends.

No sooner had she walked away, I turned and smacked Domenico across the face. "You're fucking disgusting," I seethed before turning to leave.

He grabbed my arm before I could get away and yanked me back. As my body slammed into his, my arm was twisted up behind my back with one hand while the other grabbed me by the hair. I winced from the screaming pain in my shoulder combined with the tight fistful of my hair he held.

From a distance, he probably looked like he was pulling me into a tight embrace. His head lowered so that our faces were nearly touching. "So you can show any fucking man with money what's mine, but I'm the one who's fucking disgusting?" He asked.

"They don't touch what's yours," I growled back.

"You're still letting other men fucking see your body, Anastacia," he seethed.

"At least I'm not fucking them, Domenico. Now let me go before I really fucking embarass you," I threatened as my girls started to move closer to us.

"This isn't over," he stated.

"Oh, this is fucking over," I barked back, stumbling back-wards when he suddenly released me.

"You good, Taze?" Spider asked, as she caught me.

"I'll be fine. Let's go get fucked," I replied, smirking at Domenico's pissed off expression as we walked away. As soon as we were out the door my phone buzzed again inside my bag. Thinking it was probably Domenico, I ignored it.

By the time we were in the car again, my desire to go out had waned significantly. Seeing him with another woman had ruined my mood in ways I had not expected. It wasn't even that he wasn't apologetic, but the fact that he tried to make it about me. He knew what I did before we started seeing each other.

"Where to, ladies?" Our driver inquired as we pulled away.

"Any recommendations," Charity asked, leaning over the seat toward the man.

"There's a place on the other side of town. Not quite as high end, but you'd have fun," he offered.

I rolled my eyes. The only places on the other side of town were dives that tourists got roped into to get ripped off. My phone buzzed again inside my bag, and I ignored it. I only had to look at Cherry and Spider for them to shut down whatever thoughts the driver had. Both offered a different location, but places we frequented.

The others weighed in, and we chose a club further down the road. By the time we got inside, my high had come crashing down and I was not feeling it any more. Olga and Spider went straight to the bar to order our round of drinks while the rest of us occupied a table. It wasn't so much that we had found an open one, but that we moved in with our numbers and quickly took one over.

"What was that about?" Elektra asked, sidling up close to me.

"A situation that I had misread," I commented.

"Did he not have the same understanding of said situation?" She asked, her voice just loud enough that only I could hear her over the music ringing in our ears.

"He knew what the situation was when we met. I don't know what the fuck his problem is," I stated, not wanting to get into it with her in the club.

"So that's the guy?" She asked instead.

"You mean *was* the guy?" I retorted, grabbing one of the drinks Spider set on the table and taking a sip.

"What did we miss?" Olga asked, eyeing Elektra and I.

"Discussing situations and opportunities," Elektra replied, elbowing me.

I couldn't help rolling my eyes. "Wasted opportunities," I added, taking another sip of my drink.

"Well whatever was, is done. Let's get fucked and have some fun," Cherry threw in, holding up her glass to toast.

I couldn't help the small smirk as I clinked my glass with everyone else's and repeated, "To getting fucked and having fun!"

The rest of the night was a blur of drinks, dancing and little white pills. By the time we made it back to my apartment I was fucking lit. Olga and Charity left with the driver, while Spider, Elektra and Cherry decided to stay at my place.

I kicked my heels off as soon as I walked in the door, and went straight for the mini bar to pour us more drinks.

"Can we smoke, Taze?" Elektra asked.

I pointed toward a balcony and the other three shuffled out another door. I took a huge swig of my drink and then walked into my room to change out of my dress. By the time I joined the girls in my trainers and t-shirt, they were half way through a blunt.

"So you gonna tell us what happened?" Cherry asked, passing it to me.

"Easy. He decided to fuck around because I dance. If I want to take shit further, I have to give up dancing," I explained, taking a deep pull before passing it on.

"Didn't he know you dance?" Elektra asked.

"Yep," I replied, exhaling slowly.

"He looks familiar," Spider added.

"He's picked me up at your place before. I haven't been hiding him," I commented.

My phone started ringing in the house. And I rolled my eyes. Cherry ran into the apartment and grabbed my phone, hoping to hear a showdown between Domenico and I.

"Taze, you have like eight missed calls from your sister and your aunt. Something happen?" She asked, passing me my phone.

It wasn't the first time she had called. After Mami died I found every reason to not be with them. I found an apartment in Philly and surrounded myself with the shit I didn't have with my family: a fancy car, expensive clothes, nice things, and a wild social life. I worked crazy hours for all they knew, and I was too fucking busy adulting to make the trips to visit them.

Before I could give her a response, my phone started ringing again. Spider reached over and accepted the call before I could reject it again.

"Anastacia?" Titi's voice echoed from the phone. I gave a shitty look to Spider and walked back inside to hear what my aunt wanted.

"Hola, Titi. Como estas?" I asked, sitting on the sofa.

She didn't pull any punches and got right to the point. *"It's been a year, Stacia. Come home and spend the holidays with your family."*

"I have to check my schedule, Titi."

"Anastacia! No one has seen you in a year. We're worried about you, sobrina," she admonished me.

"Titi, I have work-" I started with the usual excuse.

"Cállate. Don't feed me more of your bullshit. Visit your grandparents for Christmas dinner!" She yelled through the phone.

I looked over at my calendar and sighed. I had volunteered to dance for a private party on Christmas Eve. The client had specifically requested me, and the money was going to be good. Best part of not giving a shit about the rules, the opportunities that opened up and the money that poured in.

I didn't want to hear my family talk about life without Mami. Going home just meant it was all real. She was gone. I knew it. I knew that she wouldn't be there, but going back there and spending a Christmas that she wouldn't be in felt...

"Titi, I am working late Christmas Eve-"

"Good, then you have no excuse not to come home for Christmas dinner at your grandparents. I will let them know to expect you, Anastacia," she confirmed, even though I hadn't said yes.

"Titi-" I started.

"Rob is coming with his new wife, and he is excited for you to meet her. I will text what time we are sitting down to eat so that you don't forget. Te amo, Tace," she said quickly before disconnecting the call.

"What the absolute fuck?" I said out loud, staring at my phone.

"What happened?" Cherry asked, plopping onto the sofa next to me.

"My aunt wants me to visit for Christmas," I sighed, tossing my phone onto the side table.

Cherry gave me a knowing look. "Guess you are going to dinner then. Stop avoiding them. You all need each other," she added, giving me a hug.

My phone pinged again, but I shut it off.

* * *

Everything flashed white before my eyes as my head jerked from the impact of his hand on my cheek. Before I could realize what had happened, his hand came down again and knocked me to the floor. My ears were ringing from the jolt to my head, while my eyes struggled to focus. Domenico hit me.

Staggering to stand, I was pulled to my feet when he suddenly grabbed a handful of my hair. I couldn't think. My heart was racing and my mind desperately trying to make sense of what was happening to my body. Domenico had me by the hair and was dragging me into the bedroom. I was in shock.

This man just hit me.

The man who had shared my bed, and made sweet promises about all of our future days together, just hit me.

My mouth filled with the metallic taste of blood as he threw me face down onto the bed. I struggled to get up but he had my legs pinned with his, where they hung over the side. My arms were trapped under my body because they had instinctively gone out to brace my fall when he threw me forward. Chest heaving as the adrenaline began to increase, I couldn't see what he was doing. Would he kill me? Did I mean so little to him?

Domenico had been waiting in my apartment when I got home from work. He was sitting on my sofa, staring at the door when I walked in. He didn't need to say a word for me to know that he was drunk. We hadn't talked since I caught him at the club trying to get a hookup. He had tried to message me, but I didn't want to hear his reasoning. I didn't want to hear him putting me down because I danced.

"If you're here to talk I don't want to hear it right now. I've had a long night, and I just want to sleep," I had told him as I took off my shoes and placed my bag on the entryway table. I didn't want to hear whatever bullshit lies he wanted to feed me for cheating.

We weren't dating, but I was monogamous. I thought we were on the same page after a year together.

"You were at work?" He had asked. Something in his voice should have kicked up a red flag, but I ignored it.

"Yeah. Christmas is coming up and I need the money. My family wants me to visit them, and I can't show up empty handed," I sighed, hanging my coat up.

"How much did you make shaking your ass for all of those fucking perverts?" He asked, voice still low and gravelly.

"Not more or less than usual. It was a normal night," I had said.

"Did you entertain any private *requests?*" He had asked, standing up from the sofa and moving toward me.

My back was turned as I fished my gloves and things out of my coat pockets so I didn't realize how close he was until I turned around. Domenico was less than an arm's length from me, staring down at my face.

"Yeah, I had three VIP tickets tonight. They pay the best so I try not to turn them down when I get them," I stated, looking up at him. "You know how it works, right?"

That was when it had happened. There was no warning. No preamble for what was coming. His hand had flown out and cracked across my face, stunning me speechless.

I was in a fucking daze until I heard his belt unhook behind me, and then something in me snapped. I wrenched myself out from his grip and kicked at him with all that I had in me, terrified that he was going to try and rape me. When he grabbed my leg, I was already coming up and swinging my right fist at his face. It landed on his jaw knocking him back enough that I could scramble from the bed and get to my feet.

"Who the fuck do you think you are?" I screamed, lunging forward to hit him again. "You break into my house drunk, fucking hit me, and thinking I'm just gonna let you rape me?!"

My next swing caught him in the ribs before he grabbed me by the hair and slammed my face back into the bed.

"You're fucking crazy! This is why shit can't work with you!" He yelled back at me.

With my head smashed into my sheets, and his body weight holding me in place, I was seething. "Get the fuck out of my house, Domenico. We're done!"

He leaned forward so that his chest lay on my back, our bodies pressed together. "Why? You gotta another dick waiting in the wings? You think I don't know what a fucking whore you are?"

"I'm not the one picking up pussy in bars, you fucking asshole!" I tried to yell back, but it came out muffled when he pushed my head further into the blankets.

There was a moment of silence. Neither of us moved. I honestly didn't know what was going on, until I heard his breathing change. The mother fucker had passed out on top of me.

"Get off of me!" I screamed, trying to roll his heavy ass off of me. I started to panic when he didn't move, and began thrashing underneath him.

"Shhhhh," whispered from his lips, as he rolled off of me and tried pulling me with him to cuddle.

"Are you fucking kidding me? Get your hands off of me!" I yelled, still trying to escape his arms and the death grip he had on my body.

"Just let me sleep."

My body stilled. This man had broken into my apartment, hit me, accused me of being a whore, and now he wanted to *sleep* with me? *In my bed?* My brain couldn't handle the fucking roller coaster and shut down, because I nodded.

What else could I do? He was so out of his mind drunk, I doubt he even knew what he had done.

"Okay. Sleep," I whispered, allowing him to hold me in place.

My eyes burned with tears. I wanted to call Mami, and tell her to come get me. I wanted my sister to come and make this man go away. I wanted to bury my head in the sand and die from humiliation and heartbreak. I cried myself to sleep.

When I woke up late into the day, Domenico was gone.

I stumbled out of bed to the bathroom. I couldn't even bring myself to look at my face in the mirror. I didn't want to see the woman who had let a man lay his hands on her, and then let him walk away. I didn't want to see the evidence of what happened.

Turning the shower on, I made quick work of stripping out of my clothes I still wore from last night. The water burned my skin, but I needed it to burn to feel clean. I scrubbed my body, as fresh tears began to roll down my cheeks. A sob wracked my chest before my legs buckled and I dropped to the floor of my shower and cried.

* * *

I woke up, my head pounding, and my body aching. The room was dark. I had cried in the shower until the water went cold, before finally climbing out and crawling back into my bed.

My phone rang, snapping me out of my daze and prompting me to get out of bed. I found it on the floor where I had dropped my bag when I got home. There was no one living that I wanted to talk to, so the call was rejected without even registering who was calling me.

Everything I did was like being on autopilot. My bed was stripped and the bloodied blankets thrown into the washing machine. I grabbed a spray bottle of cleaner and a rag from under the kitchen sink and started cleaning every surface in my home. Every drop of blood, the evidence of what had happened, erased with each spritz and swipe as I went. It took nearly an hour to wash everything.

By the time I was done, I made myself a small bowl of cereal and sat on my sofa in the dark. What the fuck was he thinking? Did he really think I was a whore because I danced in a gentlemen's club? *Fuck.* It was how we met!

My phone vibrated on the table in front of me with a message from Domenico. I set my bowl down, and looked to see what he had to say for himself. Nothing could have prepared me for the messages that filled my phone.

[We need to talk about last night.]

[There's no excuse for what happened.]

[I was so out of my mind drunk, I couldn't think straight.]

[You mean the world to me. Please respond.]

[I have been falling in love with you since the day we met. I know that things are complicated with us, but we can make this work.]

[I see a life with us, but we need to be on the same page.]

[I don't know what I would do without you. You make me want to be a better man, despite the demons I carry.]

[I'm not even mad that you hit me back. I deserved it.]

[Talk to me.]

[Anastacia, I know that we both carry shit from our pasts, but I want to move past that with you. I don't want to be the situation in your life.]

[Please talk to me when you are ready.]

[I don't want to lose what we have.]

I had no idea what to feel reading his messages. Domenico said he was falling in love with me? He admitted that he was wrong. He knew that what he did violated something between us, and he was fighting to make it right again.

Before I knew what I was doing, I called him.

"Anastacia?" His deep voice called my name before I could even say a word.

"Don't hang up. I didn't know what happened last night when I woke up. It took a bit for my fucking brain to sort shit. Baby girl, I can't take back what happened, but we can make it right going forward," he pleaded quietly through the phone.

"I'm not a whore, Domenico. Not yours or anyone else's," I whispered, unable to find my voice to tell him to fuck off.

"No. You are not. You are one of the fiercest women I have ever met. Please, let me make this up to you."

"I'm not really up to going out, and I need some time," I said, feeling the swelling in my cheek throb as I spoke.

Domenico was quiet for a long time before I heard him exhale. *"Let me bring you dinner at least,"* he offered.

"I've already eaten, and I am about to go to bed. Give me some time," I repeated.

"Okay. You're right. I'll give you some space," he replied.

Even after everything, there was something about his voice that curled itself around my heart and my core. It massaged away my doubts and had me wanting to go back to the comfort of *us.* The comfort I felt when his arms wrapped around me, and we talked about the shit hands life had dealt us.

That comfort I felt when my soul was bared in front of

him, was a drug like no other. Would I get that same feeling with anyone else? Would I ever feel that peace with all of my demons being with another man?

"I don't know what to think right now, honestly," I finally said. I wouldn't give him more than that. I couldn't. Not yet.

Chapter 22

I should have left earlier. I should have not agreed to go at all. The traffic out of Philly was not moving. How the hell were this many people heading out of the city on Christmas day? I had moved exactly four miles in one hour.

Suddenly my phone started ringing.

"Hello?" I answered it, sounding every bit as annoyed as I felt.

"You're still coming right?" Jada's voice filled my car.

"Yes, Jada. As soon as I get out of the parking lot," I seethed. She had already called me three times today to verify that I would be coming down for Christmas dinner.

"You haven't left yet? Where are you?" She asked, sounding somewhat frantic

"Sitting in the parking lot that is 95, J. I'm sitting in fucking traffic."

"Okay," she responded before talking to someone else in the background. *"She's on her way, but the traffic is bad..."*

There was a pause as I listened to shuffling and voices on the other end. It didn't take long to realize that she was already at our grandparents' house. *"Nana said we're having dinner at six so you have plenty of time. Don't stress, Tace,"* she assured me.

"Thanks. I will let you know when I am closer, okay?" I offered, wanting to end the call.

"Pops said don't text and drive!" She threw in before I ended the call.

I didn't want to hear them talking about how amazing everything was going to be. Christmas with the family was always amazing. It had been a standing rule for who knew how long. Christmas was the only day that no one fought. There was no drama between my aunts, and everyone pretended to be happy and healthy.

I glanced into my mirror at the make-up job I had done before leaving. The swelling had gone down, but there was still a little yellowish discoloration to my cheek which I hid with a shit ton of make-up.

It had been a week since that night. Domenico and I had texted back and forth, but I still refused to let him back into my apartment. I had the locks changed just to make sure he couldn't let himself in after another drunken bender. We weren't together, but we were working things out. It was so fucking hard not to cave when his words were so damn sincere.

"Fuck! Finally!" I cheered as traffic eased and I sped up to a whopping 45 from the crawl of 10.

I drove another five miles when my car stuttered. "No!!!" I screamed, staring at the glowing light on my dashboard. I was out of gas. How the fuck had I forgotten to fill my car?

There was barely enough left in the tank to pull off to a shoulder before it died. This felt like the universe telling me that I should have stayed home. How many things could go wrong? I couldn't call any of the girls in Philly because they were already with their families. The traffic going toward

341

Philly was still locked up which meant calling my family was out of the question. It would take them three hours to get here.

I swore under my breath as I took out my phone. Roadside assistance charged an insane fee for shit like this, and although I had the money, my pride prohibited me from calling in and being the woman in an expensive car who ran out of gas.

[My car ran out of gas. Can you help?] I texted. Reaching out to the one person I knew would jump through their ass to show up felt like a shitty thing to do, but I didn't care.

Not even a minute had passed before my phone was ringing in my hands.

"Hello?" I answered.

"Tell me where you are," the deep voice purred.

"I'm sitting on 95."

"North or South, Anastacia," he prodded.

"South."

"I'll be there as soon as I can."

"You don't have to-"

"I was already headed that way. I need to be in Baltimore for a meeting tomorrow morning. I'll see you shortly," he said, disconnecting the call before I could argue further.

The butterflies in my stomach became agitated. Why the fuck did I call him? This was going to blur all of the lines and boundaries I had set between us. I tried calling back but the call went directly to voicemail. *Shit.*

Thirty minutes later, a sleek gray Mercedes SUV pulled up behind my car. I was sitting in the passenger seat, so I wasn't seated on the traffic side when the vehicle stopped. I set my phone back into my bag and stepped out, stopping in my tracks when my eyes connected with someone I was not expecting.

"You're lucky we were already headed this way," Roman informed me.

"I didn't know you had company," I stated softly, my eyes not moving from the man still seated in Roman's car.

Roman looked over his shoulder and shrugged casually toward Domenico. "He doesn't get a say. He knows I always look after my people."

I nodded nervously, finally breaking eye contact with the man I had kept at arm's length for the past week. Roman pulled a small canister of gas from the back of his vehicle and made quick work of emptying it into my tank.

"It might be just enough to get you down to the next service station. Where were you headed?" He asked.

"My family is having Christmas dinner at six," I responded absently, trying my hardest not to look at the man in his car staring holes into body.

His head canted to the side in thought. "How much further do you need to go?" Roman asked, twisting the cap closed.

"Um, about twenty miles," I responded.

His jaw flexed in thought. "Shit. Give me a second," he said before returning to his Mercedes.

I don't know what he said, but two men suddenly climbed out of the back seats and started walking towards me. "What are you doing?" I asked, panicking slightly as they approached my car.

"My guys and I are going to take your car, you're going to take mine. Do you need help moving gifts or anything like that?" Roman stated.

I nodded dumbly and popped the boot open, revealing

343

several neatly wrapped gifts and bags. The two men gently collected all of the gifts and moved them to the back of Roman's SUV. They returned to my car, placing two small travel bags from the back of his vehicle into mine.

"I can't take your car, Roman," I whispered, panicking that the fourth man had not yet moved from his seat.

"Sure you can," he chuckled, grabbing my key fob out of my hand. "Do you need to get your purse or anything else?"

I shook my head, but still moved like I was in a daze to grab my purse and travel cup from the front of my car. Before I finished turning around Domenico had moved into the driver's seat of Roman's vehicle.

"What's he doing? What are you doing?" I asked, my voice coming out pitchy and aggressive as I fired off questions at the two men.

"One of us needs to know where to pick you up," Roman replied, as if that made any sense to me.

"Can't one of these two do that?" I asked, pointing at the other two men.

"No, ma'am," one of the men responded before Roman could.

"What? Why?" I stuttered, eyebrows furrowed in discontent.

"Security precaution. Domenico will make sure you arrive safely to your destination," Roman stated, turning me toward his vehicle and giving me a gentle shove in that direction.

Fuck.

I glanced over my shoulder one more time to see Roman waving goodbye to Domenico before climbing into the back seat of my car. The door had barely closed before my car was driving off without me in it.

Shit.

My back straightened, and I inhaled a deep breath before climbing into Roman's vehicle with Domenico.

"Here. Put in the address," he stated, passing me his phone.

I pushed his hand back. "I know the way. I'll tell you where to go," I stated.

He nodded, dropping the device back into the console. Then we were moving back onto the road and weaving through traffic. Neither of us spoke for what felt like an eternity. My stomach felt like it was on the verge of eating a hole through itself, my anxiety just escalating higher and higher.

"You look beautiful, Anastacia," he stated suddenly, breaking the silence.

I didn't respond to his flattery. "Take the next exit."

He nodded subtly in my peripheral, and indicated the car to leave the freeway onto a smaller highway.

The clicking of the turn signal sounded like thunder booming in the stillness between us. He decided to keep talking despite the frozen shoulder I was putting up.

"I was drunk. It's not an excuse. I know, it's not an excuse. You mean a lot to me, and I would never intentionally do anything to hurt you. I hope you know that," he stated.

I didn't want to look at him. I didn't want to see the sincerity in his eyes. "I know that you broke into my apartment, and accused me of being a whore. You hit me and then tried to have sex with me. That's what I know," I replied softly.

"Anastacia," he said.

"How many are there?" I asked, turning to stare daggers at him. "It's obvious that I'm not the only one you're fucking,

345

so I went I got tested for STDs. Thankfully nothing came up positive. Take the next right, please."

Suddenly, the vehicle pulled off the highway and Domenico found a small side road before stopping. His hands grasped and clutched at the steering wheel. "I don't know how to do this. You didn't want to be with me, but you said we had to be monogamous. I asked you to move in with me, and you laugh at me. Now I am the bad guy in everything. What the fuck do I have to say for you to understand?"

I stared at him, mouth agape. "When did any of that EVER fucking happen? You made one comment about how inconvenient it was to come to my place and I was supposed to understand that to mean *we should move in together?*" I shouted back at him.

"I told you I was clean. I told you you were the only one in my bed, but were you fucking other people, Domenico? I am not a fucking side piece you get to dust off when you want. It's all me or nothing," I continued.

"It's all you, Anastacia," he responded, turning to look at me.

"What does that mean?"

"It means it's all you. Only you. If we do this, we're it. No other men, no other women, we move in together," he said, staring into my eyes. "I'm falling for you, dolce. I don't want to go another week without you."

"Don't think you can just spout shit and I will fall blindly at your fe-"

My words were cut off as he grabbed my head and pulled in to kiss me. His lips were soft and gentle, coaxing my own against my will to kiss him back. He reached down and unfastened my seat belt before dragging me out of my seat to sit on his lap.

I gasped and his tongue delved into my mouth, silencing any protests I would have made. Any thoughts I had of protesting, melted away as he kissed me like I was the most precious person in the world. His hand gently caressed my face as he pulled back from the kiss to stare back at me.

"I'm falling in love with you. I don't know how to do the relationship shit, but I'm willing to do it with you. Tell me what you need from me, I'll give it," he whispered.

I bit my lip, silencing every doubt I had. "Take me to my grandparents, please."

My words seemed to take the wind out of his hopes, his body sagging back into the seat in defeat. Seeing him compliant like this made my walls come down.

"I've never brought anyone to meet my family before, so don't embarrass me," I continued.

I watched as realization settled in and his eyes lit up. "Is that a yes?" He asked, hugging me tighter, and peppering my face with kisses.

I couldn't help the smile on my face. "Maybe," I chuckled.

"Damnit, Anastacia…" He growled, pressing his forehead against mine, before kissing me like he wanted to steal my breath away. "I want to fuck you so bad right now, but I will be a gentleman-" he growled, pulling back from the kiss.

"No," I said, shaking my head.

"I know. I will be a gentleman," he repeated, exhaling slowly to control his breathing.

My breath was picking up, staring at him. "No. I meant, I want you to."

His eyes danced, staring back at mine. The thought of

going to visit my family, freshly fucked, was not something I had ever imagined wanting before that moment. He bit his bottom lip before shaking his head.

"You are something else, Anastacia," he sighed. "We're going to meet your family, so we're not going to be late. Get back in your seat before I change my mind."

I couldn't help the giggle that bubbled out of me. I leaned in and gave him a soft kiss on the lips before scooting back into the passenger seat and buckling up.

Domenico shifted his bulging erection and exhaled loudly. "Ok. Where do I- we need to go?"

I pointed at a house across the road. "That's their house right there," I said, causing him to cough violently.

"You wanted to let me fuck you in front of your grandparents' house?" He practically screamed at me in shock.

Seeing him like this, eyebrows up, eyes wide and mouth gaping, I couldn't keep a straight face and laughed so hard that I nearly cried.

"I'm just fucking with you!" I laughed.

"Jesus, Anastacia! That's not funny!" He practically yelled, but he wanted to laugh.

"Take the next left up ahead," I directed once I had calmed down enough. "We're about two miles away."

The rest of the ride was filled with Domenico's grumbling and my persistent giggles; the stress of the reunion forgotten for at least a few minutes while he drove.

Pulling up to my grandparents house, however, sobered me up. The house was decorated with lights, like they did every year. In the front yard was a tree that had been planted in the last few months, decorated with a purple ribbon in honor of my mother's fight with pancreatic cancer.

"I don't know if I can do this," I whispered, my emotions rising to the surface.

Domenico didn't hesitate to take my hand and hold it to his lips, kissing my knuckles. "I'm with you. If it's too much, say the word and we leave."

I nodded absentmindedly, transfixed by the purple ribbon softly billowing.

"Hey. Look at me, dolce," he prodded, taking my chin and turning my head to face him. "I'm right here."

I exhaled a staggered breath and nodded. "Okay. Let's go before they start crowding the door."

Domenico glanced back at the house and started chuckling. "I think it's too late for that."

My eyes followed his stare to see Aunt Maria, Titi, and Jada crowding the door, trying to see who was in the SUV. I couldn't read their lips or hear their cackling, but I didn't need to. They knew it was me, and they were placing bets on whether I would actually come into the house.

"Ughhh," I groaned. "Let's just get this over with. Just don't tell them anything, okay?"

"Like what?" He asked, unbuckling his seatbelt.

"Like what I do, how we met, or where I live."

"Seriously? What the fuck am I supposed to talk about?" He asked, laughing.

"Christmas shit," I muttered, unbuckling and climbing out of my seat.

We both walked to the back of the car and took out the gifts I had prepared for everyone. It would have easily taken me three trips to this by myself, but with Domenico helping, we managed to carry it all.

"Feliz Navidad!" Nana called out, opening the door for us

as we came up the path to the house.

"Feliz Navidad," I responded, smiling back at her. She looked so much older since the last time I had seen her.

"Quien es?" Titi asked, taking some of the gifts from my hands as soon as I walked in the door, and stashing them around the tree with everyone else's.

"Mi novio," I responded, helping to put the remainder down before turning to help Domenico unload his arm full.

I had barely taken a breath before the introductions started. Titi, Bruja, Maria, Jada, Nana, Pops, Rob and his wife Eliza, two other cousins and their spouses, then a hoard of children.

"It's nice to meet you, Domenico," Pops said, offering his hand.

"Thank you-" Domenico started.

"Pops. Just call me Pops. It's what everyone calls me," he said, smiling.

Domenico nodded and smiled in return as he shook his hand. "It's nice to meet you, too, Pops."

"Okay, dinner is ready, so let's eat while it's hot!" Nana announced from the kitchen.

I held back while everyone filed in to fill their plates before finding places to sit around the table. The children were set up in another room watching Christmas films while they ate, leaving the adults to fill the table.

There was a hush that fell over the room as everyone was seated. Without thinking I held Domenico's hand on one side, Jada's hand on the other, and bowed my head as Pops thanked God for his many blessings.

The mood wasn't nearly as somber as I thought it would be, which hurt all the more. It felt wrong to laugh and be joyful when Mami wasn't here to celebrate with us.

Lost in my thoughts, I was startled when two arms wrapped around me from behind. "She would be so happy for you, Anastacia. She *is* happy for you. It's okay to live on. Be happy, love," Nana's quiet voice whispered in my ear.

I felt the tears burning my eyes. "Thank you," I whispered, my voice hoarse with emotion.

"Your family seemed nice," Domenico commented as we drove south toward Baltimore. By the time everyone had finished eating, opening gifts and getting drunk, it was nearly eleven. I had no intention of staying the night and used Domenico as my excuse to leave.

"Yeah. They're good people," I smiled.

"I don't get it though."

"What don't you get?" I asked, staring out the window at the night sky.

"You seem like you have a good family. You have people who love you, a nice house. How did you end up becoming a dancer and not a lawyer?" He chuckled.

I rolled my head back on the seat to look at him. "I didn't grow up with that. Yeah, my family loved me growing up, but my sister and I didn't have any of that. My mother raised us in poverty, too proud to ask for help and too nice to keep a dollar saved for a rainy day."

Domenico's brows furrowed. "Your family has money and they let your mother raise you in the ghetto?" He asked in disbelief.

"What can I say, my mother was amazing at keeping secrets and spinning her tales. I started dancing because there was no money to pay for medical bills at the end when she was dying."

"Fuck, dolce," he cussed softly, reaching out to hold my

hand. "I'm sorry you had to go through that. It couldn't have been easy…. But it made you into the woman you are, and I can't be upset about that," he whispered, kissing our intertwined fingers.

The woman I am. I thought to myself. What would my mother say about my falling for a man who hit me? Would she really be happy for me? Would she tell me to give him the second chance I was giving him? Would she be angry for me and swear to have him taken out? I couldn't know what she would say, because she was gone.

"I'm tired," I murmured, closing my eyes. I wasn't really, but I didn't want to talk to Domenico anymore. I just wanted to be alone in my thoughts.

"Get some sleep, dolce. I'll wake you when we get there," he said.

* * *

"Happy New Year!" Everyone cheered as the clock struck midnight. I turned to find Domenico but he wasn't behind me.

I pushed my way through the throngs of people crammed into Roman's house. I had made a round of the entire first floor without finding him, which was weird. Then again, he was pretty drunk. The thought of him trying to sleep one off through the stroke of midnight made me chuckle.

I ran up the stairs to the guest room we were staying in, and opened the door without thinking. How could I have possibly imagined that in under five minutes my boyfriend would balls deep in a random woman's throat.

"You SON OF A BITCH!" I screamed, launching across

352

the room to hit him.

He reared back and fell on the bed.

"Fuck, Anastacia! I thought that was *you*!" he shouted, clutching to protect his cock.

I turned on the woman and snatched her by the hair, and started dragging her out of the room as she screamed and thrashed.

I had barely made it to the hall when Roman and several others from the party came running up the stairs.

"Who does this whore belong to?" I shouted, wrenching her hair up to show her face.

"Anastacia, let her go. I'll deal with this," Roman stated calmly, holding his hands out to show that he wasn't holding a weapon.

"Who. Did. She. Come. With?" I asked again, through clenched teeth.

"Domenico! I came with my boyfriend, Domenico! You got the wrong room!" The woman cried, as she clawed at the hand gripping her hair.

"Fuck!" Roman breathed out.

I couldn't say how many hits I laid into her face before I was being tackled to the floor by Roman and one of the bouncers from Infinity.

"LET ME UP!" I screamed.

"Get her the fuck out of here," Roman barked at someone.

"I'm gonna press charges on that crazy bitch! You're all my witnesses!" The woman was screaming back at the crowd now gathered to spectate.

Roman turned to say something, and I reared my elbow back into his jaw. The shock caused him to loosen his hold enough that I could get loose, and fly at the woman again.

"What did you say?" I shouted, causing her to turn to me wide eyed.

"HELP!"

I slapped her so hard she fell onto the floor. "I arrived with that man. From the moment he woke up this morning in my bed, to when he stepped away to relieve himself, he has been with me. So tell everyone here again what the fuck you were doing in our room sucking off my man," I growled at her as I pointed at the door to the guest room.

"You thought you could sneak in there and he would suddenly what? Drop me? For *you?* Roman call the cops, I just stopped an attempted rapist. She sexually assaulted a drunk man without consent," I stated.

"Get the fuck over yourself!" She laughed. "Do you honestly think anyone is going to believe that?"

Roman turned to one of his guys and nodded. "Call the cops."

The woman, whose name I still didn't know, turned wide eyed in an instant. "You can't be serious! Roman! You know me!" she shouted as two guys stepped forward to detain her.

"I know what I saw, and I'm not willing to believe a fucking word you're saying," he stated firmly, before turning to me. "Go take care of him. The cops will be here soon."

I turned and stomped back into my room. Domenico was passed out right where he fell on the bed, cock still hanging out of his pants. I took a deep breath and crawled up on the bed. I gently tucked him back into his pants and sat back on the bed.

There was no way of knowing what kind of evidence the police would want so I didn't want to touch him too much. I sat there staring at him as tears streamed down my face.

He would be mortified to know that this happened. If he woke up in a hospital, a victim of a sexual assault it would demasculate him.

I returned to the door, and found Roman standing by with two of his men. "Make it go away. This never happened," I whispered.

Roman stared at me, a wash of conflicting emotions flashing across his eyes. He didn't say anything and nodded. I turned back into the guest room, closing and locking the door.

"Come on, babe. Let's get you cleaned up," I cooed at Domenico, pulling him up from the bed. He staggered, leaning most of his weight into me. "Come on. We'll clean up and then we can go to bed."

"Okay, Stacia. I love you, dolce," he slurred.

"I know. I know you do," I whispered, leading him into the ensuite bathroom.

This never happened.

Chapter 23

"I have a meeting tonight, and I want you to go with me," Domenico announced, while we were eating breakfast.

We had agreed to move in together, but I still had my own place and he still had his. I didn't like any of the places he found, and he didn't like my choices, so we spent each night at my place.

"I'm supposed to work," I countered, taking a bite of my toast, and watching his jaw tense up before relaxing again.

"It's important to me. To have my woman by my side."

I expected him to start an argument about my dancing again, but he let it go. My dancing was one of many things we argued about, and it never ended well.

"You need to give me more than that," I stated, finishing my coffee and pushing my plate forward.

He dropped his fork on his plate and stared at me for a minute before speaking. I wanted to hear what excuse he had this time for needing me to call out of work. *Again*. Because it happened a lot since Christmas. So much so that I stopped answering my phone or even turning it on while I was at work.

"I'm meeting with clients. When I show up alone, they try to throw women at me, and I don't want the distractions. If you go with me, they have to talk business."

I was not expecting that answer. "You want me to call out of work to be your cock shield?" I asked, arching an eyebrow at him.

"Fuck it. Never mind. I don't know why I thought you would be supportive," he grumbled, pushing back from the table and marching to the kitchen.

This was his reaction. He was such a man child about the things that mattered to him, making such a fuss over stupid shit. Maybe it started after New Year's, or maybe it was after Valentine's Day, but he was moody whenever he had to ask for my help. It became my favorite button to push, egging him to admit that he needed me to protect him.

"Can't you just admit it?" I called behind him, gathering up our used dishes from the table and taking them to the kitchen.

"I'm not doing this with you," he growled, pushing past me to go back to the bedroom.

Following him, I wrapped my arms around his waist and laughed. "Just say *you* need *me,* and I will consider taking off work," I whispered against his back.

"No. Just forget about it!" He argued trying to pull my hands off of him.

"Domenico, admit that you need me," I whispered, letting my arms drop to my sides. He didn't say anything and stomped off to the bedroom, slamming the door behind him.

I didn't follow him this time, and stood where I was. I took off the shirt that I was wearing and sat in a chair facing the door to the bedroom. I don't know why I thought it was so hot when he was like this, but it made me wet for him.

When the door opened again, he was dressed in his black pants and button down white shirt. The shirt bunched a little around the muscles of his arms, which had me biting my lip. Whatever thoughts he had before opening that door ceased to exist upon seeing me naked on the chair waiting for him.

"Tell me you need me," I whispered as my hand trailed down my body. "Tell me, Domenico."

He swallowed hard as my fingers slid between my slick folds. I slowly circled my clit, eyes locked on him as I did so. Instead of answering me, he unfastened his belt and pants, and grasped his growing erection.

"Two can play this game," he huffed, beginning to stroke himself in front of me.

"But your hand doesn't feel as good as I do. Does it, baby?" I cooed, dipping my fingers lower to tap the place he loved to bury himself in. "Right here."

"Fuck," he exhaled, stroking himself faster.

"Tell me you need me, Domenico. I'll give you what you want. All of this is yours. Just say the word," I coaxed, as my fingers began circling my clit. I had never masturbated in front of him before. Never needed to. But I'd be damned for lying if I said it wasn't a huge fucking turn on watching him wrestle with his pride as a he beat his cock.

"Anastacia," he warned me.

"Say it. Hmmm?" I moaned as my core began tightening under my ministrations. *Fuck this was so hot.*

"Tell me. Tell me," I repeated, beginning to sweat as my orgasm continued building.

"FUCK!" He shouted, before crossing the room in three steps and dropping to his knees before me. I stopped him from having his way, one hand holding him back as he watched me continuing to pleasure myself.

"Say it, baby," I whispered, arching my back.

"Fuck, I need you. I need you, Anastacia. God strike me down, I need you like a fucking drug," he admitted.

I stopped pleasuring myself, and lifted my soaking wet fingers up to his mouth. He didn't hesitate to suck my slick off of them. I threw my hand around his neck and pulled him into a kiss just as he buried himself inside me in a single thrust.

My legs were draped over his arms, his hands firmly holding my body in place as he relentlessly slammed into me. I was so close I teetered on the edge of coming undone already.

"I need you," he grunted again, capturing my mouth in a punishing kiss as I came around him.

I need to call out of work.

* * *

Dressed in a black bodycon dress that stopped just above my knees and a pair of thigh high, red boots, my assets were all on display. I straightened my hair down my back and created a smokey eye look with my make up. Domenico walked into the bathroom just as I finished applying my lipstick.

"*Fuck, dolce,*" he hissed, coming up behind me and hugging my body against his. "Are you hoping to find a new man dressed like this?"

I smiled at him in the mirror. "Just making sure all the women know what you have at home," I chuckled. "And their services aren't needed."

He kissed my hair and we left shortly after. By the time we reached the parking garage, his car was waiting. I recognized one of the guys in the back, but the two up front were new.

"Who are they?" I asked, nuzzling against him so that only he could hear my words.

"Insurance," he replied, giving me a chaste kiss so as not to smear my crimson red lipstick all over his face.

"Yours or theirs?" I continued as we climbed into the vehicle.

"Both."

There were no delusions about the type of businesses Domenico was involved in. I knew enough to know that at least one of the two men seated in the front would not hesitate to end my life. I didn't say a word the entire ride, staring absently out of the window instead of snuggling against my man.

Yes, I was his arm candy, but I was also a possible weakness. I had to be available, but not clingy. Forward, but not pushy. And if it came down to it, I could be as violent as I wanted to be if anyone crossed my bottom line and touched me without my permission.

We arrived at a club I had seen a few times while out with the girls, but always avoided. There was nothing outwardly sketchy about the building. It had great placement, clean curbside, but there were absolutely no lines to get in. Any other club in Philly would have a line on Friday or Saturday nights, but this place never had one. No lines meant it was either a dud inside or the club was a front for other shit. I knew it couldn't be the former, which only left the latter.

"I've always wanted to see the inside of this place," I commented, as the vehicle came to a stop and the security

360

moved to open our doors.

"Try to manage your expectations," Domenico muttered as we climbed out of the car.

Beyond the front door where the bouncers were stationed, the inside was nothing like any of the clubs I had been to. The whole place was set up more like a casino than anything else.

"Will you win me some money?" I asked, tugging on Domenico's arm. My coquettish behavior was rewarded with a light chuckle.

"Business first, then pleasure, dolce," he murmured, pulling our clasped hands up to his mouth and kissing my knuckles.

I nodded happily and followed him between the tables to a back room filled with smoke. Four men sat around a table playing cards. I didn't recognize three of them, but one, the youngest looking at the table, seemed familiar. They didn't pay attention to either of us until the hand had finished.

"You wanna buy in?" One of the men asked. He had dark olive skin, thick black hair and dark brown eyes. I didn't squirm or look away when he ogled my body, too used to the attention from creepy men. When our eyes locked, he looked away first, obviously uncomfortable under my own scrutiny.

"I'm not here to play with you, Omar," Domenico sighed, pulling me to sit on his lap near the wall.

Knowing enough to know that I needed to be seen and not heard, I sat quietly and played with the soft locks of Domenico's hair and drank whatever alcohol was served to me. When the game finally finished, the man named Omar remained seated at the table, while the other two stood up and left the room.

361

"Such a pretty woman you have. What is your name, pretty one?" Omar asked me.

"Anastacia," I informed him, keeping my face as neutral as possible despite feeling tipsy as hell. *What the hell was in those drinks?*

"Tell me, Anastacia... Is this man trustworthy?" Omar fired off while shuffling his deck of cards, staring intently at Domenico as he asked the question.

Domenico physically tensed beneath me, no doubt recounting all of the times he had broken my trust. All of the times I knew about, and those I certainly didn't.

"It depends what you need to trust him with," I responded, still playing with Domenico's hair. "I trust that he will make my toes curl when we are alone tonight, but I don't know if I trust him with my heart yet."

I felt the man beneath me stop breathing for half a second, like he held his breath to keep from arguing with me, or with Omar. He brought me here for a reason, and I was going to find out why.

"But if I am alone in the dark and he is the one I call, I trust him to come for me without hesitation or questions," I concluded, placing a light peck on Domenico's forehead.

Omar glanced briefly from me to Domenico. My eyes never wandered to my man's for permission to speak, and he made no moves to stop me either. Finally, Omar set down his deck of cards and jutted his chin toward us.

"Consider our bargain struck, old friend. Philadelphia's distribution line is yours, exclusively," Omar informed him just before the two other men returned to begin a new game.

"My men will be in touch," Domenico stated, lifting me off of his lap.

362

For a moment, I thought Domenico would want to stay and play a round of cards or something, but he just wanted to leave as quickly as possible. He grabbed my hand and began leading me back the way we came, until Omar called after me.

"I'm happy to be someone you *trust* upon, Anastacia. If ever there is a day he fails to curl those toes, call me."

I didn't say anything, didn't nod, didn't even acknowledge what he said, and continued walking out the door, pulling Domenico with me.

There was no hesitation in my step, as I exited the building and climbed into our waiting car. I didn't want to stay another minute in that place with Omar ogling me like a side of meat. Domenico took his seat beside me, and didn't say a word or move until the driver had shut his door.

"What a creep," I sighed, buckling my seatbelt.

The back of Domenico's hand suddenly connected with my cheek, causing my head to reel. Unlike the last time he put his hands on me, I wasn't going to sit and take it. Ripping off my seatbelt, I twisted my body in my seat and kicked him in the jaw with my bared foot.

He wanted to fight? *Game fucking on.*

"What the fuck is wrong with you?" I yelled. "I did everything you wanted, you got what you wanted. What the fuck, Domenico?"

"You think I didn't see you making eyes at him?" he shouted back at me.

My eyes widened to the size of saucers. "Are you fucking kidding me? He's a fucking creep!" I screamed back.

"I'm not doing this with you, Anastacia," he breathed out, obviously trying to reel in his anger.

363

He started this mess, and then wanted to put the blame *on me?*

"Stop the car!" I yelled at the driver.

"What are you doing? We'll talk when we get home," Domenico growled at me.

"No. No! I'm going to *my place* and you are going to fuck off! You fucking hit me for no fucking reason. STOP THE FUCKING CAR!" I shouted again.

The car suddenly jolted to a stop, and I scrambled out before Domenico could stop me. With a rough idea of where I was in the city, I started walking for the nearest train station. There was no way I was going anywhere else with that man tonight.

"Get back in the car!" he shouted from the window. "Anastacia! So help me I will leave your ass right here in the middle of town!"

"Fuck you! Do you think I am some weak bitch who can't take care of herself? I did just fine before you came into my life, I'll make it home without you!" I started yelling, my voice trailing off toward the end.

The car door slammed and I started running, afraid that he would get out of the car and try to pull me back. When I had made it two blocks I turned to see that the car was gone, and with it my ride home.

I hadn't brought any money with me because Domenico was taking me out. Thankfully, however, I had my phone. There was no one that I could call this late at night. If I called anyone at work, they would know I had lied about why I didn't come in. Cherry, Spider, and Elektra were all at work, and wouldn't answer their phones until they finished at 3am.

There were only a few people I could trust, and the names

of people I would be able to get a hold of at this time of night…. Equaled two.

Biting my lip as I walked, I dialed the one person I never expected to call.

"Hello? Why are you calling me this late?"

"Hey, it's me," I said.

"Tace, I have known you your whole life. I know who you are. Why are you calling me? Did something happen?"

Jada's voice went from groggy with sleep to interrogator in two breaths, making me chuckle.

"I was supposed to meet up with friends and I forgot my wallet. My ride left me in the middle of the city, and I was hoping you could come and get me," I admitted the half truth.

"Where are you?" she asked.

I rattled off a couple of street addresses and she hummed. *"I'll be there in 20."*

"Where are you?" I asked in return, wondering how she was going to get to me that quickly.

"I'm… visiting a friend. So I'm in the city," she explained.

There was rustling in the background, as I assumed she was throwing clothes on. Then I heard it. A man's low voice talking to her. She was with a guy and I had interrupted their night.

"J, if you're busy, it's okay. I can get home," I stated, trying to now talk my sister out of coming to get me.

"Shut up. I'm already dressed and walking out to my car. You stay on the phone with me so I know you're safe until I get there," she chuckled.

I heard her car start up, and then the sound of her voice changed as what I was assuming was the bluetooth in her car kicking on and taking over the call.

"Is it just you? Coming to get me, that is?" I asked.

Jada chuckled. *"Yeah. Just me."*

I bit my lip at the awkwardness of my ill timed call. "So you're seeing someone, huh?"

She chuckled again. *"It's new. I don't know what we're doing, but we enjoy hanging out with each other."*

"Hanging out, huh? Is that what the older people are calling it these days?" I asked giggling.

The sound of Jada's laughter filled my phone. We were practically the same age, but she was always my big sister. Listening to her tell me about Trevor and how they met was all news to me. It hit me just how much I missed having my sister in my life. Sure, I had my reasons for being angry at her in the past, but that was not now. We only had each other in this life.

I wanted my sister. Needed to be able to talk to her again.

"Is that you?" Her question suddenly pulled me from my thoughts. I looked up to see her car pulling up to the curb where I stood. Hanging up the call, I got in and threw my arms around her neck in a hug.

"Whoa. Tace. Are you okay?" She asked. First shocked by my sudden affection, then further unsettled when a quiet sob left me. I nodded against her shoulder, and continued to hold her until I could get my emotions under control.

"What's going on, Tay-tay?" Jada murmured, rubbing my back.

"I missed you, Jada," I admitted.

Her body shook a little as she chuckled. "Sure. You missed me. Get in your seat and buckle up. Tell me where I need to take you," she coaxed.

Reluctantly, I pulled away and sat up in my seat, wiping

my tears away with the back of my hand. When I could talk without crying, Jada pulled back onto the road and drove me to my place.

"This is a nice building, Anastacia. You find yourself a sugar daddy up here in Philly?" she asked, chuckling.

I snorted. "Hardly. This is all me, J."

There was an awkward silence, and I wasn't sure what to say to explain how I had moved into such a nice neighborhood with minimal education.

"Okay. You can either invite me in to see your digs, or awkwardly get out of my car and you pretend that this didn't happen. What are we doing, Anastacia?" Jada asked, turning the car off and turning to face me.

I rolled my eyes at the drama, but smirked. "You want to come in and see my place?" I invited half-heartedly.

Jada pursed her lips like she was debating on turning me down. "I don't know... It's kind of late," she feigned hemming and hawing.

I swatted her leg laughing. "Don't be a shit. Come in and see my place," I stated and started climbing out of the car.

"Fiiiiiine," she groaned. "Twist my arm about it. I guess I'll come in and see your digs!"

"I missed you, J," I whispered, wrapping my arm around her waist when she came up next to me.

"I missed you, too, Tay."

Five minutes later, we were walking into my apartment, and Jada was squealing with delight. It wasn't huge, but it had an amazing view of the city at night. Except for the two bedrooms with their own ensuites, the whole apartment was open concept.

Gray wood flooring, white cabinets, and stainless steel

appliances made up the kitchen. It wasn't super high end, but it looked high end because of the contrast of colors and clean lines of everything. In the lounge area, I had a dark blue sofa, sleek white coffee table with dark blue wing-backed chairs for seating.

Then there was my pole. I had a space set aside where a dance pole was installed so that I could practice my routines without needing to go to the club. Domenico thought it was a great idea when I first got it, even begging me to give him a private show.

Then, somewhere along the line, he came to despise it, saying it was unnecessary to constantly remind him that I shook my ass for other men. When he realized I wouldn't take it down, he stopped looking at it. Stopped asking me to dance for him, and just pretended it didn't exist.

Jada dropped onto the sofa and leaned back. "You are such a bitch, Anastacia! I have been so fucking worried about you, thinking you were up here struggling to make ends meet on your own… and you are living like a fucking pimp! Tell me your secrets to wealth and success!" She said, holding her hand out toward me like she held an invisible microphone

I dropped onto the sofa next to her, and leaned my head on her shoulder. "I don't want everyone to judge me, Jada." I sighed, a dry laugh escaping my lips.

"Try me," she prompted, wrapping an arm over me and poking me in the ribs.

"Promise you won't judge me or start lecturing?" I asked, jerking from the tickling sensation and giggling.

Jada sat up and pushed me back so that she could turn and face me. "Anastacia, you can say it. I know you dance," she informed me.

My whole body tensed like someone had poured ice water down my spine. "What do you mean?"

Jada snorted. "Please. You are so fucking toned up and you have a stripper pole in your living room. If I wasn't sure before, I'm pretty sure now," she laughed, pointing at the pole ten feet away.

"I don't want everyone to know!" I exclaimed, suddenly feeling vulnerable when my sister laughed and pulled me into a hug.

"Oh, sweetie. There are only so many jobs that pay in cash like you had when Mami was sick. You either held up a bank or you were dancing," she said.

"I could be some sort of mafia kingpin! You don't know!" I argued back, eliciting another round of laughter from my sister.

"Anastacia, you dance. Who cares? You aren't doing anything illegal. If it makes you happy, who are we to judge?" she stated.

"What do you mean *we?*" I asked, my eyebrows shooting up. I suddenly felt like my stomach was rolling with butterflies as my anxiety shot through the roof.

Jada looked at my reaction and laughed even harder. "Oh my god! You actually think we didn't talk and put two and two together? Pops called it when your friends came to pick you from their house last year. Then Nana said something about you being cagey when she asked to come see a show. It's the worst kept fucking secret!"

"Fuck!" I exclaimed, suddenly feeling like an idiot.

"Is this why you wouldn't move back home? You didn't want us to know?" Jada asked, her voice softening.

"Well, kind of," I admitted.

"Tace, you do you. We don't care as long as you are happy and healthy, and not into any illegal shit. You don't have to hide from your family, sissy," she whispered, pulling me back into a hug.

I suddenly felt like an immense weight had been lifted from my chest. "I was thinking about moving back to Delaware when my lease ended," I admitted to her.

"You should do that. And if you need help moving, you know we are all happy to help you. Just stop shutting us out. Now," she stated seriously, releasing me from another hug. "Tell me why you really called me in the middle of the night, and why your face is fucking swollen."

How the hell I had forgotten about the swollen lump on my cheek, I didn't know. But I did know that I was not about to let my sister in on that little bit of my life. She didn't need to know what happened.

Seeing my unwillingness to answer her, she reached forward and caressed my cheek. "Did your guy do that? Domenico?" She asked.

I smacked her hand away and snorted. "Yeah. I let a man hit me. I fell getting out of the Uber at the club and I was too embarrassed to meet up with my friends. I called you because I didn't want to tell anyone what a fucking klutz I was," I lied.

Jada looked at me for a minute before nodding, seeming to accept my answer. "Well, let's get you cleaned up and then we can have a girls' sleepover. Where's your bathroom by the way, cause I really have to pee. You got any snacks in this bougie crib of yours? Cause you're going to have to feed me for the taxi service," she spouted out, jumping up and pulling me from the sofa.

"Bathroom is behind that door," I said pointing toward the spare bedroom. "And you'll have to see what's in the cabinets. I think there's some popcorn and apple chips."

Just like that, my night was filled with giggling and whispering with my sister. All of the shit from the past melted away, and we were once again thick as thieves sharing secrets and talking about our futures. Did I like lying to my sister about my shit with Domenico? No. But I would never admit that I stayed with a man who hit me.

Never.

Chapter 24

"Let me in, Anastacia. We need to talk," Domenico called from the other side of the door.

"What do you want to talk about?" I asked, not opening the door.

"About the other night. Open the door," he pleaded.

Why was he here again? He had come to my place every day for the last week, messaging me about all of the things that were wrong between us. Telling me all of the things I did to make him crazy seemed to be his way of explaining why we were so toxic together.

"Unless you have an apology for me, go away," I stated, holding my ground.

"Please open the door so we can do this face to face. The neighbors don't need to hear about our drama."

The last comment made me snort. He wasn't wrong though. If the neighbors complained about my drama, I'd be out of an apartment. I sighed, leaning my forehead against the cold wood of the door.

As the latch clicked to unlock the door, I heard him exhale. He didn't hesitate to enter my apartment as the door opened, walking in and kicking the door shut behind him.

"Cara, I lost my temper. Please just talk to me," he cooed,

pulling me into his arms.

The urge to pull away was there, but I let him hold me. No matter how much I fought it, something about him kept me coming back.

"Why'd you hit me?" I asked.

"I don't know. I was fucking angry?" He explained, sighing against my neck.

"I didn't do anything wrong."

"You almost broke my jaw, Anastacia," he retorted, pulling back to look at me.

Whereas the bruise on my cheek had healed enough to be covered with makeup, *his* had turned to that sickly yellow green and covered half of his right jaw line.

"You shouldn't have hit me," I repeated, pulling away from him.

"I was embarrassed, Anastacia! How the fuck are you going to tell an absolute stranger that you don't trust me?" Domenico growled back.

"Huh…. See I could have sworn that I said you were the only person I trusted to have my back…" I chuckled, walking to my kitchen.

"Bullshit!" Domenico yelled, causing me to pause in my step.

"You can leave," I whispered, continuing to walk away.

He made some growling noise before exhaling loudly. "I didn't come here to fight with you," he stated, sounding a bit calmer.

He sounded it, but I knew him by now. Inside he was seething with rage and frustration because I wasn't falling in line and listening to his bullshit. I had been with this man for well over a year and half. Whether he cared to admit it or not, we were addicted to each other even though it wasn't healthy.

When Mami died, something in me didn't care to live and I wallowed in that dark place. The only time I felt alive was when he loved me. The way he touched me, whispering his admiration of my body, it made me feel whole even though he would shatter me.

"I need you, Anastacia," he murmured, suddenly standing behind me.

My breath caught, expecting him to hold me or turn me, but he didn't touch me.

"You've made it clear you can have any woman you want. You don't need me, Domenico."

"You know I do," he whispered against my hair, moving to stand so close behind me that my body was pressed between his and the counter in my kitchen.

"Why do you need me?" I asked, refusing to look at him because I knew I would crumble if I did.

"I can't sleep without you, Stacia," he murmured, one hand caressing down my arm and causing goose bumps to follow behind his touch.

"Yes, you can. Try again," I stated.

"You're going to make me say it?" He asked, wrapping his arms around me. "I'm falling in love with you."

"Heard that one. Try again," I replied.

"I can't live without you, okay? You've fucking ruined me for anyone else," he whined.

There was something in what he said that tickled the back of my mind, but I didn't focus on it. I wanted him to fucking beg.

Like he knew my thoughts, Domenico lowered to the floor

until he was on his knees. His face pressed into the crack of my ass and he whined. "Please, dolce. Don't do this to us. We're still figuring shit out. I'm still trying to figure this shit out," he admitted.

"What do you need? You can have any woman you want for arm candy, Domenico. I'm not doing this every time."

He turned my body and rested his head on my stomach. "I have never been with one woman, Anastacia. This with us, it's all new and crazy, and I'm a jealous man. You know this about me. The thought of you being with anyone else fucking wrecks me."

"So you came to make sure I wasn't with someone else?" I barked back at him.

He gripped my body tighter. "No. I don't want to lose you. Just let's talk about it, okay?"

Talk. He wanted to talk.

* * *

I woke up feeling like my body had been through one of Cherry's workout sessions. Muscles I didn't know I had ached in protest as I tried to roll out of my bed. What the fuck did I do last night? My brain stalled when a warm arm pulled me back against a warmer body.

"Don't leave yet. I'm not ready to let you go," a deep raspy voice whispered against my neck.

I turned my head slowly, unsure of who or what I was going to find in my bed. I had gone to work yesterday. I remembered leaving for work.

I remembered dancing my first number. I remembered the VIP-.

375

"Domenico? How did I get home?" I asked, not remembering anything about the remainder of my night.

"Somebody spiked some drinks at the club. You called me to come get you, so I did. I've been here with you all night," he assured me.

I heard his words but they didn't make any sense. "How did my drink get spiked?" I asked, trying to understand.

He yawned and exhaled loudly, rubbing his face. "I'm not really sure. Whatever it was, it's new. Made it past the security, and whoever it was was able to dose eight of you and take down that bouncer named Charlie."

Fuck.

"Did… Did you? I don't-" I stuttered to get my thoughts across, causing his eyes to shoot open and stare at me.

"I brought you home and put you in a cold bath. Your body was overheating. I took care of you, but we didn't fuck if that's what you're worried about. No matter how hard you begged me, I didn't fuck you last night," he assured me.

"I begged?" I tried to ask, but he just smirked and pulled me back into his chest.

"You weren't in your right mind, Anastacia. I know how you feel about consent, and being sober. I just held you, dolce. God help me, I just held you," he promised again.

Domenico hadn't been in my bed in two weeks. While we had been talking through our shit, I made sure to keep him at arm's length because my traitorous pussy would have had him back at *hello.* To wake up with him in my bed, my body feeling fucking ravaged, and no memory of what happened… I had to ask.

"Why am I so sore?" I whispered.

"That's the drug. It burns so hot, your muscles ache. It's

why I had you in the tub to cool you down. You just need to replace your electrolytes and you'll feel better in a day," he assured me.

My body stilled. "I thought you said it was something new. How do you know so much?"

Domenico laughed darkly, releasing me from his hold. "Anastacia, it's my fucking job to know what everything does. They can change the look, change the name, but the effects on the body are just what they are. Seeing how you were acting and your body reacting, it's the same reaction you have when you've had too much molly."

My thoughts went a hundred different ways all at once. I scrambled for my phone and started dialing before I even realized what I was doing. Charlie had been the first person to have my back at Infinity. He wasn't just a bouncer, he was like a big brother to me.

"Hello?" Olga's voice answered.

"It's me, I just woke up. Is Charlie okay? What happened?" I asked, sitting up and moving away from Dominco.

"It's not good, sweetie. It's not good. Right now he's in the ICU, and the doctors are talking to his wife and kids about the next steps-"

My mind blanked out everything that followed, with only some words registering.

Excessive temperature...

Heart attack...

Brain activity...

Neurologist....

Somewhere deep in the recesses I recognized what Olga was saying, but the conscious part of my mind was in denial.

Unlike me, Charlie didn't have someone who knew to

377

throw him into an ice bath and bring down his core temperature.

Unlike me, Charlie would not be at work again.

Unlike me, Charlie was gone.

I dropped the phone and ran to the bathroom, the bile
hitting the back of my throat before I could even get to the
toilet. I turned quickly and threw up what little remained
in my stomach into the shower. I choked out a sob once my
stomach stopped retching.

"Come on, clean yourself up," Domenico said softly, turning the shower water on.

I nodded numbly and let him move me around like a doll.
Yesterday was a normal day at the club, and today my work
bestie was dead. Yesterday I was trying to keep Domenico
at arm's length, today he was taking care of me like I am the
most precious person in his life. As I was falling apart, this
man was pulling the pieces back together and holding me
up.

Domenico washed my body from head to toe. He used my
favorite conditioning mask in my hair, and worked the comb
through all of the tangles before rinsing it clean. He gently
washed my body, treating me sweetly rather than sexually.
Maybe what I needed was a sexual distraction. Something,
anything to feel something other than empty filling my chest.

I followed along as the water was shut off, and one towel
wrapped around my hair and another my body. My feet
padded softly across the floor as Domenico led me back to
my bed, and began rubbing my arms and legs down with my
body butter.

"Your friend said she'd call you back later," Domenico
informed me, as he pulled a t-shirt over my head.

I thought I nodded, but I was still shaking my head in denial.

Charlie.

"Do you have someone you can call, dolce?" He murmured softly, pulling a pair of loose pajama pants up my legs.

My body was trembling, the cool air of the apartment too much on my damp skin.

"You need to eat something and get some fluids in you," he continued, leading me to crawl under the covers. "Come on. Get under the blankets."

Everything after that was a blur of time passing. I closed my eyes and slept. Domenico woke me up to drink or eat, and then I slept again. The sound of a phone ringing stirred me from the dark, but then I drifted off again to the sound of Domenico's quiet murmuring.

When I finally woke up it was dark outside and I was alone in the room. It took me a minute to realize that I was in Domenico's apartment. *Had he moved me while I slept?*

Small snippets of memory filtered through chasing the wisps of a dream. Domenico took care of me while I was sick. Judging by the time, I had definitely missed my shift. Maybe if I messaged Charlie, he could cover for me.

Charlie.

No sooner had the name entered my thoughts, my eyes began burning with unshed tears. I was missing something. But I couldn't remember what it was about the name that filled me with grief.

I started rummaging around the room to find my phone. Flipping blankets, pillows, and dumping my handbag on the floor beside the bed, my phone was missing. I wouldn't have left it at work, because it never left my bag. Without thinking

I began searching the bedroom for my cell.

Nothing was left untouched, from the nightstand tables, to Domenico's closet and tall chest of drawers. I emptied the cabinets in the en suite bathroom and rifled through the neatly folded towels and toiletries.

"What the hell are you doing?" A deep voice broke through my intense focus.

Startled, I turned quickly and almost fell over as the room began to swim. Domenico quickly stepped forward to brace me before I could tip over.

"Anastacia, what are you doing? Why are you ransacking my apartment?" He asked, taking two crumpled towels from my hands and refolding them before setting them on the counter.

"I- My phone. I couldn't find it," I stuttered lamely, looking around to see the chaos of destruction I had caused.

Domenico jaw clenched for a moment before he reached into a pocket and retrieved my phone.

"It was dead, so I plugged it in for you."

This was so fucking embarrassing. I felt the heat in my face immediately. "Thank you."

"Leave this here for now. We need to talk. It's been a rough couple of days, and I can't continue like this," he admitted, taking my hand and pulling me from the bathroom.

I didn't really process his words until we were sitting in the living room. He said *days*.

"How long was I asleep? I need to call work and tell them I'll be late," I started.

"You don't have to worry about that. The club is closed tonight," Domenico explained, reaching forward to tuck a loose strand of hair behind my ear. He stared at me for a moment, his dark eyes more intense than I had ever seen them. "You scared me, dolce. I don't know what I would have done if you had died."

"Dramatic much?" I scoffed, but the words stuck in my throat. Domenico was many things, but dramatic he was not. "What happened?"

"What do you remember?" He countered.

I shook my head as though it would loosen a memory into place, but there was nothing concrete. I couldn't remember how we got here, or what I had done before that. It was just a murky hole of time with no clear memories attached.

"Okay, let's try this a little differently. What's the last thing you remember clearly?" He asked instead, holding my hands and caressing my knuckles with his thumbs.

The gesture was sweet. Intimate even. It made every hair on the back of my neck stand on end as my brain struggled to remember. I remembered stuff, but there was something missing. It was important.

"Start with Wednesday. You went to the gym with Cherry?" Domenico offered.

Had I gone to the gym with Cherry? Snippets of memory fell into place. The two of us giggling together as we downed our protein shakes. Cussing Cherry out for making me sweat to the point of my legs shaking....

"Yes, I went to the gym with Cherry," I confirmed.

"Then what did you do?" Domenico prodded.

"I-" I stared at him for a solid moment with my mouth agape before I could formulate a sentence.

"What day is it today?" I asked instead.

"What do you remember?" he insisted, holding my hands a little tighter. It wasn't enough to hurt me, but the pressure was becoming uncomfortable.

"No, what day is it today? You said, *"Wednesday,"* so what day is it today?" I repeated.

"Just tell me what you remem-"

"What fucking day is it?!?" I shouted, yanking my hands from his grip.

"It's Monday. Today is Monday, Anastacia. And before you ask, you've been here for four days, in and out of consciousness. So, I am going to ask again… What do you remember?"

"I. What?" I asked, my brain failing to process what he was saying. "Why can't I remember anything?"

"I'm not surprised to be honest. Drugs will do that, dolce. They mess with your memory," he tsked, pulling into his lap and holding me.

"I don't understand," I repeated, shaking my head, desperately attempting to make sense of his words.

Rather than answer any of my questions, he leaned forward around my body to retrieve the local news paper. I didn't need to ask any more questions because the headline left nothing to chance.

'FOUR DEAD, THREE MORE REMAIN IN CRITICAL CONDITION. POLICE INVESTIGATING WILD NIGHT GONE WRONG AT LOCAL GENTLEMEN'S CLUB, INFIN-ITY.'

"What the *fuck?*" I gasped.

Domenico leaned back into the sofa, pulling me with him so that I was tucked against his chest. "Now, you know. So let's start all over again. What do you remember?"

There was nothing. No matter what he said to jar my memories, it was all a blank. Like someone had gone in and wiped my mind of everything. We went round and round for hours, but there was nothing.

After sobbing in exhausted frustration, Domenico finally told me everything that had happened at the club.

From what they had gathered internally and some grainy surveillance footage, a man dressed in dark clothes had wandered around the club spiking drinks. They had not uncovered the man's identity nor his motivation for such an act.

The drug was a hybrid of molly laced with fentanyl to create some nouveau drug that had erupted across major cities around the country. Domenico called it an advertisement, but the authorities and the news had dubbed it domestic terrorism.

"What happens next?" I asked, blowing my nose as I faced him sitting on the couch.

He tipped his head back and ran his hands down his face with an exacerbated groan. " I don't know, dolce. I feel like whatever I say is going to make you upset, and I'm fucking tired of fighting with you."

"Domenico, I can't help if I don't remember-" I started, but he cut me off.

"Do you have any idea how fucking scared I was? You almost died, Anastacia. I almost lost you for real! I can't keep doing this. What if I hadn't gotten to you in time?" He yelled, his voice breaking with emotion.

"This wasn't my fault!" I yelled back

"Fuck! That's not what I'm saying!" He said, jumping up and snarling at me.

"Then what the fuck did you mean? Huh?" I snarled back. He moved so fast I barely registered it before he wasin front of me again, pinning me to the sofa.

"You almost died. You could have died and I would have lost you. Do you have any idea how much that fucking wrecked me?" He asked, holding my chin so that I could stare into his eyes.

"I don't want to lose you, Anastacia. Fuck, I'm so in love with you, dolce…." He confessed. "But I can't support you dancing. Not at Infinity or any other club. It's not safe. You have to see that. Right?"

Fuck. What the hell could I say? He wasn't wrong. Handsy customers were one thing, but someone getting into one of the most exclusive gentlemen's clubs in Philly and killing people was another. If Infinity wasn't safe, which club was?

"Ok," I whispered tentively.

Domenico suddenly looked like I had crushed his soul. And flopped into the seat next to me.

"So that's it? We're just done?" He asked in an equally low whisper, refusing to look at me.

"Yeah," I agreed.

"Then get the fuck out. I can't do this."

It was like I had been slapped into an alternate reality. What fuck was wrong with him? I agreed with him. I was willing to quit dancing *for him*. *For us*.

"What the fuck is wrong with you?" I screamed in sudden humiliation and rage. "Do you enjoy fucking with my head? You gave me a choice and I fucking made one. Now you are telling me to get the fuck out? What the fuck do you want from me?"

"I want you to fucking choose me! How fucking hard is that to understand?" He yelled, grabbing me by the throat.

A burning rage coiled in my stomach. Was he fucking

gaslighting me? "I did choose you! I said *OKAY* and you told me to get the fuck out anyway. So *you* tell *me!*"

"I want you stop FUCKING DANCING, ANASTACIA!" He screamed in my face, squeezing my throat tighter. He was furious, but I wasn't backing down. I didn't know what kind of fucking mind games he was playing now, but I was over it.

"AND I SAID OKAY! WHAT MORE DO YOU FUCKING WANT FROM ME?" I screamed against the vice around my throat, shredding my vocal chords.

And then, just like that , like a switch had been flipped, his mouth was sealed against my own. My hands flew into his hair and pulled as his lips claimed mine. There was nothing sweet or loving about this embrace. It was rage induced and carnal. My body was lifted and slammed against a wall, crushed between it and his body.

Clothes were torn and left shredded on the floor as we clawed, nipped and licked at each other's body. My legs were pulled up and apart by the knees as he thrust himself into me. There was no foreplay or warming up. He bottomed out immediately, causing me to scream with the mix of pain and pleasure.

This wasn't about making love or showing our sweet sides. It was all of the emotions we couldn't say; the almost losses, the regrets. It was fear. I had nearly died and that had scared the shit out of him. I couldn't claim to be naive about the world I walked in. I couldn't pretend it was safe because it wasn't. People had died. *I* almost died.

His pace was relentless as he worked my body to the point where pain and pleasure rode side by side, mixing and mashing, driving me to a peak I swore would kill me.

When my orgasm tore through my body, it felt like I had been rolled under by a wave. My vision blurred, my head swimming, as my body came undone around his.

Domenico had stilled, buried deep inside me, chest heaving to catch his breath. His face was buried in my hair, his haggard breaths hot against the skin on my neck. "We can't go back, dolce. I can't. Make damn sure this is what you want, because there's no going back. I won't keep sharing you, worrying about you," he quietly informed me.

This wasn't a threat. It wasn't an ultimatum. It was his bottom line. He would rather let me go entirely than risk feeling the fear of losing me again. He would rather see me gone from the world than share my body with another man, and in my sick warped mind it was the greatest declaration of love. He loved me, beyond the words he whispered. He was as addicted to me as I was to him. We just kept coming back, like two moths burning in flames, unwilling to fly away from the warmth of the fire.

"I won't go back. I can go back to doing nails," I offered.

"You could do nothing, you know. Let me treat you, let me take care of you," he countered.

"What would I do? Sit around waiting all day for you to come back from work? Clean your house? Make you food? That's not me. I can't be caged up so that you feel safer, Domenico."

"I could just take you to work with me. Keep you by my side, then I could fuck you whenever I wanted," he chuckled, kissing my neck.

"Not if you are going to accuse me of eye fucking fat ugly old me," I grunted, remembering the last time I had joined him for *work*.

"I apologized for that, dolce. It won't be like that," he promised with a deep sigh.

Nothing about our relationship was normal. Not how we met. Certainly not how we fucked. He was possessive and I was a ticking time bomb of controlled rage. When it was good, my god was it good. But when it was bad, it was bloody savage.

And I had almost lost it all. Not just him. My life. The little lie of an existence that I had carved out for myself had nearly ended and I hadn't even seen it coming. The question had been in the back of my mind since I woke up, nagging and gnawing at me. I hadn't asked the one thing that he hadn't said. I was alive, but at what cost?

"How bad was it? Really?" I asked as my voice betrayed the raw emotions I was barely keeping under control.

Domenico, still pressing my body against the wall, shuddered. "Bad, dolce. I thought-" he choked out. "I thought you were fucking with me. I wasn't going to come," he admitted.

As a warm trickle wound its way down to my shoulder blade, I realized that he was crying. Domenico was crying. *For me.*

"You couldn't have known," I comforted, holding him closer. "Fuck. If Roman and Charlie didn't even know, how could you?"

The rest of the night was quiet. A quiet bath, followed by a quiet dinner, before we quietly crawled into bed and held each other in silence. I didn't know how long we laid there before I fell asleep again. When I woke up, the sun was shining in the window and I was alone.

"Domenico?" I called out, slowly crawling out of bed. The apartment was dead silent.

387

Trundling out to the living room, it took me a minute to register what I was seeing. Everything had been cleaned up. The clothes from yesterday, the dishes we had used to eat dinner, the sofa we sat on, the table we ate at; it was all gone.

I stumbled numbly from room to room trying to make sense of what had happened. The entire apartment aside from the bed I slept on had been cleared out. I ran back to the bed and started scrambling to find my phone, but it was missing. The only other thing left was a safe in the closet.

My brain immediately began to spiral out of control, like two demons arguing for dominance

Domenico left me.

No. He cried on my shoulder last night.

But he cried after we had sex. Was that his goodbye then?

What the fuck happened while I slept? Why did he change his mind? I told him *yes.*

He left me.

No. *NO!* He wouldn't have left me like this. Something must have happened. *Right?*

My inner debate was interrupted at the sound of men entering the empty apartment. What the fuck was I supposed to do? I darted for the closet and prayed I remembered the code for the safe. Heart racing, adrenaline pumping, I scrambled to shut the door as quietly as I could before crawling to the safe.

I cringed at the loud beeping noise echoing through the walk-in each time I pressed a key.

"You hear something?"

I froze, the sound of a man's voice coming into the bedroom.

"No. Just get the girl and let's get out of here. Boss doesn't like to be kept waiting," another responded.

Fuck! Were they here to kidnap me? I held my breath waiting to hear the footsteps coming toward me, but it didn't happen. Holding my hand over my mouth to muffle my own whimpers, I quickly typed in the remainder of the code and opened the safe with a loud click.

The footsteps returned, and I nearly choked as my heart raced. *Where the fuck was Domenico?*

"She's not here. You check the bedroom?" the second man asked.

"Not yet. Tidy up the rest and I'll grab her," the first responded.

Oh shit. Shit. Shit. Shit. They were here to grab me! My eyes remained trained on the door as I pulled the 9mm from its place. I had no idea if it was loaded, and I couldn't risk the noise to check.

Holding the weapon as best I could with increasingly shaking arms, I pointed it at the door. If they were coming for me, I wasn't going out without a fucking fight.

"Fuck! She's not here! Call the Boss!" the first man swore.

"Fuck, man. Did you check everywhere? Bathroom? Closet?" the second asked, his voice suddenly much louder. They were both in the bedroom.

I listened as one ran into the bathroom while the other approached the closet. My finger on the trigger, the safety disengaged, I pulled the trigger as soon as the handle twisted. The sound of the shot made my ears ring, but I had his attention.

"FUCK! FALL BACK! SHE'S IN THE CLOSET WITH A FUCKING GUN!" The second man was barking at the first.

"CALL THE BOSS AND GET BACK UP!" The first yelled

from the bathroom.

I thought there were only the two, but a third responded that the Boss was already on his way. I would die before I let these sons of bitches come near me.

"You picked the wrong bitch to fuck with," I growled more to keep myself from falling apart than trying to scare anyone.

The apartment fell into silence. There was no more running back and forth or shuffling around the room. It felt like hours had passed instead of the few minutes that had gone by. For a moment I thought they had left. Then a board squeaked, followed by quiet cursing.

The asshole had taken his shoes off and was coming to the side wall of the closet. I turned and fired without a second of hesitation.

"FUCK!" the man swore loudly before dropping to the floor. "IT DIDN'T HAVE TO GO DOWN LIKE THIS!" He yelled, I assumed for my benefit.

Despite the overwhelming urge to say something snide in return, I kept my mouth shut. Any noise I made would tell them exactly where I was in the closet. I couldn't risk them opening fire on me.

"Fall back, man. The Boss is here."

Hearing the two men run out of the room like their asses were on fire made me laugh, a small chuckle escaping my lips. "Pussies."

The sound of the bedroom door swinging open violently stifled the laughter like a bucket of ice water over a roaring flame. I waited to hear who was so fucking brazen.

"What the fuck is taking so long? The Boss is waiting, just go in and grab her," an unfamiliar voice barked.

There was no point playing docile lamb anymore. They

knew I was here, and I wasn't going to be a weak lamb for any fucking wolves.

"I may not have enough rounds for all of you, but the first one in is getting a bullet in the head!" I said loud enough for the people outside the closet to hear me.

"Anastacia, come out of the closet. No one is going to hurt you, dolce," Domenico called out.

The sound of feet shuffling echoed across the hardwood floors. "I asked you to let her know that I was waiting. How did it turn into her hiding in a closet, fighting for her life?" He asked whoever was waiting for me.

"Sir, we did everything as you asked. But she just started firing off rounds-"

"You said you were here to *grab me!*" I corrected him. "You were just here to grab a woman under a boss's orders!"

"Dolce, I'm going to open the closet. Don't shoot," Domenico encouraged me, his voice just outside the door.

I didn't say a word but kept the gun pointed in that direction just in case it was a trap. My heart pounded in my ears as the knob slowly turned and the door was opened. Domenico knelt down, staring at me over the barrel of his 9mm. "You don't know what this does to me, seeing you like this, dolce. I could fuck you right now," he whispered.

There was no hesitation as I dropped the gun and threw myself into his arms. The moment I was pressed against his chest, enveloped in his embrace, the tidal wave of emotions broke the dams and I sobbed.

"I woke up all alone, and then these people came in, and I thought you left me. Everything was gone!" I quietly sobbed against his neck. "You said it was me and you, but I woke up and you weren't here. What the fuck was I supposed to

391

think?"

Domenico chuckled while he rubbed my back. "I had a few of my employees move our things to our new home, Dolce. I wanted to surprise you. Don't be mad. It's my fault for not telling you what was happening," he murmured sweetly, picking me up and carrying me out of the room.

"I could have killed them," I whispered so that only he could hear me.

"I know, and now so do they."

Chapter 25

I thought we were going to a new apartment, but it was an enormous house in Bryn Mawr, an area I knew to be filled with money. I stared at the sprawling yards with enormous houses around us. I knew that Domenico had money, but this was...

"What is this?" I asked as his vehicle came to a stop in front of a gorgeous mansion. The exterior was a beautiful white stone brick, with huge windows that took in all of the sunlight they could. I could only imagine how bright and sunny the interior would be.

Domenico leaned next to my ear and chuckled. "This, dolce, is your new palace. A place fit for a queen," he whispered, caressing my hand.

I turned quickly to stare at him wide-eyed. "Are you serious? This is a freaking mansion, Domenico!"

He laughed again. "I can afford it. Come on. Let's get you inside so you can check it out. If there is anything you don't like, just let the staff know and they will change it to your liking."

I had to consciously concentrate on closing my mouth as my jaw kept dropping open. The house was massive when we walked inside, with a huge sprawling staircase taking center of a huge entryway. The stairs split off to the left and right about halfway up leading one to the left or right. It was like something I had seen only in movies.

"Domenico, this is insane," I gasped, slowly spinning to take in the high end furnishings and decor.

"You like it?" He asked, stepping up behind me and wrapping his arms around my waist.

"Jesus Christ. Are you serious? This is..."

My words trailed off. I couldn't process the lavish display of wealth before my eyes. How the hell did I not know that he had this much money? Why did he pretend to be poor when we were together? *Shit.*

"You hid how rich you were?" I asked, turning to face him.

To his credit, Domenico looked slightly guilty. "I've had women take advantage in the past. It makes you a bit skeptical about the people who come into your life."

"Why are you telling me? Why all of this? Why now?" I asked, my voice cracking, thinking of everything that we had been through as I buried my face against his chest. "Why me?"

Domenico pulled back enough to tip my head up to chin up so that I had no choice but to look at him. "You are one of the most honest, hard-working women I have ever met. Your moral compass is about as straight as they get. If I can't trust you, there isn't a woman in the world who would be worthy of standing by my side."

I shook my head. "I don't understand."

The smile that crept up on his face, revealing rarely seen dimples, was swoon worthy. He looked mischievous, reaching down to take my hand.

"Not everything I do is on the up and up, if you know what

I mean," he stated quietly, pulling me to follow him up the stairs. "If I wanted a trophy, my clubs are full of women who could fill the role. I want a partner I can trust. Someone who won't plot behind my back because they want what I have."

"And you think that woman is me?" I asked, still not believing everything my eyes were taking in as he led me to a room on the second floor.

Pulling my hand still clasped in his up to his lips, he kissed my knuckles, lingering on my ring finger.

"I know you are," he whispered, opening the door. "I hope you don't mind, but my men also moved your things here and ended the lease on your apartment."

The door swung open to reveal what had to be the master bedroom. Center of the room was a massive king sized bed with a four poster frame. It looked like the whole thing was carved out of black granite, the surface sparkling like stars reflected in the midnight sky.

"Holy shit!" I gasped, stumbling into the room behind him. "Are you serious?" I asked again, squeezing his hand. "Domenico, I don't want to be with you because of your money. You could have kept all of this away from me, and I never would have known. Why now? Why are you showing me all of this?"

Domenico responded by sealing my questions with a kiss. His lips were soft, coaxing my own to respond in turn. When his tongue slid across my lower lip, I opened up to him, my own tongue tangling with his turning the kiss from sweet to passionate in an instant.

His arms tightened around my body, my own wrapping around his neck. My fingers threaded into his thick dark curls and gripped it tightly, eliciting a growl from him.

395

Neither of us said a word, soft pants passing between us as we took turns kissing necks, nipping collar bones, or squeezing the other closer.

I gasped in surprise when the back of my legs hit the bed and I tipped backwards, Domenico following. His hands pulled at the night shirt I was still wearing, the thought suddenly jarring me back to my senses.

Pushing him back I stared in horror. "I'm only wearing a t-shirt, Dom! I just came marching into a freaking mansion in nothing but a t-shirt and panties! I look like a damn homeless rescue!"

Domenico's laugh filled the room as he rolled over on the bed and pulled me on top of him. The sound was absolutely infuriating.

"Don't laugh at me!" I protested, swatting his chest as I sat back so that I was straddling his waist. "I don't want people to think I am a charity case, or worse that I am here for your money!"

He grasped my hands and held them against his chest. "I don't give a fuck what anyone else thinks. *I know* that you aren't after my money. That's all that matters."

"You know I'm not from money, right? People will talk."

"Then I will cut out their tongues, Anastacia," he joked, pulling me back down so that my head rested over his heart.

"This is insane, Domenico. What the hell am I supposed to do in this giant ass fucking house?" I asked, looking around at the enormous bedroom.

"Dolce, you can do whatever you want. If you want to go shopping, go shopping-" he started, making me laugh.

"When have you ever seen me spend money like that?" I cackled.

"Do what you want, Anastacia. As long as it isn't dancing, I will support whatever you want to do," he whispered, tucking my hair behind my ear.

"I can do anything?" I asked.

"Anything."

"So I can stay here and rule over all of your people like a queen on a throne?"

"If that's what you want," he chuckled.

"What if I want to tear down the walls and build a giant bouncy house?" I asked, chuckling.

"Do it! Sounds like fun."

"Our kids will have an amazing childhood," I laughed, imagining what it would have been like to grow up within such wealth. To have a bouncy house inside our home.

So lost in my own personal fantasy of what our future would be like, I didn't notice that Domenico had stopped laughing and stilled beneath me.

"Anastacia, that won't happen," he said.

"What? The indoor bouncy house? You just said I could! No take backs!" I squealed as I sat up.

I expected to see the same dimples. I expected to see his eyes still dancing with joy. What greeted me instead was the hardness reserved for a fight. Everything in me prepared to fight back, my mind whirling with how I could escape this place if things went wrong.

"Dolce, I can't have children."

My brain hiccuped, like I hadn't understood his words. "What do you mean?" I asked.

"We will never have children together, dolce. It's not possible," he stated, watching me for my every micro reaction. In my mind the jump from his words to a natural conclusion

397

was the most severe: he didn't want children with someone like me.

"So I'm good enough to fuck and treat like a queen, but not good enough to have children with?" I growled, my eyes burning with tears and unspoken humiliation rolling inside my gut.

"Fuck. I can't have kids, dolce," he repeated.

"Why? Don't you trust me to keep them safe? I would make a good mother!" I swore as the first tears rolled down my cheeks.

We sat in silence staring at each other for what felt like an eternity before I slid off of the bed and stomped toward the door.

"I'm such a fucking idiot. Take me the fuck home," I murmured half to myself, my voice barely holding back the tremble I felt bubbling up.

Domenico was behind me in an instant, arms wrapped tightly around me. "What just happened? Why are you reacting like this, dolce?" He whispered against my hair.

"I can't just be someone to warm your bed. You don't want everything with me, then let me go," I cried, struggling against his hold.

"Anastacia, you misunderstood, love. I can't have kids. Not with you or any other woman. I *can't*. I would love nothing more than to make beautiful babies with you, dolce. But for me," he murmured, turning me again to face him, "it will only ever be a dream. I can't get you pregnant no matter how much I may want it."

"I don't understand. You made this big deal about me being on birth control and being clean, why the fuck did you care if you couldn't get me pregnant?" I asked, now feeling like I was being gaslit.

Domenico's head tipped back as he exhaled. "I had a vasectomy ten years ago. Do you know how many women would try to baby trap someone like me if they thought it would keep them by my side?" he asked.

"Well, I'm not like that!" I screamed in outrage.

Before I could say another word I was swept up in his arms and pressed against the wall, my legs naturally wrapping around his waist.

"You," he whispered, pressing his body against my own, "are nothing like any woman I have ever met. If I had known that you would be in my future, I wouldn't have had myself snipped. If I had known that you were my future, I'd have found you sooner and kept you knocked up every day of your life."

"What?" I asked, confused by this turn of events.

"Dolce, the thought of you pregnant is a wet dream. You strutting around our home with a round belly, carrying my heir," he whispered as he began kissing my neck and jaw. "I could come right now, imagining it."

My body responded where my brain and mouth had glitched, a soft moan escaping my lips as he ground his erection against my core. It was the only encouragement he needed, turning and making quick steps to the bed. No sooner had my back hit the soft comforter, Domenico was pulling my underwear down with one hand while the other unfastened his belt.

"You swear it?" I asked breathily, my hands reaching between us into his boxers to grasp the silky rod waiting for me.

"Fuck, dolce. You are everything to me," he groaned as I

399

gave him a couple of firm pumps.

"Show me. Show me how much I mean to you," I begged, wrapping my legs around him.

Domenico ripped my hands off of his shaft and pinned them over my head as he leaned over my body, taking one of my nipples into his mouth as he kicked his pants off. My body bowed as he sucked so hard I was gasping for breath.

My nipple came out of his mouth with a pop, and he turned to nearly swallow up the other, lathing my pebbled nipple with his tongue. One hand kept my arms pinned above my head while the other trailed down to squeeze the breast in his mouth.

"The thought of these filling with milk," he whispered, pulling away from my now reddened nipples. "It's enough to make a grown man cry in remorse."

"This pussy?" He said, his free hand trailing down to my drooling nether region. "I would worship at this altar, begging for you to get pregnant."

His thumb circled over my throbbing clit as two fingers slid up and down my soaking lips. "Fuck, you're so wet for me, Anastacia. Always this wet for me," he murmured, his eyes watching my lower half as his fingers slid between my folds.

I was a panting mess, my legs spread wide so that his eyes could see every part of me, take their fill. I wanted to beg him to just fuck me until I couldn't see straight, but this was about him saying what needed to be said. He knew where I stood, I needed him to tell me where he stood.

"I need you, dolce," he almost whined, pulling his fingers from my pussy and grabbing my hip.

"You have me," I whispered back, trying to pull my hands

from his iron grip so that I could touch him.

"I'm not going to let you touch me, dolce. I want you like this," he murmured, squeezing my thigh so that I would stop squirming. "I'm going to fuck you until you can't leave my bed, Anastacia."

That was the only warning I had before my hips were rolled up and he bottomed out inside me in a single thrust. I half screamed, half moaned from the sudden fullness of him taking me the way he wanted. Before I could gather my thoughts, he pulled back until barely the tip remained and then slammed into me again.

"FUCK," we both swore at the same time.

"You are everything to me, Anastacia. I want you so much it makes me crazy," he admitted, thrusting into me again and again.

"You have me," I panted, meeting his every thrust with a grunt.

"I want all of you, Anastacia. We can adopt if you want children," he promised, capturing my mouth with his own in a punishing kiss before pulling away again.

Did I want kids? I couldn't honestly say whether I wanted them or not. I just wanted to be loved wholeheartedly by one person. "Love me."

"I love you, Anastacia. I see you. There's only you," he swore, thrusting hard between each declaration.

My hands still pinned against above me, I dug my heels into his ass and rolled my hips up to meet his punishing pace. I wanted to combust as the tip hit the same point over and over, the ridge of his cock rubbing the right spot with every thrust.

"Tell me," I begged again, needing to hear his affirmations

all over again.

"I want you, dolce. You and you alone. *My queen*," he grunted, his pace quickening so that our bodies were slamming into each other.

"Tell," I moaned again, unable to form a coherent sentence as I felt myself getting closer. No one knew my body like this man. No man had my core tightening in ecstasy like Domenico. I was about to combust under this man, from his words and cock alone.

"I love you." Thrust. "So." Thrust. "Fucking." Thrust. "Much."

"Yes," I writhed beneath him, reveling in his words and attention.

"Come for me, dolce. COME NOW!" he bellowed, slamming into me one last time as we both fell over the edge together gasping and shaking.

My vision blurred to bright white as my orgasm rolled through my body, an electric current zipping from my core to my fingertips. Still deep inside, Domenico rolled his hips grinding against me as if he could will his dick to go deeper. The friction against my clit and ravaged lower lips left me a shuddering mess beneath him.

Domenico released my hands to hold both sides of my face, his thumbs caressing my cheeks. "I'm in love with you, Anastacia."

"Don't ever leave me again," I whispered, as my brain retook control of my body.

"Never," he promised, kissing me like it was the last thing he would do on this earth.

Hearing his words sealed with a searing kiss, I couldn't lie to myself anymore. I had fallen in love with his man. He had my heart entirely.

* * *

Two years later...

"Is everything all right, my love?" Domenico asked, tapping softly on the door to my bathroom.

Tonight was his night, and he wanted me by his side. Tonight he was meeting with the heads of the eastern seaboard gangs as their new leader. The first man to unite the various families under one house. It had been a bloody war filled with countless battles to get here, but he had finally won.

My phone buzzed softly from the counter. I didn't bother to answer it, knowing it wouldn't be anything good.

"Anastacia, we're going to be late," he huffed from the other side of the door.

I checked myself over one last time in the mirror before finally opening it. Domenico's face quickly turned from one of irritation to one of awe. The dress I had chosen for tonight was a nude champagne color. The top hugged me in all the right places, with criss crossing strips of tulle over a silk corset. The skirt was cut at the knees in the front and then flowed to the floor behind me in a small train.

"Do you like it?" I asked, smiling coyly.

Domenico turned me around slowly, barely caressing the long locks of my hair cascading down my back. His eyes trailed from my head to my toes, taking in my narrow waist and pushed up breasts. "You have to take this off," he said finally.

"I'm not taking this dress off," I laughed.

"Dolce, I'll go to prison with you dressed like this!" He swore, turning me to face him. "I will kill any man who looks at you!"

"No one would dare to look at your woman," I giggled, placing my hand over his chest. "Weren't you worried about being late?"

Domenico shook his head as if trying to clear the dirty thoughts filling his mind. "I'm going to rip this dress to pieces when we get home, Anastacia," he promised, taking my hand and leading me through the house to the awaiting car.

I had been swept away like a treasure, my every wish and whim indulged by a man who had promised to love me forever. I attended to his every need, stood by his side through thick and thin. When a rival organization opened fire on us at dinner, he hadn't hesitated to shield me with his own body; taking the bullet that was meant for me.

Arriving at a luxurious hotel, I checked my makeup one last time before the door was opened by the valet. Domenico tossed the man the keys to his Bentley and took my hand to lead me inside. Every eye was on us as we stepped into the grand ballroom. As far as the hotel was concerned, this was a corporate fundraiser for some local charity, but every guest on this list was a hardened criminal.

"Boss, it's good to see you," several men said, stepping forward to greet Domenico as we walked through the crowd.

"Regina," a few whispered, nodding respectfully to me. The reference stunned me for a moment. Though Domenico might refer to me as his queen, it was insanely presumptuous to acknowledge me by that title in front of Domenico. It was tantamount to calling me an equal to the man every person in here feared.

Domenico might have missed it the first two times, but he heard it by the third. My hand resting on his arm, I felt him stiffen, muscles tensing, each time it was repeated. There was nothing I could say to correct them that would make this less awkward or aggravating for the man beside me. When a waiter walked past with a tray of champagne I grabbed two glasses, and passed one to Domenico.

As we neared our table, I leaned my head against Domenico's shoulder and smiled warmly. "Long live your king," I said, raising my glass to the room.

Every man and woman in the room cackled and cheered, quickly downing their own beverages of choice.

Domenico peered at me from the corner of his eye, and smirked. "You think yourself very clever?" He whispered, turning to face me.

"They would see you live a thousand years, babe," I replied, giving him a sweet peck on the lips. "And I just want you to die in my embrace."

"You may just get your wish. Seeing you in that dress and not being able to rip it off is going to kill me, dolce."

* * *

I stared at the newest tattoo wrapping around the left side of my ribs and waist. It had started with a small mark on my skin. A piece of flash on the inside of my wrist meant to symbolize my love for Domenico. Now I used the tattoos to hide the ugly scars I carried on my body and inside my heart.

"Is everything to your satisfaction, regina?" The artist

asked, eyeing me nervously.

"Don't call me that," I corrected him, as I looked over the new ink welting on my side. "It looks fine. Will you still be able to finish it today?" I asked, returning to lie on the table.

"Uh, yeah," he nodded.

"Good, get done then while we still have time," I reminded him. Domenico might have loved my ink, but he hated any man who touched me. It made getting elaborate pieces extremely difficult to schedule. If I couldn't get the piece completed in one sitting, it wouldn't be finished by the same artist.

The tattooer would either turn up missing, or I would receive a message that they'd 'moved back home with family.' Gabriel was unknown in Philadelphia, because he didn't have a shop with flashing lights. He tattooed by appointment and through referrals. I had seen his work, and knew he needed to be the one to complete the mishmash of incomplete work on my torso.

We had been communicating through intermediaries for nearly a month, exchanging pictures of the incomplete ink on my body and the design ideas he had to tie them together.

Getting on his calendar without Domenico knowing had been hard, but I had convinced his shadows that I was spending the day at my sister's. It wasn't a complete lie. I just had Gabriel meet me at Jada's apartment. She had let him in before I arrived and then gone to run errands while Gabriel did his work. His men were not permitted to follow me when I visited family, so we were left alone for the most part.

"You said there was something else you wanted added?" Gabriel asked, finishing in the shading of scales fading into a sakura blossom.

"Yes, a teardrop," I confirmed.

"Where did you want it?" He asked, wiping the excess ink from my side and lathering it clean before wrapping it.

"Here," I stated, pointing to my throat and the tattoo of an eye staring back at the world.

Gabriel stared at my throat for a moment, assessing my previous work. "You sure? It might mess with the symmetry of it. I'd have to do something else to keep the balance."

I waited until he was done wrapping my side, before laying back on the table again, my head tipped back.

"I trust your judgment. Make it work," I stated quietly. On the outside I may have seemed calm, but inside I was dreading the pain he was about to inflict. Tattooing my throat was the worst pain I had experienced among my many pieces.

It was one part sensitivity of the thin skin, and one part trust that the person working on my throat wouldn't kill me. Gabriel reset his station up and then leaned over my body, staring intently at my throat. I couldn't handle the intensity of his gaze assessing me, and closed my eyes as if I was ready to sleep.

The lightest touches of a pen slid across my throat. I couldn't tell what he was drawing, but it felt like a series of soft arches.

"You're sure about this?" He asked, repositioning himself so that my head practically sat in his lap.

"Just get it done," I murmured, keeping my eyes closed. I let my mind drift away to the soft buzzing of the needle.

* * *

"What did you do at your sister's?" Domenico asked, from the other side of the bathroom door. I had stayed the night and the better part of the following day at Jada's so that he wouldn't question me on the tattoos as soon as I walked in the door.

"What we normally do. Drink, gossip, eat junk food. How was your meeting in Baltimore?" I asked as I applied the cream to my freshly cleaned ink.

"It was what it was," he sighed. "Are you going to make me come in there, dolce?"

My movements froze. *He knew.* It was the only thought I had at that moment. If he knew, then it made no sense to pretend he didn't.

"Let me finish cleaning up and then you can come and inspect, ok?" I offered.

I heard him chuckle from the other side, half expecting to hear the sound of his footsteps leaving my room. They did not.

Drying my hands, I checked one last time to make sure that I hadn't missed a spot and opened the door. Domenico's intense gaze met mine as soon as I stepped into the bedroom. He was seated at the end of the bed, leaned forward, arms resting on his knees. He was getting ready for a fight. I stood there in only my bra and panties, watching and waiting for his reaction.

"Do you like it?" I asked, tipping my head back slightly and turning around.

"It's stunning. Just like you, dolce," he stated, eyes raking over every inch of my body. "Come closer so that I can inspect."

I couldn't help the smirk teasing at the corner of my mouth.

Domenico and I had a love-hate relationship. He hated it when I challenged him, but I loved the domineering sex that always followed. I stalked toward him like a predator, unwilling to show him any fear.

"Who did the work?" he asked, sitting up as I moved to stand between his legs.

"Does it matter? They won't be inking me again, right?" I couldn't stop the sass in my question. I had kept quiet up until now about his efforts to keep me in the dark, so why was I rubbing in the fact that I knew what he had done? It was easy pretending to not know how controlling he was, all of the measures he took to keep me hidden away from the world. I loved him, but at the end of the day I loved myself more. He couldn't control me, and he needed to know that.

Domenico stared at my face for a moment before smiling. "Right."

There was another long moment of silence before either of us said a word.

"I need to go out of town for a few days, my love. Will you promise to stay here with the security detail until I get back?" he asked, placing a feather light kiss on my chest.

"I can't do that, and you know it, Domenico," I sighed. He started to argue with me, but I put a finger over his lips to silence him. "Cherry is picking me up on Friday, remember? We're doing a girls' spa weekend. You promised it wouldn't be a problem, and had your guys go through every second of the fucking itinerary. I'm not staying home, again," I argued.

Domenico's whole demeanor changed. Normally I would cave and let him make a big show of trying to keep me safe. This was different. Cherry was throwing me a birthday party, because even after all this time, *she* remembered my birthday.

A fact that seemed to elude the man sharing my bed at night. It was something that broke a piece of my heart whenever I thought about it.

"We've had this planned for two months. I'm not backing out at the last minute, Dom. I'm not spending the whole weekend alone without the girls," I argued.

"It's not last minute, you have three days. And you are never alone, dolce," he argued back.

That made me laugh. "Really? Who is going to talk to me, hmm? Sure as fuck not your babysitters. The maids you have running around here won't even fucking make eye contact with me. No. I'm not backing down on this!" I stated firmly and turned back to my closet to find some clothes to wear.

I had barely stepped into the massive walk-in when the bedroom door slammed, causing me to flinch. I wouldn't stop him this time. I wouldn't call out for him or text him as he marched out of the house. He wanted to throw a temper tantrum, I wasn't going to stop him. Rather than going to sleep like I had planned, I pulled a suitcase from the back of the closet instead and started throwing clothes in it. If I didn't leave now, Domenico wasn't going to let me leave while he was out of town.

It took all of fifteen minutes before I was dressed and dragging my luggage out to the garage. I could hear a flurry of footsteps running through the house, but I wouldn't run. I opened the back of the Rover and threw my shit into the compartment like I didn't have a care in the world. His detail could lock me in the house, but they couldn't lay a finger on me without facing Domenico's wrath. A fact that was well known.

I slammed the hatch closed and climbed into the driver's

seat. We'd talk about all of this when he got back from wherever he was going. As far as I was concerned, I was going on a vacation with my best friends.

* * *

I spent the next few days with my grandparents and helping them with odd jobs around the house. Initially, Nana was shocked to find me standing at her door, but then embraced me like a long lost child who had finally come home. I only really saw them at Christmas or the occasional visit with Jada. The days flew by gardening, drinking coffee and rearranging furniture. By the time Friday rolled around, I had forgotten about the argument with Domenico and I was ready for the weekend.

Friday morning started with a limousine ride to an upscale day spa in New York. Cherry hadn't lied when she said that she had gone all out for this girls' weekend. We drank mimosas and snacked on assorted fruits, laughing at each other's stories along the way.

I squealed when we entered the hotel and Marjorie, Lacy and Angel greeted us in the lobby. Cherry quickly made it clear that this would be a reunion weekend with a lot of the girls from the Marquessa. Marjorie pulled me into a tight hug before passing me over to Lacy and then Angel.

"Look how grown you've become," Angel gushed as we embraced each other.

I couldn't help but laugh. "I've been grown for as long as you've known me!" I corrected her.

"Bullshit. I just watched you walk into this hotel like you owned the place. Confidence looks good on you, Tace," she

411

said, tucking a loose strand of hair behind my ear.

I had to turn my head quickly to stop the tears from burning my eyes.

"Don't make her cry!" Cherry laughed, pulling me toward the elevators across the lobby.

"Don't we need to check in?" I asked, looking over at the concierge desk confusedly.

"Marjorie already took care of it. You, sweet birthday girl, need to just relax and let go of the control for a couple of days. We have the whole penthouse floor this weekend, and all you have to do is enjoy yourself. No stress, no planning, no coordinating. Just eat, sleep, laugh, drink and have fun," Cherry stated as the elevator doors closed.

"So what is first on the agenda?" I asked, looking at the other women expectantly.

"We're going out on the town, Marquessa style," Lacy grinned.

"Won't that affect your work there, Miss public defender?" I asked, smiling back at her.

"Please," she laughed. "I'd like to see someone try to fire me for having a girls' night out on the town. I'd sue their asses into bankruptcy courts."

We were all laughing at her bravado just as the doors opened to the penthouse suite. Elektra and Spider came bounding through the room to greet me, the two squishing me between them in an impossibly tight hug.

"Guys! I can't breathe," I wheezed, laughing at them both.

"Oh my god, look at you, Tace!" Spider squealed.

"This ink is fucking amazing!" Elektra added, tipping my head to get a better look at the tattoo work on my neck and shoulders. "Fuck that is hot."

412

"Give her some fucking room!" Cherry yelled, pushing the two away from me. "We have the birthday girl for the whole weekend. That's plenty of time to catch up. Right now, we need to get her ready for brunch!"

The women nodded and pulled me into a side room where a small team was standing by to do my hair and makeup. By the time they were finished with me, everyone was dressed to step into the NYC socialite circles. The dress Cherry purchased for me was a high collared maxi dress that pulled in around my waist but flowed down to my ankles. Instead of long sleeves, the dress was paired with a chenille cardigan that wrapped around my back and only covered my arms.

"All we need now are some fascinators or big hats, and we're ready for the races," I giggled, seeing everyone else dressed similarly conservative.

"I told you she would figure it out!" Spider cracked up, pointing at Cherry.

Wide-eyed I turned to face Cherry. "Seriously? Are we going to the races?" I asked, unable to hide the excitement on my face.

"This is your bucket list weekend, Lilly-bear. Whatever your heart desires, we are going to get it done!" Cherry smiled back. "This weekend you are the queen, and we are your ladies. You just say the word, and we'll take care of you."

I had to fan my face to stop the burning sensation in my eyes, tears threatening to smear my makeup. "You guys are too much. I don't know what I ever did to deserve women like you in my life," I choked up.

Marjorie was the first to step forward and give me a hug. "You are the most selfless woman I have ever met, Anastacia. This is just us showing you how much we love you for being

413

you."

Rather than stopping the torrent, Marjorie's words turned me into a blubbering mess, as the women laughed at me. I felt like I'd been a horrible friend to them over the past two years. I rarely got to see them, and often had to resort to contacting them on the sly to avoid Domenico's lecturing. When I agreed to step away from exotic dancing, I had only meant the job. Domenico, however, wanted me to break all contact with anyone from that chapter of my life. I refused. These women were like sisters to me.

After a quick touch up of my makeup, we were out the doors of the hotel and on our way to the races. The remainder of the day went by in blur. We wagered, lost, and won some on the horses. After the races we went to an upscale restaurant for dinner. I couldn't remember the last time I had laughed that much, and truly felt the joy of those around me.

Saturday was another day of pampering and a shopping trip on Fifth Avenue. Jada and I had always fantasized about shopping on this iconic strip of New York. Mami had laughed with us, and we pretended to be billionaire socialites buying up the stores in one go. Now I was standing inside those iconic high end shops, while the staff fawned all over us.

I already had enough clothes at home, so I opted for a new pair of heels and a set of cuff links for Domenico. When it was time to check out, I was the last one at the register.

The attendant looked embarrassed passing my card back to me. "I'm sorry, miss. It seems your card was declined."

Too busy laughing with Elektra, I hadn't heard her the first time. The woman cleared her throat, and repeated the words.

"Your card was declined, miss."

"What? That's impossible," I laughed, pulling out my phone to show her the account balance on my accounts.

Everything after that was a blur. My friends rushed me off of Fifth Avenue and took me back to our hotel room. I didn't know what to say.

I couldn't believe it, standing in the shop staring at my bank app. I didn't want to believe it, staring at the evidence in front of me for the third time.

Everything was gone.

Chapter 26

"Hi, baby. The girls and I are having a great time in New York. I wish you could have been here for the baby shower. We have so much to tell you, so call me back. Okay?" As soon as I ended the call, my voice went from sickly sweet to sobbing again.

"Shit, Tace. You're pregnant?" Cherry asked, staring at me wide eyed along with the rest of the group

I snorted. "Not a fucking chance. We can't have kids, but nobody is supposed to know. It's our code for emergencies."

I pretended not to notice when the women all exchanged glances with one another. They didn't know who Domenico was, and I wasn't going to tell them anything now that things had come to this. But we had all been around enough thugs and trouble makers, heard them talking in the clubs, to know that the man I stood with was dangerous.

"Why do you need a code for emergencies?" Marjory asked first, her voice barely above a whisper.

Of course she was the most perceptive. I opened my mouth to tell her what I could, but my phone rang, interrupting us.

Dommy calling...

"Hi baby!" I answered, staring at the women around me.

"Where are you, dolce?" His voice came through calm and

416

reassuring, as if nothing had happened.

"I'm in the hotel with the girls. Are you busy? I didn't mean to disturb you, baby," I cooed.

Spider shook her head as if to shake off a chill, and Elektra left the room with Angel and Cherry following behind her. I would have stopped them, but Marjory shook her head at me, rolling her hands as if to tell me to keep talking.

"I wasn't feeling well," I continued. "Like everything I have just suddenly drained out of me."

"Is that so? That's a shame. I know how much you were looking forward to this weekend," he responded, his words causing my brows to furrow.

"I was thinking of coming home early. I miss you," I lied.

There was a moment of pause, before Domenico responded.

"I don't think coming home will help, dolce. There's been so much going on, I think your body needs this vacation, dolce. Stay where you are and enjoy yourself. You deserve this time with your family."

His words trickled down my spine like ice settling in.

"You really don't mind if I extend my stay?" I asked tentatively.

"I think being with your family is the best thing for your health in your condition. Don't even think about coming home. I insist, cara."

I didn't stay on the phone much longer, and mumbled a few sweet words before Domenico ended the call. The entire room began spinning, and I couldn't think straight. We had talked about so many things over the years. There plans upon plans in case something happened to him, but this was the worst case scenario he had anticipated.

417

Elektra returned with a tray of drinks and set them on the table. No one said a word as she passed everyone a glass and took a seat on one of the two massive sofas in the lounge of our suite. We sat and down the glasses of whiskey before anyone said a word.

"What's happened?" Marjory asked.

"I seemed to have overspent my savings on this trip," I stated numbly, relaying what Domenico had said to me.

"Shit," Lacey swore before reaching to refill her glass.

Cherry and Spider share a confused look before turning to Lacey to explain. "What does that mean? We don't get it," Spider said.

Lacey looked at me and I gave her a slight nod, letting her know it was okay to explain the situation from a legal point of view.

"It means that someone has been investigating them, and there is enough evidence to warrant freezing the assets to prevent anyone from attempting to get away, flee the country, or bribe officials," she explained. "It's a last resort reserved for people with access to immense resources and power. It means they have enough evidence to point to someone, but not quite enough to put them away. And in this case, they are looking at our girl here."

"What the hell did you get into?" Cherry blurted out pushing my shoulder back so that I would turn to face her.

"Cherry...." I wanted to tell her. I wanted to tell them all but anything I said would taste like ashes in my mouth. I couldn't lie to them.

So we sat there in silence, the seven of us, for what felt like hours but was really only several moments. At this point, anything that I said could be used against me or them. If

418

things continued to go badly, they could be implicated in my mess.

"You're right," Lacey said, breaking the silence. "You can't tell them a thing without pulling them into your situation, but you can tell me. As your attorney, let me handle this."

Lacey quickly scribbled one word on a piece of paper and held it up. No one said a word.

"Lace-" I started but Marjory stood up suddenly, like she had been shocked.

"You know, I think we should go to the movies together. My treat. Angel, what was the name of that show you wanted to see again?" Marjory asked, walking toward the kitchen.

"Do you really think that's wise?" Spider asked, obviously not understanding the diversion techniques at play.

Angel patted Spider's back and smiled. "It wasn't a movie, Marj. I said I wanted to see Chicago at the theater," she corrected, smiling.

"That's what I said," Marjory insisted from the other room.

"No. You said going to the movies. I was talking about the theater," Angel insisted, trying not to laugh.

Cherry looked confused as hell and added her two cents to Marjory's defense, "They play movies in theaters, Angel. They literally say, '*In theaters now.*'"

"Oh my god, seriously?" I muttered, shaking my head.

"What? It's true!" Cherry argued back, causing Lacey to nod in approval.

"Are you kidding me? Yes, movies are in movie theaters," Angel laughed. "But *the theater,*" she said, making air quotes, "refers to a show. Like a play, or in this case a musical off broadway."

"Really, you are so dumb, Cherry," Spider threw in, pretending to look at her nails.

"Stuff it, Spidey! You didn't know either!" Cherry huffed, storming into the kitchen to join Marjory.

Angel and Elektra followed, dragging Spider with them, leaving Lacey and I to stare at the piece of paper now lying on the table between us. Lacey was smart. She had picked up on exactly what the problem was in an instant, and the others had followed her lead without hesitation.

"Have you seen Chicago yet?" Lacey asked, sipping her whiskey casually.

I shook my head, causing Lacey to point at the piece of paper.

"No. I have to admit, I've never been to a live performance," I added.

"Not even a concert or a comedy stand up?" Lacey asked, raising a brow.

My cheeks heated up, but I shook my head again. "Nope."

"Do you hear that, ladies? Lilly-bear has never seen a live show!"

Angel immediately came running from the kitchen and pounced onto the sofa next to me. "Seriously? Oh my god! Marjory, we have to get this woman out into the world!" She yelled, turning quickly toward the others, knocking my phone off of my lap and sending it skittering across the floor.

"It's not that big a deal" I said, laughing as I got up to retrieve my phone.

What happened next, was nothing short of a comedy action shot from the bygone days of silent movies. Elektra, running into the room at Angel's words, stepped on my phone and slipped forward. As she tried to right herself from the impending fall, my phone was kicked out from beneath her foot and launched further across the smooth floors of the suite toward the kitchen.

Cherry, who was a few feet behind Elektra, was hit in the foot with the projectile phone and instinctively kicked it away, launching it airborne.

"Catch it!" I yelled at no one in particular, dashing to grab my phone.

Spider, rather than catching my mobile, dove to the floor to keep from being beaned in the head with it. The phone ricocheted off of a pillow that Angel held. Instead of ending the phone's flight, it bounced back and flew over Lacey's head.

"Fuck, Angel!" Lacey screamed, diving to the floor.

My phone hit the wall behind Lacey's head and shattered.

"What the fuck just happened?" I yelled, looking around the room at everyone in shock.

No one said a word as we looked at each other. Spider was laying in a ball holding her head, Elektra sprawled out on the floor where she had fallen. Cherry was holding her foot cussing about the pain, and Lacey lay in a heap on the floor shaking.

I didn't know who broke first. Whether it was a whine, a wheeze or a snort, it didn't matter. The suite was suddenly filled with the sound of us laughing hysterically.

"That was fucking awesome!" Lacey laughed, gasping from the floor. "Holy shit! I wish I had that on camera!"

"Lil, I'm so sorry!" Angel apologized. "I thought the pillow would catch it!"

"HA!" Elektra laughed harder.

"That's like asking a tennis racket to catch the fucking tennis ball!" Spider wheezed, crawling toward the couch.

"Oh, god! That's pure comedy gold!" Lacey laughed harder.

When we had finally calmed down a bit, Marjory and I cleaned up the remnants of my phone. I moved to dump the pieces into the trash but Lacey stopped me. She took what remained of the phone's body and removed the small SIM card.

"Angel would buy you a new phone, but she's on a strict budget. Let me cover this, since it was my fault it fell" she said, dropping the card into her glass of whiskey.

Angel looked indignant for a moment. "Spider could have caught it instead of ducking like chicken shit!"

"I wouldn't have had to duck for cover if Cherry *Beckham* over there hadn't launched it at my head!" Spider retorted, pointing at Cherry.

The giggles started up again, and soon we were all panting from laughing so hard. "You have to admit, that was such an amazing fucking kick!" Cherry giggled.

"It was," I agreed, wiping the tears from my eyes.

"So what do we do now?" Elektra asked, taking the glass of what I thought had been whiskey and a now dissolved SIM card.

"We'll have to run and get a new phone for Lilith on our way to see the show," Marjory stated, smoothing nonexistent wrinkles on her skirt.

"It's too late for that," Lacey interjected, looking at her watch. "All of the stores are closed until Monday at this point."

"Well, I guess I'll be unplugged until Monday then," I sighed, not feeling the least bit upset about the wait.

"No you won't. Lacey has two phones. She can just lend

you her personal phone until we can get you a new one on Monday," Spider argued, causing everyone to turn and look at her like she was an idiot. "What??" she asked, staring back at us.

Lacey just shook her head and sighed. "If you need to reach anyone, or anyone needs to reach us, they'll find a way. For now let's just get changed, and get ready to go see Chicago."

↞�⊱⊸✕⊸⊶⊱↠

For an impromptu outing to the theater, we managed to get center seats overlooking the stage from the balcony. Sitting between Lacey and Marjory, I was completely enthralled within the opening number of *All that Jazz.*

"So you like musicals now?" Lacey asked, singing along with the women on stage.

"This is amazing. I love it!" I gushed, unable to stop myself from swaying in my seat to the catchy musical number.

"How deep are you in, Lil," she asked quietly, her eyes never leaving the stage nor her smile breaking.

"Association. Locations. I'm with him, not in it with him," I said, mirroring her attention on the show before us.

"Joint accounts? Assets?" Lacey asked.

"Mine is mine, his is his," I clarified.

"Where'd it come from? Your money?" She continued.

"Worked for it. My former employer gave me a really good severance package after I nearly died on the job."

"Above board?"

"To the letter, lawyers notarized and verified everything. Even threw in an NDA so the particulars wouldn't be disclosed openly," I added.

"Tell me about it," Lacey murmured, leaning back and wrapping her arm over my shoulder so that we could sway together to the music.

Over the next forty minutes, I quietly told Lacey everything about the near death fever. My memories were still blurry, but I had gathered enough from talking with Roman and the others at the club to tell Lacey what had happened. It wasn't like the incident was not known. Nearly twenty people died in Philadelphia alone. The press had taken to calling the deadly drug such as a play on the two street names for the deadly concoction: *Kiss of Death* and *Fever*.

Aside from the names of the dead, no one in the public knew the names of those of us who had survived. The nondisclosure agreement prevented me from talking about the other victims, and it prevented the club from ever revealing that I was there that night as an exotic dancer.

"That's enough," Lacey stated as it came time for the intermission.

"Champagne, ladies?" Angel asked, as she moved into the rest area where a bar and seating were arranged.

"Oooh! That sounds perfect," Lacey agreed. "Order me a glass while I run to the ladies' room."

"Wait for me! I have been near bursting for twenty minutes," Marjory huffed, quickly following after her.

Champagne glasses in hand, we found seats in a corner with bench seating on two sides of a tall table.

Angel and Elektra looked at me expectantly. "Well? What do you think so far?" Elektra asked.

"You seemed like you were having a blast during the first half," Angel noted, sipping her champagne.

I smirked because truly I had no idea what had happened during the first half due my conversation with Lacey. "It really is *all that jazz*," I sang quietly.

"I knew it! You and I are going to be *Broadway* buddies from now on!" Angel cheered, making me laugh.

"How the hell can you afford this with a hubby and kid, Angel?" I asked, knowing that the tickets couldn't have been cheap.

Angel responded by swatting at the air like it was nothing. "Don't buy tickets for an opening night, order your tickets early, and stick with one theater so that you get discounts for being a returning patron."

"What, like frequent flyer miles?" I asked slightly stunned.

"I hadn't thought of it that way, but yeah. Something like that," Angel nodded.

"HELP! CALL AN AMBULANCE!" A woman suddenly screamed from the direction of the bathrooms.

Everyone stilled, unsure if we had heard correctly. "What did she say?" A woman at the next table asked.

I shook my head, slowly standing to move with the crowd toward the screaming.

"CALL AN AMBULANCE! SHE'S HAVING A SEIZURE!" The same voice yelled again, but this time I recognized it.

"Marjory!" Angel and I yelled at the same time, beginning to push through the crowd to reach the bathroom.

"MOVE! MOVE! THAT'S MY SISTER!" Angel shouted, startling people around us as Cherry, Spider, and Elektra created a wall to help us shove our way through the throng of people.

A few guests quickly started pulling others back and out of our path. "Please be okay. Please be okay," Angel repeated over and over, her eyes glazing over with unshed tears.

We made our way through the crowd into the bathroom, Elektra slamming the door shut behind us. "How much time do we have?" Lacey asked, pulling me onto the floor.

"What are you-" I started, but my words halted in my throat as an ungodly pain wracked through my abdomen and took me to my knees.

"Quick, lay her out," Marjory barked to the others as they circled around me on the floor. Cherry braced my head and Spider pulled my legs out from under me a second before the theater's staff came barging into the restroom with two emergency medical personnel and a stretcher.

"What happened?" A man in a suit asked.

"I'm not sure," Lacey responded. We came to use the bathroom and suddenly she collapsed.

"Please give us some space," one of the EMT requested moving to one side of my body while their partner kneeled on the other. The two rapidly fired off questions to which my friends responded.

"Does she have any allergies?" No.

"Has she had anything to eat or drink?" Champagne.

"Does she have a history of heart issues?" No.

"Is there a history of epilepsy?" No.

"Are there any health issues we need to know about?"

"She's pregnant!" Lacey whispered urgently.

The EMTs shared a look, before continuing to evaluate me. I couldn't do anything but stare wide eyed at everything that was happening around me, my body convulsing uncontrollably as wave after wave of pain rolled through my body from my abdomen.

"Who is the next of kin?"

"Me. I'm the closest she has to family here," Lacey declared, grabbing my hand.

"You can meet us-" the first EMT started but Lacey cut

426

him off.

"Let me be clear, gentlemen. She is a witness in a high profile case, and I am her lawyer. Until we verify that this wasn't an assisination attempt, she doesn't go anywhere without me by her side," Lacey growled quietly.

"Fine, but if you get in the way of us treating this patient I won't hesitate to kick you out of the vehicle," the man I assumed in charge barked back at.

"What should we do?" Angel asked as they began moving me out of the bathroom.

"Clean up. I'll call you from the hospital once we know something," Lacey responded.

Marjory nodded solemnly, as the women followed the stretcher down to the waiting ambulance. I couldn't formulate a word as my body heaved again, spasms contorting my stomach in knots.

"We'll see you again soon, Lilly-bear," Marjory called out just as the doors shut.

The pain continued as my muscles attempted to wrench themselves into knots. I could barely see what was happening around me due to the agony of the repeated waves of cramping. Lacey held my hand, as I was hooked up to a heart monitor, and the technician worked to stabilize me. He administered something into my arm, promising relief, but it only made it worse.

"It's going to be okay, sweetie," Lacey murmured over and over.

Suddenly, I was being pulled from the vehicle and wheeled into a hospital. I squinted against the glare of the bright lights, wishing they would just put me out of my misery. We could have been in that vehicle for ten minutes or two hours, and I wouldn't be able to say for sure. My mind was devoid of connection to reality beyond my pain.

"Hello, my name is Doctor Sang. Can you tell me what's brought you to the emergency department?" A woman blurred by the lights asked from somewhere near my feet.

Pain. So much pain.

"We were at the theater and she collapsed. We thought she was having a seizure, but she just keeps saying she's in pain," Lacey's voice sounded from my right.

"There were no other indicators? Had she been unwell prior to the onset? Any stress or issues at home that could have precipitated this?" The doctor asked.

"We came to New York for a girls' weekend. We do it every year. She's never been like this before," Lacey informed the woman.

"Well, we'll need to do some blood work before anything else, and then we'll go from there. The EMT notes state that she was administered pain relief, but it doesn't seem to be helping. I'll order something a bit stronger and have the nurse come in to administer it into her IV."

"Thank you, doctor."

The room became quiet again, and I nearly went insane. In my head I was screaming against the pain, begging for it to stop, but nothing more than small whimpers passed my lips. I was fine until we went to the theater. A little stressed, maybe, but my health had always been good. I wanted Mami by my side. She always knew what to do in these situations.

"Mami," I whispered.

"Sweetie, I can't call your mom. She passed away. Remember?" Lacey whispered softly.

That's right. Mami had been gone for three years now.

428

The realization struck me. Hard. My mother was gone. I couldn't call her and ask her to come help me. She wouldn't show up and take control of the situation, demanding the best for her baby. There was just me. Me and Domenico.

Wait. Lacey told them I was pregnant but that was impossible. I had been on birth control pills for years, and Domenico and I were careful. Why would she say I was pregnant?

"Hi, my name is Sheray. I'm going to be your nurse. Doctor Sang ordered some morphine for you, but the EMT stated that there was a possibility you could be pregnant."

"No. No baby," I sobbed.

"We ran a quick test from your blood sample, and you are not pregnant. I'm sorry if you were trying. It's incredibly hard on a woman when she's expecting good news, and it doesn't come," nurse Sheray continued as if I hadn't said anything.

What the hell was she on about?

"Okay, that should do it. I will be back in about fifteen minutes to check on you. If you need anything just pull the red cord there, and someone will be right in to assist you."

I felt like a soothing balm was spread through my body. The muscles slowly began to relax and it felt like I could breathe. My head rolled to the side where Lacey was sitting, watching me intently.

"What did you do to me?" I whispered.

She looked like I had slapped her in the face. "Sweetie, we didn't do anything to you. When you can think more clearly, you will realize that. Whatever this is... It was done to you before you came to New York."

I shook my head. It wasn't possible.

429

"No. I was fine," I insisted.

Lacey's face became serious, her jaw clenching tightly. "Let's just see what the doctor has to say before you start coming to conclusions."

Over the next few hours I was wheeled from the room to imaging, back to my room, then back out again for some other scan. The cramping had long since subsided, but the drugs made me too lethargic to really contribute to anything going on around me.

Finally, the doctor came back into the room. "So, I have some good news and some not so good news. Your labs were a little on the suspicious side. Your potassium levels were three times higher than they should be, which in someone your age is cause for concern. I had the labs double checked to be sure. Do you take any supplements?" she asked.

"No," I whispered. I hated taking pills in general. Taking a supplement made less sense for me.

"Then I have to ask if there is an underlying substance abuse issue?"

"What? No. I rarely drink. I had alcohol this weekend because we were celebrating," I explained.

"Any history of kidney disease or diabetes in the family?"

I shook my head. There was nothing like that in my family.

"I'd like to run a scan to check your kidneys, just to be on the safe side. If that comes back normal, we are going to treat this as a one off. I'll have them change out your IV with an insulin/dextrose infusion, and we'll monitor your values every two hours. Do you have any questions?"

I was in and out of consciousness as they wheeled me here and there around the hospital. Twelve hours passed before I was finally released to leave with Lacey. It was nearly dawn when I was wheeled out the door to our waiting cab, the sky painted with the slightest first ribbons of color. Lacey and I didn't say a word to one another the entire ride back to the hotel. When the cab finally stopped, a valet was standing by to open the door for me.

I followed beside Lacey into the hotel, across the lobby, and finally into the waiting elevator. We had barely moved eight floors when Lacey moved to step out of the elevator.

"This isn't our floor," I reminded her and tried to pull her back in.

Lacey looked at me for a moment and then pulled me into the waiting corridor with her, allowing the doors to close behind us. Once the elevator was gone, she hit the button to call a new elevator.

"What the hell are you doing?" I asked.

"Buying a little more time. Tace, you need to know that we love you. There isn't a single one of us that would do anything to harm you. Every single one of us knows how you feel about not having control of your own body, and we would die before we see that power taken from you. There has been something off about you since Cherry picked you up at your grandparents. I could see it. Marjory could see. We all could see it, but you pretended like everything was fine. Then we thought maybe you were just as exhausted as you said, and really needed this weekend to relax," Lacey stated calmly and quietly beside me.

"What do you mean by I looked *off*?" I asked. "And you have *all* been discussing this? What the fuck is that all about?"

"They may not know who you are with, but I do. He's a fucking controlling, narcissistic prick. I would wager my life savings that he didn't want you coming this weekend, right?

431

Probably gave you some bullshit about being out of town, so he wanted to keep you safe? Am I right?" She asked, turning on me.

It was like a punch in the stomach. She wasn't wrong. In fact, she was spot on about everything.

"What do you know that you aren't telling me?" I asked.

"I didn't lie to you, Anastacia. He's pulled you into his shit, and he's going to make you fall."

Lacey never called me by my name. None of them did really, except for Marjory. Cherry, Spider, and Elektra stopped calling me Tace since my debut at the Marquessa. I had been Lilith or Lilly-bear to them for years.

"When I walked into the bathroom, you asked how much time we had. I felt fine until before that. If you all didn't do something to me, then how did you know I would be sick?" I asked.

"You walked in the bathroom and collapsed, sweetie. Elektra yelled for someone to call an ambulance," Lacey explained.

"No. You were in the bathroom and someone yelled, *she's having a seizure.* So we raced to the bathroom," I corrected her. "I was fine before that."

Lacey licked her lips before pulling them in her mouth and biting them. "Marjory and I were coming out of the bathroom and saw you slipping away before our eyes. Your eyes were glassy, and you weren't responding to anyone. Cherry and Spider carried you into the bathroom. Elektra was the one who yelled. *You* were seizing up. And I didn't ask how much time we had, I asked how long you had been like that," she snapped back.

"That. That's not what happened," I refuted.

"You can ask the others when we get back," Lacey stated as the elevator door opened.

There was a quiet tension between us that lasted until we reached our suite. I was prepared to question the shit out of the others, but never had a chance to open my mouth. No sooner had we walked into the main room, I was nearly tackled to the floor by Cherry, Spider, and Elektra.

"Oh my god, Tace! You scared the shit out of us!" Cherry practically sobbed as she threw her arms around me.

"You just spaced out on us! Fuck! I have never been so scared!" Spider added, wrapping her arms around Cherry and I.

"Let her in the damn door before you attack. It's not like I haven't been keeping you bitches up to date," Lacey barked at them, as she moved us further into the room.

"What'd they say?" Marjory asked Lacey, as Spider and Cherry led me back to the living room to sit on the sofa.

"There was so much going on. Her potassium was too high, and they think the pain was due to an improperly placed IUD in one of her fallopian tubes." Lacey informed her.

"Like she ate too many bananas?" Elektra chuckled.

"Like they thought she was in renal failure high. They had her on an infusion, and then drew blood every two hours until her levels were back to normal. Thankfully they had a gyno on duty…. They got her into one of the smaller procedure rooms and successfully removed the IUDs. She's lucky she doesn't have permanent fucking damage to her body," Lacey added, coming to join us on the sofa.

"Jesus, Anastacia. We were scared shitless when we saw you collapsing on our way back from the bathroom," Marjory murmured, bending over to hug me between Cherry and

Spider.

I couldn't help looking over at Lacey, ignoring Marjory's words.

"Don't feel too bad for her. She thought we did this to her, Marj," Lacey stated snidely.

The girls looked like they had been slapped. "Tace, you zoned out for like five minutes while we were talking. You just dropped off mid-sentence and sat there," Cherry stated.

"We practically carried you into the bathroom," Spider added. "You weren't responding to anything we said or did."

"What do you mean," I started, before Angel cut me off.

"You asked about getting tickets to the theater, and then just stopped talking like your brain fritzed out. You were sitting there, eyes open, but nobody was home. I snapped my fingers in front of your face, nothing. It was all I could do to get the champagne glass out of your hand before you started convulsing and whimpering."

"Marjory spotted you and yelled for one of the attendants to call an ambulance. Everyone in the area cleared out of the way to make room for us. Hell, one guy even took off his jacket and put it on the floor so you wouldn't get filthy," Elektra added.

I shook my head trying to reconcile what they were saying with what my memory was telling me. "What do you mean?" I insisted, still staring at Lacey.

Marjory knelt down in front of me. "Anastacia, you never made it to the bathroom. You collapsed where you were, knocking over one of the tables. Sweetie, you weren't in the bathroom."

I couldn't have imagined that right? Lacey clearly said that they had removed my IUDs.

434

"NO. I remember!" I yelled, smacking everyone's hands away from me.

"What color was the bathroom?" Lacey asked.

"What?"

"If you remember it so clearly, tell us what color the bathroom was," she repeated.

I opened my mouth to respond, and nothing came out.

"Stalls or booths in the bathroom, Lilith?" Lacey asked, firing off another question I couldn't answer.

"You don't know because you didn't make it into the bathroom. My cousin has seizures. On the rare occasion she has a mild seizure she can have whole conversations, and not remember it. Once, she even swore that her sister was with her, not her dad. The brain does funny shit when it is desperate to keep you alive," Elektra interjected. "It's how I knew you were having a seizure before the others figured it out. Moving you while you were seizing would have been the worst thing we could have done, Tace."

"Shut the fuck up! I'm not talking about the fucking theater," I growled. "What do you mean they removed my fucking IUDs?" I asked Lacey.

Lacey looked truly upset at my outburst. "I'm sorry I didn't ask what you wanted done beforehand. I told them to remove them if they were what was causing the pain. Tace, you have to be careful with shit like that. It could affect your ability to have kids down the road, so I told them to take them out. I'm sorry."

"What the fuck do mean? I never had a fucking IUD put in. I take the pill, Lacey."

You could have heard a pin drop.

435

Chapter 27

Lacy dropped me at my grandparents so that I could pick up my car. It was out of the way, driving past Philly from New York to get it, but I needed the drive home alone to clear my head. This weekend had not given me the break I wanted, but, instead, slapped me with the wake up call I needed. I couldn't sit and let Domenico make all of the decisions any more. I couldn't be a passenger in my own life, and have no say in what and when shit happened.

I parked the car in the garage and carried my bag back to the room I shared with Domenico. The house, normally bustling with people coming and going, was eerily quiet. I dragged my suitcase into the walk-in closet and began sorting what needed to be washed and what could be put away. Domenico had wanted to hire a woman to keep the house clean, but I refused to allow someone else into our private spaces.

I took care of clearing our room. It was me who made sure that the clothes were washed, and his suits and pants were pressed and ready in the closet. Staring at all of the work I had put into organizing and decorating our home, I didn't know if I wanted to laugh or cry.

"You're home?" Domenico's voice interrupted my

thoughts.

"Yeah. I just got back a little bit ago. How was your meeting?" I asked, continuing to put my things away.

"It would have been better if you were there with *me* instead of galavanting around the city with those women," he growled.

This wasn't the first time he had made it known that he didn't want me around them. When I agreed to leave the lifestyle and move in with him, I gave up a lot of freedoms. I couldn't go where I wanted when I wanted without security. I couldn't lounge around the house in my underwear eating ice cream and crying over stupid movies. Everything I did, from how I looked to how I spoke, reflected on Domenico as the king. If I stumbled, even once, it would look bad on him.

"Do we need to talk?" I asked, turning to face him.

"What would we need to talk about, Anastacia?" Domenico asked.

It was a loaded question, and we both knew it. There was so much shit in the air between us, and I had no idea how to process or make sense of any of it. I took a deep breath and tried to smile, hoping it reached my eyes.

"Let's start with why my accounts are frozen," I started. "My money has always been my money, and now I have no money."

I watched as Domenico licked his teeth, a tell I learned meant he was trying to find a middle ground between the lies and a truth I would believe.

"Are the feds investigating you?" I asked bluntly.

Domenico's jaw clenched, the muscles twitching before he finally exhaled. "Things will be a bit tight for a little while.

We may need to move."

His partial answer to my questions caused me to smirk. It was bad, but not enough that he felt it necessary to tell me.

"Okay. Well, I want to move closer to my family. My grandparents aren't getting any younger, and I miss spending time with them," I stated, walking past him to the bedroom.

"What's wrong with your grandparents?" He asked, pulling me back so that my body tucked against his chest, his arms wrapping around my waist.

I sighed. "I spent a few days with them before going up to New York, and they just need a lot of help getting stuff done. Don't get me wrong, no one's dying or anything like that. But…. I don't know. They aren't spring chickens, babe. Just cutting the grass takes it out of Pops. Like, nothing else is happening on a grass cutting day."

Domenico was quiet for a moment, his chin resting on my shoulder.

"Nana was talking about needing to get things out of the attic and downsizing their house, because it's too much for them to maintain. Mami grew up in that house. Hell, I practically grew up in that house. There are a lot of memories there, and being around a little more would help keep it in the family a little longer," I explained. "I just want to be closer."

"Let's look around and see if we find anything that works," he conceded.

I spun around so that I was facing him and gave him a hug. "Thank you. This means a lot to me!" I gushed, my face hidden against his chest.

Domenico sighed and hugged me back. "It's gotta be a nice area. I'm not living in some shit hole just so you can be closer to family, Anastacia," he grumbled.

I knew just the area to start looking.

←⟟←✦←※→✦→⟟→

After scouring various websites for available rentals in the area, I found a three bedroom in an area that Domenico was okay with. The building itself was in a gated community, and the building itself was another controlled area. A doorman was posted in the main lobby to check visitors in and out, twenty-four hours a day and seven days a week. In other words: no one could visit me without him knowing about it, whether his security detail shadowed me or not.

Most of the furniture was sold with the house in Bryn Mawr, but there was still enough to furnish the new place. I put the apartment in my name, to keep Domenico's name out of any more shit the feds might snoop into. As far as any paper trail went, he had an apartment in Philly and this apartment in Delaware was mine.

The neighbors were nice enough, if not a bit on the snooty yuppie side. They made polite nods from time to time if we shared an elevator, but otherwise no one really spoke to me. I had been in the new apartment for nearly two weeks and only spoke to the doorman, despite 'seeing' all of my neighbors on multiple occasions.

It had been two weeks since we moved in, and I had a daily schedule that kept me from going crazy. Rather than get annoyed with Domenico, who was always busy with meetings, I filled my days.

I woke up at six every morning and went to the gym. My workouts were just as brutal as the ones Cherry used to lead, so they lasted a full ninety minutes. By eight, I was back in the apartment showered, dressed and ready to inhale breakfast. I spent three days a week visiting with nana and pops, helping them do whatever menial tasks they needed help with.

If I wasn't at nana and pops, I was cleaning the new apartment from floor to ceiling. I couldn't help the overwhelming desire to meticulously clean every single surface. I was halfway through deep cleaning the second bathroom when the doorbell rang. Pulling off the hot pink rubber gloves and throwing them on the counter, I trundled out the main room.

"Coming!" I called out, giggling as they rang the door again.

A firmer knock pounded on the door as I got closer.

"I am on my way! Damnit! Have a little bit of patience before breaking the fucking door down!" I hollered as the door was finally wrenched open.

Standing outside was our doorman, holding a large package.

"Wow. You didn't have to bring that all the way up here! I would have come down to get it," I said, taking the box.

"The box requires a signature, and we pride ourselves on the confidentiality of our residents. If you wouldn't mind signing here," Phil the weekend doorman asked, holding out a small digital device.

"If the package has my name on it and I have to sign for it, doesn't that kind of give up the whole mystique of who lives here?" I asked, signing with my finger across a small touch screen.

"This is consent for the front desk to sign for future parcels. This should have been included in your documents, but it seems to have been neglected," Phil explained. "There are a lot of important people who live here, and it isn't uncommon to receive packages with a pseudonym."

"Good to know," I said, smiling.

"Have a good day, Miss Garcia," Phil said, dipping his head politely before heading back to the elevator.

I was just about to step back into the apartment when the elevator doors opened and Domenico stepped out, barely acknowledging Phil as the two passed one another.

"Hey, babe. How was your day?" I asked, smiling sweetly.

Domenico didn't say a word until we were both in the apartment and he had closed the door behind us.

"What the fuck was he doing in our apartment?" He growled, grabbing me by the chin.

I snorted at him, and pointed to the box on the floor. "He was delivering a package."

Domenico stared at me for a second longer before releasing me and looking down at the box. "Why are you receiving packages to our door all of a sudden?"

I couldn't help rolling my eyes at him as I bent over to pick up the box. "Apparently, delivery people are not allowed to bring shit up to the door when you live in bougie exclusive buildings. Phil asked me to sign a release so that they could sign for packages at the front desk in the future. Is that okay?" I asked, sashaying into the kitchen.

"He seemed rather flushed for someone just delivering a *package*," Domenico sneered, loosening his tie.

I couldn't help but laugh at that point. "Seriously? He was here less than a minute before you walked out of the elevator. He knocked, handed me the package, explained why I needed to sign a document, then left. He didn't even step foot into the apartment."

The package was barely on the counter when my head was wrenched back, my hair held tightly in Domenico's fist.

"What the fuck, Domenico!" I shouted a second before his other hand was over my mouth.

"If you feel that what I offer isn't enough to satisfy you, all you have to do is say so!" He growled in my ear, his voice barely above a whisper.

It took everything in me to force my body to relax, to fight the instinct to fight back. "Babe?" I said calmly. "We have been together this long, and I have never so much as looked at another man. I don't go anywhere without telling you. You can check my phone, see everything that I have done and where I have been. I knew your birthday was coming up so I ordered something special. I didn't know the rule about package deliveries."

It had taken a few hard lessons learned to know how to diffuse his short temper, but I had learned it nonetheless. He slowly released my hair, and turned me to face him.

"I'm sorry. I shouldn't have said that," he apologized, caressing my cheek.

"I know. Did you have a rough day?" I asked, hoping to divert his attention further and completely calming him down.

"No. Just the same stupid shit, dealing with the same fucking idiots," he sighed before giving me a quick peck on the cheek.

I nodded and turned back to face the kitchen island and the box as he left me to head to the bedroom. My eyes burned with fury, but I knew I had to keep it in check. Pulling a knife from the drawer, I talked instead about my day.

"It was pretty quiet in the gym this morning. Just me and

Gladys the porn star there today. She asked how my man was doing, as usual," I said with forced joviality that I *really* didn't feel.

"Who is Gladys the porn star?" Domenico asked, laughing as he came back out of the bedroom.

I smiled as I opened the box. "You know.... The woman with the bleach blonde hair, stunning blue eyes and enormous knockers."

Domenico stood beside me shaking his head, his brow furrowed as he tried to place a face with who I was describing. "I don't think I have met her," he admitted, chuckling.

"You don't remember? She was all over you when we moved in, begging for you to come check her leaking pipes," I reminded him, wiggling my eyebrows.

Domenico's eyebrows shot up and he barked out a laugh. "Are you talking about that senile old woman who fucking molests me everytime we're in the elevator together?" He asked.

"Gladys tells it differently, babe," I said with mock seriousness, shaking my head. "Apparently, you two have shared secret passionate moments when I'm not looking. I just need to know...." I trailed off, turning to face him.

"If you feel that what I offer isn't enough to satisfy you, all you have to do is say so," I repeated his words.

Domenico's smile faltered for half a second before he pulled me against me. "You are more than enough to keep me happy," he purred against my neck, trailing kisses from my shoulder up to my jaw. "Let me show you how much."

I pulled away laughing. "I would love to have you rock my world but it's that time of the month, and we both know you don't like fucking through blood," I reminded him, turning

443

back to the package.

His hands dropped from my body and he took a step back. "Why is your cycle so fucked up recently?"

I bit the inside of my cheek to keep myself calm. "Remember I told you I had to change birth control pills? Apparently my hormones are all fucked up, so my cycle is going to be a bit irregular for the first month."

Domenico sighed as he walked away. "I don't understand why you need to take those if you can't get pregnant," he commented over his shoulder.

"I told you, I like to keep my cycle regulated. It's not about the birth control aspect of the meds, but managing my cycle. The doctor said it's perfectly fine to continue taking them, she just changed the type I was taking," I explained, no longer interested in opening the box.

There were a few moments of silence before I realized that he had ended the discussion by getting in the shower. I clenched my fists as I leaned over the counter, and gritted my teeth. The back of my head throbbed where demonico had yanked me by my hair. My jaw ached, so I just knew it would be bruised in the morning.

I knew his routines well enough by this point. He was going back out tonight, and I would not be invited to join him as punishment for whatever fucking indiscretion he felt I had committed.

Lacy was still working to get my money released back to me, or at least placed under some sort of conservancy situation with her law firm. The way she explained it, I would have limited access to my funds, receiving an allowance just big enough to live on but not enough to thrive on. Unfortunately, that allowance was based on the average cost of living for the state and not the actual fucking city I lived in.

I would be lucky if I got fifteen hundred dollars a month. The rent for this apartment was nearly three thousand, and that didn't include the utilities or additional costs that came with living in the same building as some of the wealthiest mother fuckers on east coast.

The sound of the shower turning off snapped me out of my funk, and I scrambled to unbox the contents of the package. Opening small prepackaged containers of already prepared food items, I made a show of creating an elaborate meal.

By the time Domenico walked back into the kitchen it looked like I had hand rolled noodles, finely cut vegetables, and started cooking perfectly marinated and seasoned chicken legs.

I schooled my expression, and turned to Domenico with a look that I hoped conveyed some modicum of excitement. "Dinner will be ready in ten minutes! I hope you're hungry, babe," I gushed, throwing the noodles into a pot of boiling water.

Domenico stared at me for a moment before sighing. "I'm sorry, dolce. Roman called while I was in the shower. There's an issue with one of our distributors that I need to handle."

I glanced over at the stove and tried to force a smile. "Oh. Um, I can turn everything off and be ready to go in like ten minutes-"

"No. It's okay. I shouldn't be gone that long. Make the food. I can't wait to try it when I get back," he promised, leaning over to give me a quick peck on my forehead before leaving again.

I turned off the stove and started cleaning up the food,

throwing everything into the trash. We both knew damn well he wasn't coming back here to eat, and I would be damned if I was going to eat that shit myself. By the time the dishes were cleaned and the kitchen was gleaming once again, I returned to the box.

Buried beneath the packaging and paper was the real gift in the box. The phone was simple. I could call or text any one of the ten saved numbers. I could even take pictures and send them to the last number listed, if I was so inclined. The only thing I couldn't do with the phone, however, was let Domenico know that I had it. If he knew, he'd kill me.

* * *

Domenico didn't stumble in until nearly four in the morning. This had become his routine at least once a week since we moved into the apartment two months ago. I was struggling to pay the rent, let alone buy food, but he didn't seem to give a shit about how I was living as long as I lived the part of his trophy wife when I walked out the door.

Creeping out of bed, I tiptoed out of our bedroom and to the kitchen. It was six o'clock and I should have been at the gym, but I couldn't be bothered this morning. I needed money and Domenico had none. The small allowance I was getting wasn't enough to pay the bills, and I refused to sell my shit to pay my way. I lived in poverty through my entire childhood, never able to keep the money I made because it had to pay for someone else.

I poured myself a cup of coffee and curled up on the sofa with the burner phone. I hadn't messaged or called anyone since receiving the device, but now I was running out of steam, options, and patience. Selecting the last number, I began drafting a message.

[Looking for income. CV attached.]

As soon as the message was sent, I tucked the phone back into the cushions of the sofa and continued sipping my coffee. It would be at least an hour before they responded. A soft vibration from under my butt scared the shit out of me, and I yelped. I slapped my hand over my mouth and stared wide eyed at the bedroom door.

Please don't wake up. I prayed.

When no sounds or movements came from the bedroom after five minutes, I warily pulled the phone out of the cushions and looked at the message. The response was the address of a place in Baltimore with the date and time for an interview. I tucked the phone back into the sofa, and finished my coffee.

It was nearly ten when Domenico finally pulled himself out of bed. Following his usual routine, he got up, showered, and left without saying so much as a single word to me. I waited until eleven before I got dressed and left the apartment. I didn't have a car any more, as the last one was sold to cover expenses Domenico had incurred. I couldn't help snorting in disbust just remembering that bullshit excuse.

He had lost a shit ton of money gambling in New Jersey and fucking ponied up *my* car to cover his debt. Of course the excuse he gave me was that we didn't need two cars if we were trying to save money. He had even thrown my own words back at me, telling me how expensive the insurance was to upkeep for the two vehicles. Like he had any idea what my insurance was.

As I stepped out of the building, I turned right and headed

toward the small district located a couple blocks away. I had no idea if Domenico's men were still watching me, or if they had been redirected to cover their boss's ass. My regular phone pinged, and I pulled it out of my pocket.

Stephanie: [I'm in the neighborhood. Do you have time for a coffee?]

Me: [Sounds great. Meet at Starbucks off Pres?]

Stephanie: [See you soon!]

I smiled and stuffed the phone into my handbag. The coffee shop was a five minute walk from the apartment, but Lacy was already there when I walked in the door.

"Hi, sweetie!" She gushed as soon as she saw me, and rushed over to give me a hug.

"Oh my god, it feels like forever since we saw each other," I whined, hugging her back.

"I was in the neighborhood, like I said. I thought maybe we could grab a coffee and do a little shopping while I'm here," Lacy said, smiling ear to ear as she pulled me to sit at the table she had occupied.

"I'm not really in the mood for shopping. I think I pulled a muscle at the gym this morning," I said, laughing as I sat down.

Lacy gave me a look and chuckled. "You still follow the workout regimen?"

"Faithfully!" I giggled.

Lacy rolled her eyes in mock disgust and shook her head. "So what did you have planned instead for the day?" she asked.

"Honestly? I was thinking about occupying one of those beanie chairs in the back and reading a book all day," I admitted, sneaking a sip of her coffee.

"Uh, booooorrrrrrrring," she huffed, before taking her cup of coffee out of my hands. "Get your own coffee, boring girl."

I looked around the coffee shop and stopped when I noticed the bathroom. "Actually, here's ten. Can you order me a latte, no sugars or flavors? I need to run to the bathroom."

"Keep your money. This will be my treat," she said, pushing the ten dollars back into my hand.

"Thank you!"

"Shut and go pee. I want to hear about what you've been up to. It seems like a million years have passed since we got to sit and catch up."

I quickly scurried to the bathroom, and entered the second stall. Hanging on the back of the door was a backpack with a change of clothes and blonde wig. I got changed quickly and put my own clothes in the bag.

I had barely finished, when someone else entered the bathroom. There was gentle knock on the door, so I flushed the toilet and stepped out. The woman who had just come in wasted no time and rushed into the stall behind me locking the door.

"Thank you," I whispered quietly, but the woman did not acknowledge me.

I walked out of the bathroom and pulled a key fob out of my pocket. As I exited the coffee shop I hit the unlock button on the car, and caught the flashing lights of a blue sedan to my left. I turned and prayed that that was the right car as I opened the door.

As I pulled out of the parking lot, I glanced a woman with long dark hair, wearing my clothes sitting down opposite Lacy in the coffee shop. The two women smiled and sipped their coffees like nothing was out of the ordinary. I had three hours to make it to my interview and be back before Domenico's security detail sent someone into the coffee shop to ask the fake me what time it was.

⟨ᚹ᚛᚜᚜᚜᚛᚜᚜⟩

"Do you have any experience?" The woman seated across from me asked.

"I do," I responded.

She eyed me over, pursing her lips several times in disdain. Her name was Sadie, but she was known as Big Mama. She was a tiny woman to hold such a name, but Marjorie had assured me that she was a fierce boss in her own right. At the moment, Big Mama was giving my tattoos a serious look, and she was obviously not happy about them.

"Where did you work previously?" She asked.

There was no point in bullshitting since Marjorie had set this up, so I told the truth. "The Marquessa and Infinity."

"Why did you leave?"

"Honestly?" I asked, to which she nodded. "I lost friends the night of the kiss. I was in a bad place for a long time, and I pretty much became a shut in for two years."

Big Mama's entire demeanor softened. "I'm so sorry to hear that. We were fortunate not to be affected, but several club owner friends of mine weren't so lucky. It was a night that affected us all." There was a moment of silence between us before she began speaking again.

"I am very protective of the women who work here. We're the Masquarade for a reason. There can't be any identifying marks on your body, and you would have to wear a mask while working. Every dancer has her own changing room, so not even the other dancers will see your face without your mask. Will that be a problem?" She asked, arching a brow.

I couldn't help the smirk that crept up on one side. "No. Not at all. In fact, it's the reason I wanted to work here. I want the ability to earn money without being harassed for what I do," I admitted.

It wasn't a lie. If Domenico found out that I was dancing again, he would lose his shit. Shame for him that I could make money all by my self. I wasn't going to beg him for pennie when I could pull enough to cover the rent, and then some, in a single night in the right club. Traveling to Baltimore to dance was a risk, but too many people in Philly would recognize me because of being with him.

"I owe Marjorie a favor, and she speaks very highly of you. I'll let you pull a shift on Friday night. If you can pull in two grand in tips, I'll make you our Friday night special," Big Mama offered.

I smiled that time. "I appreciate the opportunity."

Big Mama looked at her watch and frowned. "Unless you have any other questions, I have another appointment coming in ten minutes. Please excuse me for not showing you out," she stated and waved her hand at the door.

"Not a problem. Thank you, Big Mama. I will see you on Friday."

↔↜↜⁂⇁⇁ᱬ↔

By the time I had made it back to the coffee shop, there was barely ten minutes left. The woman sitting with Lacy saw the car pulling into the parking lot and leaned over to give Lacy a hug. Lacy was stepping out of the coffee shop by the time I was walking in the door.

"Call me later," she whispered, holding the door for me.

"Thank you. You have a great day as well," I replied and

made for the bathroom again.

A blonde woman had just stepped out of the second stall, and held the door for me. "I'd use this one. The other two are a bit on the gross side," she stated.

"Thank you. I appreciate the head's up," I replied and hurried into the stall.

The wig and clothes came off as quickly as possible and I began pulling my clothes back out of the back pack and dressing as fast as I could. Once my clothes were on, I dropped the backpack onto the floor and kicked it out from under the stall's door.

My purse dropped over the top of the door, and I grabbed it before flushing the toilet. I had to slow my breathing, counting slowly from one to ten, before I opened the door and went to the sink to wash my hands. Domenico's man were standing in line to buy a coffee when I can out of the bathroom. He looked over at me and I rolled my eyes, before exiting the coffee shop and starting the walk back to the apartment.

His guys had now seen me go into the coffee shop, bullshit with a friend for several hours, and then leave to head home. Unless Domenico had FBI-level facial recognition pros working for him, they were none the wiser for my little slip away and decoy.

It took roughly ten minutes to get back to the apartment, and changed into more comfortable clothes. Domenico was sitting on the sofa watching a baseball game when I got home.

"Hey, babe. Why didn't you tell me you were going to be home early? I wouldn't have stayed at the coffee shop so long!" I squealed, running over to jump on the sofa with him.

Domenico smiled and caught me as I landed on his lap. "You're always complaining about my long hours, so I thought I would come home early so we could do something together. Where did you go?" he asked, pulling my hair back from my face.

I smiled from ear to ear for him. "I was going to go shopping, but then I realized it wasn't a very smart thing to do when I have so much shit already. So I thought I would sit in the coffee shop and binge a book I have been dying to read," I told him.

"That's it?" he asked, holding my chin so that I was forced to look up at him.

"Well, that was the plan... An old friend of mine was in the area, and invited me out for coffee... But other than that I can't really think of anything," I informed him.

"Oh? Which friend was that?" he asked, staring into my eyes.

"Steph. Remember my friend who went to law school?" I prodded.

Domenico snorted then chuckled. "Right. Because you have so many friends who have done well for themselves."

The smile that had been plastered on my face up to that point slowly fell. "Stephanie finished law school three years ago. I wouldn't say she had it as rough as I did, but she graduated and passed the bar.... So, yeah. I have at least one successful friend in my life," I retorted, jerking my head back from his hold.

"If you met your friend at the coffee shop, then whose phone did I find on the sofa?" he asked, pulling my burner phone out of his pocket.

"Oh my god! Where did you find that? I was looking all

453

over for that thing. Your favorite porn start left it in the gym this morning. I meant to drop it at the front desk on my way out, but I couldn't find it. I was meaning to look for it when I got home," I said, reaching for the small device.

Domenico pulled his hand away at the last minute, keeping the phone out of my reach. "So this phone isn't yours?" he asked, raising an eyebrow at me.

"No. First of all, that's a granny phone. Second, mine is my bag," I informed him pointing to my purse still sitting on the table by the door to our apartment.

He stared me down like he was waiting to catch me in a lie, and I could only pray that he didn't take this shit too far. Domenico surprised me and passed the phone back to me. "There's only ten number saved. Call the third one," he directed.

I accepted the phone and made a show of trying to figure out how to access the contacts. With some prodding from him, I *managed* to dial one of the numbers in the phone. No sooner had the call gone through, Domenico snatched the phone from me.

"Hello?" A woman's voice answered, but Domenico said nothing.

"Hello?" She asked again, when there was still no response.

Domenico just stared at me, still not saying a word or even breathing loudly.

"Hello? Gladys did you butt dial me again? Helloooooo... Glaaaaaaadys!! Fucking crazy ass woman. Clive! It's your sister..... No. I mean it's her number but I think she butt dialed me-"

Domenico ended the call "Just give it to her in the morning when you see her at the gym. I'm sure she'll need it," he said, handing the phone back to me.

"I'd rather leave it at the front desk. If she knows that I found it, I'll have to hear some whole bullshit story about how she left it for you and I got in the way of yet another one of your kinky secretive affairs," I said with mock disgust, causing him to laugh.

"Good point. We can drop it off on our way out to dinner tonight," he offered.

I could only nod in agreement. "Okay. Sounds good."

I fucking prayed the night would pass quickly, because I was tired of playing the fucking games at this point. It was hit or miss whether I got Domenico the lover or *demonico* the asshole. And this was feeling like a demonico night.

Chapter 28

Domenico's men had picked him up for a meeting in Philadel-phia. Tonight was supposed to be my first night working at Masquerade, so I was thrilled when he made it clear that my presence would not be needed and dropped me at Nana and Pops house instead.

I waited until he was gone before borrowing Pops's truck and driving over to Titi's house. Titi let me borrow her car to drive to Baltimore, and drove pop's truck to his house for me. I hated playing musical chairs with the cars, but a girl had to do what a girl had to do to get the bills paid.

It was nearly seven by the time I reached the parking area on the waterfront. I hadn't been in Baltimore without Domenico since the expo years ago. Looking back, I wished I had never met him. He made my heart race and my body sing, but he took more than he gave; chipping away at everything that was me, whether I knew it or not. I thought I would stand beside him, but he only ever wanted me beneath him.

The trip to New York had been my breaking point. Domenico had violated my trust in the cruelest way possible. I knew now why he didn't want me to continue talking with my friends from the clubs. If I had, I would have never let him touch me again.

As I entered the back of the club my mind wandered back to that hotel room. The day every lie he ever told unfolded in front of me.

I sat on the sofa, surrounded by my dearest friends, trying to make sense of what they were telling me.

Elektra had leaned over a taken my hand to comfort me. "My cousin has seizures. On the rare occasion she has a mild seizure she can have whole conversations, and not remember it. Once, she even swore that her sister was with her, not her dad. The brain does funny shit when it is desperate to keep you alive," she explained. "It's how I knew you were having a seizure before the others figured it out. Moving you while you were seizing would have been the worst thing we could have done, Tace."

"Shut the fuck up! I'm not talking about the fucking theater," I growled, slapping her hand away and turning my attention to Lacy. "What do you mean they removed my fucking IUDs?"

Lacy had looked like I slapped her at my outburst. "I'm sorry I didn't ask what you wanted done beforehand. I told them to remove them if they were what was causing the pain. Tace, you have to be careful with shit like that. It could affect your ability to have kids down the road, so I told them to take them out. I'm sorry."

"What the fuck do mean? I never had a fucking IUD put in. I take the pill, Lacy."

The entire suite fell into pin drop silence. No one breathed for what felt like an eternity.

"I would know if I had an IUD. It requires a fucking appointment with a doctor. I only take the pill to regulate my cycles, why the fuck would I want an IUD on top of that?" I asked, still staring at her.

Lacy's mouth opened and closed several times, at a loss for

457

words.

"Anastacia, don't lose your shit on Lacy. She's just telling you what the doctor's told her," Marjorie interjected, ever the mother hen.

I turned wide-eyed to look at Marjorie, completely at a loss of how to say what my brain was struggling to process.

"How?" I stuttered eventually.

Marjorie looked at me like I was an idiot. "What are you confused about?"

Before I could even attempt a response, Cherry and Angel took gasping breaths at the same time.

"Oh my god," Angel whispered.

"It's not that, right?" Cherry asked, but she directed the question to Angel and Lacy. Not me.

Angel made a sound akin to choking on something and left the room. Cherry gave me a quick glance and ran after Angel.

"What the fuck just happened?" Elektra asked, looking from the two sprinting out of the room to Marjorie, Lacy and I. "What am I missing?"

Lacy ignored Elektra and moved to sit down next to me, taking my hand in both of hers. "Sweetie," she started, caressing the back of my hand. "This is really important, okay? Have you had any medical procedures, dental work, anything that would require you to be sedated for any reason?"

I could feel my brows crunching up in confusion. I couldn't stand not being in control of my body. It's why I never got really wasted or black out drunk. "No. Never. Not since before Cherry drugged me on the plane to the Caribbean," I responded, shaking my head.

Lacy sighed with a bit of frustration. "There has to have been something, Taze. Think. You were sick. You were tired? Someone *put a fucking IUD into your uterus. You would have had to been knocked the fuck out or complicit!"*

I couldn't remember a single instance of when either of those two scenarios could have happened. I wouldn't even let the dentist put me under when my wisdom teeth were pulled, and scheduled multiple appointments to avoid taking sedatives.

"Never," I stated again. "Lacy, I'm not crazy! Why the fuck would I do something like that when he can't even have children?" I had argued back.

An uncomfortable silence fell over the room as the women exchanged awkward glances.

"What about that night?" Cherry asked.

"Which night, Cher?" I retorted, feeling frustrated.

"You said he took care of you after that night. The night your friend died."

"What? Who are you talking about?" I asked, not understanding or recalling the night she was referring to.

"Anastacia," Marjorie said softly. "The night Charlie died, were you also drugged?"

My mouth gaped open for a second before snapping shut. It had been years since Charlie died. I remembered that someone had leaked some new drug into clubs all over the city and several other places around the east coast.

"He picked me up from the club...." I said, my voice trailing as I closed my eyes to remember.

Domenico said I had called him. He had taken care of me... for days.

"No," I whispered, as my voice crackled. My eyes burned with tears behind my eyelids.

"Taze?" Lacy called.

"He did it," I murmured. "When I woke up the whole apartment

was empty except for the bed. He did it. Why would he do that to me?" I asked, opening my eyes to look at her.

"You know why," came Marjorie's response.

"Hey, girl! You new here?" a woman's voice pulled me from my thoughts.

I blinked for a moment staring at the woman in front of me. She was slightly taller than me, dark skinned with her hair pulled back into a high ponytail of locks.

"What?" I asked. "Sorry, yeah. Tonight is my first night," I mumbled as my brain caught up with the conversation at hand.

"Well in that case, welcome. I'm Danny," the gorgeous woman named Danny greeted me with an infectious smile.

I couldn't help but smile back at her. "Taze. It's nice to meet you, Danny."

"Did the pit boss give you a run down yet?" Danny asked, taking a seat at the vanity next to me.

"In so far as my music comes on, I dance?" I asked, chuckling.

Danny smiled and shook her head. "Everyone here wears a mask outside of this room. Doesn't matter if you're taking a piss, or stepping out back for a smoke. If you are on the clock, the mask stays on. Second, you'll need to cover your tattoos," she advised me, waving her hand at the ink covering my neck, chest, and arms.

"Yeah, they covered that when I interviewed. I think they said I needed to see someone named Marissa or Melissa...."

"Marissa. She's set up in the booth over in the corner," Danny informed me pointing toward a curtained area in the dressing room.

"Thanks. I appreciate the head's up."

"No worries. Women need to support women if we're going to take over the world," she giggled before leaving me to finish getting ready.

It didn't take long for Marissa to spray paint body to a delicious golden brown. Once she was done, I received a light powdering that created a shimmering effect on my skin. The paint wasn't enough to completely conceal the tattoos, but the shine of the glitter made it difficult to see them clearly under the lights in the front of the house.

"Taze, you ready?" Danny asked, peeking her head into the dressing room. "You're up in ten."

I put my mask on and followed Danny out to the main floor. I loved the layout of this club. Dancers rotated between the center stage, one of two side stages, and various suspended cages to dance. The suspended cages weren't actually suspended, but the effect of placement and lighting gave an amazing dungeon feel to the room.

Danny led me to the first side stage, where I began to slowly go through my movements while the main act had all of the attention on the central floor. I let my eyes scan over the room, checking out the clientele. Most of the men here were dressed in business suits, their ties pulled loose, and the top buttons of their shirts open. Aside from the security at the side entrance and the bartender, not a single man in here looked younger than thirty.

I just stepped onto the main stage when a party near the back stood up to leave. As the music began, the leader of the group turned and smiled at the bartender, a curvy blonde woman tucked under his arm. Her arms were wrapped around his waist, as she made an adorable pouty face at him. I couldn't hear a word they were saying from across

461

the club and the din of the music, but I knew what she was saying as if she had screamed it.

'Te amo.'

The man leaned down to kiss her, repeating the same words. My song began playing and I strutted onto the floor like I owned it.

Put down the keys, baby, why do you have to leave.

You know just what you're doing, the words you say to me.

The lyrics to *No Games* echoed across the club, as I spun myself around the pole.

All this fussin and fightin, it just don't make sense to me.

One of the men stopped and whispered something to one of the men, causing him to lean back and laugh. Another of the group turned to watch me dance. For a moment, our eyes locked and I had his undivided attention.

I looked away first, as my eyes began to burn. I continued my routine, my eyes returning to the group until they left the club.

My love is not a game...

Domenico had no idea that I was here.

You come with pleasure and pain.

He was too focused on the woman in his arms. The woman who had said she loved him, and he had repeated the words to her.

But who am I to blame?

Domenico had lied to me about where he was. What was one more lie to him? Everything about us was a lie.

Maybe I treat you the same.

Domenico may not have recognized me….. But Roman did.

The rest of my shift was uneventful. Then again, what

could top seeing the man you risked your life, the one who swore to stand beside you resolutely, through thick and thin…. Obviously cheating. In my fucked up mind, I could have excused an occasional fuck.

But that was not a fling hanging on his arm. That was another woman.

I felt like a fucking idiot.

While I was caged in an upscale apartment, he was treating another woman. *Fucking* another woman.

Loving her.

Climbing into Titi's car, I navigated the empty Baltimore streets until I reached the interstate and headed north.

I reached into my handbag and grabbed the burner. Dialing the number was a muscle memory at this point. The inside of the car was quiet except for the slight sound of the engine as I sped up the road.

"Operator," a woman answered, her voice the deep resonance that came with age.

"I need directions to the next exit," I stated calmly, glancing from time to time between my mirrors.

"Shall I connect you?" she offered.

"I'm not lost. I need directions," I clarified, hearing the woman shuffle papers on the other end of the line.

"I understand. A representative will be in contact with you shortly."

The call was disconnected, and I rode the rest of the way in silence. My eyes constantly surveyed the road for any sign that Roman might have outed my new side job to Domenico. By the time I crossed the state line, I knew that my secret was safe.

It was nearly four in the morning by the time I pulled to a

stop in front of Titi's house. Titi didn't ask questions when I asked to borrow her car, and I was thankful that I didn't need to explain my need to hide what I did.

The fact that I danced at all was the worst kept family secret. Everyone knew, but no one talked about it. The true tongue in cheek comments came from the onset of what my sister said was vertigo from an accident I survived some years ago. The vertigo, a slow onset symptom of brain injury, was attributed to the time my vehicle was rolled in a failed carjacking turned hit and run. The vertigo explained my "new" propensity for falling into things and bruising myself.

What they didn't ask was how I hurt myself. They didn't ask how I fell into the kitchen island bruising my ribs, or how I slipped in the bathroom and nearly broke my wrist. They didn't speculate on the obvious fingermark bruising around my neck, because my tattoos obscured the telltale discolorations.

Domenico and I were fire and ice in the best and worst ways. When we were good, it was steamy, sweaty, passionate, toe curling pleasure. When we were bad, it was like a volcano exploding, volatile, heated, violent destruction. There was not in between. No balance between the two extremes with us.

For the longest time, I thought that if I followed his rules, if I played the trophy, things would be better. They weren't. He would always find some slight I committed just to argue.

I opened the door to Titi's and quietly slipped inside, dropping my bag by the front door. My phone, the one Domenico knew about, was sitting on the side table next to the sofa; a neatly stacked pile of blankets and pillow calling my name.

It took me ten minutes to quickly shower and another five to make up the blankets on the sofa. My mind had stopped wandering and pondering next steps and missteps, accepting what would come to be. Come hell or high water. By the time my head hit the pillow, I was out.

The sound of my phone ringing jerked me out of my sleep. I nearly knocked a lamp onto the floor as my hand smashed and swatted at the table to find the damn device.

"Hello?" I answered, my voice groggy from sleep.

"Where are you?" Domenico's deep accusatory voice barked through the phone.

"What?" I asked, confused.

"I asked where the fuck you are!" He shouted, thereby snapping me awake.

"Babe, I'm at my aunt's. I told you I was going to visit family-" I started before he cut me off, disconnecting the call.

I barely had time to roll my eyes before a video call came in. Still snuggled under my blanket on the sofa. I accepted the call.

"Why is it so dark there?" Domenico asked, attempting to make sense of the shadowy figures around me.

"Babe, I don't even know what time it is," I responded, sounding whiny.

"Turn on the fucking lights, Anastacia! I want to see where you are."

I huffed, flinging off the blankets and sitting up. I didn't care if he could hear me cursing under my breath. I didn't care in the slightest anymore. Switching on the side lamp, my eyes shut at the sudden light.

"Fuck!" I swore, shielding my eyes.

"Anastacia!" Domenico yelled again.

"What the fuck do you want, dude? I'm sleeping on my aunt's fucking sofa. See?" I shouted at him, turning the camera to show my aunt's living room.

He'd been here several times over the last few years for various family get-togethers, so he knew where I was.

"What the fuck is wrong with you? Are you high again?" I asked, crawling back under the blankets.

"Where were you tonight?" He asked, obviously not happy with the answer he received.

"Seriously? For the last time. I had dinner at my grand-parents'. Then I came over Titi's to hang out with her. I'm going home after breakfast. Why are you being like this?" I groaned.

"So you weren't out fucking another dude?" He asked, though it sounded more like an accusation.

I snorted, tired of playing the back and forth fuck-fuck games. I was fucking tired, and this asshole was keeping me from my sleep.

"No, Domenico. I don't fuck around. That's your gig, not mine. Go ask your fucking side piece to suck your dick so you'll let me fucking sleep," I muttered, already starting to fall asleep again.

"What did you just say?!?" He growled.

I chuckled, the sound deep and raspy. "I'm not doing this anymore. If my shit isn't enough for you, then say so, so I'm not sitting around thinking this shit is going somewhere. You want to fuck a chick in every area code you control, go for it. But your STD ridden dick isn't coming near me. Okay? That clear it up for you, *babe?*"

"Dolce."

466

"Don't call me your sweetie. I'm going back to sleep now." The call was disconnected before he could utter another sound. With my phone set to airplane mode, I went back to sleep. It was the best sleep I had had in years.

Things with Domenico were over the top loving when I got back from my aunt's that first weekend I started at Masquerade. He made it a point to have breakfast with me before leaving for work, and I pretended to be busy with cleaning the house and helping family.

I had a set routine every day to ensure that his eyes, security hiding in every corner, would report back what a good little girl I was for their boss. As soon as he left for work, I cleaned. I went to the gym, came back and cleaned up. Three days a week I went to my grandparents and hung out there, moving furniture or cleaning and decluttering. Whatever odd tasks they could think of to keep me at their place.

Today was a special day though. Today was three years since our first meeting. Today marked three weeks since I saw him cheating with my own eyes. And it was three days ago that I decided to leave for good.

Tonight, Domenico wanted to take me out. He was super secretive about the plans, but I knew it would be something work related despite his insistence that it was about us. I was dressed to the nines, looking every bit the part of his trophy wife when his guys came to pick me up. I followed them out to the waiting car, and climbed in without saying a word.

The ride to the club took thirty minutes. Thirty minutes of awkward silence in a vehicle with three security details. Not a peep.

"We're here," the driver finally announced.

The two security guards quickly dismounted from the

car and opened the door for me. I followed silently as they escorted me into the club. Domenico was many things, and he could be very sentimental when he wanted. The place has been bought out and transformed from a gentlemen's club into a nightclub, but the bones of the Marquessa were still there under the bright colors and strobing lights.

The stages had been transformed into elevated VIP booth seating and the main floor was now swarmed with dancers swaying to the music. It struck me that this was the place my life had changed, for better or for worse. The women I met here were beyond any stereotype of what dancers should be. They were strong. Fierce. Driven. They were my best friends and my soul sisters.

The security detail stopped on either side of what was once a private room used for special request dances. Now it was converted into a private party room for high end clientele to drink away from the everyday people.

"SURPRISE!" several voices shouted as I stepped inside.

I honestly jumped a little, seeing Domenico, Roman, and several other men with their wives crowded into the room. My eyes immediately looked for Domenico's, and the smile on his face almost melted me. *Almost.*

"Happy anniversary, Dolce," he cooed, coming up to pull me into a sweet embrace.

"What is all of this?" I asked, giving him a sweet kiss on the lips.

"I wanted to surprise you," he whispered close to my ear, his breath tickling my neck.

"Happy Anniversary," Roman cheered from the table holding up a glass of champagne.

I smiled graciously and thanked everyone for the sweet

surprise. As I looked around the room, my heart went from feeling sweet to turning sour. The men here were all associates responsible for some aspect of Domenico's business from weapons to drugs, to money laundering. I knew every one of them, and this gathering was not about me.

The night started with Domenico holding me on his lap as we laughed and joked with *his* people. Before long the wives were sent to sit with me while the men moved to the other side of the room to discuss business. The conversations were usually dull, but this time I had no reason to pretend to be cordial.

"I'm sorry you're all forced to socialize with me when you could be home" I stated softly.A shared look of surprise went around the four or five women before they each smiled nervously.

"Please. I know that two of you have small children, you'd rather be home with. At least one of you takes care of your grandfather... I am sorry that you were dragged out for... .*this*," I said, waving a hand at the men joking and smoking in their corner.

"You know we've never really gotten the chance to talk," one of the women admitted.

"Why is that, Raquelle?" I asked, taking a sip of my drink.

Raquelle had been with her husband since they were barely teens. She had grown up on the edge of Kensington and her husband Mike had grown up in the thick of it. They jumped gangs together when they were each 14 or 15, and she stayed by his side as he climbed the ranks to stand beside the boss. She wasn't even 35, but she had lived through more violence and bloodshed than any war zone overseas. Still, she kept herself looking the picture perfect wife beside her man.

"It wasn't encouraged," another whispered.

I felt the men's eyes looking over at our table and so I held my hand out and wiggled my fingers to show off my nails. The women around me took the hint and gushed, Raquelle grabbing my hand and turning it slightly as if to get a better look.

"Why do you think that is?" I asked, taking my hand back as another woman held hers forward. On cue we all leaned in and gushed at her stunning ring.

"Look. You don't need to worry about me saying anything to the boss," I finally clarified.

There was another quick look shared around the group before we laughed and began complaining about the lengths we went through to look amazing tonight. It was amazing to sit with these women and complain about blisters on toes, body contouring underwear, and the best and worst of eye creams. It was the first time I had a real conversation with these women, who previously were ordered to only discuss wealth and status symbols: properties, cars, vacation destinations, and handbags.

It was all code for when shit was moving, from where, and the quality of the goods. I had completely disrupted the status quo by bitching about my heels, and it was a welcome change.

"Dolce, it's time to go," Domenico suddenly announced, standing from his table.

I smiled at the women around me and said goodbye.

Domenico's hand was firmly on my lower back as we walked out of the private room and into the throng of dancers in the club. He smiled and joked with me as we made our way to the car, and held my hand whispering sweet nothings the entire ride home.

I felt my heart tug. It was in these quiet moments, when it was just the two of us, that everything else felt wrong and we made sense. As we entered the apartment, his phone chimed indicating that he had received a text message. I had no idea what the message read, but as the door closed behind us, it was like a switch had flipped.

"What did you talk about with those women?" Domenico asked, loosening his tie.

I smiled. "The usual. Nails, cosmetics, pilates, and shoes. The boring shit you don't want to hear about," I chuckled, removing my stilettos.

"Let me rephrase the question. What the fuck did you say, *dolce?*"

My head was yanked back as he grabbed my hair in a fist and pulled me into his chest. I didn't wait to find out what he wanted to accuse me of and elbowed him in the gut, forcing a hard breath to exhale from his lips. When his hand loosened on my hair, I turned and pushed him away.

"What the fuck is wrong with you?" I screamed, massaging my scalp.

His response was a back hand across my face. I reeled from the impact and swung back catching his jaw as I punched with my full weight behind it. Compared to Domenico, I was waif of a woman, but years of fighting, learning how to box, made my hits land just as hard as his.

"Is that how you want it, Anastacia?" he growled, snapping back and coming at me with a fury I was not expecting.

The next hit knocked me on my ass, and his hands were once again snatching up my hair as he attempted to drag me across the apartment. I spit a mouthful of blood on the floor, the metalic taste overwhelming my senses for longer than it should have.

"Let me go, Domenico," I pleaded, grabbing his hands to alleviate some of the pain he was causing to my head. "What did I even do?"

"Do you think I'm fucking stupid?" he screamed, throwing me to the ground in the center of the living room. Before I could ask another question, a stack of neatly organized bills was thrown at my face, the money flying across the floor around me. "Where the fuck did all of this money come from?"

I couldn't speak for half a second, honestly astonished that there was cash anywhere in the apartment. Domenico routinely went through all of my shit, so I never brought anything home that I couldn't explain.

"That's not mine!" I cried, but he wasn't hearing it.

"Did you think I wouldn't find out about your fucking stripping?" He roared, throwing several more stacks of cash at me, as I scrambled backwards on my ass.

"It's not my fucking money!" I tried in earnest to convince him, but it only seemed to infuriate him further.

Rolling onto all fours, I tried to crawl away faster so that I could at least stand a chance of defending myself. Domenico closed the distance between us faster than I could get away and kicked. His leg caught my ribs, facturing them. The air wheezed out of my lungs as I rolled away. Everything seemed to go by in a blur.

He dragged me from one room to another around the apartment, yanking drawers from cabinets, dressers, and desks while screaming more accusations at me. With every new allegation I was hit, punched, smacked, or kicked.

I couldn't see straight until I could. Pinned down on a bed we had shared for more than two years, his left hand squeezing my throat, I stared up into the barrel of a gun.

"I should fucking kill you!" Domenico seethed. "Did you think I was stupid? That I wouldn't find out?"

In that moment, I let go. I let go of everything I held dear, certain that he would kill me. It didn't matter the life I could have had with him, or the person I could have been without. None of it mattered any more.

"YOU FUCKING CUNT! DO YOU THINK YOU'RE SO SMART? HUH? DID YOU THINK I WOULDN'T KNOW ABOUT YOUR LIES?!?" he continued screaming.

I stared up past the barrel of the gun, into the eyes of a man I didn't know. There was only hatred in his eyes.

"IT WOULD BE A FUCKING SERVICE TO YOUR FAMILY TO END YOUR EXISTENCE! A DIRTY FUCK-ING WHORE LIKE YOU! I GAVE YOU A FUCKING LIFE SURROUNDED BY RICHES AND YOU FUCKING THREW IT AWAY!" he continued.

There was no fight left in me. "Do it," I wheezed. My eyes closed as the last of my energy dissipated into nothing.

Without a moment of hesitation, he pulled the trigger. The barrel of his gun pressed against my forehead jarred slightly as the hammer fell forward and made a harsh metallic click. The gun wasn't loaded.

"It's not so easy," he laughed darkly. "I'm going to make an example out of you, you cheating whore."

To be continued…..

About the Author

Cave Marie is the pen name adopted by an American immigrant living her best life in Norway. While writing is her passion, it's not everything about her. She holds degrees in Education, Latin American Studies and Organizational Leadership, speaks three to four languages, and will honestly admit that she's hopelessly addicted to coffee in all of its forms. She is a combat veteran, advocate for women's rights and staunch supporter of victims of sexual assault and domestic violence. "People should support people."

You can connect with me on:

☍ https://bsky.app/profile/cavemarie.bsky.social

Also by Cave Marie

I write books inspired by the world around me; spilled tea over coffee and wine and all the drama you just can't make up. My books are a mix of contemporary, science fiction, paranormal and fantasy genres with a little romance and smut thrown in for the thirsty. I like to create emotional journeys, filled with examples of life's hardships: loss, fertility, death, abuse, and mental health. I don't pull punches. Not everyone gets the happily ever after we wish for. Grab your tissues and coffee, and settle in for a good read.

Perfect Chemistry: A second chance romance
Amidst the memories and scars of the past, Kai yearns for the one who slipped away, while Katie harbors a wound that never healed, inflicted by her first love. Fate has reunited them, but can they rekindle their passion, or will the weight of memories and heartbreaks quell the sparks of what could be a perfect chemistry?